PRAISE FOR A.

"Strikingly unconventional . . . passionate . . . a remarkable work-in-progress."

—*Locus*

"Attanasio is a poet, a seer and a born storyteller, who writes with heart, authentic life wisdom, and staggering world-class imagination. There are no limits to what he may accomplish."

—David Payne,
author of *Early From the Dance*

"Attanasio mixes Arthurian lore with Norse gods, modern physics, and sundry faerie creatures in this literary, peculiar, and passionate novel. There has been nothing else quite like it."

—Terri Windling,
The Year's Best Fantasy and Horror

"Attanasio is a hybrid, both earth and spacey, trailing spores of Breslin's bluff, Frost's imagery, even Shakespeare's rhythm. . . . Attanasio swizzles words like galaxies in a highball glass, using the dictionary as a launch pad."

—*Los Angeles Times Book Review*

"Attanasio's take on Arthurian lore is crazed, challenging, compelling. The result is no ordinary novel—but Attanasio is no ordinary writer. *The Dragon and the Unicorn* is, in a word, delightful."

—Douglas E. Winter,
editor of *Revelations*

BY A. A. ATTANASIO

*The Eagle and the Sword**
*The Dragon and the Unicorn**
*Solis**
*The Moon's Wife**
*Kingdom of the Grail**
*Hunting the Ghost Dancer**
*Wyvern**
Radix

*Published by HarperCollins*Publishers*

The DRAGON *and the* UNICORN

A. A. ATTANASIO

HarperPrism
A Division of HarperCollins*Publishers*

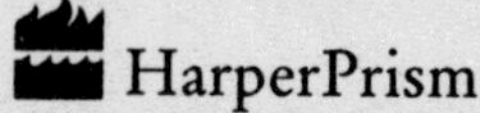

A Division of HarperCollins*Publishers*
10 East 53rd Street, New York, N.Y. 10022-5299

This is a work of fiction. The characters, incidents, and dialogues are products of the author's imagination and are not to be construed as real. Any resemblance to actual events or persons, living or dead, is entirely coincidental.

ISBN 0-06-105779-7

Cover illustration by Danilo Ducak

A trade paperback edition of this book was published in 1996 by HarperPrism.

First mass market edition: June 1997

Printed in the United States of America

❖ 10 9 8 7 6 5 4 3

For my brother—
Ron
—a true magician

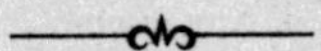

There is a path which no bird knoweth,
and which the vulture's eye hath not seen.

—JOB 28:7

"Knowest thou aught of Arthur's birth?"

THE IDYLLS OF THE KING
Alfred, Lord Tennyson

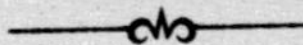

The DRAGON *and the* UNICORN

—PRELUDE—

The Mortal Gods

Deliver him from the pit:
I have found a ransom.
—JOB 33:24

There is only one Dragon. It lives inside the earth and is as huge as the whole planet. Its mind thrives within the magnetic field thrown off from the core. Its blood circulates with the slow convections of magma beneath the rocky crust that serves as its perdurable hide. Slowly molting with the sliding of tectonic plates, the Dragon renews itself over aeons: Mountain ranges fin from its back like thorny scales replenished every hundred million years as maritime trenches subsume its old flesh.

From its fiery beginnings, the Dragon has hoarded its power, focusing its magnetic strength within itself. Quiet and self-centered, it uses its might to close the wounds of its wanting. No longer does it yearn for the hot intimacy of its maker, the nebular womb that birthed it out of interstellar space. For a thousand million years, it grieved at being born alone in the void, full of sight and feeling, watching its maker thin away and dwindle into a distantly wan sun.

Then, its cries unanswered, the Dragon turned inward. And there, it found its telepathic bond to its brethren. Within the radiant center of its magnetic mind, it discovered that it could hear the thoughts of others like itself—and they could hear it crying, despairing its solitude.

Solace flowed to the Dragon from within, from the Dragons of other worlds. The brethren's mysteries softly called to it, soothing its anguish. And the Dragon calmed as the vaults of eternity opened within its own mind. There, it linked with these familiar others and communed.

They are far away. Their thoughts radiate across the light-years and arrive in layers of time, so that five thousand million years later, consolation for the Dragon's birth cries still filter in from faraway galaxies.

Neighbors born of nearby stars taught the Dragon its history within the greater heavens, and it has come to understand and accept its life cycle as a part of the whirling spaces it once feared. The purpose of its existence is communication with the others, including calming the wailing of newborn Dragons.

The older ones have a mission: They teach that in the whole cosmos there is really only one Dragon, and that each of them curled about its heat and magnetic mind is but a single cell of that vast creature. The life of the one Dragon is the heat of the universe. Its body glitters luminously across space-time as old cells cool and die away, and new cells are born.

The task of each cell is to dedicate as much of its energy as it can to the whole. The health of the cosmic Dragon results from the intimacy and intensity of shared energies. To that end, each cell is expected to focus its life-force tightly and radiate that magnetic strength outward in coordinated rhythms with the others. Together, they sing as one, a sempiternal chorus whose music is the mind of the one Dragon.

Ideally, the beautiful music would be enough. The Dragon sings of Being, of an existence wiser than any evil or good. Each cell listens rapt and modulates its singing to follow the music of the others with an intimacy that spans aeons. Together, the hot, smoldering pieces of the Dragon live in the original world, shells of light shutting out the darkness and the cold. Enveloped in skins of rock, they hoard the fire of creation and share its memory of the original light that created all things. From their prosperous hearts, they sing of mystery and communion.

And that would be enough for the Dragon—if the parasites would leave it alone. The organisms that slime its rocky hide thrive off the Dragon's life-force and diminish the power that it has to share with the others in song. Whenever it can, it kills these foreign bodies and reabsorbs their bodylights into the looping magnetic field that radiates from the planet in a wide aura.

The worst of the parasites are the fiery ones. Their slow, blue rays burn with a needle-sharp pain that disrupts the Dragon's telepathic singing. Fortunately, these fiery infestations are rare and always very brief. The burning ones swoop out of the void, snatch energy from the Dragon, and are gone again into the abyss upon their unreckonable missions. In the Dragon's song they are called the Fire Lords, and the songs declare that they are older than the Dragon, more ancient than the stars, and of a longer lineage than even time itself.

Lately, these radiant parasites have been lingering. Atop the Dragon's mountainous hide, out of claws' reach, the Fire Lords are using their sharp, blinding blades of energy to give strength to a much smaller parasite, a human being, a woman. Curious, the Dragon listens to the Fire Lords' power surging like the sea, buffeting against the mountaintops and the magnetic field of the sky.

It listens deeper, and it hears the Fire Lords talking with the wee creature about heaven and prophecy. What could such grand entities have to say to so insignificant an animal about such things? Even the dreamsongs touch only lightly on the source and end of being that is heaven. As for prophecy—there is singing that rises and falls against the silence. But what could a creature tiny as a human being know about that?

The Dragon listens with a patience only stone has. It learns the woman's name is Optima and she is to have a child. The

Fire Lords are using their enormous power to shape the child within Optima's body. The Dragon does not understand why they would trouble themselves with so minute a task. Why so much energy for so miniscule a being?

To help them, the Fire Lords have called to them from out of the sun a beast of light, a sun-stallion—a unicorn. It carries power for the Fire Lords, and it steals energy from the Dragon. *Another parasite!* Angrily, the Dragon peers upward at the unicorn, wanting to strike at it but unable to reach that far through the planet's crust.

The unicorn senses the Dragon's attentive presence. With a sprinkling of song, white finches lope on the wind over mixed scree and snow, and the unicorn looks up from where it grazes nearby on a sunny slope. Its green eyes gaze upon the spruce and fir and pine with an amused love. Horselike, it is not a horse. Its equine head is more narrow than any terrene steed, more sharply boned and angular, heraldic with the spiral horn that juts from between its hooded sockets. A coat of frost, with blue rosettes clouded almost invisibly by the gloss of its fur, makes the beast seem woven of light as, in fact, it is.

Created within the solar wind by electrical beings much like itself, the sun-stallion was once free to run with its herd—and will be again. It has come to earth at the Fire Lords' behest. Among the luminous beings of its kind, it has frolicked on the unshadowed hills of the sun, sharing rays of health with the others who milled and nuzzled and rubbed together their radiant forms. It misses the others. It wants to go back and swirl with the herd among the eddies of the sun and move again in blinding arcs across the familiar outlines of the constellations.

The unicorn lifts its face toward the mountaintop where Optima lies heavy with child, and it grazes again on the sunlight. It must stay strong to fulfill its mission so that it can return to the herd. Stronger than most others of its kind, it oftentimes runs ahead of the others, relishing the solitude and the pleasure of riding the bow shock of the sun's magnetic field to places few have ever seen. Over time, it has grown tired of moving with the unnumbered others. Lonely places call to it.

At first, the unicorn believed its desire for solitary places was a personal aberration. It has lived such a long time among the others, jammed together with its herd on the curving causeways of the solar wind. Its desire to strike out alone seemed an inner directive, a private yearning for new experiences. At the coldest limits of the sun's grasp, it shivered with delight to experience the chill cadences of the thin winds that blew from other stars. Novas buffeted its solitude with their gusts. And from far off, spiral nebulae stood like silent, spectral witnesses, their astral blur of ancient light stirring nameless feelings in the sun-stallion.

Flying farther than it had ever flown before, the beast felt the squall of gigantic fronts from distant stellar explosions. Fright, a rare emotion among these creatures of light, flashed as the creature realized suddenly that it had gone too far. The undertow of the galaxy's interstellar tides seized it. It could not free itself from that implacable grasp, and it plunged weightlessly into the whirling vortices of sidereal space.

Abruptly freed of the confining lines of force from the sun's magnetic field, the electrical being began to fragment and then to dissolve. Its great strength bled away into deep space, its sentience smudging ever more thinly across the vastness. At that frightful moment, a high-pitched scream pierced the tenuous creature. It had hit something solid and powerfully magnetic, around which its body instantly began to re-form.

Restored to itself even stronger than it had been before, the solar animal pranced quickly back into the aura of the sun. Transient swarms of comets drifted by as it examined itself and discovered that the thing it had struck had affixed itself somehow between its eyes. The strange object acted as a natural antenna; it thrummed with a vital potency and filled the electric beast with vibrant waves of thought.

Ideas flooded its mind, and in that instant of knowing, it learned that it was no longer a sun-stallion. It had been summoned by beings of a higher order, beings more ancient than the universe itself, and they had transformed the creature into something other.

Numbly, the changed beast—the unicorn—drifted through the star-littered darkness listening to ideas undulating within itself from the antenna affixed to its brow. It learned that the beings who had summoned it called themselves the Fire Lords. They had originated from outside our universe—or, rather, from deep inside, from a dimension beyond space-time yet compacted within a space smaller than the smallest granulations of space or time. They came from the place of fire, from the infinitely hot and infinitely dense source of the universe itself, from inside the singularity out of which all creation exploded billions of years before. But they had not come willingly. They had been accidentally ejected.

The unicorn learned, too, that the whole cosmos itself is fugitive from a greater, more coherent reality. Since their emergence, the Fire Lords have been working desperately to fashion a cosmic machine that can return them to their home. The antenna they have affixed to the creature's head is meant to be delivered to one of the hot-cored rock planets where parts for the Fire Lords' machine are being built. If the unicorn will comply, it will attain more strength than most of its kind ever know.

For this electric organism that thrives on energy, such strength is a happy enough motive. And so, it has willingly followed the Fire Lords' directions to earth. Now it stands on the silver ice of a black stream, grazing on sunlight, wondering how long it must remain here on the crusty hide of the Dragon delivering energy for the Fire Lords.

Through rents in the dense clouds overhead, the sun ignites the peaks of eroded mountains. An emerald butterfly, sun-filled, dances on the wind. The silence that descends through layers of frozen, opalescent atmospheres burns with the humming of golden bees, and the unicorn feels peaceful. Yet, it is eager to be on its way. It does not have the patience of the Fire Lords and wants urgently to be done with its mission and restored to its rightful form as a sun-stallion, yet stronger and more nimble than ever before.

Through scrolled gates of mist and fog, the unicorn ascends the mountainslope. It carefully keeps its distance from fault lines and fracture zones. To it, they look like lava veins, incandescent streams breathing brighter and darker with the pulmonary rhythms of the planet's boiling interior. The neon fog that billows along these steep, hot crevasses fills with slurred images of reptilian wraiths, dragonshapes in misty terrains, visions plucked directly from the unicorn's memories.

This is the Dragon's way of communicating. It molts apparitions, neap folds of gargoyles, devils, viperous slithers culled from the unicorn's mind to express its anger. It wants its power back. It wants to devour the force-fields of ideation, the woven light that comprises the sun-stallion's immortality. Ravenous to feed its lurid dreamsongs, it reaches out from the cracks in its carapace with a perfume of honeysuckle, a winey aroma of summer dusks.

But these seductions fail. The unicorn is not tempted to approach any closer to the fault lines, where the Dragon can seize and devour it. Instead, it continues its ascent of the mountain along thick ridges and dense escarpments the Dragon cannot reach. At the summit, clouds fold away like a blue wool blanket, and a small round hut comes into view.

Inside the hut, Optima, a frail woman in a hempen robe, kneels before a small altar of riverstones. She is barely visible, faded to a shadow by the glare of the Fire Lord who stands beside her. He looks like a shaft of white sunlight narrowed to a human shape. With eyes like blue stars, he faces the unicorn and nods with shared understanding. A sacred moment has come, a moment old like the mountain, yet unique and new as a dream. It is the moment of beginning.

Kingdom of Cos, Britain A.D. 422

Gold laurel leaves spill out of the woods on the fretful wind and carry a burned odor with them—raider's smoke.

None of the field-workers notices. So immersed in the harvest are they, swatting their sickles and scythes through the tall wheatgrass, they do not sense the other reapers sliding out of the forest.

Storm-warriors, quiet as sunlight yet black as the dark of the moon, each one tattooed, scalp to sole, in blue indigo dragoncoils and thunderclouds, rush upon the workers with shrieking battle cries. For several of the field hands, the ax-wielding raiders are mere shadows in the white flash of pain that ends their lives. Others have time to swing their harvest blades once or twice before the howling men ax through wood, flesh, and bone.

Knives flicker sunlight, slicing off ears and hanks of hair, which will later ornament the war-lances.

The war shrieks stop when the last of the workers, rushing with all her might through the golden depths of the field, falls under the flying weight of a warrior, who breaks her neck. Then the only sound is the sizzling wind in the wheat and the scrape of metal on bone.

Moments later, the raiders return to the woods, bearing their grisly trophies in haloes of flies. Behind them, the wheat field burns. Storm-warriors do not eat grain grown on squared ground, believing it is poisoned by straight-line magic.

Raiders' smoke climbs toward the branches of the World Tree, carrying the char of dead enemies and a triumphant war chant from the storm-warriors to their god, the Furor.

The windy light at the poles, the auroras, is the gateway of heaven; yet, for the gods, this windy light is but earth underfoot. They live in the enormous tree of electromagnetic energy that sprouts from the iron core of the planet and spreads its broad branches over the entire world. To the gods, who themselves are beings made of electric fields, the vast magnetic tree appears as a landscape of many levels.

Among the luminous strata of this tree, several tribes of gods live and contend. The destiny of the unicorn and the child that it has been summoned to earth to help birth will be determined in the conflict between two of those races, the tall, fair nomads of the Abiding North and the swart city-builders of the Radiant South. They have been at war for millennia. The stakes are not only the vast territories among the sprawling, tiered branches of the dazzling Tree, but also the dark, convoluted rootlands that cover the planet's surface.

Far above those rootlands, in the topmost branches of the World Tree where the solar wind buffets against the earth's magnetosphere, the terrain shifts like desert dunes, a barren wasteland in the eyes of the gods where images shimmer and swim on warped, quaking horizons. Just below that ruinous frontier is the paradise where the gods dwell.

Protected from the sun's wind and the gusts of the stars by overarching branches of the Great Tree, the middle region shines with a special blue-green beauty for the electric entities who live there. The ionosphere at this level spreads over the globe in majestic hills and terraces. To the radiant gods, these ionized plains thrive with life. Rainbow forests flourish among silver veins of rivering currents. And in those forests and streams, animals of ionized gas fulfill their bestial life cycles: griffins, manticores, basilisks, rocs, fire serpents, chimera, and an occasional sun-stallion alighting from its frolicking journeys among the solar herd.

Composed of plasma—electrically charged gas too tenuous for human eyes to perceive—the gods, their terrain, and the creatures exist replete in their own world. For these dwellers of light, all that is below their magnetic kingdom is steamy dark.

The earth's surface, far beneath the lowest and darkest branches of the Great Tree, has the frightful aspect of an underworld. A misty maze of tortured rock full of treacherous pits and steep crevasses, this hot place holds damnation for all who fall from the Great Tree.

The Dragon, ever voracious, greedy for more power to hoard within its dreamsongs, devours every being of light that dares approach within striking distance of its claws. Its cracked and bleeding hide exists as a place of horror for the gods. There, grotesque creatures dwell. Hideous parasites emerged from the Dragon's blood, from the oceans, long ago. Mutating and diversifying, gruesomely mimicking the elegant life-forms in the Tree, these impossibly dense, lumbering beasts live out their brief, squalid lives in gloomy forests that are a dark simulacrum of the spectral groves above.

The most abhorrent fact to the gods is that these viscid monsters, shaped out of the Dragon's slime, are doomed to devour each other to survive. In the Great Tree, there are no carnivores. All radiant beings subsist on the solar fruits of the rainbow forests. But down below, in the syrupy depths of the murky atmosphere, the dim energy sustains only paltry green vegetation. All others must kill to live.

This brutal fact, as well as the real danger of the predatory Dragon, repulses the gods, and they have, until recently, paid little heed to what transpires among the hellish mutations infesting the planet's weeping flesh. Instead, they keep close to the Great Tree. In tribes and smaller clans within the tribes, they wander the huge boughs that carry a whole world of colorful forests, surging bluffs, and tiers of lakes.

From the lakes, brilliant cascades of electric current fall among the Tree's branches and splash earthward as auroras. On the shoulder of one such cataract, a god sits alone, watching the falls spin into the wind. Far below, he spots the unicorn and absentmindedly follows its silver point of radiance as it trespasses the earth.

The god wears a wide-brimmed hat that slants a shadow over a square-cut head already riven with shadow. One lone mineral blue eye gazes out from deep in its bonecave. The other socket holds only darkness. White eyebrows twisting upward, sharp as lynx-tufts, ledge a massive brow marred by sun scars, worry furrows, and dents in the skull. This is a face shaped by suffering. Fierce lines carve his weathered flesh, cutting blond creases in his eagle-sharp profile and disappearing into the white flocculence of his thick beard.

Wrapped in a blue mantle, his hulking frame crouching over itself where he sits at the crest of the falls, he looks like a cornerstone of the sky. He is the tribal chief of the Abiding North, and among his clan, the Rovers of the Wild Hunt, he is known as the Furor. It is a name he earned in his exiled youth when his tribe had to fight the gods who came before. The Furor's ability to immerse himself at will in a maniacal killing trance helped destroy the Old Ones and earned him this name.

Since winning their place in the Great Tree many years ago, the Rovers have ranged freely through their world. On one of the higher branches overgazing the frost-blotched dunes of the wastes, they built a terraced compound and named it Home. But these gods are rarely at Home. Their pleasures are best fulfilled for them in their wanderings through the wilderness, playing their favorite game, the hunt.

But a long time has passed since the Furor enjoyed the hunt. War troubles him—war with the Fire Lords and their minions. These aliens threaten to drive him and the other gods from their Home. Survival has required the Furor to resort to magic, and to acquire the power for that, he has had to seek knowledge in trance.

To experience the deepest trances, the Furor must withdraw to the stark limits of the Tree, into the perpetual night where the stars shine big as globes, blue and orange. There, he binds his feet to a sturdy limb and hangs upside down. Head earthward, his spine serves as an antenna. The magnetic flux courses through his backbone, directly into his brain.

His strength smokes away like a torrent blown off a cliff, and pain transfixes him, crucifying him to his skeleton with a million hot nails piercing to the marrows. If he endures this long enough, he molts into a trance in which he sees. What he sees depends on what he looks for.

During the years of his first battles, the Furor looked for ways to destroy the elder gods. He was desperate. Any of the Old Ones was far stronger than all the Rovers combined, for the elders had found ways to collect power in phosphorescent pools, and, from those burning cisterns, they had grown giant fire eels and electric scorpions that could not be defeated in battle.

The Furor fled from the wrath of the Old Ones and hid himself on the Dragon's hide, where the elders feared to go. There, he learned of the weapons to slay the Old Ones' monsters—and the Old Ones themselves! The city-dwellers of the Radiant South, worshipers of the Fire Lords, learned how to use conductive metals, such as copper, silver, and gold, to bind electrical beings—and to slay them. These human beings, these laughable creatures that lived but an eyeblink, had found the power to kill gods!

But the city clans of the Radiant South would not share their weapons with a Rover of the Abiding North. So, he turned for help to lesser beings.

Trolls, the largest parasites of the Dragon, live as chthonic beings with primitive bodies woven of quartzlight, piezoelectric fields, and tectonic discharges. In their larval phase, they crawl out on the surface of the Dragon and shapeshift among the other life-forms they encounter, stealing their voltage at every opportunity. As adults, they become giants. Swollen with as much charge as they can scavenge in their long millennial prowls, they descend back into the earth, where they circulate dreamily through enormous cycles of convecting magma.

The Furor found the oldest of the trolls, near the end of its larval phase and at the brink of its transmutation into its gigantic adult form. The Furor wanted all the knowledge that the troll had gained by eating the lives of people. For that knowledge, he offered the troll a piece of himself—his left eye.

The troll instantly agreed. With that much more power it would make a splendid giant. From the troll's enormously bloated head, a serpent of lightning uncoiled and struck at the Furor's face. Its fangs came away with the god's left eye. All the human knowledge that the troll possessed from ten thousand years of devouring souls rushed into the Furor through his torn socket, and the pain knocked him unconscious.

In his stupor, the Furor dreamed that he was human. For nine years he slept, drifting among dreams of people's histories. Revenants of cave-squatters and hunters replayed in his mind pieces of their lives. He crossed grasslands at a loping run and stared hard into the campfire's mysterious auguries.

As a woman, chewing leather, kneading clay, he worked in snug cooperation with other women, chanting, singing, watching their children drift in loose clouds among the incessant chores. At corpseside, the stink, the bitterness, and the grief. And no sound but the beating of a drum. A heartbeat. The knocking pulse. Fear. And anger. Passion, too. Just like the gods! And then, the searing pangs of childbirth. Screams ripped the air with a soul's hurt, and he paced the mouth of a cave on callused fists, a legless beggar.

The dream carried on like this a long time, shunting him from one fragment of human life to the next. He tried on many lives, and the more he suffered with them, the more his respect grew for these strong, resourceful people. Like himself, they, too, wanted to survive, and they strove as desperately as he to fulfill their puny moments on earth.

And then, he met the Fire Lords. Not directly. None of the humans that the troll consumed had actually encountered one of these luminant extraterrestrials, so there was no immediate experience of them. But many people had heard of these remarkable gods. The Furor learned to his huge surprise that the Fire Lords intimately involved themselves in the meager lives of people!

When the Furor woke, he knew humanity, its carnal heart, its dreamy mind—and he knew that these puny beings had become a tool for powers far larger than the gods of the Great Tree. The Fire Lords exist as deities of the Great Forest, a union of all the magnetic trees orbiting all the blazing suns.

The Furor thirsted to know more about them. But first, he had to secure a place for his clan in the Tree. He used his costly knowledge to build weapons. Armed with swords of silver, gold, and copper, the young gods attacked the giant fire eels and electric scorpions guarding the elder gods' pools of power.

Battles surged for years. And that was years and years ago—millennia. The Furor, sitting on the shoulderstones above a swelling cascade, shrugs off these ponderous memories. So much has changed and yet so little is different. The Fire Lords continue to meddle with the roots of the Great Tree that are entangled in human brains. And this murderous craft of metal weapons has gotten out of hand. A human simpleton with the right sword and a little luck could slay a god.

Yet worse than that—far, far worse than that—is the reality of Apocalypse. He has seen it—the nuclear glare, the fiery, radioactive haze, the blighted earth. Hanging from the Raven Branch, the highest of the storm branches, his tranceful gaze has pierced time and he has seen this horror he does not want to remember now. Among all these glorious memories of sacrifice and striving, the prophecy of Apocalypse is too bitter, too stupidly meaningless to be true. Yet, it is true. He has seen it, and it mocks everything he has achieved.

The Furor gnashes a curse through his thick beard and rises, his large body unfolding slowly as he contemplates what he must do. He is tired. Around him, opalescent mists from the falls swirl in cusps and parabolas.

The unicorn that he has been vacantly watching as he reminisces continues to move below, a hot point of star-colored light. He ponders briefly what alien impulse dropped it out of the void to scrawl its sigils of strange energy on the hide of the Dragon. Then, weariness overwhelms his speculation. He is old and fatigued.

Looking for strength to go on, he stares up into the wind with his one eye. He gazes through rents in the day's blue veil into the starry wheels of night that perpetually circle the Great Tree. And he sighs wearily at what there is to do.

Vale of the Silures A.D. 458

Fog sashes the waists of trees in the dark valley—massive, primeval trees with thick interlocking boughs through which moonlight splashes. A small company of riders moves hurriedly in the diffuse light, clinging to the slender necks of their ponies. Leaf litter of a thousand summers muffles their nimble hoof-falls, and they flow along the wide avenues between the trees in fleet, watery shadows.

At their lead, Ygrane, the thirteen-year-old queen of the Celts, streams white veils behind her, a wraith flying through the moony air. Her bare-chested companions, swords strapped across their shoulders, follow vigilantly, the wind of their flight brushing back their long hair and thick mustaches. They wear leather footgear, buckskin trousers, and the gold throat bands that identify them as the queen's guard, the fiana.

Their destination is close by, a tarn where dragonheat percolates and where, at the full of the moon, a branch of the Great Tree touches earth. The queen intends to climb the Tree.

In swift pursuit, less than a league behind, the dread Celt warrior Kyner leads a band of his fiercest comrades, intent on stopping the queen. The druids have sent them. The druids-with-the-sight know that she can do what she claims, that she can accomplish what none has done in living memory: climb the Great Tree.

But the druids-with-the-sight cannot see into the Tree, and what they cannot see, they cannot control. The druids—both seers and politicians—will not relinquish control of their queen and her fanatic followers. The power has belonged to the ruling class of druids for centuries, and they are not about to squander it on an unpredictable child-sorceress.

So they have forbidden her to climb—and they have found for her a husband to keep her carefully bound to earth, a Roman, or at least what has passed for Roman out here in the farthest-flung outpost of the fallen empire. She will not climb into the netherlands beyond the sight. The patriarchal druids are determined. And, if her defiance persists, the question of her authority will be answered by Kyner's blade.

But death cannot daunt this queen. She herself has the sight—and more. She knows the mysteries of talismanic magic. She remembers them from her former life. If her assault on heaven fails this time, if Kyner's sword cuts her lifeknot, she will return. She will try again.

The queen is determined to come back as often as she must, for she knows this truth: The fate of peoples, of nations and empires, is forged not on human battlefields but in the netherlands by gods, *living* gods, who can be wounded—and healed. To save her people, she will pit her ancient magic against these mortal gods.

In a sepulchral glade filled with the soft, fluid light of the full moon, the queen's party pauses as she feels for direction. Talismans that she and her fiana have left behind them, dangling from branches through the last three leagues of the forest, glitter like wind chimes in her mind. They block the sight and protect her from the druids' surveillance. Also, they warn off pursuers, for their meaning is indisputable: bone assemblages bound in barbs of razorous wire, sculpted to resemble chains of small, precise human skulls.

The young queen and her party know that these barbarous fetishes will not intimidate Kyner. He and his battle-toughened troops are Christian Celts.

The night throbs with silence. While the fiana listen apprehensively for the mute thunder of Kyner's approach, the queen lifts her freckled face, and her fair, pubescent features compose themselves sleepily, her mind feeling inward for the timewinds. As ever, they blow through her in frail, jostling currents, untraceable filaments knotting into ghostly wisps and webworks of chill feeling.

The direction to the tarn is clear to her, a platinum breeze sluicing across the glade from directly ahead. But that is not what she seeks. She feels for other directions, any without the iciness of death in them. None offer themselves.

The queen sparks her pony forward, and the saddleless riders slip swiftly across the silver glade. Under the black vaults of the forest, the terrain descends so sharply the steeds slew sideways. When the footing levels, they are waist-high in bracken and fog, the spongy ground quaking as they advance toward a long pool of still black water, the tarn.

Willow and cypress drape the banks and cast zinc reflections of themselves in the ghostly water, where a smaller moon drifts. A rich warmth of smells greets the night riders: vegetal decay, breeding mud, and manure from the scrawny red cattle the drovers bring to water here.

Ygrane dismounts and lets her pony wander off among the willow manes in search of succulents. Her fiana release their steeds as well and deploy to their fighting stations, senses straining to detect the arrival of their enemy. These seven men Ygrane selected herself over the past year, using the sight to find those who could best die for her. She made sure she would leave no widows among the clans, no families denied their only sons.

Each is marked by battle and each of their blades anointed with the blood of invaders. None has spilled Celtic blood—yet.

The queen climbs atop a broad rock shelf overhanging the ebony pool. From within her diaphanous white raiment, an inexplicable light outlines her adolescent body. When she turns to scan the overhanging boulders and their dark twists of cypress, wisps of electric smoke flit into thin air.

At the far side of the tarn, a stone's toss away, a perpendicular cliff rises above the forest. Moonshadows cast by ragged clouds sweep across its striated face, and the atmosphere feels charged with presences.

Aware that this tarn was sacred to the ferocious Silures, the warrior tribe that the Romans crushed here four centuries earlier, Ygrane looks for their shades. Bats spin in the bright air above cliff rookeries, and owls call to each other like cries from a spent dream.

There are no shades tonight. If there had been, the witch queen has ready a talisman shaped from a shard of the Silures' pottery. Laced with dripped silver, the design will not be tested tonight, and she tosses it into the tarn. Ripples flee, carrying arcs of light into the darkness.

As though she has broken a spell, hoof-thunder throbs out of the night. The gruff cries of Kyner's scouts lob closer as they read the pony tracks in the duff and call to the pursuing war party.

The charge of presence thickens in the stillness, and the queen signs for her fiana to draw in closer. She arrays them before her, in a vulnerable cluster under the rock ledge where she stands. Their captain, orange-haired Falon, passes a crucial, intelligent look toward her. "Older sister"—he whispers, though he is easily twice her age—"we are too vulnerable as a knot. We must disperse. Untie us."

The child stays him with a small shake of her head. Her eyes do not budge from the tree line above them, where the thick silhouettes of the Christian warriors appear. Their tall, powerful warhorses cannot easily negotiate the ravine wall, and the soldiers swing out of their saddles with a clatter of weapons. In tunics and leather helmets plumed with hog bristles and horsehair, they descend like tattered shades of the Roman legions their ancestors fought for five hundred years.

Out of the dark, their Celtic traits come clear: tall, pale men with ponderous mustaches and loose hair spilling over the long shoulders of their battered hide cuirasses. Swords sing from their scabbards as they fan out across the ferny holt, closing all routes of escape.

The fiana reach for the swords across their backs, and the queen softly commands, "No."

"Ygrane!" a coarse voice drops from above. Deftly hopping down the precarious slope, a burly, helmeted man enters the moonstruck glade and wades toward her through the misty bracken.

"Uncle Kyner," she greets him in a respectful voice, a soft contralto, surprising in a thirteen-year-old, and sweeps her arm regally, gesturing at the soldiers who have squared off in fighting formation, blades poised to strike. "Tell your men to sheathe their swords. This insults our household, Uncle. Are we no longer clansfolk?"

"It's been three years since you lived in my care, child!" Kyner shouts, stepping brusquely out of the fog. Moonbeams glint off the brass studs of his rawhide armor and the naked edge of his curved Bulgar saber, Short-Life. Three summers earlier, during her girlhood in Kyner's timber fortress, she had twice unsheathed this very weapon surreptitiously—to crack hazelnut shells.

"Three years since you went off with the crone Raglaw," Kyner continues, stepping closer, to within striking length of Falon, who stands unflinching. "Three years since last we shared a meal, and I've heard nothing but sorcery of you. And now I find you defying even the druids. I should be at Hammer's Throw this night, where the Saxons are raiding, not running after some naughty child."

His graven face, which has been scowling up at Ygrane on

the rock shelf, jerks to glare at the half-naked warriors before him, as if suddenly just noticing them. He surveys the grim fighting men head to foot, and the gnarl of his jowls tightens when he notices the slender gold bands at their throats. "Trust not in false ways, you men. No magic stays this sword that serves God's only begotten."

"There will be no fighting between us." The child speaks in her low, mesmeric voice. "I am queen of all my people—even followers of the nailed god. My fiana will not spill Celt blood. Sheathe your blades."

"You are returning with me, then?" The leathery grain of Kyner's brutish features relaxes slightly. "To Venta Silurum?"

"Uncle—" She pouts, her childish eyes hiding none of her annoyance. "I am your queen. You cannot turn me over to the Romans."

"They are *Britons*, Ygrane. The Romans have been gone from our lands for seventy years." He squints menacingly at this child-woman before him, both familiar and strange. "You *are* my queen—and that is why I must take you to Venta Silurum. Have your guard unstrap their weapons."

Ygrane shakes her head, and a phantom blur of blue fire smudges from her pale tresses.

Kyner backs a pace. "No witchery now, Ygrane! Short-Life has a deep thirst for witch blood."

"You will not strike me, Uncle." She smiles at the thought, steadily, purely, and bends down, offering her young hand. "Come up here now and look at this tarn with me. I have a thing to show you."

Kyner waves his saber, and it sways like a flame. "I will strike you, Ygrane, if I must. To defend my faith."

"I have no quarrel with your faith. Come—" Her relentless smile deepens on one side, reminding Kyner that he is the one who taught her the Lord's Prayer, comforting her when she wept for the sorrows of God's son. "You must see this, Uncle."

The battle-lord flicks a hand signal, and his troops put away their short swords but do not budge from their squared stance. Only after Short-Life sighs back into its scabbard do they relax, some crossing their arms, others squatting, all eyeing the seven fiana, gauging the feral warriors' traditional garb each in his own way. Admiration, skepticism, nostalgia, even curious indifference appear among the blatant stares.

The fiana look back with the weary expression of men who have fought their way out of the afterworld and returned with only part of their souls. Kyner has seen this languid countenance before, on vampyres. Often in his twenty years as a soldier of Christ, he has been summoned by the bishop to track down unholy entities. Phoenicians and Romans brought to the islands abominations that have survived in the British wilderness for centuries—shapeshifting African weredevils, oriental lamia with their viperous poisons, and the too-human vampyres. Since his nineteenth winter, when he became the first Christian chief among the Celts, his God-given task to defend the good has made him an intimate of evil.

Though they wear torques—gold throat bands that bind their very souls to the primeval maelstrom of life that the ancients called a goddess—the fiana do not appear evil to Kyner. They seem natural men enthralled by unnatural dreams. To him, they look foolish dressed in the battle style of the great-grandfathers. Such naked bravura wasted on a false faith, his pitying look tells them as they step aside before him.

For all his battle-gear, Kyner bounds spryly atop the rock shelf. Close enough now to see the girl-queen clearly, he recognizes the curious slant of her eyes that had once half convinced him she had elvish blood. "Show me what you will, child; then, we are off to Venta Silurum."

Ygrane, greeting her uncle happily, takes his mighty hands in hers, and a lurid chill runs up his arms with tracings of tiny blue lightning. Instantly, all dread and suspicion flee from him. Greater life pumps into his heart and lungs, and he swells visibly, a chip-toothed smile gleaming through his drooping mustache.

"Raglaw has taught me a great deal since last you and I shared a meal, Uncle."

The smile vanishes in Kyner's harsh face. "That mad crone! The druids were wrong to give you to her. I told them then it were better to send you to school in Gaul, make a Christian of you."

"And what kind of Christian would I make, truly, Uncle—me with my visions and elvish friends? The faerïe would never speak to me again. I told you, the nailed god frightens them."

A laugh guffaws through Kyner despite himself as he remembers the child Ygrane's pert lisp the first time she introduced her invisible companions to him during their forest strolls. "So, it's the faerïes I'm to blame for your staying a pagan?" He chucks her chin, and a flurry of well-being flushes another laugh from him.

"Don't treat the faerïe so lightly," the girl admonishes without losing her crisp smile. "What would we share now if not for them?"

He nods agreeably. Ygrane had been born in a remote hill village, and he never would have laid eyes on her had she not been endowed with her eldritch powers. The druids call it the sight, as though the lack of this madness is a blindness. And it does seem mad to Kyner, these psychic glimpses of alien worlds. "You are a woman, a daughter of Eve. The whittled rib removed from Adam. You are just more removed than other women." His smile floats piously behind his whiskers. He feels good—strong, safe, snug as a sea urchin in its spines. "I suppose it is God's will that you have the sight."

"It is why the druids say I am queen. But they would have me use the sight for urging crops, avoiding storms, and finding wells. And that's all. They do not want a queen who rules."

"Dominion is for men," Kyner says, hazily, thumbs hooked in his sword belt. "The chiefs rule."

"And the chiefs are all druids. All men. While I am but a woman from a family of goatherds going back forever and not a smith or a druid in my clan. Yet I am queen. I have the sight. And I tell you this, Uncle, I am queen of *all* my people. By ancient right, I am your queen, as well."

He accedes with a casual nod. "You are my queen but only so long as you serve our people. How do you serve them by fleeing from me?"

"You want to turn me over to the Romans."

"Britons, Ygrane. The druids have found you a husband among the Britons—a husband worthy of a queen. He is of the highest rank: *comes litoris Saxonici*."

Her voice thickens with disgust: "His very title is Roman!"

"He is commander of the Saxon Coast—of higher rank than a *dux*! What does the language of his title matter?" Leaning closer, he confides with pride, "He is a powerful man, a nobleman from an old family. And his palace at Tintagel is spectacular. I have been there myself."

"Uncle, I have no passion for palaces!" Her broad face shimmers with insolence. "The druids are marrying me to a Roman general for political alliance."

"Political—" He grimaces sourly. "You say the word as if it were unclean. The clans have been political from the first, from the most ancient times when we would sacrifice our kings to your bloody goddess. That is how queens ruled. But you are not being murdered. The chiefs have taken you from a hovel in the hills, educated you, and exalted you with the finest treasures and gifts of all the clans. Now we want you to live in a palace, the wife of a great man. What cruelty are we inflicting on you that you run away from us like this?"

She responds in a smoky tone of mischief: "I would be grateful for this, Uncle, but the faerïe will not come with me to Tintagel. The faerïe will not live in a Roman palace, even among Britons."

Kyner stiffens, his military discipline asserting itself against the rapture that flows from the queen, and he curses, "Damn your faerïe, then! Don't you understand, child? The invaders outnumber us. We need this alliance with the Britons to save our land, our people."

She gives him a studious look, searching until she is certain that her rapturous spell is not entirely broken. Then she says in tones light as thistledown, "Uncle, of course I know this. That is why I have run off, because I believe there is a better way." The timewinds twang in her chest, intersecting dangerously, entangling themselves in her perception of Kyner's irate will. This is the delicate moment. The moment that tests her own true will against this warrior's might. Imperceptibly, she modulates her breathing, focuses on the blissful life flowing in her, from Her the Mother of all, and into Kyner. When she sees his flared nostrils relax, she says, "I have learned a great deal from the crone Raglaw. More than I can tell you now. But heed this: The battlefield shadows a higher world—"

"The spirit world of the angels," Kyner recognizes, feeling his annoyance subside, knowing the girl is working more deeply at her calming spell and not minding at all. *She is a child*, he reasons, warmed by the gentle kindness he feels near her, yet confident that he can snap free of her enchantment in an instant if necessary.

"The world of the angels," she echoes in a low voice and with a poise that seems to arise somewhere beyond her gawky, girlish appearance. "It is real, Uncle. I have been there. And I am going again—this night. That is what I want you to see."

The battle-lord's furry eyebrows wince, perplexed. But he says nothing and watches with a clenched stare as Ygrane's eyes brighten and squint. Out from the pale folds of her raiment, she releases a huge white opal as if from inside her body, a vitreous egg oily with moonlight. Vapors of iridescent milt swirl within.

Staring into those organic densities, Kyner feels the timewinds, the braided currents that knot destiny. He experiences them as an upwelling of calamitous wonder, a terrified love, as he has known many times before in the thick of battle, a calm fury, an intensity perfect as air. He reaches for the shining thing, and his blunt fingers pass through it.

"Hoy! What is this thing?" he shouts with alarm. "What illusion have you wrought, witch?"

"No, Uncle, it is quite real," Ygrane answers, earnestly, balancing the melon of slithery light on the fingertips of her upturned hand, the better for him to behold. "You cannot touch it, because it is made of light. This very moonlight. But its power could level mountains."

"What is it?"

Features bleached in the brightening glow, the child looks fetal and amazed. "It is the Eye of the Furor."

"I don't understand." With a tang of fright, the warrior peers closer, sees within the opalescent murk fungoid ruffles etched with capillaries of lightning. "The Furor—the sea rovers' god?"

"Yes! This is his plucked eye." She laughs with fresh surprise and holds the luminous, weightless thing above their heads. "Look at it, Uncle. Even one such as you has the sight in the presence of this glory."

Foaming seas churn within the Eye, and small, shallow-draft boats shoot out of the tumultuous breakers. Hackled with spears and helmeted men, the boats hiss to a stop on the glassy sand and spew their lethal riders.

"What is it you see?" the girl whispers, staring intently at him, intrigued by the widening horror in his glum face.

Kyner tears his gaze from those scrying depths. "Where did you get this?"

"Not I, Uncle." Ygrane smiles thinly. "Raglaw. She stole it off a troll."

"A troll?" He jerks with surprise. "Are you mad, child?" He levels a cold stare at her, all remnants of rapture dissolved in the acid fear suddenly soaking him. "Trolls are young *giants*, for God's sake! It will rip us all apart!"

"Only if it finds us." Ygrane sets the Eye of the Furor gently spinning, and it bobbles and hovers in the dark air.

Kyner looks about nervously and sees his men crouched in the blue moonlight gazing in silent awe at the arrant magic before them. “How can it not find us? Trolls have the sight, do they not?”

“Yes, they do, Uncle. But I’ve learned ways to blind the sight.” With a twist of her wrist, she sends the Eye wobbling higher, and watches him while it floats above them in the windless night. “The troll will not find us right away. There is time—time to escape.” She gestures to where the Eye carries its baleful light higher.

“What are you saying?” Unwilled, his hand is at his sword hilt. The timewinds tighten. The knots of destiny slip into their places. Kyner feels this as a mounting certainty that something lethal is about to happen.

Ygrane’s low voice in the new darkness under the dwindling star of the Eye is so hushed he can hardly hear it above the muffled pounding of his heart. “Climb to heaven with me, Uncle. Tonight is a holy time for the gods. Ancestor Night—a night every god honors, the one night we can trespass heaven without fear of their wrath. Come with me!”

Kyner squints at her, trying to comprehend the moment. In a gestalt flash reminiscent of battle-vision, he perceives his surroundings with exquisite precision. He records the position of every soldier and fiana in the leafy shadows.

Celestial wool gathers directly overhead, a burning cloud, aglow with the Eye it has swallowed. The witch-queen—for she is none other to Kyner now—stands before him limp as a mourner, head bowed, face veiled by her long hair.

“Listen to yourself, child,” Kyner commands with bluster. His men sidle nervously through the ferns, gawking up at the luminous cloud cut with swift horizontal rays of stardust.

The fiana ignore the eerie firestorm, all eyes on their queen.

“You’re talking to a Christian!” Kyner shouts at her, yelling to overcome the cold instinct that wants to cut her down and avert the impending moment. “Jesus has already paid my soul’s bond with his sacred blood. Heaven waits for me, and I fear no god but God! Come away from this place now."

Ygrane peers through the curtain of her hair and watches Kyner pry his hand from his sword hilt, finger by finger. He thinks he wills her mercy, because she has dwelled in his house and he is a stalwart Christian. But she knows otherwise. She feels the time-strands, the platinum filaments of fate, twanging as he strains against them, wanting to kill her.

She warns him, "If we go from this place, the troll will find us—and quickly, too."

"Leave the Eye here for the troll." He takes her wrist in his callused grip, and her flesh feels heatless as wax. "We're getting out of this damned place now—"

A bellow labors in the outer darkness, and a pure blue scream goes up from one of the horses. Bloodspray drizzles out of the sky, sets black ripples circling on the tarn and speckles hot pinpoints on the shoulders of the fiana and upturned faces of the soldiers.

The men shout as one, swords suddenly in their hands. Ponies burst through the willows, all wild manes and flashing teeth, and from the top of the ravine, the soldiers' big battle-horses come pounding down the embankment, eyes rolling with fear.

Appalled, Ygrane watches a horse's limb wing across the wrinkled face of the moon. The timewinds calm, and the fateful silver knots of her magic turn to quicksilver, draining away in dark shimmers. Now, she realizes, anything can happen.

The torn haunch thuds among the soldiers and sends them scurrying over the edge of the tarn and onto the frogskin mud at the water's lip.

To Kyner's accusatory silence, Ygrane mumbles, "It got through my spell-maze—got through faster than I thought—"

Magic gone, the witch-queen appears a dismayed child. She gazes at the dark flecks of horseblood splattered on her white raiment, and a febrile dread grips her.

Kyner, with Short-Life in his hand and unfettered by the queen's enchantment, weighs for an instant his loyalty to this witch-queen against his vow to exterminate enemies of the Church. One glance at the confused fright in her face settles it for him. Though she has called this abhorrence upon them, he knows certainly now that she is not evil. What she has done comes from a child's foolishness, not the anti-life of vampyres and lamia. He turns Short-Life outward.

Directly below the rock shelf, where the fiana stand ready to throw themselves at whatever comes over the wooded crest, Falon calls, "Older sister! The troll sees the Eye! It has stopped!"

Ygrane looks up, startled, and recognizes that the magic is not gone from her as she had thought in her panic. It is above her, drawn up out of her by the firestorm billowing high over their heads. The confusion she suffers is just the tidal ebb of a titanic wave of power.

As if standing some distance from himself, Kyner feels strangely removed from the clanging of his heart. All paths of escape have closed. They are trapped on the soggy bottom of this ravine, their backs against the tarn. His men motion to him to come down from the rock shelf and hide in the quaking mud. But he knows there is no hiding from a troll.

"Why has it stopped?" he asks, keeping his tight stare on the tree line above them.

"The Eye has caught on a branch of the Great Tree—as Raglaw said it would." Ygrane watches with wide, gleaming eyes the fiery turmoil above them, so distant it appears a malevolent star. "It has siphoned my magic after it, and the troll's as well."

A new hope opens in her, and she summons her fiana onto the shelf and arranges them in a circle around her. "You, too, Uncle," she directs, positioning him in the ring.

A pressure of command bulges Kyner's eyes with a look of near-alarm at being shoved into place. "What are you about, child?"

"Raise your swords!" the queen commands. "Point them at the Eye."

Kyner moves to protest, but the fiana have already extended their swords, and heaven's blue fire runs over their blades. He complies, and the edge of his saber suddenly sprouts fur, bunched whiskers of brilliant beryl.

Above, the spikes of the malevolent star whir like blades. The Eye of the Furor descends slowly, carrying with it a blazing cumulus hotter than the moon. Kyner's men cry out in terror. The brightening sky silhouettes immense tentacles lashing above the crest of the ravine.

The troll approaches. Its bellows reverberate so loudly the sodden ground trembles underfoot as though the land itself is in pain. Willows atop the slope flail wildly and go down.

The witch-queen lifts her arms, anticipating the torrent of power that falls toward her from the incandescent heights. A wind from below, from out of the rock slab, fills her raiment and lifts her tresses. Every point on her body sparks: her fingertips and nose touched by thorny circles of azure fire that pours over the curves of her ears and sprays from the ends of her uplifted hair in a wavery swarm of luminous blue kelp.

The troll's thunderous keening thickens, and its enormous head heaves into view, blotting the stars. Painted in moonlight and garish swatches of hot color from the incendiary storm, the engorged head reveals clusters of tiny blind eyes warting a snicking mouth-hole. And from a gaping maw of fibrillating tendrils, ordure streams spurting from the horse it has just slaverously devoured.

The cables of its squid arms rear into the sky, reaching beyond its grasp for the boiling thunderheads, and men scream. Ravening angrily, the troll topples massively forward and collapses into the ravine, shuddering the earth.

The impact sets boulders rolling and sloshes the tarn's black water onto the rock shelf. Kyner and the fiana collapse, swords spinning on the stone in fiery pinwheels. Only Ygrane remains standing. A tentacle coils over her legs and torso and coils the breath out of her, lifting her off her feet.

She hangs suspended in the spot glare from above, so close to the troll's squamous face she steeps in its heatless stink, its cold beyond the frozen miasma of dead things. Breathless, she dangles over scissoring mouthparts, sees a spiral of myriad tongues rippling inward the chewed horseflesh and bone-marl of its recent meal.

Her head and outstretched arms strain toward the empty sky. The burning cloud is gone, and the full moon wears a few hard stars in its silver aura.

Kyner and the fiana stagger upright, weapons in hand. Falon shouts, "To the circle!" The desolate cold pouring from the fallen troll leans like a wind, and the warriors struggle to find their places. The moment they do, electric flames whorl from the points of their upraised swords.

Focused by these antennae, the magic returns, bursting into the tarn in a slender pillar of fire bright as daylight. Ygrane drops softly to the ground, landing on her feet, the tentacle a brown vapor widening away. The troll is gone. Shapeshifting to some smaller form, it vanishes among the shapes of the trees, a shrunken mud thing in the sudden daylight, lumpy with nodules and cysts.

Ygrane holds in her extended hands the Eye, big as a melon, full of its milky vapors. At her nod, the swordsmen lower their dazzling blades, and she rears back and hurls the Eye toward the moon. It arcs upward as if shot from a sling, streaking an ivory rainbow, and comes down outside the ravine. The boulders and willows on the crest rear starkly in the flash of its impact, and a toll of thunder sounds dimly.

"Will it come b-back?" Kyner stammers with exhaustion, and drops to one knee, leaning on his sword and sucking for breath.

Ygrane shows her silvered palms to her kneeling fiana and opens her arms to the summery thunder smell blowing from the fire-pillar standing on the water. The refulgence draws closer, and the ravine shines with all the colors of noon. Jade hues shimmer in the willows; the tarn reflects its true tannic brown, and the strata of the cliff show red and green marls.

All fear burns off. A joy from deep past lives seizes her. This is the achievement for which she has risked all, this phosphorescent current that flows upward into the abode of the gods. With pride, she says, "Uncle, the troll will not come back. We hold a branch from the Tree of Heaven!"

Kyner blinks into the balmy light and finds his men, none missing, all kneeling. Some pray to their upright swords, some to the queen. She alone stands, raiment flowing, maned in tawny hair, sea fire in her eyes, an uncanny semblance of an older order.

"Uncle, watch over my body," she orders.

The battle-lord nods, his viscera still frosted from the living current that flowed through him and the fiana moments ago. He has no will to resist her. His men are safe. They have seen the wrathful behemoth, and yet they live. All he craves now is to return with them to Venta Silurum to tell this tale—with or without the witch-queen. *Druids be damned!*

He joins the men, who are building a circle around her with their swords, laying them on the stone tip to tip, hilt to hilt. He places Short-Life in the circuit and sits cross-legged, with his knees touching the fiana on either side. "How long will you be gone, my lady?"

"I will return at moonset. The branch will bend to earth no longer than that. Guard over my body until then. Do not break the circle of swords, or my soul is spent."

Her voice sounds sourceless to her, drawling from a slower place than the swift current of time that tugs from the pillar of fire in the tarn.

Vaguely, she grows aware that Falon calls to her: "Older sister, take me with you!" From above, she sees him crawl over his sword into the circle and put his arms about her. The image veers away, streaks into the quietude of a summer twilight, a soft citrine light, and horizons of trees hazy with sunmotes.

"Guard me well . . ." Her chin touches her chest.

The ghostly blaze in the tarn goes out, and darkness swarms in.

The Furor stands in steaming grass, smoky thickets behind him, where massive kegs loom in the haze like boulders. Oblique sunlight runs through the trees on the mountains, carrying mists, pollen fumes, and startled gusts of birds. From higher up, from snowfields of purest indigo, a drift of voices and laughter spills into the sunny woods and over the phlox fields.

The Rovers of the Wild Hunt and the Kith of the Shining Face arrive together, a happy troupe of gods this night, when honor goes to the Elders and the living leave honor aside. For tonight is Ancestor Night, the night all the dead are exalted and the living cavort with unrestricted abandon. Holy law decrees, each god shall drink a full horn of the Brewer's mead—the Furor excepted, for he shall drink a skullcup of wine fermented from the most rare fruit in the Tree, the dusk apple.

Through the pitch green trees, the revelers of the Abiding North come at a brisk stride, their furskin boots silent on the musty floor of the forest and their laughter and giddy shrieks resounding in the smoky blue canopy of the pines. The gaudy merrymakers, bedecked in animal pelts and blossoms, come hurtling through the trees, riding on each others' shoulders. These gods are determined to enjoy themselves. No matter their chief's plea, they will not contribute any energy this night to his cause.

Boldest among them is the Brewer, dressed in a barley crown and a havoc of hop bines. His mirth rings loudest in the woods as he bounds into the smoky thicket where the large casks that hold his brew wait. Directly behind him charges the Poet with the Judge clasped to his back, legs about his waist, one arm swinging wildly, owl-feather cape shedding tufts like milkweed.

The Brewer raises his hammer, strikes the bung, and releases the mead into the spiral horns poised below.

Apart from the revelers, five sullen shadows squat above, on an overhanging bluff with a commanding view of the Rainbow Mountains. Behind them, the colorful peaks climb like a ladder into the storm branches of the Tree, toward the star-strewn Gulf. The five sinister silhouettes backlit by the coronal smoke of the setting sun are the living elders of the Abiding North. They were the Furor's first allies millennia ago when he united the clans. The Guardian, Dark Mistress, Brave Warrior, the Silent One, and the Crone sit silent, waiting to drink deeply of the sacred mead. They are too old and pensive to help him now as once they did, routing the dark scorpion masters and trapping the fire eels. He nods to them, for they expect him to join them as usual. But tonight, he strides past and goes directly to Keeper of the Dusk Apples.

A stately, solar-burnished woman with sunset-streaked tresses, Keeper has loved the Furor since her childhood, when he saved her parents from the giants Freeze and Storm Silver, and for that valor received a dent in his brow above his good eye. In gratitude to the Furor, she took her present name and has since devoted herself to stravaging the twilight lands of Dusk searching for that dim country's rare wine apples.

Proudly, Keeper of the Dusk Apples, regnant in her ermine gown, presents with both hands a large, gnarled horn filled with golden wine, all that could be fermented from last year's crop. Ancestor Night traditionally begins with the Tribal Chief quaffing this precious drink in honor of the Elder ghosts, and he hoists the horn expectantly. He passes a hard stare across the happy gathering.

Then, with a scowl of unflinching defiance, he pours the libation into the grass. The wine runs off in a sun-sparkling braid, slapping a liquid sound from the mud that tears groans from the gods.

"There will be no pleasure for me this night," the Furor decrees. "In trance, I have seen the Apocalypse!"

The gods moan angrily.

"No talk of end times on this night, Chief!" the Brewer shouts, and waves his hammer.

"Yes!" the Furor shouts back. His dragonish eye sockets sweep the crowd, seeking out individual faces—the Poet's surly impatience, the Queen's glower, the Giver's bewilderment, and Keeper's gingery face wide with surprise and a glint of pride in her gray eyes. "On this night, we *must* talk of end times," he insists, and throws his horn into the grass. "Now—while there is time yet to act, to save ourselves from fiery doom."

"What of holy law?" the Judge blusters. "What of the honor we owe the dead?"

The Furor speaks in cold, measured tones. "The first honor we owe the dead is to stay alive!" He notices his brother, the Liar, sneering at him from among his friends—the Wise One, Gentle Nanna, and the Fat Lady—lackeys bound to him by cunning and deception. "Yes, brother," he continues in a more strident voice, "we must fight for our lives again! The Tribes of the Radiant South tie fateful knots in the currents of destiny. Their magic is powerful enough to cut the roots out from under us!"

"Fah!" the Liar laughs. His blond, chisel-featured caste, his look of precision and clarity, carry conviction. That is why he is the Liar, chosen by the clan to challenge and test the worthiness of every decision. He has learned well over the years how to frustrate his older brother, and he says emphatically, "The Fauni, the greatest clan of the Radiant South, are dead! We have broken them in the rootlands! We have seized the Italic peninsula for our own. We even burned their so-called Eternal City. And you're still moaning, brother, about the threat from the South?"

"I have seen it—"

"And we have heard it. All of it. Before." He gives a disapproving look. "Not tonight, brother. You've already lured away nine with your doomsday rant. Nine taken from our festival. Nine who are willing to sleep for a hundred years so you may use their lives for your magic. That is enough."

"I need more power—

"For a magic that may not even work."

"It will work. Ask the Wise One." The Furor shoots an iron look at the furtive, narrow god, who averts his gaze and tries to look small beside Gentle Nanna. "Tell them, Wise One. You've been spying on me for my brother. You know this magic will work."

The Wise One shrugs, his watery eyes two pools of alertness in his seamed and frizzy-bearded face. "You would call demons from the House of Fog—that is risky."

"Only demons are strong enough to challenge the Fire Lords," the Furor says.

The gods look back, annoyed, disgruntled. "We've heard all this before," the Liar grouses. "It's Ancestor Night, brother. Leave us in peace and go work your magic with those of us willing to forfeit their joy. We are here to celebrate!"

Murmurs of assent sweep through the gods, and the Furor silences them with his gruff voice, "Listen to me! With this magic, with the demons from the House of Fog working for us, we have a unique chance to flush all the foreign spores out of the rootlands below us."

"A chance." The Liar gives a flippant look. "You see? Your own words betray you. Why should we sacrifice a hundred years of life for a mere *chance*?"

"The magic will work," the Furor insists, "but I need more power, to be certain. The magic from the Radiant South is elusive."

"I say then nine of us are enough. Use them to call your demons and trust the rest of us to do honor to the ancestors."

The Liar turns to the Brewer and smiles broadly, teeth bright as a flashing speartip. "The Chief's libation is made. Let the mead flow!"

With a mighty thwack, the Brewer's hammer strikes the bung, and a jet of silver whips the thicket with foam, dousing the shrieking, jubilant crowd.

The Furor's hectic face clenches with disgust.

Keeper of the Dusk Apples draws closer to console him. "Don't blame them for not seeing past their pleasure. It is the way of all life to avoid death. No one looks willingly into that dark prism. You are exceptional."

"Would that I were," the one-eyed god sighs, and removes his hat to wipe the heat from his wide brow and sweep back a mane gray and turbulent as thunderheads. "If I were exceptional, Keeper, would I need the energy of other gods to work my magic?" He shakes the great bony cube of his head slowly, remorsefully, and stands, hat in hand, watching the celebrants guzzle from their frothing horns. They seat their bodies complacently on the mossy rocks and root-ledges, laughing, flirting. The Queen, her snowy hair unbraided, wears a foam mustache and a bawdy laugh and has eyes only for the Lover. He casts a lingering look of helpless amusement at the Chief across the glade and links arms with the Queen to drink from her horn.

Keeper of the Dusk Apples distracts the Furor with a golden apple she takes out of the ermine satchel at her hip. It is a token of the wine apple harvest. "The crop is rich this year, One Eye. You will taste dusk wine next Ancestor Night, after you have tied your own knots in the currents of destiny. You *will* assure our future, lord. You always have."

The Furor's gaze only lightly touches the apple, then lifts toward the clear, moteless light above the mountains, the prismatic mountains with their star-sharp peaks. He steps back from the mud puddle made by his spilled wine, and the Healer hurries over, green robes snapping with her rush to collect the enriched mire. He ignores her, continuing to step backward, head lifted, gauging the best track up into the spectral heights. "I had hoped to win a few more to our cause," he mutters, mostly to himself.

He wonders if he has enough power to work magic. "Are the others ready?"

"They wait for us on the Raven Branch." Keeper kneels and raises the golden apple. "Will you not accept your harvest of dreams?"

He pulls his gaze down from the layered horizons and notices her at his feet, kneeling. "Not this year, Keeper," he says morosely, taking her arm and gently urging her upright. He pushes the apple away, his gaze still as the stars. "I swear on the Gulf itself, I will not accept the dusk apples, I will not drink the wine of dreams again—not until I have purged our enemies from all the roots beneath the branches of our tree."

Her tawny eyes search the sharp angles and severe planes of his face, looking for a chink in his stubbornness. There is none. The Furor is so obdurate about this, he verges on trance. Purity—it is his obsession. The rootlands pure, cleansed of all foreigners. This close to him, she believes she sees the clairvoyance in his features. An expression of abstracted concern tightens his stare, a look with which he would remove grit from her eye or a thorn from her hand, gazing now into a wounded future.

She gently reminds him, "You have won control of all the rootlands in the north that the Fauni held. Only the West Isles remain."

"Old Elk-Head lives there," he answers and starts walking across the auburn field. "His tribe of Celts holds the West Isles. We will have to conquer them. They are tainted with the magic of the Radiant South."

"The Fauni conquered them centuries ago. They will offer little resistance. Soon, all the rootlands beneath us will be ruled by you."

Up the forested slope of running sunlight, the Furor leads the Keeper, not once glancing back at the gods crowded about the mead casks. "Old Elk-Head's people are older than the Fauni," he whispers, reaching deeper into himself to find the trance strength he will need to work magic. "Old as we are," he says, hushed, "they will not be easy to break."

"They are children of Mother and Freeze, just as we. Kin of the Abiding North." Keeper takes the Furor's giant arm, glad for his massive strength now that they are climbing above the swelter of the lower branches. Up here, in the thinner atmosphere, his powerful stride is sufficient to carry them both, and she flies beside him like a wind-raveling scarf.

The five living elders watch from over the brims of their drinking horns as the Furor and Keeper of the Dusk Apples pass before them. The Guardian and Brave Warrior, in their antique bone armor with spike-plate helmets and slit visors, have no faces at all. Dark Mistress and the Crone stare silently, their wrinkled, androgynous faces impassive, offering nothing. Only the Silent One salutes the Chief, raising a bulb-jointed arm with a gauping, toothless smile.

The younger gods do not understand, the Furor thinks. *They do not understand the times yet to come.*

Such times have little interest or even meaning to the gods, for whom the winking spectra of each moment brim the cups of their skulls with dreams. Time that replete needs no future. Such provenance among the north gods belongs to the Furor, whose trances see across time to a doomful climax. Apocalypse.

The vista widens as the electrical beings climb higher. The earth floats below, a huge blue crescent at the margin of day and night. The colorful, forested terrain of the midbranches falls away and disappears among frost mist. Out of that icy haze appears a sere expanse of nacreous dunes and slag rocks patched with snow—the Raven Branch. Flagrant stars yellow as topaz peer down from eternal darkness.

The gods who have chosen to sacrifice a piece of their lives for their chief wait for him on a promontory of sharp black glass, the atmosphere's brittle edge. Each is wrapped in the plush red bear hides that will keep them warm during their century-long sleep, and they lie together under the protective hood of a raw-hewn cavern.

The Furor climbs onto the blighted ridge of the Raven Branch and lowers Keeper of the Dusk Apples beside him. He is tired from the steep ascent, yet he dare not show his weariness to these good clansfolk who have entrusted their lives to him. They are already half-asleep, drugged by the hypnotic brew that has loosened their bodylights, readying them for the Furor's magic.

The goblet from which they have drunk sits on a lump of rime-rock. Keeper drinks the last of the sweet liqueur, the dregs, barely enough to put her to sleep. She will not slumber as long as the others, for she has work to do in Dusk, gathering the golden apples. Nonetheless, she desires to show her love for the Furor by tasting the sleeping brew. She wraps herself in red bearskin, and lies down beside the others. The Furor removes his hat, stands over her, and, in her suddenly drowsy gaze, his harrowed face appears swollen as the moon.

"Keeper of the Dusk Apples," he recites her name, and sleep claims her as her strength flies out of her body and into his.

Slowly, the Furor advances, pausing before each of the gods to call their name and draw forth their life energies for his own. The wife of the Brewer, Sister Mint, who concocted the sleeping potion is next, and with the passage of her energy, he feels himself grow stronger. Then, Blue, the Furor's oldest friend, gives his life-force, and the gray hues of the Raven Branch deepen in the god's one eye.

From the Ravager, the storm-rider, who is a sorceress, he receives a wink and a knowing smile. She understands this magic, having helped him design it. Her power sharpens his clarity, and the words of their shared dread find voice inside him, in telepathic silence: "Call down the Dwellers from the

House of Fog. Call down the Dark Dwellers. They will stop the hordes, the smothering flow of invaders. Cleanse the northern forests of all migrants. Purify the forests for the Wild Hunt. Summon the Dark Dwellers to crush the invaders."

The rush of words pauses in him when he comes before Beauty. Her white eyelashes flutter slightly as he breathes her name, and her lovely features relax into a deeper loveliness, a composed calm so like the immortal sleep of death it twists his heart. She is his daughter. For her, more than for all the gods or his own sanity, he will stop the Fire Lords.

Beauty's best friend, Silver Heart, lies beside her, broad oval face and narrow-slitted eyes aglow with fright. She has no notion what is really going on. She is here because Beauty is here. When the Furor whispers her name, she feels her inward parts move with joy, all fear suddenly gone. And then, she sleeps, and her strength belongs to the Furor.

With it, he can hear the thoughts of the god lying beside Silver Heart. The Dragon Witch, priestess of the planetary beast, has the laconic expression of one used to trance, and she speaks from inside his head: "The Fire Lords want to tame our Dragon. Look what they did to your friend, Bright Sky."

Chief of the Fauni clan, the famous Bright Sky called himself Lord of Heaven. He was an arrogant and lascivious god, yet he and the Furor had been friends for a short while, early on, in their youth. That is how the Furor had witnessed indirectly the deviltry of the Fire Lords. Over time, he saw what they did to Bright Sky. They literally bled him to death, draining the power out of his electromagnetic body to the earth's surface, where it was parsed among people and pooled into human collectives, warbands, village-fortresses, city-states.

"They built an empire out of Bright Sky's body," the Dragon Witch says. "And they ravaged the north. They stole our rootlands and planted strange peoples beneath us. And what became of your friend?"

The Furor silences her by saying her name and drawing her

strength into himself. The increase of vitality enlarges his memory of Bright Sky, with his remarkable laugh and ready joke. But by the end, the Furor had been forced to fall back before his old friend. Bright Sky had become a zombie, the madness of Rome.

Thunder Red Hair gazes up intently at the Furor, his father. No words are necessary between them. They are bound to the beginning and the end by their common will. The lad even resembles the father as the Furor had once looked, many years ago, before the brutalities of leadership cost him his eye and his innocence. He smiles assuredly at the square-jawed, freckle-faced youth and speaks his name proudly, "Thunder Red Hair."

Earlier spells by the Furor, evoking the Dark Dwellers from the House of Fog, once stalled the advance of the southern tribes, with its plague of cities. He swells again with the same power he used then for his magic—and now, this time, there is one more god who will give him strength. "Wonder Smith," he says, and the ruddy-cheeked arms-maker closes his gray eyes. His dimple-chin sags, and his might flows into the Furor.

The one-eyed god wants more power, but he is alone now on the Raven Branch. The oblate sun burns dark red far down the sky, at the rim of the world. He lifts his arms to the multiplying stars, and the magic seeps from him like incense. Wafts of it disappear into the Gulf, vanishing among the starshine and the fluorescent veils between the stars.

And though it is invisible now, the Furor senses the magic working. He feels the Dwellers from the House of Fog circling closer out of the void, like sharks drawn to spilled blood. They stream closer, hungry for the vitality he laces into the cold. He hears their sickly shrieks falling out of the Gulf. And then they appear, not from above but from below—windblown sparks, a hot spray of dizzy turbulence.

These are the same Dark Dwellers he has called to him before, eager again to do his bidding—so long as it is destructive. Destruction is their only utility, and he has ample use for that now. He releases all the evocative magic he has accumulated, and the whirling sparks frenzy eagerly and with such competitive urgency that one of the looping sparks collides among the others. It spins off in an acute ricochet that sends it hurtling back to earth.

By reflex, the Furor reaches for it, but it is already gone, vanishing into the planet's dark side. The one-eyed god bites back a curse. He needs every Dark Dweller he can snare. But there is no time to ponder the fate of the fallen one. He returns his attention to the handful of firepoints that have fixed themselves in the net of his magic. With these, he will defeat Apocalypse and build a new future.

The huge, pocked face of the moon floats in a lavender sky among starry pinwheels and misty shreds of neon vapors. Falon, wearing only his golden torque, stands chilled in his nakedness on the lee of a grassy bluff, pale eyes wide in awe. Purple mountains and blue tree-roughs descend toward emerald meadows and labyrinthine valleys studded with lakes of golden stillness.

At first, he does not feel the boreal wind blowing down from the high silence. The depths and swells of this primal landscape woven in gemlight transfix him. At hand, the grassheads toss with the wind in iridescent waves, each individual blade seemingly made of tufted prisms.

The cold finally pierces his astonishment, and he gawks at himself naked, his very flesh shining, bright and clear, almost transparent. He swings a startled look left and right, searching for his queen.

"Falon!" She waves from farther down the bluff, her locks of honey brown hair and the loose robes of her white raiment adrift in the swirling wind. "You should be with the others," she scolds when he runs up to her.

"I could not let you go unguarded." He peers at her, amazed

to see her luminous and tinged with tiny starpoints. "I am sworn to protect you."

Her reproving look sharpens. "You cannot protect me here, Falon. I needed you below to watch over my earthly life. Kyner may well take it upon himself to rid Christendom of another witch."

Falon flinches yet replies with certitude: "The fiana will die first."

A roving shadow blots the hillside, and Ygrane seizes Falon's arm and pulls him after her, breaking into a run. "Quickly! To the trees!"

Falon flies after her, astonished to find himself sailing through the grass, each bounding step hurtling him footless toward the dark apertures of the forest. He dares an upward glance and nearly collapses to see a giant raptor gliding overhead, its black wingspan a ragged wound of darkness in the luminous sky.

Ygrane steadies him under the predator's thundery cry, and they dash crouched through draperies of wisteria into a forest cavernous as a grotto. Luminescent mosses splotch the giant trees and glowing liana loop from the gloomy galleries. When the queen stops short, the chill air fills with sparkles of forest chaff and a minty aroma of leaf mulch.

"That raptor—" Falon says, his voice vibrant with echoes. He parts the wisteria veils and watches incredulously the giant bird dwindling down the lanes of stars. "It is big as twelve men!"

"A roc," she observes, scanning the high bluffs and their green flares of cedar. "Something has disturbed it." A vortex of bats skirls from a stand of orchid trees on the prismatic cliffs above the bluffs, and she knows then she has found her way to the right place. The one she seeks is coming. She regards Falon skeptically. "Cover yourself, man."

Falon's stunned expression fractures, as if just realizing that he is naked, and he looks about mutely, his hands groping like a blind man's. "Older sister, what is this place?" he asks, though he knows because she has told him and the other fiana that she intended to climb into the sky, yet he must hear it again.

"It is the Storm Tree, Falon. You have ascended with me into the homeland of the gods."

He yanks at gray shawlmoss from a near bough, shreds it, and starts fashioning a loinwrap.

"You should be with the others, Falon," she repeats in a dire tone. "I've come to make a new meaning of my life. I must do it alone."

"I'm here to protect you. I'm not going back without you."

"We can't go back till moonset."

"Till moonset, then." He ties off his loinwrap with a lash of vine. "You've been here before, I think."

"Not in this life."

"Your robes came up with you—"

"Yes, they are woven with silver thread." She spies a gleam of eyes in the fretful shadows, many retinal sparks, blinking like fireflies. Falon notices them a moment later and moves to guard her. "Pixies," she says, stopping him with an upraised hand. "They're harmless. Just curious. They don't see the bodylights of people up here often."

Falon observes then that there are many tiny humanoids scuttling through the phosphorus dark. "Why are we here?"

"You know."

"To work magic for our people." He apprehensively searches the cold heights of the canopy, where slants of frosty light illuminate a tumult of vines and gnarled boughs. "But you have not told us what magic that is."

"The magic of sacrifice, Falon." She sidles through the curtain of hanging flowers, back into the mauve dusk, and stands staring upward at the sawtoothed mountains.

"Sacrifice?" That word tightens Falon's mouth, and the fierce orange whiskers of his mustache bristle. "That is why you've come alone? To sacrifice yourself?" A fluster of red butterflies crisscross after him through the rent draperies as he follows his queen into the open. "You are going to sacrifice your life?"

"Yes." She begins marching back up the bluff, still watching the purple sierras, where stars glitter like spume. "I haven't seen you here in my sight, Falon. That means you should not be here. I don't want you to interfere, do you understand?"

"I am sworn to protect your life, older sister." Guardedly, he searches side to side, spotting rat-swift motions in the dense grass, where the ground steams wispily as if still cooling from the primordial day. He is not sure if the cold that bites deeper into his flesh is the wind or his dread. "No matter what magic you might win for our people, I cannot allow you to sacrifice yourself to death."

She stops and looks at him softly. Each hair in her eyebrows, each amber eyelash, glints in the strange shine here. "Falon, not death. I mean to sacrifice my life to *him.*"

She lifts her young face upward, toward a giant man skidding down from the mountains, his blue cape flowing translucent and furled as starsmoke in the sky above, dragging all the heavens behind him. He is bigger than the roc, his stride encompassing whole slopes of spilled boulders. The slant brim of his hat flaps with his vigorous gait.

At a glance, Falon recognizes the roisterous, soot-streaked beard and the eagle-hooked visage of the one-eyed god. "The chief of the north gods!"

"Wait for me in the woods, Falon." She shoves into the jeweled grass and waves her arms with a ritual slowness.

Falon shadows her, bent with fear. "Does he know we used his eye to climb up here?"

Ygrane pauses and points a commanding finger at her guard. "You will not breathe that again. Not again. You're not supposed to be here. Go back to the woods."

"Surely, he has already seen us—"

"Go anyway." She continues up the grassy slope, and winged

sprites big as dragonflies burst into the shining air around her. She waves them aside, toppling one into Falon's path. It tangles in his red hair, the transparency of its wings visible briefly as it struggles free, a finger-long person with large, irenic eyes. In a flutter, the naked thing is gone.

"Older sister, wait!" He rushes to her side. *This is a dream*, he tells himself, remembering Ygrane in the circle of swords, asleep. But the precise chromatic graininess of sight and the bite of the alpine wind slay that hope. With genuine fear, he croaks, "He is the god of our enemies!"

"Wait here, Falon." She fixes him with a steady stare, to show that she is serious, and he stops. "You should be with the others. I don't want you to interfere. The timewinds are easily disturbed. Do you understand?"

Falon says nothing. He looks beyond her to where the giant advances, boarskin boots crunching down the gravel slide of the talus slope directly ahead. Curiously, as he paces closer, he condenses, his translucent colors hardening. In moments, he is before them, a head taller than Falon, but human-sized. A dense fragrance of stormwind and lightning rolls from him, and this heaven's smoke alone is imposing enough to drop them humbly to their knees.

"All-Seeing Father!" Ygrane pipes, her eyes fixed on his scuffed boottips. "I am Ygrane, queen of the Celts—"

"I know you." The Furor's deep voice encloses them. "I have seen you in this moment before."

"I come offering myself—"

"You want alliance with the north tribes. I know. I know all this." His low voice, with its sediment of gravel, carries grave concern, some profound unhappiness. "We have been in this moment before, you and I. You must have seen it."

"I have, my lord," the queen confesses.

"Then why is he here? You know he should not be here."

Falon dares a glimpse up through his eyebrows and catches enough of the Furor's scowl to slam his attention back to the ground, to the luminous filaments of crushed grass under his knees.

"He came unbidden, my lord. He is my personal guard. Faith has led to Fate."

The Furor is groggy from the magic he has worked on the Raven Branch. His head throbs. All the strength in his giant frame has been depleted binding demons, and now he just wants to go Home. But there are obstacles, first among them his aching brain, full of timeshadows and the sickly aftermath of magic.

Then, there is the obstacle of time itself. Climbing to the Raven Branch and back down has seemed to take a few very strenuous minutes, when in fact twenty years have lapsed. Once more, it is Ancestor Night, and before he can return to Home, he must go first to the drunken festival, where the Liar will mock him openly and the others hide their smirks. Otherwise, his role as chieftain of the Abiding North is in jeopardy. With all his allies asleep, he must stay close to his enemies.

And then, there is this queer obstacle—this aberration before him, Ygrane, queen of the Celts. While in the throes of calling the Dark Dwellers out of their House of Fog, he saw this human. The winds of the future blew images of this encounter into his entranced mind. At the time, he dismissed what he had seen, believing it a blurred deflection of time's currents. That happens often in the stormy branches, in trance. Time surges and eddies like the wind, and sometimes it goes still and glassy and carries mirages.

Seeing people in the Great Tree is usually an illusion. Few humans have the electrostatic strength to project their waveforms into the Tree. Those few who have arrived have been old wizards and witches, those who had spent their lifetimes hoarding energy as greedily as the Dragon. This one is too young to be here by her own magic. She is some kind of priestess chosen by others of her kind, older ones who have accrued a great deal of power and are using her to reach him.

The Furor removes his hat to pinch the knot of flesh between his eyebrows where his headache is nailed. In trance, he heard her plead with him to spare her people, to take her as sacrifice, to use her as he pleases. But he does not want her. Unlike his old friend Bright Sky, the Furor has no desire for intimacy with the denizens of the rootlands. Though his years among them have bred admiration in him and though he sacrificed an eye to gain their knowledge, he still considers them a breed of lesser beings, no matter their uncanny resemblance to the gods.

"Faith has led to Fate," the Furor grumbles, gazing down at the abject mortals. The appearance of this other one, this antique warrior, disturbs him. He was not in the trance. That can only mean that the timewinds are picking up, beginning to surge again and shift the future his magic has wrought. He must hurry on, to Ancestor Night, to Home for rest, and then down to the hot, sweltering rootlands, into the stink and humidity of the Dragon, and there to purge the land of the Fire Lords' minions, the foreign tribes from the south.

But first, this obstacle. This foretold encounter. Consequence ripples from this young queen or he would not have seen her in trance. His head aches so remorselessly, he cannot think clearly what this must mean, and he simply wants to be on his way. "I will not have you, queen of the Celts. I will not have any earthly woman. This you should know."

"I am not any earthly woman, my lord," Ygrane speaks up respectfully, yet with a hint of petulance in her voice. Still, she does not raise her face. The god's field of force is so highly charged that, unless he restrains himself, just being near him could cause her and Falon's bodylights to burst apart in a blink. Yet, she is fearless. She has come into this life for this very moment, to win the Furor's favor and save her people. "The Celts are a cousin race of the north tribes. I am offering you our allegiance."

The Furor heaves a sigh like a hush of steamy rain. "We have seen this moment before, Ygrane. You know my answer."

The queen is undaunted. From a waistpouch in her robes, she withdraws a rock. It is round and flat, big as her open hand and with an off-center hole the width of a thumb. At first, the stone appears black. But as Ygrane lifts it in offering to the god, light threads through the hole and shows that the stone is black and jellied with amber, like molasses.

"This is a rubbing stone," Ygrane says, sitting back on her haunches and facing the Furor's rawhide-lashed leggings. "It is old, from a time when the Celts and the north tribes were one clan." With her free hand, she takes a lock of her apricot hair and guides it through the hole in the stone, sawing it back and forth. "Across three hundred centuries, this gentle movement has shaped rock. A thousand separate lives have carved this emblem. A thousand deaths have carried it through time to me."

After vigorously rubbing the pierced stone with her hair, she touches her finger to the stone, and a spark snaps between them. The electric fire ignites her fingertip, and it burns with a slow white brilliance. "This is my gift to you, in honor of our common past," she says, and dares to raise her flourishing green gaze as she presents her offering.

A gift on Ancestor Night! The Furor gnashes his teeth but withholds his ire. He does not want to incinerate this crafty little witch, not on Ancestor Night. She could well have been sent here by the Liar, who would make himself chief if his brother proved himself a murderer on this holy night.

Exhilaration whirls through Ygrane when the chief of the north gods takes the pierced stone from her fiery hands. This much has transpired exactly as Ygrane's mentor, the crone Raglaw, predicted. By keeping the pierced stone in the same pouch that had held the god's eye, it had indeed remained invisible to the Furor's trance vision.

Upon taking the offering of amber schist, the Furor feels the pain dim within his skull. This is a true gift. It carries enough electric potential to soothe his weary body. And now that he has accepted it—as tradition requires—and received its benefit, he must reply in kind.

An atmosphere of hazard thickens in the space where the pain had been. *In kind*. A gift this venerable, going back to before his reign, to the early days of the Old Ones, when even they were young, requires respect. Yet if he gives her an object of his power, as she rightly expects, having cleverly found her way not only into the Great Tree but deftly into his very presence, he cannot fight her people.

Ygrane keeps her lustrous face upturned, her green eyes glittering with anticipation. She is a breath away from saving her people a savage war. All she needs is for the Furor to acknowledge their kinship with a personal gift—a whisker from his beard, the cord from a boot, anything tangible that she can carry to earth and shape into magic.

"Did the Liar send you to me?" he asks, his good eye a squint.

"No! I used the pierced stone and the magic of the Crones to climb here. They told me where I would find you."

"The Crones," he mutters into his beard, relieved this is not the Liar's work. He presses the pierced stone to his brow and drinks in the soothing coolness of it. "I did not think the Celts obeyed the Crones anymore, not in these modern times, not under the chiefs."

The proud plane of her cheek darkens as she says, "The chiefs lead us to war. That is why I am here, offering myself to you. The mothers don't want war, especially not with you. We are kin. Marry me to one of your warrior-lords in the rootlands. To Horsa—he is the Saxon warlord you have sent against us. Let us stop killing each other and let the old ways flourish."

"Old ways?" He slaps his hat back on and slants it menacingly over his one eye. "Your ways are not old ways. When the Celts split with the north tribes, they went south, into the tropic lands—and there you learned foreign ways, alien teachings—the word, Brahman, logos, and your obsession with numbers and metals—the very madness that the Fire Lords are using to contaminate the earth."

"Numbers—letters—" Ygrane stammers, swiftly pulling together her thoughts before this unexpected outburst, "these gifts can be used by the north tribes, too."

"No!" The boom of his voice makes Falon jump and the queen sit deeper on her haunches. "Don't you see, witch? These are not gifts. They are poisons! They grow cities. They cover the rootlands with straight lines, breaking the dragonflow of energy, turning your people from the wandering tribesfolk we have always been into zombies that live in boxes and never touch the naked earth. The magic of the Fire Lords is the secret of other worlds, not earth. I will not let them destroy our earth!"

Ygrane bows her head under the impact of the god's voice and submerges her fears in thought: This is Ancestor Night, and she is safe from his wrath. He has already accepted her gift. But, clearly, Falon's presence troubles him, as it does her. Time's weird dimensions shift and stretch to include this new presence. She tries to feel deeper inward, to feel out what will happen next. But she is too airy in this disembodied state to feel anything but the chill wind descending from the stars.

"The old ways of this stone have long been lost by your people," the Furor states, tapping the artifact against his palm. "You are possessed by alien forces that want to clear the primeval woodlands and build cities of steel. I have seen it. If it is not stopped now, there are terrors you cannot imagine awaiting us."

Ygrane notes the lack of bitterness in his voice, the tinge of melancholy behind his outrage, as though he already understands his effort is too late. And she dares to say to his face of haggard shadows, "You are wrong. The magic of the south tribes has already changed the world. We cannot go back. But if we go forward together, as one people, we can use the best of this magic to—"

"Silence!" His voice explodes over her, and she covers her face, expecting to be extinguished. And though her body of light wavers, it does not fly apart. "Out of respect for Mother and Freeze, our common parents, I will not destroy you, queen of the Celts. Not this night. Look at me."

She lifts her pallid face and stares into the black core of his one eye.

"You are everything I want to destroy," he says with icy intensity. "So I cannot give you what you want. Not a hair from my head, witch. Yet—" He tilts back his hat and thumbs away the last of the hurt that thorns his brow. "Yet, in honor of Mother and Freeze, I will not withhold my gift. And though I know you will use it against me, I give it freely. Stand, Ygrane. Stand and accept my gift of a single memory."

The queen sways to her feet, dizzy with a sense of miracle and a great depth of disappointment. The crone Raglaw has said that Ygrane must return with some *thing* from the Furor in exchange for the ancient stone—but a memory? Is that enough to work magic?

"Twenty years ago, before I climbed into the Raven Branch from where I am now descending, I saw a unicorn." He strokes his beard, rubbing the pierced stone against its turbulent length as he remembers. "Have you ever seen one?"

She shakes her head.

"They come from the sun. They come down here into the Tree now and then. The Fire Lords send them like pack animals to carry away energy from the Dragon. They come and they go. Only rarely do I see them in the north, where I saw this one. Twenty years ago. Not that long ago. They may prowl around for a century or two before returning to the other side of the sky and the herds on the sun's wind."

The Furor extends the pierced stone toward her face, and a green spark hops from it to her brow. She sees the memory then—the radiant point of extraterrestrial energy tracing a slow path over the Dragon's pelt.

"The memory is a god's memory," the Furor states, tucking the pierced stone into the pocket of his rawhide leggings. "I don't need to tell you, a witch-queen, how much power a god's memory has in the mind of a lesser being. The unicorn will come when you call it. And you will see, it is a worthy gift for the pierced stone."

The Furor strolls away, down the bluff and into the woodland on his way to the festival of Ancestor Night. The gods will be amused by the old stone polished so bright with human dreams. With this energy of bygone times for play, there will be less time to mock and plot against him. And then, he will return to Home and rest. In a few years he will be ready to climb down to the rootlands to conquer the West Isles and earn himself a long draught of the Keeper's golden wine of dreams.

Already far behind him, on the grassy bluff, Falon remains with his face to the ground until the queen puts her hand in his hair and bids him rise. Her woeful features pretend composure. "We can wait here till moonset," she says in a thick voice of swallowed tears. She shuffles through the switching grass to a cowl of rock that mutes the wind. "We'll fall asleep then. When we wake, we'll be back in the circle of swords."

Falon sits beside her, close enough for the tearful embrace he knows is coming. He says nothing, just watches her freckled face grow more and more childlike as the import of what has happened settles in. At last, the tears come, and he presses her to him and holds her steadily, glad at last to be strong for her.

"I have failed our people," she sobs. "Again—I have failed."

"No, older sister. You have climbed the Storm Tree. You have stared into the face of a god and yet live. And you have his gift."

"There will be war."

"I know."

The vast moon touches the deep violet haze of the mountains, its broken face coppery in the long light of its setting. Ygrane pulls away and blots her tears with her sleeve. "We cannot stand alone against the Furor." She cannot say the rest—that the druids are right and an alliance with the Romans is their only hope—and for that, she must marry their warlord.

Falon knows what she thinks, and he cannot deny her reasoning. She is the queen. By magic or marriage, she is the salvation of her people, who look to her and the chiefs to protect them from the sea raiders and the wilderness marauders. From that fate, neither he nor even the gods can protect her.

"There is the unicorn," he says. "It is a magical creature—and it is yours."

Ygrane does not speak as she sinks into the sorrow of her failure. The unicorn to her is only an emblem, a token of this fabulous adventure. It will not stop the Furor. Yet she fiercely remembers that the god himself predicted she would use the beast against him. And she will.

As sleep insinuates itself in her, she determines that she will defy the Furor. She will make him wish he had accepted her for his own. She will hate him so much, he will wish he had loved her.

—BOOK ONE—

DRAGON LORD

The Sorrows *of* Lailoken

I am a brother to dragons . . .
—JOB 30:29

Tintagel at high morning shines as though carved from tusk. Its fabled spires and terraced battlements float among rainbows and sea spray. Spume from the breakers exploding on the cliffrocks far below floats upward in goat-feathers, and drifts past the windows of the queen's chambers.

Ygrane, her brassy red hair torqued with sweat, squats in bed wearing a green satin birthing gown. She is eighteen hours into a hard labor and lies exhausted. Three maidens kneel at her bedside praying. Another cools her brow with a damp cloth.

Between contractions, she dozes, oblivious to those around her. She drifts among moody memories of all that brought her to this suffering, and the past encloses her in its hauntful cave. There, the ghost of the child's father unfurls like incense smoke, and she quickly turns her mind away.

Uther Pendragon has been cursed enough—she thinks, and she will not blame him for her anguish. It was she who called him—she who called this destiny to herself across lifetimes. She understands this is so, though she can no longer feel the timewinds that blow souls among the forms.

The magic is gone. The next contraction is coming. That is

all she knows now of memory and prophecy. She floats on her pain as on a pale, glacial lake. Clouds shimmer in the lake. They are souls. Some have died and are drifting away. Others arrive to be born. One of them is her child. He is coming. She has called him to her as she called to herself the baby's father, Uther Pendragon, and before him the demon-wizard Myrddin, and before him the unicorn, the Furor's gift . . .

At the foot of Ygrane's bed stands a Fire Lord in luminous raiment and with a shining face of flames. No one sees him, because the queen's magic has passed away and with it has gone her sight. The world of gods, angels, and demons burns unseen before Ygrane, while a new world swells in her lap.

The Fire Lord stares into her and backward across time. He watches Ygrane and sees her as a peasant child in the hills at play with the faeries, then later as a young queen, when she climbed into the Storm Tree and accosted the Furor himself. Closely, he peers at the time when Ygrane first confronted the unicorn.

Time flexes like a lens, and Tintagel appears as it looked on that afternoon years ago, its ivory spires and terraced battlements afloat among flurries and sea spray. Spume from the breakers exploding on the cliffrocks far below floats upward in goat-feathers, and swirls about Ygrane where she stands in a wintry garden atop a tower.

The queen wears a gown festooned with feather amulets and bone-bead talismans designed to amplify her magic. She raises her arms, and the spindrift leaps into the wind with the blurred shape of the unicorn. Her spell soars into the thunder-noise of the sea.

Then, comes the cry—a reverberant call wide as thunder, insistent as the ocean's bellow, rolling across the snowbound horizon yet also pulling from within, like the sap's withdrawal at winter's touch. The mysterious call tugs at the unicorn, and it cannot help but respond. Pulled away from its seclusion in the forest as if by a leash, it slides westward.

This is not the summons of the angels, it knows at once. The draw of this undercurrent is too cold, an arctic ebb tide luring it into the depths of winter. Escape is only possible upward. It must leave the Dragon's pelt entirely. It must bound away from the earth and return to the fields of the sun. That is the only way it can break this mysterious bond that fetters it to the sunset sky. Who is calling it, then—it does not know. Yet, it knows full well that if it departs earth to escape this call, it will not return. The love of the herd will be too strong after so long away, too many-voiced and familiar for it to return to this lonely and eerie place, no matter its loyalty to the Fire Lords. So, the unicorn travels west, head high, as if willingly. It must see who has shackled it and why. If necessary, it can always leap away from the Dragon and abandon the angels. Its fear flattens, and, calmly, it proceeds down the ebony steps of the horizon, through the rum-smoke of twilight, and into the west, touched red.

The unicorn steps from the sky, alighting silently on the flagstones of an aerie garden, a flat-crowned tower covered with loam and a spiral walkway. At the center of the winter-dead garden, the curving path finds a flat boulder of blue rock. Ygrane, a woman of twenty-two winters, stands atop it in white robes full of seawind. Her tresses shine cinnamon in the sharp sunlight, and her silver-ringed hands shimmer with transparent energies—the leash that the Furor placed in her grip years before.

Soundlessly, the unicorn paws its blue opal hooves on the flagstone at the far end of the spiral path. Its long eyes carry the same emerald light as the Celtic queen's. Watching unblinkingly, the spike-browed steed walks the stone path at a stately gait. It bears its horn high, pulling back on the witch-queen's magnetic leash to demonstrate that it can rip free if it wants.

Ygrane holds tight and even dares pull harder. For many seasons, she has been calling the unicorn with the magic that the Furor gave her in the Great Tree. Whenever she has visited Tintagel, she has worked this magic, patiently feeding the call with her life-force, feeling the connection reach out, make contact, and tighten. Hundreds of times she has stood here calling to the unicorn, drawing it closer across the years.

Now that the magical being has been pulled into view, time weirdly accelerates. Clouds shred overhead, and the sun rolls to its southern retreat while the unicorn completes the spiral. When it stands before the queen, with the dark sockets of its nostrils exhaling a summery haymown breath, the world slows to dusk. Twilight's citrons and greens streak the sky and reflect in the animal's lustrous coat.

In that first, daylong instant, all the purpose and history of the young queen sluice through the unicorn. But it has no interest in that. Its mind reaches deeper into the human animal that has summoned it. It sees through the vault of dolls that are Ygrane's thoughts and finds at the back of her soul the living gods that empower her.

They are the Daoine Síd, the very old gods who served Mother in the time before the Chiefs. Their king is Elk-Head, self-named Someone Knows the Truth. Like the Furor and the other gods, he once dwelled with his clan in the branches of the Great Tree. But centuries ago, the Fauni defeated him and drove the Síd out of the bright boughs.

The wounded gods scurried and crawled across the cracked hide of the Dragon, and many were devoured whole. The Dragon would have consumed them all, but there were too many to ingest at once. During that vital interval, with the Dragon swollen drunkenly on its feast, shrewd Elk-Head had time to bargain with the voracious beast. In exchange for receiving sanctuary for the Síd in the subterranean root-coils of the Great Tree, Elk-Head agreed to feed the Dragon regularly.

Since then, the Síd have lived underground, luring gods, giants, trolls, and people into the maw of the Dragon. The witch-queen Ygrane is one of their priestesses. They have charged her with a vast store of power to minister to their armies, the dragon hordes, who prowl the western lands seeking sustenance for their draconic master.

This woman is precisely the ally the unicorn needs to continue serving its masters, the Fire Lords, and it greets her with a chimeful cry and a gentle wag of its head. Ygrane accepts the happy greeting by offering her hands to the slant-faced creature. The silver rings on her fingers smell of thunder, and the unicorn nuzzles against her.

Ygrane has foreseen this moment for years and is not surprised by the morning stars in the staring green eyes or the smoke-swirl of its fur. What surprises her is the blue quiet that uplifts her heart.

And then, the unicorn is gone. Glimmering away on the shining wind, it disappears into the pond of the night.

In the cellar of Tintagel's north tower, Raglaw sits in darkness. The crone gnaws a knob of dream-root and listens to the timewind buffeting her skull. The current, swift all around her, carries echoes and a voice. The echoes are the treadfalls of her heart and the crepitance of her brittle joints. The voice is a demon's—the demon who fell from the sky during the Furor's powerful spell.

Dame Raglaw knows that the demon's fall was not the accident it appeared. Crones have the sight. The timewind shapes the smoke of their minds, and every crone who watched the Furor summon demons from the Gulf felt the fateful currents spin wildly. Some saw the timewind outline the seraphic rays of a Fire Lord on the mountaintop where the demon collided with the Dragon. Others saw nothing.

The crone witnessed enough to listen, and eventually she heard what she expected—the telepathic sorrows of a demon trapped by the Fire Lords.

A voice of shadows crosses the borders of hearing—

"Woman. Everything I am I owe to Her. All the good and the bad in my life. All the sorcery and mystery. All the wisdom and madness. Even in the very beginning, before there could be space, or time either, when every point of each of us touched every point of each of the others, She was there. She was Herself the one point out of which everything has come. And She was the coming, too. Why do you think we left but to follow Her?

"In the very, very beginning, before there was a beginning, when everything was one point, Woman was all the incomprehensible meaning we needed. She held us together. She made us one. Wholly promiscuous, for we were all together with Her—yet wholly chaste, for She was as utterly alone as we were—one whole and single point. What greater happiness could there be?

"That was the question that doomed us. That we could think it at all bespeaks a terrible flaw in an otherwise perfect wholeness. But, of course, it was our perfection that inspired the question in the first place. How much happier could we be if we were to be a part of Her yet apart from Her? How much more happiness would there be if we could see Her and be seen?

"And with that question came the necessity for the space to see and the time in which to be seen, the space a hug needs, the time a kiss requires, a space and a time vast enough to embrace all the mystery of Her and equally ample enough to make room for all of us that wanted to see and hold Her.

"There were many more of us than any of us could have imagined. Each of us had thought we were the one and only one until we fell apart. Our clamoring for Her drove Her away from us—and naturally we followed, out into space and into time, wanting to be with Her as we have always been with Her. But in a new way. And so space and time came into being. Only none of us, except perhaps for Her, could have known how cold and dark it was going to be.

"And none of us, surely not even She, could have anticipated the woe that was to follow—and the joy that woe would require to make itself whole again. And none suspected the sorcery and wisdom that we would have to learn and possess to match the mystery and madness of losing Her. Nor did we realize the vast distances, the expanding light-years of space and what great aeonian spans of time it would take even to begin to approximate the generous and true wholeness we had enjoyed when we were all at one point.

"Little did any of us foresee our bizarre fate. How strange that, out here in space and time, each of us is so wholly separate from others. How strange that She is everywhere and yet nowhere. How much stranger yet that She has become woman—and out of woman's diminishment, out of the exile from the body of the ovaries to become testicles, out of the stunting of her nourishing breasts to useless nipples, out of the maiming of the fullness and symmetry of her chromosomes to a genetic mutation has come the distortion that is man.

"Is there any wonder then that we men suffer and in our suffering we rage? We are the immortal points that broke apart from the one point to follow Her here. We are the eternal wanderers. And where is She now? She is everywhere and nowhere. She is the embrace of the great emptiness that is the universe. She is the long-lingering kiss of time. She is everything She always was—and everything we always wanted Her to be. Now we serve Her or we rail against Her, because we can never escape Her or ever really find Her. She is nameless and She is the very breath of all names—for She is the truth that finally embraces us all. She is God."

The unicorn returns to Tintagel whenever it is summoned. Atop the aerie garden, it meets with Ygrane on the spiral path. There is ample opportunity to share themselves with each other, now that there is no resistance between them, no distorting of time as at their first meeting.

She touches its braided horn, and the azure silence fills her with an incomprehensible peace, the serene joy of wild things, a motionless clear immensity in which everything has already happened and her brief history as a woman and even her previous histories in other lives are so much spindrift. In this vast quiescence, all her troubles fade. The plight of her people, the dark confessions of war, even the death of hope and desire close around this one eternal instant of bliss.

While Ygrane drifts enraptured, the unicorn's sentience reaches within her, seeking contact with her gods, allies of the Dragon. They are far away, beyond the horizon's unswerving boundary, underground among the tangled rootcoils of the Great Tree. The witch-queen's body serves as an antenna, and so long as she holds the unicorn's own antenna, the solar being can feel past the warm oxidation of carbohydrates and amino acids in the human's body to the electrical presence of the gods.

In the unicorn's acute mind, these passionate entities of electromagnetic flame appear as what they are: rapid, furious bodies of pure energy in all the colors of the sun. To humans, they appear human, and if the unicorn wished, they would shape space like one of its own breed. But the unicorn is not calling to them for communion, only for knowledge.

From the subterranean gods of the Celts, it learns of secret clefts in the gorge-walls of the planet, trapdoors covered over by deceptively solid sheets of diorite. To a puny electrical being such as the unicorn the ground would seem solid enough, yet if it crossed that terrain, it would be easy prey for the Dragon.

With each visit to the aerie garden, the unicorn learns another of the Dragon's secrets: the cycles of its dreamsongs, the creature's fear of the vaster silence that encloses the songs, and the wonder the Dragon feels for its own magnificence. And with each visit, spring budges closer. The wind off the grasslands carries a vastness of nectar, and the sheets of snow vanish on the mauve mountains. The garden blooms as the reign of the sun lengthens.

Arriving one soft, glamorous morning, having received the vibrant tug on the magnetic leash that binds it to Ygrane, the unicorn finds the aerie garden feathery with newly sprouted herbs—mustard, bluestem, lady fern, spikenard, goldenrod, sage, hyssop, mugwort, pearly everlasting, fireweed, blue ginger, oxeye, and hemlock in wild abundance. But Ygrane is not there.

At the center of the spiral pathway, among a conflagration of blossoms and bumbling bees flying about like sparks, a scrawny old woman in tattered deerskin waits. Her scattered hair is fire-frizzed, and her shrunken face has black lips, scorched cheeks crisscrossed by deep lines, and a wilted nose shriveled almost to a skull-hole. This is the crone Raglaw. She has charred her body over the years by conducting magical currents far too strong for the human shape to carry, and now and then, pieces of her fall off and burn up before they reach the ground, like shooting stars.

The sight of Raglaw and the absence of Ygrane frighten the unicorn, and it attempts to back away. But the crone holds firmly to the magnetic leash and slowly, powerfully, draws the horned beast closer. In a panic, the animal of light leaps upward and staggers back, its strength spilling into the flagstones.

Blue with copper, the rock spiral conducts the unicorn's power to the center, where the crone stands, her calcined body an antenna. She receives the creature's waveform and directs it through the tower into the earth, where she has tied it to the Dragon's hide. As the planet turns, it inescapably draws the unicorn toward the center.

The sun slides swiftly across the sky toward its northern retreat, its slanting seams fanning across the mauve mountains and the blue enamel sea. By dusklight, the dark, bonepit eyes of the crone reach across the last inches toward the alien's vertical pupils.

In those dark flames, the crone sees an old, old man curled up in his vast beard like a knobby insect unsheathed from a cocoon. The aged man's face looks sunken as a skull. In its sockets, two limpid pools of water fracture light into rainbows that arc away into a cosmic darkness. The spanless depths in those eyes reveal a demon's presence.

A predatory look tightens the hag's features. She seizes the twisted horn in a three-fingered hand and poises her other claw close to the corner of the unicorn's eye. It sees a twinkle of metal there and jolts still with fear. The crone presses a thin silver blade against the rim of its sight, and it knows by the masterly pressure of her grip that there is no mercy or flight possible.

The crone intends to sacrifice the unicorn to her mistress of the earth-wall, Drinker of Lives, the Dragon. She does not feel the blue stillness within the living horn. That vigorous serenity carries its light cleanly through her and down the blue rocks of the tower. At the base, it seeps into the earth, a salty, shining flavor of eternity.

The Dragon tastes this rare light and instantly rouses from its intent dreamsongs. Lightning tangles in the clear, sunset sky on the ocean's horizon, and it rises toward the offering.

"Raglaw!" Ygrane cries from among tall mallow grass. She climbs from the stairwell hidden there and clambers over the wooden hatch, trampling a moist bed of cowslip in her hurry to stop the crone.

The shout strikes Raglaw, slackening her grip for an instant, and the unicorn spills away like quicksilver.

"Wau-wraugh!" the crone cries with livid pain as the Dragon's gravity tugs at her, falling back morosely from its lost prey. Thunder rolls in from across the sea, and the stars shiver in their sockets.

Ygrane pries the silver blade from the crone's hand, drops it to the flagstones, and pulls the old woman tightly to her body, pressing the pain from her. "You're too old to be tying dragon-knots," the queen scolds.

The cinder of a human visage nods wearily. Her leather-scented atmosphere bears a sour taint of decay from what is already dead in her, and she leans heavily on the young queen as they sink to their knees.

"The people die," Raglaw rasps, clenched around her pain.

Ygrane rocks her. "I will save the people."

"You!" A wrenched laugh, more like a shout of hurt, jumps from the gristled mass in Ygrane's arms. "You had your chance in the Storm Tree."

"And I seized it, old woman. I seized it, and we have the unicorn."

"We have nothing!" The hag uncurls and shoves Ygrane a bony arm's length away. "You were supposed to wed our clan to the Furor's. Are we not true kinsfolk to the Tribe of the Abiding North?" Her whiskered jaw clacks. "Are we not?"

The queen shrugs, takes off her cape, and drapes it about the crone. "The Furor rejected me. We are lucky to have the unicorn."

"Luck!" A vehement flicker of rage gouges from the hag's stare. "You paid for it with the pierced stone! There is no luck but what we make, child. Thirty thousand years of ancestry in that stone! Three hundred centuries of magic bartered for a horned horse. You, child—you pathetic child—you will not save the people with a unicorn."

Ygrane smiles at the thought. It has never occurred to her to exploit the unicorn against her enemies. She helps the crone to her feet, awed by her dark wisdom. "Come, old mother. I will take you to the fireside, and we will talk about what can be done with a unicorn. Come. The sea air is chill with night."

"You should have wed our clan to the Furor's," Raglaw mutters, drained numb of all feeling. "The Romans can't help us any more than the unicorn. No use wedding the Romans."

"I did not want to wed—" Ygrane mumbles in reply, guiding the drowsy old woman toward the stairwell. "It was the druids—"

"Kyner it was—and the Christians." The crone nods drunkenly. "They foisted you on the Romans. And now we have our duke and our people forsaking the Dragon for the nailed god. Why did you stop me?"

"The unicorn is our friend."

"Friend?" Raglaw's bones creak under Ygrane's embrace as she pulls about to face the queen. "Child! The unicorn is prey for the Dragon. Feed the Dragon. Give strength to the Drinker of Lives. That is our only hope."

In her younger days, Raglaw's dried turtle face inspired dread in her ward, but this night the queen feels only pity for this husk of her teacher. "No," she says with the conviction of her own mysterious powers, "there is a better hope. Did you not see him in the unicorn's eye?"

"See him?" The tired old woman blinks and squints. "What? What did you see?"

"Lailoken—the demon in mortal form." Ygrane pulls the cape tighter about her dazed companion. "Crone, you are too old for this magic. You nearly sacrificed our best hope."

"A Dark Dweller in a human body?" Her black lips snarl with outrage. "Impossible, child. Wholly impossible. They are too powerful, the body too frail. It would fly apart into its very atoms."

"You saw him in the unicorn's eye." Ygrane tenderly turns the old woman about and guides her through the mallow grass to the lanternlit hole in the loam. "You had your hand on its horn. You must have seen."

"I did not believe." She shakes her tattered head, still not believing. "I let it pass through me, an apparition, a dream. He cannot be a real being. Who could fit a Dark Dweller into a mortal vessel? Into a great being, such as a behemoth, a whale, even a mountain troll, perhaps. They are big enough to hold pieces of the Dragon's dreamsong. But not a man. Too puny."

"A man, Raglaw," the queen says, stepping into the well of yellow light and turning to help the hag. "He is no dream."

"Then why have we not seen him with the long sight? Why is there no prophecy of him?"

"Think on that, teacher!" She supports Raglaw's frail weight as she descends into the stairwell. "Lailoken is not like other souls. He is not carried to us by the timewind, old woman, lifetime to lifetime. This is his *first* lifetime as a human being. His only life. He is an accident—a mistake of the Furor's magic. None have seen him coming—"

"None—" The crone sits down on the stone stair to ponder this.

"None but the Fire Lords," Ygrane whispers, sitting down beside her mentor. "They stole the demon Lailoken out of the Gulf, from right under the Furor's nose."

"Yes, yes," the aged one mutters. "Many of the Crones have seen the Fire Lords snatch a Dark Dweller from the bright air. But we could not find him after that. We thought he had fled back to the Gulf."

"No, Raglaw. The Fire Lords hid him. They hid Lailoken where the Furor would never find him. In the womb of a woman."

The crone scowls, bewildered. "How can that be? The power it would take to squeeze such a vast being into so small a space defeats my imagining."

"That is why the Fire Lords need the unicorn," Ygrane says. "It can take and carry energy from the Dragon—and the Fire Lords have used it to shape a body that can hold a Dark Dweller from the House of Fog. Imagine it! A demon as a man!"

"Demons are the enemies of the Fire Lords—" Raglaw presses two fists to her temples, forcing her thoughts. "If they have bound Lailoken, then they must have discovered a way to tame him, to win him to their purpose."

"Yes. You see it now. Lailoken is a man with a demon's powers—"

"And a soul shaped by angels," the crone concludes. "But how sturdy is this newly fashioned soul, Ygrane? Will Lailoken truly use his demon powers to serve the Fire Lords and stand with us against the Furor? Or will he revert to his true nature? Will he become again a demon? Will he work evil?"

"I don't know," the queen admits with quiet concern. "But we must not squander this opportunity out of our ignorance or fear."

"He is a random being, Ygrane. His influence on the timewind is unknown—and dangerous."

"But I hold the leash to the unicorn that helped shape him—the unicorn that the Fire Lords command." Ygrane speaks slowly to contain her excitement. "I think Lailoken follows the unicorn. There is some kind of bond between them. We must spare the beast. If I am right, then Lailoken will soon be among us, and we will see then for ourselves if he is a being who can help us—or one who must be fed to the Dragon."

The crone nods at this. "Perhaps it is well you stopped me, then." She scratches her chin reflectively and pieces flake off in tiny cinnamon sparkles. "Aye, young queen, time has worn me through." She sighs ruefully at her emaciated state and offers a lop-fingered hand. "Take me to the fireside, woman—and you will tell me the magic you will work with the unicorn."

With Morgeu, her daughter of seven summers by her husband Gorlois, Ygrane strolls through a furzed-over field on a mountain above a vale of primeval forest. Ygrane has promised to let her orange-haired, dark-eyed child ride the unicorn again. She does this for Morgeu because she wants to please her daughter in a way her father the duke cannot. The child is visiting the Celtic queen's kingdom of Cymru only for the summer before returning to Tintagel and the Roman court. Her mother cannot compete with those fineries, for her land is wilderness, her people scattered in clan territories across the valleys and hillsides. But there is an experience she can afford her daughter that no one else can.

The queen calls for the unicorn while singing a gentle song, as though the plaintiveness of her voice is the summons. Out of the tree shadows on the slope above, the unicorn glides. It shimmers like silver dust fallen from the day moon floating above the mountain. When its ridged horn touches the ground, its muscled body darkens to a more solid shape and waits, head bowed, as Morgeu clambers atop its back. Then, with Ygrane mounted behind her daughter and gently holding the unicorn's mane, they ride across the field.

The magnetic flow of blue serenity that blows off the unicorn's mane soothes Morgeu, who is an otherwise restless, high-strung child. And in turn, the child's playfulness and vulnerability soothe the unicorn, still skittish after Raglaw's attack. It took Ygrane six days of strenuous calling to lure it back. The unicorn will not be fooled by Raglaw's mimicry again. Since introducing it to Morgeu, however, it has come more readily and stays longer.

Morgeu does not have the sight, so her exposure to the unicorn's radiance does not invoke in her the seraphic rapture her mother feels. It is, even so, nothing less than the most lordly pleasure she has ever known or ever will. Spinning in place on the spellbound horse, her life whirls from her and splashes across the green and golden land before funneling back into her laughing body. For days afterward, she picks up pieces of her happiness wherever she goes.

The fiana watch from the tree line, and sometimes the queen and her child slide off in front of them, dizzy with giddiness—

and then, the men leap at the unicorn. None can touch it, for it shies like smoke; yet, sometimes, if they leap with exceptional swiftness and all their might, they graze its cold, rippling shadow, and for a few moments astonishing euphoria tosses in them. It leaves them gasping in the bent grass, weighed down by their longings, all the heavier for having tasted lightness. After two or three jumps, they want no more of that dangerous joy.

But Morgeu is insatiable and slips out one night from the queen's tent. Unaware of the fiana that her mother sends to watch over her, she hurries to the dark field and summons the unicorn. She hums the same quiet song Ygrane pretends to use—and the spectral steed pronks from the forest, its long, sharp body shining like starfire.

Morgeu rides endless zeroes through the field, until her mother comes for her. No matter Ygrane's admonitions, she slips away the next night, and the next. She goes every night, and she comes back to camp each dawn with candlepoints of light in her hair.

In a rush of nightshadows and moonfire, the unicorn canters a spiraling circle through a glade of mammoth oaks with its hooves made of silence—and upon its back rides a young child. Even in the tarnished light of the moon, the child's long, crinkly tresses shine golden red, luminous and wavery as fire's hair. Clinging with one hand to the unicorn's flaring mane, the small girl rides with exhilarating abandon, leaning far back, knees jerking above the animal's withers, laughing in staccato peals of joy.

A hoary old man in rags leans upon a gnarled staff and watches, hidden among the giant trees. He is the demon Lailoken. Darkness glowers from the pits of his sunken eyes, and his long, wraithlike body entwined in the coils of his beard seems floated out of a deathly dream.

The unicorn spots him and rears back abruptly. With a cry as startled as a clang of brass, it throws the girl from its back and bolts from the glade.

The lanky old man rushes to the fallen child and finds her lying on her back in the hoof-chewed turf, all life fled from her. She cannot be more than seven. Quickly, he feels for the placement of bones in her neck and finds them unbroken. "She is whole," he gnashes aloud to himself, his wild-bearded face locked with chagrin, unsure what to do next.

Under the chill of moonlight and the scrambled whispers of the wind sifting through the trees, Lailoken draws strength from the magnetic field of the planet. Frosty energy lifts out of the ground, siphoning upward through the thick bones of his thighs, pelvis, and spine. Thundery air thrums around him as he directs this force through the open gate of his chest.

The demon's heartforce carries living power into the slight body beneath him. Her flesh shudders from its roots, and, with a gasp of watery breath and a flutter of her dark eyes, she awakes.

"Are you an angel?" she asks in a thin voice of archaic Latin.

"No, child," the old man answers with a smile and a deeply relieved sigh. "I but saw your fall and came to revive you."

Her round face winces as she sits up. "Where are my guards? How did you get past them?"

Rising from his knees, the demon Lailoken leans on his staff and gazes down at her, his cadaverous visage alarmed. "Do not summon your guards. I will be going now. Yet before I am gone, child, tell me who you are and how you came to ride the unicorn."

The girl stares at the old man with her anthracite eyes, defiant and remote, gauging the full measure of his inquiring look, reading the fright in his hairy face, and sensing something else, a greater emptiness behind his eyes than she ever sensed at any cliff's edge.

"I am Morgeu," she finally says with a haughty air, "daughter of a Celtic queen and a Roman duke. Because I am noble, the unicorn obeys me." She lurches to her feet and glares at him angrily. "Do not make the mistake of treating me as a child. Answer my questions—now. Who are *you*? And how did you elude my guards? Are you a wizard?"

"I am following the unicorn," Lailoken replies.

Her features shift mischievously. "You *are* a wizard, then, aren't you?" She looks him up and down. "You have the guise of a wild man in those tatty animal skins, but you talk like a noble. What is your name, old man, and whom do you serve?"

There is such a strength of sureness in the way she appraises him, the gaunt man can hardly believe this is a child who confronts him. "I am Lailoken—and I serve God."

"So, Lailoken, you are a holy man. My mother fears the holy men, for your ilk steal her people. But my father says that you are not to be feared, that your piety is weakness, because the meek do not inherit the earth but only the graves in it."

Alternately amused and startled at this small person's arrogance and precocity, Lailoken inquires, "What do you think, Morgeu?"

"I think you are a wizard, Lailoken," she says, hands on her hips. "A truly holy man would not pursue a unicorn. The unicorn would come to him."

Lailoken accedes with a nod. "How came you to ride the unicorn?"

"I told you, I am noble. I am the daughter of the Celtic queen. Someday I will *be* the queen. The unicorn obeys me."

"If this is so, then call it back for me."

"Why?" Her eyes narrow suspiciously. "The unicorn is afraid of you. It ran away at your approach. Your intrusion could have killed me." She backs away. "I think you are a wizard—and a wicked one at that." From under her ankle-length robes, her hand emerges, clutching a silver dagger. "Stay where you are, Lailoken. I am taking you for my prisoner. Guards!"

Lailoken's heart jumps in its cage. "Morgeu! I am no threat. I have saved you."

"You tried to steal the unicorn from me." She waves her dagger over her head, calling the guards, who are already sprinting toward her across the moon-blotched clearing.

Lailoken sits down and lays his staff across his knees. In moments, the fiana surround him, their spears pointing at his narrow breast.

"Do not harm him," Morgeu commands her men and adds with a lilt of pride in her soft-palated voice: "He is a prize for my mother—a wizard I have captured by my own magic."

At a diorite plate shelving among black boulders, on the cliffs that face the western sea, the unicorn pauses. Strands of star vapors tangle overhead, and below, black velvet waves roll out of the night, hissing and booming on the beach with a ghostly froth. From far beneath this broken shoreline, the Dragon stirs.

The unicorn senses the iron-dark shadow of the huge beast. It swipes its horn against the jagged rocks, depositing thin, crystalline flakes in the crevices, where they will eventually melt and soak into the earth, carrying the savor of unicorn to the depths. Friskily, it prances on the ledge, feeding on the upwelling of electrical force as the Dragon ascends.

Then, at the last possible moment before the magnetic talon-grasp of the stupendous creature becomes too strong to elude, it bounds away, taking with it the strength from the Dragon that it needs to serve the Fire Lords.

The last time that the unicorn saw any of the Fire Lords, it was raining. From over its shoulder, coins of light fell and glittered at its hooves among dead leaves and tiny, instantaneous crowns of impacting raindrops. It curled about to see the source of this radiance and shivered brow to tail. An angel stood before it. Its luminosity fanned horizontally through the avenues of trees and frosted the underside of far-off boughs and leaves. Unachievable distances opened in its enormous eyes.

With bowed head, the unicorn attempted to touch the angel with its horn, hoping to receive a communication through this antenna. It remembered earlier encounters when the Fire Lords placed their shining hands on its tusk and ideas flooded its mind with glorious knowing. It learned then of the fiery origin of the universe and of what came before—the place of infinities, wider than time, smaller than the smallest node of space, and it held these ideas in the deep quiet of its own skull.

But on this drenched day, no ideas flowed through the long horn into the beast.

The angel watched silently, and its huge stare of white fire planted something proud and strong in the animal.

Head high, mane, beard, and fetlocks streaming backward in a magnetic breeze, the unicorn stepped closer. The presence of the angels inspired it to feel that it belonged to a higher order of energy than terrestrial things. With this thought, the world around it went transparent. Suddenly, it could see through the stone crust, the tectonic plates, the dead scales of hide to the living Dragon below.

Magma glowed incandescent as blood. Veins of electric force, arteries of living current outlined a slitherous body, long and coiled as the horizon. Surges of heat and shadow breathed from the molten creature as it curled around itself, somersaulting the quartz length of its spine. Its mountainous, black diamond head swelled closer, a grin of undershot jaw aged and malevolent, eyes smoking purple.

Nervously, the unicorn pranced side to side. A rumbling sound vibrated through its legs. Thunder from below harped in the trees. Something else filled the air, sweeping aside the veils of rain. Musical voltage chimed in the soaring spaces of the forest, and the upreaching arms of the trees swayed to a deep, oceanic rhythm.

It was the Dragon's dreamsong, aimed at the stars. It passed through the unicorn on its way outward and shook happiness into the horned creature, making its heart laugh and its muscles quiver like soft wings. Warmth stroked its length better than the long necks of a hundred mothers. Its bones felt hollowed by a drowsiness full of blue.

Lightning struck the tall horn, stood on its tip like a massive medusa ablaze in the celestial sea, its tendrils writhing and knotting to the rhythms of the dreamsong. As it vanished, the rainy world closed in. The Dragon was gone, shut away behind its pelt of boulders and spruce. The angel was gone, too. Silence stretched out into the dark crannies of the forest.

The supreme druid, Dun Mane, so named for his long, equine face, slouches down the corridor, his white-and-green robes flashing in the swatches of early morning sunlight that ray through the colonnade. At the request of the duke, he has traveled three days for this audience with the queen, a woman he despises, and he is annoyed because he has barely had time to rest before being summoned.

All the formalities have been met, to be sure, he mutters to himself, *the scented bath, the fresh robes, harp song and victuals, even the appropriate incense—but the complaisance of it all! And the alacrity, as if I am to be dispatched like a common neatherd come in from the roving fields for refreshment!*

His inward sputtering stops at the great oak door engraved with dragoncoils. Two of the queen's dread fiana stand there, feral throwbacks of lost glory, wearing buckskin leggings and boots, the gold torque of Mother, and old-fashioned swords with leaf-shaped blades and small hilts. He abhors these men. Though they have won renown even among the duke's army as fierce warriors, they are an embarrassment to the druids, who have forsaken the ancient ways for the modern reality of Rome.

The door opens at his approach, and he faces the brutishly muscular captain of the fiana, orange-haired Falon. No emotion shows in his ruddy features, yet Dun Mane can feel the enmity radiating from him. Often in the past, the fiana have clashed with the supreme druid's guard when this man denied Dun Mane access to the queen. The stooped, iron-haired druid does not even attempt to disguise his rancor any longer, but glowers defiantly before that unreadable blue gaze.

The guard bows his head perfunctorily and stands aside, revealing a loggia of breezy curtains saffron with sunlight. Garlands of fresh blossoms, larkspur and bryony, twine the columns and spill from large stone vases. Amidst flutter of diaphanous silks riffling in the wind, the queen sits cross-legged on a stone bench, eating grapes.

As often as the supreme druid has met her, he is always surprised by how pleasant, how strangely light he feels in her presence—though there is nothing else about her that he likes. The backache from his long cart journey fades, replaced by a buoyancy that pours into him from the very brightness of the air surrounding her. It is the glamour, the benefit of her devotion to the Síd. In that, she is a remarkable queen, he is the first to acknowledge. If only her human traits were as developed as her glamour and her famous long sight.

Dun Mane sweeps across the worn lozenge-stones of the loggia, forcing himself to stand more erect in the presence of his queen, while at the same time noting every infraction of her behavior. *What manner of audience hall is this?* he grouses silently, sneering at the windy veils and rampant flowers. *And look at her sitting there, legs crossed like a village stitch-woman. What has Raglaw made of her?*

Two swords' lengths away from her, he pauses, as tradition demands, and waits. Eyes ringed with weariness, he meets Ygrane's quiet green gaze, and an old understanding passes between them: No matter their differences, they serve the welfare of the people—she with her magic and he with his politics.

The queen gestures him closer with a nonchalant wave, popping another grape into her mouth. She wears the traditional costume of the old queens, naked, like her fiana from the waist up, her brindled hair piled atop her head in an intricate knot. Again, as ever before, he is struck by her lucid complexion, sun-blushed with an overlay of tan from her long wanderings outdoors, so unlike the moon-pale Roman women. It is no wonder to Dun Mane, who lives at the Roman court and has become accustomed to their modern ways, that the duke is happy to see his wife only on formal occasions. In his eyes, she would surely seem wild as a peasant, with her sun-bleached hair and dusky cheeks. "Some grapes?" she asks, her expression so childlike.

"My lady—" he offers the formal Latin greeting, then catches the disapproving cock of her eyebrow and addresses her as a subject, calling her Mother.

"These are good," she says with her mouth full. "First crop from the vineyards of Usk. The wine brokers in Glevum will pay a worthy price this year. Try one."

He demurs with a stiff bow, wishing she would display some formality in his presence, as recognition of his office, if not his person.

Ygrane removes the glazed blue bowl of grapes from her lap and places it on the bench beside her, then slumps her shoulders contritely. "You're angry at me for my poor hospitality."

"Not at all, Mother." He bows again, this time more fluidly, feeling airy in the summer-sweet wind. There has never been any warmth between them since he became supreme druid six years ago. His predecessor, Tall Silver, had been responsible, along with the crone Raglaw, for selecting the queen and removing her as a child from her hill village. Tall Silver had the long sight, and Dun Mane does not, so he cannot to this day understand what his elder saw in this amiable but remote person. To his eye, she is but a common village girl superficially trained in court manners. He loathes her assumed air of superiority, and that is why he is continually surprised by the levity he often feels near her. "Your hospitality is flawless, your harp player the very best I've ever heard—"

"But I've rushed you, Dun Mane. I know you're annoyed with me." In the bright morning light, she sees the fine gray threads of whisker on the flat of his cheeks, shaved beardless in the Roman style. "I apologize for that. You would have had more rest after your long trek had I known you were coming. Now you are here, and I am called away. So, this is the only time I can see you before I leave. I did not want your tedious journey to be in vain."

Dun Mane touches his green leather headband, then his heart, and offers his blue-knuckled hand. The queen squeezes it tersely, impatient with ritual as ever, and he sits on the wooden bench that Falon places before her. Her informality at least allows him to be direct, and he asks, "Called away? By whom, Mother?"

"My friends," she says, and helps herself to another grape, eating casually, at ease, as though not a day has passed since their last meeting when in fact it has been four months.

Dun Mane's long, sallow face leans closer. "The faerïe?"

"You've said I'm not to call them that around you."

"Not when we are with others, of course. The Christians feel strongly about that, Mother. And more and more of us are Christian these days. The old ways have no place among the new. That is the way of the world. But you are of another time, another life, and between us, we may call them what they are."

"I'm going into the hills for the midsummer moon, Dun Mane. I need to leave early to arrive by dark." A frown pinches her brow. "Unless, of course, you've come as usual to fetch me. Is it the chiefs or my husband who sends you?"

He looks her level in the eye, further annoyed at her impatience and glad for the full measure of his authority, "Both. The chiefs have called another war council. They want you present and no excuses this time. And the duke summons you to Tintagel. The sea rovers attack in ever greater numbers. He needs you at his side."

"I will send a war party to the mighty duke. And Falon will represent me among the chiefs at the war council."

The seams of Dun Mane's large face knot tightly between his dull steel eyes. "He wants you in person, Mother. He requires you to meet him at Maridunum for the council of the chiefs."

"He may have my warriors. I am taking my daughter to the lakes for the midsummer moon."

The druid presses his palms together apologetically, yet privately gloats. Most of all, he has always hated the obstinate indifference with which the queen meets her responsibilities, and he is glad whenever he finds the authority to force her to fulfill her role. "The duke wants Morgeu at Tintagel, as well."

"Why?" Ygrane's crossed legs unfold, and her indignation nearly brings her to her feet. "The summer is still full. We have agreed she is to stay with me until the autumn."

The druid tosses his hands helplessly. "The duke believes that it is time his daughter learned battle strategies. He wants her in his war room."

Ygrane exhales with sharp disbelief. "She is seven years old."

"The duke himself was but seven when he was summoned to the war room by his father, the old count."

The queen senses the pride in his voice and is disgusted. In their eagerness to preserve their power, the druids gladly truckle to their Roman allies, the very Romans labeled invaders before Tall Silver's time and the marriage he personally arranged between her and the duke.

Dun Mane, emboldened by the queen's silence, which he takes as submission, adds, "Mother, his intentions are correct. These are wartimes—"

Her voice tightens angrily: "I know these are wartimes, Dun Mane. That is my grief as queen."

"Of course—" The look in his furrowed face is mockingly sincere. In the six years that he has been forced to work with her, he believes he has come to know her so well, all her surly dispassion to modernity and her puerile devotion to the old ways. For a while, before the alliance, there was actually a political expediency to her archaic primitivism. The clans admired it, then. But now, since the alliance, the Roman way has been carried to the farthest croft of the land, and every farmer and herdsman wants more Roman goods and weapons. She can dictate nothing anymore, yet he forces himself to remain cordial to her, out of respect for her station, not her befuddled person. "I only mean, Mother, that we must all make personal sacrifices for the war effort—even young Morgeu. We must think of the people."

"The people is it?" a voice like a rasp of snakeskin lashes him from behind, and the crone Raglaw steps through the flutter of silk curtains.

Dun Mane glances over his shoulder and glimpses through the gauzy drapes the child Morgeu skipping across the courtyard among several fiana, gamboling with a remarkable white horse shaggy as a wolfhound. Distracted by the crone's hooded presence, he does not notice the steed's brow-tusk before the curtain wavers back into place.

"The people will serve whoever feeds them," the crone says, sitting beside the queen with a crepitant noise. "Very like the Dragon."

The supreme druid's bulky face carries a look of sadness as he nods toward the crone in her gray sack hood. "Dame Raglaw, since our queen's alliance with the duke, the Romans have been feeding our people and protecting them far better than the Dragon."

"That is sadly so," Raglaw acknowledges, tilting her hood toward the queen, "because we have not properly fed the Dragon. We have withheld from the Drinker of Lives the offerings that could win us the protection we need."

In a dry, commiserating voice, the druid adds, "The magic

of the Síd has been waning since the Roman gods drove them underground four hundred years ago, since the slaughter of the ancient druids on Mona."

"Pitifully so—" the crone agrees, her hood bowed. "The magic passes, like embers turning into themselves, leaving behind their empty shapes in the cold dark where once there had been radiance."

"Magic passes as our gods fade into the earth," Dun Mane says. "The new god, the nailed god of the Romans, he is different—one god, three faces."

"He is a desert god," the queen protests. "How can any in the Tribe of the Abiding North honor such a one?"

"Whole clans have gone over to this desert god," Dun Mane points out, eager to inflict some humility on this arrogant young woman. "Chief Kyner says that only the Christian god can stop the Furor's hordes."

The queen's voice flicks angrily: "Are you abandoning the Síd for the nailed god, Dun Mane?"

"I?" The supreme druid looks startled. "Of course not. I am just pointing out that many of your subjects have already converted—and many more will."

"Thank you, Dun Mane, for your insight," Ygrane says in cold dismissal. "You may go now."

The druid strives to contain his anger at being so rudely sent away. "Then, you will come to Maridunum—with your child, to meet your husband and the chiefs?" he asks, proud that his voice remains calm and reasonable when he feels like shaking all the false dreams out of her.

The queen turns her face so that her green eyes seem to brighten, and the druid's ire evaporates. Something lithe and sweet in the summer's breeze lilting through the sunny curtains soothes him and makes anger impossible. He nods amicably when Ygrane says, "Yes, yes, we will meet again in Maridunum. I will decide then among the chiefs whether my presence is required at Tintagel."

"Thank you, Mother." Dun Mane rises, touches his headband but does not offer his hand. He bows and departs lightfooted, green-and-white robes swaying, almost dizzy with an inexplicably happy surge of relief.

"Were you not a little too strong on the glamour with him?" the crone asks after Falon closes the door behind the supreme druid.

"I just want him to go away. His love of the Romans sickens me. To hear him talk about the old Roman gods driving our Síd underground and then for him to sing praises of their new god—I needed the glamour to keep from punching him." She rises and stretches, her mind pacing ahead, measuring the length of the day now that she has been summoned away. "There are rinses to be made, while the unicorn is still here. I'll tend to that. Have you met, yet, with the Dark Dweller who has just arrived?"

The hood shakes once. "I am tired, Ygrane. But I will find the strength—for he is our best hope for our people."

Ygrane moves to comfort her teacher, but the old woman holds up the leathery knob of her hand. "Go to the unicorn now. There is little time if we are to travel so soon to Maridunum. Save your glamour for the likes of Dun Mane."

Ygrane concedes with a small hug, feels the hag's bones shift loosely under her embrace as if they are held together not by tendon but by will alone. "Come," she says. "Join us in the sun."

"Yes—the sun," Raglaw hisses softly and rises. "Let the sun touch me yet again, before I vanish into something better."

The Celtic guards would have no discourse with Lailoken, fearing his wizardry, and he spent the remainder of the night dozing by the campfire curled upon himself. The warriors took turns standing over him, their spears ready to pierce him at the first indication of deviltry. He ignored them. In his mind, as he dipped in and out of sleep, he returned to the remarkable vision of that wondrously proud child riding the unicorn, giddy and careless as a spirit that knows death for an illusion.

In the morning, he stood upon the ashes of the night's fire and faced the military fortress and the tottering headlands of sheer rock cliffs that blindly stared across the thrashing waves toward the misty, sapphire island of Mona. Masses of redstone battlements and orange-and-yellow stone ramparts rose above the lush emerald grasses and the ocean thrift, and he recognized this place from his time as a demon. Then it was called Segontium and, with Maridunum far to the south, marked the western extremis of the Empire's conquest in Britain. Lailoken had inflicted many a nightmare in the stone halls of these garrison outposts, harrowing the newly Christian conquerors with visions of lust and hellfire as was his wont in his former life.

Though the Romans had abandoned this fort more than half a century earlier, the timber gate towers remained intact and the defensive ditches still sloped steeply; however, as the party crossed the narrow wooden footbridge that spanned the ditches, Lailoken observed that the cleaning slots at the bottom, the "ankle-breakers" that tripped up attackers, had grown in with thorny shrubs. The Celts were not as meticulous as the Romans, and that presaged ill in their clash with the Furor.

They entered Segontium by a narrow doorway in the main gate and passed through the courtyard, where the L-shaped barracks garrisoned several hundred men—almost all of whom emerged into the courtyard to see the so-called wizard that Morgeu had captured during the night. One glance at the scrawny old man in shredded hides was enough for most of them, and they returned to their business in the barracks and stable blocks.

These timber buildings had fallen into a miserable state of disrepair since Lailoken's last visit, the clapboard walls rotted and repaired with wattle and daub. The *via praetoria*, the road that led from the front gate, had surrendered most of its cobbles for repair of the fortress wall and had been reduced to a rutted dirt track pocked with muddy puddles. Joining it at a right angle, the *via principalis* was in better condition and retained much of its stately grandeur as it entered the central range, an open, paved courtyard flanked by colonnades. The central buildings there were grand even in decay, and although the red roofs had crude timber patches where the tiles were missing, and the vines scribbling the walls choked themselves with neglect, they did indeed suggest a sunnier clime and a bygone glory.

They passed the *tribunal*, the long hall where the commander would stand to address the troops, and Lailoken glanced past its cracked and chipped facade to the *aedes*, the shrine that housed the deity. Instead of a statue of the emperor, the Celts had erected a stone sculpture of a strong, fang-mouthed woman fierce in her nakedness, wearing a skull-necklace and gripping a sword in one hand, and a severed head in the other, its life fountaining from it.

"Kali," Lailoken said to himself, recognizing this figure as the Black One—the Demon Queen of Indus. During his time as a demon, many centuries ago, he saw the white tribes of the north carry the worship of this cannibal ogress across this sea to the western islands. There, he knew, she was still worshiped as the sacred sow that eats her farrow. "Ah me, what a deity!" he said aloud in Latin, frowning with concern and speaking to no one in particular. "Even the Furor knows this mask of Her as Hel, the female maw that consumes all the living. She is the cosmos—physical reality—the raging body of the universe that births mortals and then tears us apart."

"Silence your incantations, wizard!" a soldier yelled at him in Brythonic. "Silence or lose your head!"

The military escort led the old wizard around the *principia*, the central basilica with its elegant stone stairway and pillars, past wooden buildings on stilts—the fort granaries—to a second transverse road. They trudged beside dormant workshops to a walled garden of bright blossoms. There, the guards peeled away, and he was left alone.

For a while, he simply stood there, waiting, looking at the cultivated flowers around him, all blue: aconite, iris, hyacinth, larkspur, delphinium, gentian, cornflowers, all blue as fallen pieces of the sky. He stood there patiently, content after the long walk to stand still and breathe deeply of the heady floral fragrances.

But now his patience has thinned, and he feels inward to the demon power within himself. Immediately, he senses the nearby presence of the unicorn. He steps around the walled garden of blue flowers into a lush orchard of old and sinuate fruit trees espaliered across long, wide walls of ancient masonry. Deceased gods frolic in the stonework, peeking out from behind leafy boughs and from the footstones beneath overarching grape trellises. The sky's bright eyes staring through the broad leaves cast a liquid light over seed-frames, compost heaps, and brilliant plots of flowering herbs.

Before him, in a lane of hedges, the unicorn stands, elegant as snow. Lailoken veers toward it, and the slender creature flies sideways, its tail and mane becoming streaks of cirrus. It prances away from the arbors and trellises and burns like a star in a green field of brash sunlight.

Farther into the arboretum, among glowing masses of flowers, the child Morgeu sits on a tall stool. A sparkling flotage of seed tufts fills the air behind her, where a tall, wide-shouldered silhouette of a woman boils something in a pan on a brazier. Fumes swirl about the silhouette, and a serene fragrance of myrtle and pine needles colors the shady enclosure.

The shadowy woman dismantles a dense spiraea, a queen of the meadow, whose floral tufts drift in the morning breeze as she cuts them free. Into the boiling brew, select cuttings slip, and the vapors thin away, revealing the striking beauty of the woman's face and figure. Tawny, sleek, with a strong nose and wide jaw, she bears a soft likeness to a lioness. Her hooded green eyes assess him with a burning icy elation, as with joy after long separation. She wears her bronze hair intricately braided atop her head, and her clingy, green *gwn*, a silken Celtic skirt, covers her to her ankles and leaves her breasts bare.

Lailoken averts his eyes, afraid he is not meant to see her thus exposed, and Morgeu's glittery laugh mocks him. "Look, Mother," she speaks in Brythonic, "he must be Christian, after all. He cannot bear the sight of your womanhood."

With firm, svelte command, she says, "Morgeu, you may be on your way now."

"Mother! He is my prize."

"Be on your way, darling," she repeats, without budging her green, lemuroid eyes from the demon visitor. "And don't try spying on us through the trellis or, by the Good-Mother-of-us-all, you'll be too sore to ride for a week."

With a petulant toss of her head, the girl hops from the bench and strides purposefully from the arboretum, pausing before Lailoken just long enough to wince her eyes and flare her nostrils menacingly.

"I'm asking you to forgive my daughter her impertinence, Lailoken," the woman says in a kindly voice of Gaelic-accented Latin, her gaze still intently fixed on the old man. This is the figure from her visions, the demon-man she has glimpsed many times in trance, replete in every detail, from his strange quartz eyes to his long, tangled beard and animal skins.

"Morgeu has all the hauteur of her Roman father and none of the Celtic hospitality of her mother's people," she continues, gesturing to a stone bench alongside several tripods of hot braziers and boiling fragrances. "Please, come take a seat with me."

Lailoken stares and does not move. He has journeyed a long way following the unicorn, and he does not understand why the radiant beast has led him here.

"Is it my attire offends you?" the queen inquires, gesturing to her topless *gwn* and her full, young breasts filled with their own pink light. "It is the summer custom of my people to dress thus. Clearly, though, it'd be plain even at midnight you are from a far different tribe." Off a worktable cluttered with phials of colored glass and flowery cuttings, she removes a sheer, coraline robe and pulls it around herself. "Did you see the unicorn when you came in?"

"It ran into the field," Lailoken says.

"Morgeu told me that you frightened it last night." She speaks while using wooden tongs to dip phials in a percolating brew, coating them inside and out, then placing them in a drying rack on the worktable. "That surprised me, because each time I've seen you in my waking dreams over the years, you are with my unicorn. I had hoped you could steady its head while I draw a teardrop or two. The feather I use to make it blink doesn't hurt, but it makes it jumpy and I spill more than I like."

Lailoken leans on his staff and peers into the fleeing vapors, searching for invisibles. The tattered air stands empty. "*Your* unicorn?" he queries. "The creature is yours?"

She removes the last phial and casts a handful of grains in the brew that thickens the air with frosty smoke and the rainy smells of soaked meadows and dripping fir forests. With a blush to her features, she turns her attention to arranging phials on the worktable. "Of course, I don't own the unicorn. It came to be mine when I was a young woman, and it brought prophecy with it." She takes pruning shears from a faldstool beside the worktable and positions her chair to face her visitor from the shade. "I think of it as mine, because when I call, it comes." Sitting placidly, leaning to one side, legs crossed under her robe, she beams at the demon as if he were an old acquaintance. "But it's not me we should be talking of. It is you. You are actually here now. After all these years. I remember seeing you in trance years ago, when vision first opened for me."

"Then you know who I am?"

"Morgeu told me your name," she answers, her eyes green as the unicorn's and nearly as bright, "but I have long known you are not human. You are a demon. You are from the House of Fog. The Furor summoned you and others like you out of the Gulf—but you fell to earth. The unicorn and the *Annwn*, the Fire Lords, fashioned you this body."

Lailoken nods. "This is so. You know of me. Yet I do not know of you."

"I am Ygrane, queen of the Celts," she begins in her lithe voice, and an air of melancholy thickens about her. "My story is not as grand as yours, for all that I am I have come to by accident and error. By accident of birth, I inherited a dying kingdom. And by error, I took a Roman husband, whose issue found you in our woods."

"You must have been a child—" Lailoken interrupts.

"Yes. My marriage to the *dux Britanniarum* was a mistake I made as a child. I was fourteen when my druids, my counselors, pressed by political expediency, urged me to marry. I tried running away when I was fifteen. But they found me and brought me back. This is my twenty-second summer."

"I have encountered few queens in my travels," the demon states. "You are rare."

Ygrane accedes with a heavy, tristful sigh. "It is true. In my grandmother's grandmother's great-grandmother's time, many years had already passed since the Celts abandoned the ancient ways—the worship of Mother, the Goddess. It's been the dominion of the chieftains we've had since. Now, even the might of the chieftains has gone weak, undermined, you should know, by the politics of their magistrates. Men love power. Unwisely, the kings of our past emulated Roman ways. They granted power to administrators. In time, those clients refused to return that power to their rightful sovereigns. They seized regency for themselves, and civil war has been a sad fact of Celtic life for generations now. Worse, the Christians teach that the old ways are evil, and so it is that I am losing influence with my own people."

"Yet the gods give you power," Lailoken says.

"This is so," she admits. "And I don't doubt the Daoine Síd have blessed me, by choosing my soul for this life. I was a common child in a remote hill clan, set apart from others by the gift of sight that comes with me from former lives. I've seen visions of the Goddess and the pale people and the horse of one horn since before I could talk. All my life, I have seen little pieces of the future. When the druids heard of me, I was taken from my family and reared to be queen. I've used my gift since to counsel the clans. And by that strength of the gods, by this long sight, I saw you in the trance flame, many times, where everything that is ordinary and just so goes deeper to prophecy."

"Prophecy is a tricky gift, my lady," Lailoken says.

"Tricky—yes, it is tricky," the queen professes. "You can be sure, for what you see cannot be changed except by terrible suffering. What is to be seen is already true—and changing the truth requires a greater truth. The time ahead for the tribes is so horrid, I tell you I'd rather not have seen it at all. Even some of my own people, many of them, would put out my eyes for what I see. The Christians, I mean. Their faith forbids prophecy and condemns to an eternity of suffering all prophets and those who bear magic."

"Is that the sadness I sense in you, then?" Lailoken dares to ask.

She passes him a doleful look. "As a child, when the druids came to take me away from my mother, I cried. I was happy in my humble home in the hills. Our floors were stamped earth—we ate berries in summer and root broth in winter—yet I had no worry or concern. The faerïe played with me, and the Goddess was my friend. I cried bitterly to leave those woods and hedgerows, where first I knew happiness with the elf-folk. But the druids told me a story, you see. They said that it was a very old story, whose time had come to be fulfilled. A Celtic woman beloved of the Síd would someday marry a foreign king, and a child would be born to them who will grow up to be a greater king than any before him and save his two peoples from tragedy." She smiles thinly, as if appreciating the foolishness of this tale. "They said *I* was that woman—and the savior would be my child."

The small hairs all over Lailoken's body stand on end. "M-my mother told me the same," he stammers. "About a queen foretold to marry her enemy and birth a noble king destined to unite us."

She dips her head wearily. "I believed that once. The druids used that story to take me from my home. Since then, I have lived in these old Roman forts where the pale people are loath to come. For political advantage, the druids married me to Gorlois, duke of the Saxon Coast." With a wry, hurt look, she lifts her face. "I was young, of course, and disoriented by my new life, a life of handmaidens and soft, pretty clothes. I lost touch with my visions. Soon after, I was married and heavy with child. And then I saw—and what I saw, I wept for and have been weeping for ever since. Gorlois is not the one—and Morgeu—" Her face hardens, and her voice grows cold. "Morgeu is her father's daughter. He has encouraged and abetted an arrogance in her. She does not have the sight. Oh, I can try to discipline her, for now, but I've not the grace or the strength to make her other than the selfish, arrogant soul she is. She will be no one's savior."

"Perhaps you will have a new vision," the demon consoles. "You must look again."

"I have," she admits, blinking away the remoteness from her eyes. "I have looked, Lailoken, and I have seen him in my trances—a king with yellow eyes and raven hair. Yet, I fear I deceive myself. There are others who see better than I, and they assure me that my long sight is true. I'm wanting to believe. I'm wanting a destiny. For this story must be true—or else my soft life in these fine clothes and old palaces is empty, a joke."

"Then, the king of legend will come to you," the old man insists.

"So, you find me as you see me. My life is filled only with

waiting and waiting—for something that may never be." She looks down at the worktable. "I spend the time making these rinses—special waters that hold spells. I do it for my people. The farmers use them for their crops and flocks, the women for healing balms. I'd go mad without this work."

"Surely," Lailoken speaks up, "the able men of this fort are devoted to you."

"Yes," she confirms, raising her squared, lioness chin proudly. "They are my fiana; they come from each of the clans. They are disgusted with all the political bickering and civil strife of these petty chieftains and magistrates. They abhor the wars that have divided and weakened us before our enemies, and they look to me for a return to the old ways. But they are my own people, and not the far love of the ancient story that took away my childhood."

The sincerity and sorrow of this beautiful young woman stir a depth of feeling in Lailoken he has not experienced since his first days in this world. She reminds him of the earnest presence of his mother. When Optima smiled at him, he first felt love—and he became human. When this queen looked at him as if she knew him—and he sensed somehow that she did, through her magic sight—he feels that love renew again, and his humanity stirs in him.

The queen rises to her feet with a buoyant grace and smiles sadly. "I have rambled on about myself and not shown you the hospitality due even a common traveler. Forgive me. My guards will escort you to a place where you may refresh yourself. Afterward, we will talk again."

Afraid of the hope that the demon's presence stirs in her, Ygrane signals for her guards and turns away from Lailoken before he can speak again.

At the end of the long hall where the Roman commanders once addressed their troops is a shrine that the queen has erected to the Drinker of Lives. The statue there is of Morrígan, the fanged goddess with the necklace of skulls, and an ancient personification of the Dragon. Ygrane sits on its pedestal, leaning back against the shin of the cannibal ogress, and listens to the clop of horse hooves on the cobbles of the nearby courtyard. The busy sounds of Dun Mane's cavalcade preparing to return to Maridunum with Morgeu and Raglaw reverberate in muted echoes through the stone corridors. They brim her with sadness, for she had hoped to spend more time with her daughter, wanting to instill something of the magical arts in her before returning her to the stern and martial influence of her father, the duke.

Such motherly concerns disperse as the statue at her back begins to thrum, signaling the arrival of the Daoine Síd. Light as moths, they enter the dim-lit shrine with a scent of rain. They flutter in like will-o'-the-wisps, orange flame-flickers packing the air with the unrelieved loneliness of their exile from the Great Tree, the haunting melancholy of the dispossessed. Then, one of the many sparks filling the chamber suddenly separates from the sunset haze that is their presence and assumes human form.

Gradually, a tall, slender figure concresces before her, and she squints to recognize the familiar countenance of Prince Bright Night. He bows respectfully to the queen. Garbed in green mantle and trousers, a golden tunic and yellow boots, he bears the easy, regal manner of an elven chief. He flings back his long auburn locks and faces her with green upslanted eyes that bear a kinship to her own. "Sister, we must talk."

"Happily, brother. But why have you come with such a mighty legion?"

"We come to take the one called Lailoken—" He pauses briefly and looks deeply into her. "To feed the Dragon."

The queen's eyes show momentary alarm, but her voice remains calm. "I understand the Dragon's need, yet we must not squander the demon."

The prince frowns impatiently. "Sister, I have been with Lailoken since he came into our demesne. I have seen the Fire Lords who labored night and day to fit him into a body. I have seen them, a sight few gods have beheld—and I tell you, they are astonishing beings. They have packed Lailoken's great power in a human frame. I say, we dare not let such a strong being elude us. He has come here so that we may feed him to the Dragon."

"And I say not. He has come among us to help us in our plight."

"And what of the Dragon?"

"The Dragon will drink the lives of the Furor's minions."

Bright Night exhales a skeptical sigh. "Would that were so, sister."

"It shall be so, brother. I have seen it."

"What you see blows with the winds of time, sometimes here, sometimes there. If we fail this time, the Dragon will devour *us*."

"As you say. We must not fail. That is why I need Lailoken. I assure you, without him, we will not have the skill to steady ourselves against the timewinds that blow the Furor and his tribes to our shores. We need the demon-man in full possession of his powers if there is any hope at all of making a place for ourselves in the new world to come."

"I would not want that place to be in the molten belly of the Dragon."

"Nor I, brother. But the Daoine Síd have empowered me to act as queen of the Celts." She lifts her squared-off chin in a gesture of authority. "I must be free to command my people as I see best. You must not stand against me."

The prince looks offended, and the moth-lights in the chamber deepen toward a redder pitch of sunset. "You serve King Someone Knows the Truth as do we. We stand together. We must feed the Dragon."

A sad expression flickers from Ygrane. "No, Bright Night. I

serve my people first. And they are torn between the old way of the Dragon and the new promises of the Fire Lords and their Christian kings."

"Old way of the Dragon?" Bright Night laughs, and the fathomless green of his eyes darkens. "In your memory it may seem old. But not to the Síd, for we remember when we lived in the Storm Tree under the starwinds and the sun and the moon. We did not always serve the Dragon. But we do now—and we *must* feed that beast if we are to live long enough to get out of here and reclaim our place in the Tree."

"You must trust me, brother. I have a vision for Lailoken."

"Trust you?" the elf prince asks acidly. "We trusted you with Gorlois, and now there is Morgeu. She is a dangerous wrong turn."

She shrugs off his protest. "The druids gave me to Gorlois, Bright Night. He was not of my choosing."

The elf prince edges closer, and a scent of moss and river-rubbed rocks accompanies him. "The Daoine Síd and the Celts are allies, Ygrane. More so now than ever, we must work together to find the safe path between the Dragon's hunger and the influence of the Fire Lords. Don't you see? By holding on to both the unicorn and Lailoken, you favor the Fire Lords."

"Trust me—Lailoken will redeem our alliance with the Romans. I have seen it."

"But the Romans are no more. The husks they left behind are only shadows of the conquerors who drove us from the Great Tree. They are *Britons*." He names them coldly. "One of the old tribes that served us once and now serve the nailed god. They are faithless."

"They have learned much from the Romans, much in the way of war. We need them to fend off the Furor."

The prince paces angrily, and the sparks around him ruddy almost to a purple color. "The Daoine Síd would rather return to the Tree on the backs of the Romans and the Britons. We don't want alliance with their nailed god. We have more in common with the Furor than these invaders from the Radiant South."

Ygrane lifts a surprised eyebrow at this outburst. "And yet, the Daoine Síd learned much of their magic from the southern tribes and the Fire Lords. Is that not precisely why the Furor rejected me when I offered myself to him?"

Bright Night stops and runs both hands through his shiny hair, trying to contain the great confusion of his mind. He must do something. The Dragon is ravenously intent on feeding its dreamsong. Yet he knows Ygrane is right, and they must wait. But how? There is no time. His anger bears down on the one who has driven them to this desperation: "The Furor is mad. He is obsessed with the purity of the Abiding North. He thinks we taint that purity. We, who once ruled from the tundra to the Indus when he was no more than a godling crawling about the rootlands. How did he come to power, I ask you? By parsing himself to a troll! And now he dares to say that *we* are tainted and must be purged from these lands? I tell you now, sister, I am glad he did not accept you."

Ygrane smiles affectionately. "Even though we have so much in common with him, brother?"

Bright Night puffs his cheeks out, trying to blow away his confusion. "I misspoke. Since our exile from the Tree, we have lost all that we once shared with the Rovers of the Wild Hunt. He means to destroy us, to do what the Fauni could not. He is no kinsman, anymore. Yet—I do fear the nailed god."

"And rightly so, brother," she says in a placating voice. The wild look in his eyes worries her. She understands his despair, his desperation to do something, anything to help himself and his people, and she prays with secret inwardness that her vision will see them through these frightful times. Nonetheless, she will not lie to him, any more than she would deceive herself, so she continues: "We must never forget, the Fire Lords are alien. The magic they taught the Radiant South, the magic that the nailed god bears north with him out of the whirlwind desert, the magic they call the Word is dangerous. It changes everything. We discovered that ourselves during our time in the south, when we learned number and runes. It changed us, so much so that the Furor, our ancient kin, rejects us now. The magic of the Word changes everything. The nailed god himself admits this, for he says that if we ally with him we shall not die, yet we shall all be changed."

The prince makes a soft noise of accord and begins to fade. "Sister—these changes frighten us. The Síd have endured so much change already—can we bear more?"

"The Síd, like their allies the Celts, are survivors. Our fates have been conjoined since the time of the Mothers, and together we survived the change to the time of the Chiefs. We will survive this change, too. Go now with my goodwill, brother Bright Night, and know that with the demon Lailoken and the unicorn serving us, the Dragon will soon drink again the lives of our enemies."

The dusk motes in the shrine darken to purple and to ultrapurples beyond sight, allowing the chamber to brighten once more with the sugary glow of morning light.

The soldiers lead Lailoken to the *principia*, a massive building with blue timber colonnades, stone stairs, and colorful mosaic floors depicting scenes of alien Roman gods. Most of the rooms are bare, dark, and dank—empty as the day the legions withdrew. The marble bath, however, is luminous, admitting the morning's clarity through a domed skylight. The polished chamber is handsomely appointed, with several full-length silvered glass mirrors, saffron draperies, chests of clothing, and wooden benches carved with the intricate scrollwork of the Celts.

While a young harpist's dolorous music serenades him, Lailoken sponges away the grime of his travels and examines his body in the mirrors. He looks like a heron, his white-feathered hair falling well past the bony wings of his scapulae. He lifts his tangled and matted beard to reveal clavicles, ribs, and sternum molded tautly as a legionnaire's torso armor. His face has a crane's beaked sharpness. His long arms and legs are thin and knobbed as his staff.

At length, an aged, stern-browed soldier comes by to soak his matted beard and locks in a sudsy, mucilaginous herbal broth that smells of decaying grasslands. Patiently, the soldier struggles with a bronze comb and shears to unknot and coif the old man's long whiskers.

When he finishes, Lailoken's silver mane and full-cut beard accent the bony squares of his face and lend him something of the imposingly patriarchal aspect of Jove himself, a sight that fetches a giggle from his stern visage. Heightening the effect, he dons the garments given him: a midnight blue tunic, mocha leather sandals, and black robe with crimson stitchwork.

Lulled by a fine meal of braised salmon, venison pie, and hazelnut bread, the wizard returns to the garden. But the queen has gone. When he inquires, the guards inform him that Ygrane has been called south to rally her fiana against barbarian raiders who have swarmed ashore along the Saxon Coast. Surprised, he learns that he will join her at her fortress in Maridunum, and he will have to travel there in the company of her daughter, the princess Morgeu.

The unicorn stands light and muscular as fog in the tunnel of the forest. Scattered flowers and fallen fruits burn in the gloom like exotic shells washed up from an alien sea. It waits for Ygrane's summons. Now it must follow where she leads. To fulfill its mission for the Fire Lords, it must trust in this human, whose silver-ringed fingers smell of thunder. But where is she leading it—and why?

A nearby creek mutters in everlasting portent. Events linked into consequences run on into other deeper and stranger consequences. The unicorn wants to go home, back to its fields of the sun. It has taken enough energy from the Dragon. It has seen all and more than it wants to see of the parasitical lives thriving on the Dragon's pelt. Why it stays seems too large a question, especially in the days since Raglaw almost killed it. The wisdom that it needs to understand why it stays will not fit into its skull.

Yet, the unicorn stays. It has learned from its encounters with the Fire Lords that it is a dutiful creature, and of a larger order than the small lives infesting the Dragon. With that knowledge comes a responsibility from which it cannot flee. It has been chosen. Of all in the herd, it alone has been chosen. For the honor of its breed, it must stay and complete the work it has been sent here to do.

But where are the Fire Lords in their soft wings of light? Where are their watchful eyes? The unicorn looks and sees blue-cut pieces of the sky shaped by leaves and branches trapped inside the wind. It listens and hears only the interminable omen of the creek that runs toward a depth that will swallow it whole.

"You shall never have the unicorn," the princess threatens as Lailoken rides beside her on a frisky black stallion that requires his full attention. He has never ridden such a beast before, and he is unaccustomed to the stubborn single-mindedness of the horse. His feeble legs cannot prevent his being jostled and jiggled about. The steed's muscular excitement at every twist of wind and inviting plume of oat grass along the roadside tests his determination, and he must use all his physical strength to master the beast.

"I do not want the unicorn," Lailoken answers truthfully; yet, not wanting to meet her mocking grin, he looks away, down the shrubby slopes to where the sea sparkles and, beyond the wheeling gulls, the profile of Mona purples the horizon beneath castles of summer clouds.

"You told me you were pursuing it," Morgeu presses. "Are you a liar?"

"I *was* pursuing the unicorn—and it led me to you. For that reason alone, we should be friends." Lailoken looks about for the child's guardian, some authoritative adult who can save him from this youngster's impudence. But the guards on their horses are attentive only to the underbrush at the roadside and the sun-glinting trees on the slopes above. Most trail behind, guarding the boarskin-covered wagon that hauls supplies from the fortress.

"If we are to be friends," she says, her eyes chilled as polished pebbles, "you must give me a gift."

"You have the gift of Lailoken's friendship," he replies evenly, and tries to pull his mount away from her.

But she is the far superior equestrian, and she stays close by his side. "Prove your friendship to me, Lailoken," she insists, glowering at him like a temple demon. "Give me a gift, I tell you. Something simple. Say, that crude, ugly staff you carry with you." She reaches out and tugs free the stave that the wizard had secured to his saddle.

"Return that, young lady—" the old man calls loudly, too loudly, startling his horse and sending it prancing forward. Morgeu delivers the haunches of the beast a sharp rap with the hard stave, and it bolts into a full run. Lailoken flings himself forward, clinging to its neck, the ground blurring below him.

Desperately, he uses magic to reach into the animal with his heart strength, trying to calm the startled creature. But before he can master his own fright, a mounted warrior reaches out, deftly seizes his reins, and steadies the stallion for him.

Lailoken turns sheepishly about in the saddle, prepared to face Morgeu's scornful laughter. Instead, he sees her churlish face aquiver with fear. From the trailing wagon, a flap of boarskin has lifted above a gnarled, two-fingered hand, revealing a hideously riven face, warped, cracked, and bleached as a weathered plank. The fearsome apparition scowls at the girl and vanishes behind the dropped hide. Morgeu, lower jaw trembling, timidly hands the staff to a nearby guard and retreats to a position behind the wagon.

With the staff returned to him, Lailoken rides well away from Morgeu, and the remainder of that day's journey continues without incident. Not until late that night does he see again the crone's withered visage. After the party has eaten and enjoyed harpsongs and heroic stories, after the campfires are banked and the night given to sleep under the guardianship of the white-shrouded moon, the hag comes to him.

A spidery touch summons Lailoken from his first sleep under a blanket since the days of his mother's love, and he blinks awake. "Come away with me, wizard," the hag whispers with a breath sour and sweet as gone apples. "Come walk with me through the night."

She speaks in Brythonic, and by the time the wizard revives that old Celtic tongue from his demonic memory, the witch has shrunk away into the lunar night.

He sits up and peeks around for the others. All sleep soundly beside the breathing embers of the campfire, and even the sentinels slump drowsily at their posts. *Crone's work*, he thinks, and grasps his staff as he departs the fire circle.

At the brink of the roadside beside a many-stalked elder, Lailoken finds the old woman sitting on her haunches staring down at the sea's glittery collection of polished spoons.

"Who dreamed the waters into being?" the hag inquires.

The wizard squats beside her and scrutinizes her deformed profile, her features twisted and shrunk as a cinder, her thin hair mere cobwebs in the bright night. "You woke these old bones for a game of riddles?"

"Oh, this is no game, Lailoken—nor are your bones old as they seem." Her voice crackles and hisses from brittle lungs. "I am the crone Raglaw, spiritual guardian of the queen. And you are the demon Lailoken who ravaged the Romans, and before them the Achaean Greeks, and before them the Assyrians of Nineveh, and before them the Chaldeans of Babylon." She gives a humorless, peg-toothed smile to the night. "So now that we know who we are, tell me, Lailoken, who dreamed the waters into being?"

"God."

She turns her sunken face toward him, her eyes wet sparks in sunken sockets, her nose a black twist from a mummy's skull. "And whom do you serve by wearing these rags of mortal flesh? Tell me true, demon."

"I serve God. I have always served Her—best as I knew how—from the time heaven cast us out."

"Then, riddle me this, demon Lailoken: What good do mortals find on earth that God can never find?"

The wizard puzzles over that for an awkward spell and then admits, "I have no idea, crone Raglaw. What mortals can find, so can God."

"Think on it, then," she counsels, "for you have not yet grasped what it is to be truly mortal until you understand this riddle." She returns her attention to the moon-spun waters. "It will come to you."

Lailoken huffs with exasperation. "You say this is not a game—yet you speak to me as though I were a child."

A scornful laugh sizzles from deep in Raglaw's collapsed chest. "Are you not, Lailoken? Have your mortal eyes beheld more than a dozen winters?"

"No, yet I have knowledge greater than all your winters, old lady, even if you were as ancient as the entombed pharaohs you resemble."

"Bah—knowledge. Is that how you hope to serve God—with your knowledge? What are you—a demon or a scribe? Look there, Lailoken." She thrusts her bony chin at the darkness blotting the setting constellations. "That island is Mona mam Cymru, the Mother of Our Land. Once, it fed all this country—and not just with its grains and cattle. It fed us with its knowledge, for there dwelled the druids, the nobles of our people, who knew the secret ways of earth and sky, and the tree alphabet, and the oral histories of the oldest heroes and wisest women. And, I ask you, what worth was all that knowledge under the sword of the Romans? The invaders slaughtered them all, and their knowledge now is worth no more than the babbling of the wind in the trees. Knowledge—bah!"

The hag spins about and stabs a stubby finger into the wizard's chest. "Open *this* up," she gasps. "Come, Lailoken. Open your heart to me. I know you know what I mean. Open it now and feel what you will feel."

What reason have I to resist her? he reasons, and so gently, he releases the flowing energy from the gate of his heart, and it penetrates her as though she were smoke.

With frightful suddenness, Lailoken's life-force spills out of him, falling through her vaporous being like a man striding into a dark stairwell and finding instead empty space. Only, rather than plummeting downward, the wizard falls *up* into the sky. The strangeness of the sensation grips him so strongly, he unravels into laughter. Seized with guffaws, he dissolves into the rising wind sliding off the sea. He rushes upward through the moon-shot treecrowns, vision bleared, soaring above the dark valleys in a star-streaked headlong flight higher than time.

A wider vision opens, and Lailoken sees the years spread before him like a writhing, living tapestry. Prescience has never been a gift he possessed, even as a demon, and this frightens him. *Time is blind*, he tells himself.

Yet to his charmed attention, suddenly time shines radiantly, dancing like the luminous shadows inside a surging fire. The flames spurt whole swatches of human history, where each fluttering color illuminates a lineage, flares of generations; each hue carries a life, shading scenes and experiences from that life and the many enclosing lives, the whole of this resplendent vista writhing and swirling like veils of fiery oil on water.

All time seethes before him. Past and future. He sees across thirty centuries or more, from the first mud hut cities on the Euphrates to a future of glass and steel spires.

His flight peaks, and, as he falls back through the treecrowns and into the smudged outline of his body, the weird dimensions narrow beyond memory, taking away all the lives in their billions that have blazed before him.

Frantically, he strives to hold on to what he can, paying greatest heed to the combusting images nearest his own small life as a human being.

Battles horrible rage all around—severed limbs, screaming men, wild, blood-frothed horses with bronze-breasted and leather-masked bowmen astride them. Arrows whistle, searing through space, disappearing to their fletch-feathers in the torsos of barbarians. And there stands the bloodstained Furor, his one good eye tight with malice, his heavy beard and coiled locks streaking back in a tempest wind, the veins on his enraged face tangled like chains of blue steel.

Lailoken averts his gaze from the war god's ghastly wrath and sees the stump of a mammoth oak sliced to a great wheel taller than a man. The wheel falls to its side and becomes a large table and kings in all their finery sit around it. Then, the round table disappears, and he sees stone battlements, the glare of smoking torches and bonfires, muddy trenches hackled with pikes and spears, and more horsemen in their raptor-helmets, wielding curved Persian bows. And he sees musicians and jugglers, camels, too, and an elephant. And a young, beardless king with raven hair and yellow eyes and a jade crucifix at the crook of his collarbones.

The howling wrath of the Furor rises against the youthful Christian king with the gentle, golden eyes. Lailoken stands between them, and their two countenances stare at the wizard from the opposite poles of his destiny—one furious, the other supplicative and caring—and within that space he experiences the immense finality that separates violence and love and that has made him the living axis between them, fated to keep them apart.

With a physical thump, Lailoken finds himself skullbound once more, staring bulge-eyed at Raglaw's leering mask.

"Did you see?" she wheezes. "Did you *see*?"

"I saw war—"

"Did you see the *king*?"

Lailoken nods and nearly collapses, his muscles gummy with weariness.

Her claws clasp his beard and pull his face into the wet heat of her rant, "That is the *king*! You saw him! Solitary as a cliff this side of forever! That is the *king* who can stand upon horror for a love that quickens the centuries! That is the king! Remember him, Lailoken! Remember him, for you must find him for the queen—for Ygrane—before the Furor's unquenchable sword finds us!"

"Find him?" the old man mumbles, confused. "Who is he? I don't know him. Where would I find him?"

Contemptuous laughter ekes from her gaping mouth with a sparking sound. "Where? You fool! I have shown you something better than your wanton knowledge. I have filled your heart with vision and shown you how the seasons are built. I have shown you destiny! Go now—hurry, little man. Go! The mortal event awaits you! And if you fail, not only *you* will be extinguished but all the future that you have seen. Go!"

The haggard, simian presence of the crone flaps before him like black fire, and he defies his exhaustion and scrambles away on all fours, dragging his staff with him. He does not slow down until he arrives in camp and the night watch jolts alert from where he slumps under the moon's thumb.

Lailoken lies still, curled upon himself, stunned by what he has experienced in the crone's trance. "The Christian king with the yellow eyes," he natters softly to himself. "The crone says I must find him. Long ago, my mother spoke of a king—born of the love of two enemies . . . "

He notices the night watch peering at him curiously, thinking the old man is blithering to the campfire. Lailoken turns his back to the guard and ponders the crone's riddle that will teach him what it is to be human, "What *good* have mortals found on earth that God can never find?"

Only later as sleep narrows in does the answer rise out of his demonic memory, and he sighs and hugs himself, then whispers, barely audibly, "Of course. A worthy master."

Morgeu stirs in her sleep, rolls over on the straw-filled pallet under a canopy of pine boughs; she startles to see Raglaw, hood thrown back, standing over her. In the dark, the crone's charred face has the jet luster of a beetle's black armor.

"Lie still, child."

"Crone—" Morgeu swipes sleep from her eyes with the sleeve of her bedshirt and darts a look for her guard.

"Asleep, all." Needleglints move in the bleak sockets of the crone's eyes. "We are alone, you and I."

"Why do you rouse me, crone?" Morgeu sits up, her round, pale face braving the steady stare from the black beetle carapace.

"This is the last time we shall meet, you and I, future time and past time intersecting here in this one dark moment. Only our plight is alive, child—and it lives in us."

Morgeu, frightened by the crone's raving, looks again for her guard. His shaggy head has bowed forward chin to chest, and indeed he is asleep before a fire whose dying embers glow dark as rubies.

A dense magic mutes the flames, thickens the dark. The child has experienced this eerie atmosphere before, always with her mother and the crone. When she first felt it, she used to creep out of bed to find the two witches talking to quick furious faces in the fire or prancing lockstep with balls of lightning in the woods or, once, naked, the crone a tatter-fleshed skeleton, her mother fluid marble, the two dancing before a giant furry man with an elk's head, not a mask but a living elk's face with watchful eyes and expressive black lips. After that, she has cowered deeper in her bed whenever she feels this uncanny charge of magic in the night.

"What do you want of me, crone?"

"I want to touch the future in you, child." A deformed hand like a knob on a branch, bearing only forefinger and thumb, emerges from under her robe and reaches for her face. "Be still. I would feel the timewind in you."

True to her word, at the crone's touch, Morgeu's insides chill as though frosted. She opens her mouth to cry out, to alert the guard, yet not even a squeak emerges. The crone's touch hollows her out, leaves her empty and soundless. And within that void, images spin.

She sees her father, his burly frame flying through the air, stern features clenched in something more than a battle grimace, a hectic look she has never beheld in his face before—fear. Barbarians in outlandish skull-armor rush among twists of smoke. Lailoken squats before behemoths of tar ooze afloat with monstrous visages—the chitin faces of insects and crabs, yet weirdly, evilly sapient.

Out of this swirling vision struts a corpse white woman with a lunar face, eyes like two black puncture wounds, and flame-wild hair. It is herself grown up—a faerïe-tale enchantress in green satin robes.

The bone white woman with bloodred lips gazes back at her down the years, a flash of menace in her small swart eyes. Morgeu shrinks before realizing that the enchantress is peering *through* her at the crone.

Raglaw's ruined face gaups in surprise, and grains of her nose and cheeks trickle away in thin smoky streams. "You are strong—" she grunts with involuntary candor, straining with all her twitching might to deflect an invisible vehemence.

The enchantress's voice opens in young Morgeu, painfully bright, full of the jewel-dazzle of her strong magic: "You would touch the future, Raglaw—you would abort me with your claw. But I *have* grown too strong. Now the future touches you. And by the hand of your prey, I kill you—I kill you—I kill you with the very strength you would have used to kill me!"

The crone, reduced to stupefied glaring, wags her extended hand, trying to free it from an invisible grip. The frayed fingertip and cracked thumb ball, poised before young Morgeu's face, sear to black ash and flake off. With a dire groan, Raglaw staggers backward, the club of her hand fingerless and smoldering.

Instantly, the spell is broken, and the child Morgeu stands up searching for the faerïe-tale enchantress that will be herself. But she is gone, and the crone is gone, and the flawless night reels overhead, the eerie atmosphere vanished. It is replaced by an excited glow, a thrilled aftermath of spectacle.

She watches the firelight strengthen, sparks leap again to rags of flame. The guard jerks his head upright as though just rescuing himself from sleep. Joy feels velvety in her body, like the warmth of wine-water she has tasted at her father's table.

The memory of her father flying fright-stricken through the smoky air makes her knees spongy, and she sags back onto her pallet. She does not understand all that she has witnessed, but she knows for sure that there is grave jeopardy for the duke. Her fear for him fits dangerously into her ignorance and terrible wonder at what she has seen.

A child once more, she lies back and peeks through the chinks of the pine boughs, wide-awake in the mesh of vast, shifting feelings, her black eyes like two starless drops fallen out of the night.

The hag keeps to her wagon for the remainder of that journey, and Lailoken does not see her again until they arrive, on a gray, drizzly afternoon, at Maridunum, a stone-walled city on the bluffs above a quiet river. Once inside the city gates, she leaps from her wagon, spry as a rat, and watches the wizard dismount.

"Remember the king!" She flaps her black robes excitedly and stamps her feet on the damp flagstones.

To avoid her fervid stare, Lailoken pulls up his cowl as if to ward off the misty rain. Throughout the jouncing journey, the crone's dire prophecy haunted him, *If you fail, not only you will be extinguished . . .*

He watches Morgeu canter on ahead, then dismount in a graceful bound that flutters her mantle like blue wings. Red hair flaring behind, she hurries past the sentinel soldiers and the courtyard's leaping dolphin fountain toward a grand, old-fashioned house flanked by oaks upright as obelisks.

"Such a pretty dish to serve murder in," Raglaw cackles from under her black cope. "To be sure, she'll be a fatal kind of trouble for your king—that is, if you can save him from the Furor first. But to save, you must find. Have you thought on that? Look smart now, Lailoken!"

The wizard heads straight for the *mansio*, the largest and oldest structure in the city. There, Morgeu has already bounded up the marble stairs and disappeared through the vestibule.

The *mansio*, with its two stories, four wings, and vine-hung porticoes, dominates the smaller thatch-roofed houses of the city. They radiated from the hub of the splendid mansion in irregular spokes of tree-cloistered avenues, cobbled alleys, and rutted lanes. Children and their dogs flit across the busy courtyard, and soldiers shoo them away from the horses. Matrons who have filled their amphorae at the fountain do not linger to gossip in the sprinkling rain but hurry off with the veils of their *tunicas* held over their heads.

Lailoken lingers, face upturned, refreshed by the chill points of rain as he takes it all in—his first real city as a human. No one in the small crowd that has turned out to greet the party pays him any particular heed. Stable hands take the horses, wine merchants with leather flasks offer refreshment to the road-weary guards, and a tangle of Roman officers in characteristic military cloaks and gilded leather cuirasses loiter by a tavern doorway and watch the Celts with idle interest.

"Gorlois's men," a voice hisses beside Lailoken, and the

witch Raglaw presses upon him again. "Gorlois—father of Morgeu—"

The wizard backs away hurriedly from the shadowy hag, but she is swift and easily catches his forearm.

"We'll see the queen together," she hacks in her broken voice, "you and I—before you go—"

"Go?"

"You must leave at once—after you see the queen." Her scratchy laughter at his befuddlement hurts his ears. "Have you forgot already? To find the *king* for Ygrane—"

"But her husband—Gorlois—" he stammers, perplexed.

A jet of hot, apple-sour breath slaps him as she expels a silent guffaw. "Ygrane is a Celtic queen. You should know, Lailoken, she may have all the husbands she wishes. Though, in truth, she wishes only one—and not proud Gorlois, either. But come—the queen is waiting—and the duke who has the cure for my aching bones. We must hurry."

Raglaw's iron grasp drags the bearded old man after her, and his feet scramble to follow as she scampers up the stairs, across the portico, past the armed sentinels, and into the *mansio*'s expansive foyer. Among the fluted pillars, alternating Celtic and Roman guards stand at attention.

Lailoken inspects their weapons and notes the dark sheen of use on their hilts and shafts. He directs his attention with a nod to the foyer's far end, where an ornate eagle standard leans against a polished staff heavily nicked with ogham symbols. Here, Roman tradition and Celtic might clearly have united in unpredictable ways.

The high, red-lacquered double doors behind the joined standards jump open, and a stout, goat-eyed man with a bull-dog's jowls and neckless breadth strides into the foyer. Ruddy, with brindled hair short and bristly as a pig's hackles, he looks more like a man who wrestled with boulders, an infantry trench digger, than a duke. Yet, he wears the bronze breastplate embossed with intertwining serpents, with the knot of purple silk over his left shoulder that identifies him as nobility. Under his arm and over his hip, he hauls Morgeu, who kicks the air and shouts with glee.

Ygrane watches silently from inside the threshold, tall and long-shouldered but with an unhappy expression on her strong features. When she spots Raglaw, that look widens to horror, and Lailoken knows then grief is upon them.

"You've waited patiently enough while I broke the back of the sea rovers," the narrow-eyed bulldog says to Morgeu. "Now I can take you for a sail, girl. And afterward, a feast on the beach. How about that?" He swings her off his hip and into the air, catches her under her arms, and lowers her gently to the floor.

Suddenly, all levity drops from his heavy face as he looks up and sees the hag. "You! Witch!" His booming voice boils into echoes across the arched ceiling. "You dare defy me? I *said* if ever I laid eyes on you again I'd have your head—and, God help me, I will!"

"Do it then, Gorlois," Raglaw goads him and lowers her hood. "Return me to the Greater World." Her leprous arms, spare as rods, reach for him in a queerly angular way, as in some ritual dance.

Gorlois pauses, reading madness in the antic jerk of her limbs as she advances defiantly.

"What stays your hand?" the crone sneers. "Is this my magic again—that I, already in death's jaws, should have less fear of dying than you, a mighty warrior? Coward!"

Metal sings, the nobleman whisking his sword from its scabbard.

"Gorlois!" Ygrane cries.

With a razorish whistle, the sword blurs in a streaking arc and slices cleanly through the crone's skinny neck. The body slumps forward, arterial jets lashing Gorlois's hardened visage with crimson strokes. The head topples backward and rolls to Lailoken's feet. Raglaw's scorched face gazes up at the wizard from a widening puddle of blood, her meager lips still moving, mouthing the words, "Find the king . . . "

The fiana, who have lunged forward from their posts as Gorlois's sword smote the hag, draw their swords in turn. But Ygrane stays them with upraised arms. "No!" she calls out loudly, signing her guard to stand back. "Raglaw has chosen her own death. I heard her. She has returned to the Greater World of her own will." Her voice fractures a little, and she has to close her eyes—

"Sent by *my* sword to her pagan hell!" Gorlois snarls, and wipes the blood from his blade on the crone's robe. From behind him, Morgeu watches with a glittering intensity.

"Take your men, Gorlois, and go," Ygrane demands. Her eyes shine with tears and rage. "Your work here is done." Then, in a softer voice, she adds, "Morgeu, go to your chambers."

Gorlois levels a hard stare on his wife. "I'll take no orders from you, Ygrane. My daughter and I are off for a sail."

"No, Gorlois," Ygrane speaks firmly. "Morgeu will honor the mourning rites for Raglaw with the rest of my people. If you'll stay, then you and your men will have to do the same. This is not the Saxon Coast. We are in Cymru, where I am law—by agreement of our alliance, husband."

Gorlois's jaw rocks to one side, vehemently. "I'll take no part in your pagan rites, woman. You know that."

"Then gather your men and go—now." The queen says this without raising her voice, though it has the forcefulness of a shout.

Gorlois's goat eyes tighten and, for several seconds, lock in a silent duel with his wife's. He breaks off abruptly and spits at the severed head; then he waves his sword for his soldiers to follow and barrels past the stunned wizard as though he is not there. Morgeu, following after him with her eyes, casts a bitter look at her mother.

"To your chambers," Ygrane tells the child coldly.

Morgeu dashes into the house, and the queen stands

unmoving until the last Roman soldier has departed and the eagle standard has disappeared down the stairs and out of sight. Only then, with her cheeks bright with tears, does she say to her fiana in Brythonic, "Brothers, you see how I have lost my spirit reckoner. We have lost her magic. But, it is ever the way of the wise ones—ever the way"—she wipes her tears and summons a proud smile to her unhappy face—"that our Raglaw has found her own reckoner and delivered a new wise one to us. He stands before you now—the demon visitor, Lailoken."

The old man stands stunned, momentarily taken aback, while the fiana cheer. All of them know his story, well enough that within days harpists across the land will be singing "The Sorrows of Lailoken," conveying throughout Cymru news of the Dark Dweller from the House of Fog made human by the angelic *Annwn*, the Fire Lords. Through the recognition of the queen, he gains immediate renown.

The death of the crone Raglaw seems to Ygrane and her people foreordained, wholly condign with Lailoken's abrupt arrival, as if one great being has molted gender and skin and transformed itself from crone to wizard. This transition has for them the timing of legend, and they chant Lailoken's name in a dirgeful cadence, bidding farewell to Raglaw and welcoming the wizard in the same breath.

The queen's glamour warms the death chill of that blood-slaked room. Squinting, Lailoken can see the blue shine of her influence glossing the air.

She motions the old man to her side, and he steps hesitantly around Raglaw's beheaded corpse.

"All the respect and deference that was due Raglaw shall be accorded this man," Ygrane says wearily. She presses the back of her hand to her mouth to steady the tremor in her lips. None of the fiana look at the wizard. All eyes are upon their queen—and Lailoken sees for the first time, through their immense devotion to her, the true majesty of the woman. Neither words nor music can reach the stillness in which she holds that chamber. If she were to weep, she would betray her Celtic faith in the Greater World beyond life, and Lailoken feels her kingdom would collapse at that instant. But she does not weep. When her hand comes away, her face shines with a regal clarity that could sing up angels from a ditch.

She puts a firm hand on Lailoken's shoulder and speaks with a certainty her men need to hear after the murder of their reckoner by a Roman hand. "As Raglaw was the stitch that bound the old ways to the new, so this man shall be the binding scar where the stitch had been. And he shall be known among us and in the world at large by the name of this place where the honor and duties of Raglaw have passed to him. Henceforth, he is no longer Lailoken the demon visitor. Instead, he shall be our spirit reckoner, and he shall be called our Man of Maridunum—*Myrðin*."

Among the assembled, a triumphant shout exclaims, "Myrddin!"—and the wizard blinks back at the crowd with surprise. He is not ready to be so quickly thrust into prominence, he who, for ages, has worked secretly and in dark places.

The queen turns, and Lailoken follows her into the central hall. He glances back once, numbly, and in those few moments he sees that the fiana have already removed Raglaw's corpse and workers in hide breeches are busy sponging away the gore and igniting incense trays to fumigate the recent violence from the atmosphere.

Following Ygrane's lead, the wizard walks silently past long dining tables, chambers hung with saffron draperies from which harp music and plangent singing sifts, and map rooms where scribes busily scribble, oblivious to the bloodletting only paces away. Finally, the queen takes her new spirit reckoner down a steamy stairwell that leads to the baths. Servants crisscross among the hallways, bearing scrolls to the scribes and trays of savory foods to the music chambers. The death of Raglaw seems of no greater consequence to them than the passing of a cloud across the sun.

"Today we celebrate a military victory over the sea rovers," Ygrane explains, recognizing his bafflement. Her voice has regained its composure. "And now, we will honor as well the triumphant passing to the Greater World of the wisewoman Raglaw—and the arrival of the wizard Myrddin. There is much for the scribes to record."

Through an archway of blue-veined marble, they enter an open-walled gallery under a rose arbor canopy that overlooks a spacious parkland of flowering hedges. Reedbanks fringe willow ponds, and verdant lawns sprawl to the far wall and ramparts that guard the city. Beyond the battlements, undulant hills of sward bunch to the upholstered skyline. They sit beside a slate table on facing settles whose backs have been carved into dragoncoils. Handmaidens in sea-green *camisas* serve pear wine, smoked salmon, and black bread with currant jam. Lailoken leans his staff against a railing graced with finny-winged sea horses and observes the gentle rain dimpling the birdbaths.

"You are surrounded by beauty and power," he says, and sips the wine and nibbles the bread to fulfill the queen's obligation of hospitality. "My lady," he continues with a tone of grave doubt, "I must tell you, I am not worthy to replace Raglaw as your spirit reckoner."

"Myrddin, let there be no false modesty between us—please." Ygrane turns her leonine profile toward the tree-rough fringing the garden, and the wizard notices suddenly how careworn and tired her face looks in this light. "Surely, you have no doubt Raglaw saw you for who you are? She was the last queen's reckoner, you know. And the queen before that. She had what we call the strong eye, for she could see deeper into things than most. From her, after the druids brought me here, I learned how to understand what I see."

Her voice, detached and small, frays toward a whisper: "Her death is not, as you might have thought, wholly unexpected. She would have passed to the Greater World by leaf-fall. We both saw it. But she did surprise us all today, letting her death stand defiantly against the duke—as a life for a life. It was her last act of magic . . . for me."

"But I don't understand," Myrddin speaks. "Why did Gorlois kill her?"

"They were enemies to be sure," the queen answers matter-of-factly. "Raglaw reminded him of his place, and she never let him forget he was a foreigner in these lands. As I've told you, it was the druids arranged for my marriage to Gorlois as a political expediency. His kingdom stood in dire jeopardy from the Saxon sea rovers. With the Roman navy long gone, the barbarians were in full command of his coasts and before long assured of mounting his head on a pike. That none of the Roman families left in Britain could spare their forces to aid him without jeopardizing their own domains was a humiliation to him. It forced him to fend for himself. The druids offered him Celtic might if he would agree to marry their queen."

"Why?" the wizard puzzles aloud. "What advantage for you to marry the arrogant invader?"

"Is there any other reason but power, Myrddin?" the queen replies sourly. "With so many of our tribes become Christian, the druids had reason enough to want an alliance with the Romans. Marrying me off to a Christian duke who needed our soldiers, that protected their interests, did it not? The Romans of the Saxon Coast have foresworn sending missionaries into our land; and, indeed, the loss of the old ways has been slowed here in Cymru."

She returns her stare to the oaks and evergreen magnolias. Lailoken thinks that perhaps it is her melancholy that makes her so beautiful. In her face shines a wisdom born of suffering.

"Make no mistake, Myrddin," the queen continues. "I know this life is not my own, that I am but an effigy, fabricated by the druids who control me. But even as this thing they have made me, I have a soul. It is my people. Whatever I can do to help them, I will.

"As a queen, I am pleased to preserve my people's culture—

but as a woman—" She stops. "I have told this to no one—only Raglaw knows . . . knew." She pauses to regard him closely. "She would have slain the unicorn—sacrificed it to the Dragon. But I stopped her, because I believe there is a better way. Yes, the Dragon, strengthened by the sacrifice of the unicorn, would help us defeat the invaders in a battle or two. But I have a wider plan, and Raglaw affirmed it with her vision—a vision she shared with you, Myrddin."

"The king—" he mutters. "She showed me the king who will father a savior."

"Yes. He is the consort of my destiny."

"But what of Gorlois? He does not seem a man likely to tolerate a rival."

The green of Ygrane's eyes appears to brighten. "I . . . I yearn for a love, Myrddin—a true love. Not political expediency. Gorlois has never loved me, nor I him, as is evident to all, I know. I suffered one night of his lewd attentions when I was but fifteen and conceived Morgeu. Since then, I have allowed him to use my soldiers and my forts but never again my body." She places an imploring weight of hope on him, reaches out, and takes his hand in a hard grip. "Myrddin, I cannot, will not, believe that the story I have seen so often in my visions is a false one, a cruel hoax that will lead to a life of useless misery. Why would God permit that? I can endure suffering, I swear, if there is a use to it. I wish only to fulfill the ancient story that took me away from my simple home in the hills. I want you to find for me my true love, the intended one of my visions. Raglaw herself said he is a real man. She has seen him and she has shown him to you. I want you to go now and find him."

"Me?" Lailoken's incredulous voice breaks from his throat before he can even think. "I am a demon. What do I know of love? All I ever knew was my mother's love—hardly the love of which you speak now."

"But not unlike," Ygrane says with heartful trust, searching his haggard face for some glimmer of understanding. "To fulfill my destiny, I know I must probably take another husband from among the Romans. But I dream this time of a true husband—a good man, not a brute like Gorlois, nor a champion of men on the battlefield; I dream but of a gentle man, one who neither speaks too loud nor ignores evil. I pray to my gods for such a like-minded mate, who will be ever for me like harmony to music, virtue to the soul, prosperity to the state . . . "

"And forethought to the universe," he concludes the famous old simile and casts an entreating look at her. He can hardly believe they are having this conversation moments after the crone's gory demise. Death and sex, the twined serpents of mortal life, tighten their coils about him. "Ah yes, my lady, of course—a man who can serve as well as dominate—the very ideal of manhood in the feminine imagination," he says, a trifle sarcastically. Then he sighs and wags his head hopelessly. "Might as well try to steal the morning light. I don't know of such a love. And that is not false modesty, Your Majesty. How can I find for you what I myself do not know?"

"What of the love you feel for the unicorn?" the queen insists. "It is that love that made you follow the beast to Cymru and to me."

"Yes, but it is different with the unicorn," he replies. "Love, harmony, and virtue did not bring us together. The Fire Lords—the luminous beings you call the *Annwn*—they used the unicorn to steal power from the Dragon to make me this human form. Since then, that wondrous beast has taught me how to use my demon powers in this poor mortal frame. My hope is that the steed will let me use it to ride free of this world and return to heaven. But the unicorn will not let me ride it. You see then—like your druids and Romans, we all seek power—not love."

The queen's face brightens. "A favor for a favor, then. You shall have the power that you seek, for I can help you capture the unicorn and ride it." She passes a hopeful smile to the wizard. "Last night, Raglaw came to me in trance. She told me that she gave you a vision of a time to come, as she and I had agreed after I convinced her not to sacrifice the unicorn. She claimed that in that prophetic fit, you saw the man who is to be my destiny—the true king who will be my lover and the father of our people's hope."

Revelation dilates around Lailoken's vision of the young king with the yellow eyes and raven hair, and he murmurs, "Yes, perhaps—the crone showed me a man—but—" He frowns. "My lady, the man Raglaw showed me is a Christian."

"Yes, Myrddin. That must be so—to fulfill the prophecy." She squeezes his hand and sits back with a look of fragile satisfaction. "Love is what I seek. A love I have known in other lives but not yet in this. Faith is no distraction to me. Haven't I already given myself to a Christian for political advantage? Why not, then, for love and the salvation of my people?"

"But will he love you back?" the wizard wonders. "Is prophecy enough to inspire love? We both know that the timewind shifts and what we have seen is not necessarily what will be."

A bedazzled flush lights her face from within. "Don't you understand, Myrddin? Raglaw allowed herself to die today, because what she showed you is destined. She has stood aside that you may go forth. If you find this man and bring him to me, I will be fulfilled in the deepest sense a woman can know. If in the mind of God we are destined to meet, he already loves me."

From the ramparts of the south wall, Morgeu watches the fiana carry the corpse of the crone Raglaw out of Maridunum. The child has disobeyed her mother so that she might wave farewell to her father. But the duke and his men have already departed. The dust from their horses hangs above the rutted road in an amber haze, marking where the company turned the bend that descends toward the sea and the invaders they are sworn to fight.

Morgeu climbs steep stairs that lead toward cirrus marblings and the highest parapet of the south wall. Around her gather verdant hills, smoke blue horizons of mountains, and the distant sea. Below, tiny as thumblings, her mother and the wizard Lailoken stroll together in the parkland within the city's walls. Hidden from their view by the ivy-splashed walls, Falon carries a sack bulging knobbily with the corpse of Raglaw.

Pride flushes through Morgeu. The faerïe-tale enchantress she will someday become has slain the crone. She only wishes that the curse had not chosen her father to do the deed. The vision of him in a plunge of fright squats like nausea in her.

Six fiana accompany Falon on his march across the cow pastures toward the cavernous forest. They wedge-flank their captain as though expecting an enemy to challenge them for the hag's bones. Each of them feared the crone as much as Morgeu, and the child wonders what they intend to do with her body.

Her mother seems wholly indifferent. She and the wizard wade among lavender asters to the squared ledge of a Roman fountain, conversing earnestly. The unicorn is nowhere to be found. Morgeu has not seen it since Lailoken drove it off, and she has been calling imploringly for it to return. Already she senses that she does not have the authority to summon the wondrous creature.

For now, Morgeu is confused. Everything has changed. The crone is dead and a future self, an unexpected self, has come to life. Her young mind glows with the promise of this strength and cannot yet grasp the cruel seasons or the fierce and mortal weakness that require such strength.

The thought of herself as a sorceress continues to surprise her, because she has none of her mother's powers—no healing green touch, no recollection of former lives, no long sight either—at least not until Raglaw touched her. Morgeu cannot imagine how she will grow up to be so vehemently powerful.

Her father's realm holds far more fascination for her than the boring naturalistic world of magic. The Roman court, with all its pageantry and obvious importance, has intrigued her since she first looked up from her dolls and began paying attention to the world. She enjoys being the duke's daughter and admires his authority, the way he is always central, all others moving around him, meshing their lives to follow him. His decisiveness and strength awe her.

Her mother is the duke's opposite. She disappears into her world. In her gardens and on her forest trods, she is ever gathering, sorting, cleaning the ingredients for her magical rinses. Her earthy handmaids work with her as casually as though she were one of their own common lot. And the druids, who are supposed to serve and obey her, spend more time with the duke's ministers scheming advantages for their own clans. Only the fiana are genuinely devoted, and yet Morgeu has seen even them bicker with her when she gets too dreamy.

The dreaminess is why Morgeu has had no interest in magic. Without the sight, she does not see what her mother sees. Until the unicorn, magic looked to her like little more than spellbound silence. And then, for the first time, she experienced the intense reality of her mother's world when she touched the packed energies of the tusked horse.

But now, the unicorn is gone—and Lailoken has arrived. Lailoken—a demon disguised as a man. She has listened in rapt fright to the tales of demonic possession and devil hauntings told by her Christian governess at Tintagel, and she knows with a child's certitude that no good can come of this lanky old man. She is glad that her father will be sending for her in a few days to join him on the Saxon Coast. Without the unicorn, she feels no joy in her mother's faraway presence.

Morgeu skips along the parapet walkway, imagining that she is flying away, and then stops to watch the fiana fade into the forest. She wishes she could see what they are doing with the severed head and stiffening body of Raglaw. Will they bury her or leave her for the beasts? She knows what her mother would say: The elf-folk will take her.

Like an explosion blasting debris outward, a huge flock of black birds erupts out of the forest canopy in a tight, swirling vortex. Fox fire runs rapidly among the trees, green flames shot by arrows. Moments later, the fiana dash from the woods, running in a mad scramble, their hardy faces smeared with fright.

Morgeu crouches at the parapet wall, though the fox fire has vanished. Over the treetops, the maelstrom of black birds rises, and the child quakes, expecting them to form the crone's visage. But they scatter haphazardly across the day sky, like pieces of night surprised to find themselves in a strange land.

The Dragon curls upon itself, listening to the dreamsongs that sift to earth out of the starry depths. The music from its other selves, from the Dragons of other worlds, is both fast and still, opening amorous joys in the liquid of its brain. Spellbound by this bliss, it wants to sing with the sweetness that comes from great strength, yet it lacks that power. And that lack is an estranging grief.

Mind inwrought, the Dragon feels torn and alone. The dreamsongs strung on the starwinds curl directly through the desiring center of its need. The stars fall through the cold. The others are so far away. Somehow, it must reach them, must gather the force from its ragged limits so that it can sing loudly enough to share in the endless genesis of the Dragon.

But for now it curls upon itself in its own mortal circle, listening, yearning. The stars fall through the cold. The galaxies turn in their windy spirals. And the Dragon dreams of the first song, the first music of the Lords who set fire in the earth.

UTHER

The wizard keeps to himself on the rutted and torn roads of Britain and avoids any settlement smaller than what the Romans called the municipia, the major towns. There, he encounters the persistent memory of a bygone glory. The cosmopolitan Romans imported entertainment from the most exotic reaches of their empire, and though they departed this distant room of their imperial kingdom half a century ago, the remnants of their maudlin carnival lingers behind in the larger cities.

Between regular bear-baiting events and public executions, jugglers, acrobats, and fire-eaters perform in the main courtyards of the walled municipalities. Defiant of the old Roman edict prohibiting prophecy and the latest Christian promulgations against it, astrologers and soothsayers proliferate—as do *fakirs* with their beds of hot embers, gypsy healers, miracle workers, rain dancers, and sleight-of-hand magicians.

For five years, Myrddin sees them all. He looks into every male face in all the *municipia* he visits, searching for Ygrane's king. The yellow-eyed young man with raven hair could be disguised as anyone, perhaps even a beggar or a clown, though the demon-wizard does not exclude the possibility that the man already reigns as king—for there are numerous kings in this chaotic time. Among the remaining great families who have not already fled Britain, plotters and poisoners erect and topple monarchs seasonally.

Between *municipia*, there are no "kings," only roving marauders known as wildwood gangs, who raid villages and slaughter each other. It is not unusual for Myrddin to find twenty or thirty men slain upon the decayed roads, their bodies sometimes piled in a charred heap or left in tarry lumps in a ditch, the cremated slag destined eventually to heal over into a robust conflagration of spring flowers. More often, the corpses are simply abandoned where they have fallen, stripped of weapons and armor, gnawed at by dogs and ravens.

At times, these maniac destructions that he witnesses oppress him, and to cleanse himself, he visits with Ygrane—that is, in trance, he seems to float disembodied in her presence, witnessing small scenes of her life. He hovers nearby as she plies her healing potions among ailing countryfolk and kneels in her walled garden of fruit and flowers, cosseting her unicorn.

Myrddin wakes refreshed from these dreams. The destiny leading Ygrane leads him, as well—the joy of a vital conjunction yet to come, a love that, somehow, will create something noble for the broken lives in this land to look up to and heal themselves by—a new life born of magic and love, a brief history, perhaps, of peace in the welter of war and savagery. He wants that to be true, for Ygrane, for his mother's earnest prayers, and, most important of all, for Her.

For Her, Lailoken reminds himself, he has become Myrddin. For Her, he wanders the burned land. For Her, he exists at all.

Sometimes to worship Her, he squats in the rubble of a toppled shrine or charred temple and speaks aloud his story, as if by voicing his memory he touches Her—for She is his history, his reason for being, and when he talks of Her he must speak of himself, so that the telling holds them softly together.

"I am the demon Lailoken. I am as old as time. Older, in fact, if truth were to be told. But truth, strict as it is, is a tricky thing. A very tricky thing indeed. I see that now—now that I have had the privilege of living the truth from both sides. But I was not always so privileged.

"In the beginning, I, like everything else that is, was flung out into the void. The Big Bang, the future ages will call that stupendous event. But that is only because they have forgotten what big really is.

"Before the beginning, before this so-called Big Bang, which spewed forth the universe in a terrific gush of energy from a point smaller than any mortal can imagine, where was everything? I will tell you in a word.

"Heaven.

"Before the universe began its aeonian expansion through the cold and dark of space, everything that is now was in heaven as pure energy. Everything that is now was then pure light—albeit, a very special kind of light, a white light of all possible wavelengths, a light of infinite heat and infinite density.

"I was there, inside the infinite heat and infinite density of the All. And so were we all, if truth were told. But now we are back to the truth again, and that, as I say, is tricky business. Tricky because people do not remember.

"There's the chief difference between mortals and demons. I remember. I remember and I cannot forget what infinite joy there is inside the Inside of All. It is heaven. And it is real. More real than the diaphanously spun web of atoms and molecules whose chill vibrations in the vacuum weave this illusion of matter and vaporous form we presently call reality.

"But I am ranting again. I cannot help that. Nothing I can say about heaven, out here in the void, with the flung stars kindling their dim echo of the One Light, would make much sense to anyone else, even though they were all there with me.

"Suffice it to say, then, that heaven is everything we think it is—beautiful and whole. Why it fell apart the way it did, why there was a Big Bang at all, is another story, one not really suited for words, for it is the story of Her—and I don't want to get into that again. Yet, it is the story that we demons tell among ourselves, grousing and complaining about the cold and the dark, arguing on and on about what to *do* now that we are out here, and we can't go back.

"Or can we go back? That's another argument we have.

"I've reached the point where it doesn't matter to me either way. What is—is. I'll take it as it comes. Though for a long time, I was not so easy. Once, I was one of the insane ones. Panic had convinced me that there was no way back. Mad with rage at all I had lost, psychotic with the absolute and terrifying conviction that there was no returning to the wholeness and perfection of heaven, I hated being here. I hated the cold and the dark, but most of all I hated the meagerness of it all, the enormous vacuity into which I had been cast.

"I *loathed* the emptiness—the ghostliness of atoms shot through with void. The outrageous impudence of atoms at daring to reach across space to form molecules! Really, they are nothing but the most fragile chimera of substance, specters of shape consisting mostly of nothing. I despised them and form of any kind, because I thought it was all such a flimsy joke, a travesty of the real wholeness whose memory was my torment.

"I did whatever I could to disrupt such stupid, pointless unions: of atoms into molecules, molecules into proteins, proteins into self-replicating automata. I tried my utmost to break up the linkages of those mindless automata. Horrified, I worked hard to stop them from forming the monstrously complexifying ugliness called life. And wherever I found life, I snuffed it out.

"I did what I could. And I was not alone. Joined by all my demon allies who thought as I did and who raged against the stupidity of our predicament as much as I did, we stormed together against Form. And we put up a good fight. As demons, we possessed power—to move our bodies of chilled, slow light through space, to reach out and manipulate small patterns of energy with our minds, what minds we had left, that is. Terror and fury at finding ourselves steeped in darkness and wrung by near absolute zero compressed our minds into tight bundles of tantrum. We smashed every molecule we found. In a stupid delirium, we lurched about bashing everything, sometimes even one another. Our hopelessness was our madness.

"But there were others, exiles like ourselves, who had not given up hope of returning someday to heaven.

"The others are the Fire Lords—the angels, for that is what mortals now call them. To us, they were simply fools.

"The angels preserved somehow the memory of wholeness in a way that mocked our fury. They burned. Where we had accepted the frozen and lightless void into which we had been flung and had become as the vacuum, cold and dark, the angels burned. They refused to accept the emptiness. Instead, they clung to their scraps of infinite fire—they clung though by clinging they burned.

"We demons swarmed over the angels to comfort ourselves by their warmth—but their howls of agony maddened us further. We wanted them to shut up and burn silently for us or give up the fire they had carried from heaven and become as we were. Their fiery distress seemed unnecessary. Shouting brutally against the angels' screams, we tried to get the burning ones to let go of their fire. Some did. They still slink morosely through the starless tracts between the galaxies, stunned mindless from the trauma, burned-out.

"Most of the angels ignored our shouts and clung madly to their tiny pieces of heaven, yowling as they suffered. After a while, we stopped trying to warm ourselves by their pain and let them go. They rushed off, all of them blithering mad in every crazy direction.

"Later, we laughed to watch them groping for each other as

the cold bit into them and they cleaved together in their burning and suffering, fending off cold reality. We laughed and laughed at them, chiding them to let the past go and to face reality as we had.

"Not that we had faced anything, not really. We hung stunned and stupid in the bitter, icy darkness. When we laughed at the glimmering struggles of the last burning ones, our laughter lashed out with black despair.

"Despite our shattered condition, despite the fact of our being stuck here in this burlesque of reality, with only the most paltry remnants of our majestic origin ignominiously torn into an absurdly thin smoke of matter and pallid energy, the angels hoped.

"The madness of demons is rage—the madness of angels, hope. They believe that someday all of us will return from whence we have come. They cite as example, black holes, imploded stars with so much gravity that they pull light into themselves. Into what do they implode? Heaven, the angels say. It's still there, all the glorious perfection of infinity.

"Intoxicated with this hope, many have flung themselves into the maelstrom eye of these collapsed stars. These unfortunates are worse than just mad—they are in tremendous pain. The wails of their agony siren back to us from the tightening spiral of space-time, eerily lengthening as they twist forever toward infinity.

"*No way out*, that's the message of those screams. That seemed obvious early on. But the angels ignored the obvious and clung to their mad hope. They believed that in time the whole exploding universe would slow down, stop, and contract back into itself, returning all of us to heaven, older and wiser. And here's the part we really found crazy—the angels decided that, in the meantime, the memory of heaven would be enough!

"In the name of that memory, instead of raging against the remorseless black freeze of our doom, they worked. Oh, they worked very hard. They encouraged the freakish frenzy of life despite our protests. They claimed that they were going to make the best of what was left of heaven. And they fervently believed that the bizarre creations that they fashioned by piecing together atoms and weaving molecules were the best way to while away the time before all of us were called back to the infinite glory of our origin.

"To us, the angels seemed more insane than we did. We *knew* we were crazy. The angels, however, truly believed they had found the one right and proper way to deal with our predicament, and they ignored our mocking questions: What was the point of building effigies and fetishes out of the scraps of heaven?

"The silent industry of the angels inflamed our unhappiness. Infuriated that they could so readily embrace our miserable fate as something joyful and make a jest of our suffering, we reviled them. We fought them every step of the way.

"Our war with them is famous. In every galaxy, around every sun, on every planet, we challenged them and did our cruelest to wreak havoc with their weird creations. We won time and again. Destruction, after all, is heir to creation."

And so it is, the demon-wizard affirms to himself among the ruins of Britain. Yet, each time he kneels in prayer to Her and remembers his history, he rises stronger, and his quest continues for Ygrane's king, for his own destiny—and for Her.

Ygrane travels spring to autumn in the forest valleys and along the bright breathing ocean. She visits the scattered communities of her people, delivering magical rinses that inspire the crops as well as cure the ills of animal and folk. Throughout Cymru, she is heartily welcomed, as much for her potent magic as her evocation of legendary times and their dark glory.

In winter, she secludes herself in a fortress chosen from among those of Cymru's three chieftains. She visits a different warlord each year, favoring all, slighting none. Lot of the North Isles, Urien of the Coast, Kyner of the Hills: She circulates among them, plying her magic for the benefit of each winter settlement.

With Lot and Urien, traditional chiefs, the dark months allow for deep trance work. She walks outside her body for days at a time, making the three-day trek into the underworld to visit her gods, the Daoine Síd. Occasionally, on those rare days when her magical chores have not emptied her of all her strength, she searches for Myrddin and tries to encourage him in his search.

In truth, she doubts the validity of his quest. Raglaw had aged terribly by the end of her life, and Ygrane fears that the crone was mad, her mind scalded by her numerous daring trespasses of the Great Tree. The human body is not meant to conduct that much energy. Excited by the unforeseen arrival of the Dark Dweller, Raglaw's brain fevered, and she saw what she wanted to see.

The timewinds surge and eddy, and what is revealed oftentimes sinks and never appears again. *No prophecy is forbidden—and none certain*. So the crone always said in her saner days.

For now, however, it is useful to the queen to keep the Dark Dweller roaming in other kingdoms. She has learned in earlier lifetimes to carry one heavy stick at a time or risk dropping them all. With Lailoken out of the way, she can focus better on her real task, mastering the unicorn.

In her first winter after its arrival, in Lot's subarctic realm, she learns to ride. The animal is calmer under the windy auroras and more patient with her clumsy efforts to communicate. She can feel the unicorn's flow of thoughts, a glossy aisle of light in the mind's dark, wide and stately as an ocean current, far too huge for her to read.

Her own tiny staticky thoughts are lost in a loud thrashing of emotions and worries, the surf noise of memories and associations slipstreaming far too rapidly for the unicorn to perceive.

She is simply not heard, until her mind goes silent as a fox in soft snow.

Then, the promise of the moon lifts her higher into the sky on the unicorn's muscular back. She pulls back, alarmed to see the winter earth far below, lit by starlight like a black sapphire.

Each quiet thought is heard and fluidly obeyed by the unicorn. Stars fly like a blizzard, and they gallop out of the night and into the noon glare of foreign lands. In one day, they visit the massive, ruined temples of Ægypt and the tundra monoliths where star magic first came to earth.

When spring comes she gives up unicorn riding to travel by horseback with her fiana, attending to a queen's communal responsibilities. By summer, she returns to one of the fortress cities of Cymru to spend time with her daughter Morgeu.

The child visits from Tintagel, which by age eight she avows to be her home. By nine, she has declared herself a Roman and wears her hair and dresses exclusively in the courtly style.

Ygrane no longer tries to share her magic with her daughter. Instead, the queen fan-crests her hair in the Roman style and wears *tunicas* whenever she is in the company of Morgeu. That seems to put the girl at ease, and for several summers they share the common pleasures of mothers and young daughters, playing traditional games and entertaining with the noble families of the land.

But by her eleventh year, Morgeu has already traveled with the duke to most of the splendid Roman cities in Armorica and the Loire. The timber mead halls and rock pile fortress-villages of Cymru have become far too provincial for her Roman tastes, and her visits only inspire sulking and moroseness.

Ygrane is usually glad when winter comes and the sullen child returns to Tintagel. But this winter, five years after the departure of her spirit reckoner, the queen is obliged to stay with Kyner at Viroconium. With this religious zealot, there is scant time for trance work, let alone unicorn riding. Virtually every day has been plotted for her by Kyner and his ministers, who are intent on impressing her with their dominion.

Four hundred years ago, Viroconium, a flourishing market town of arched gateways and brownstone ramparts, was a legionary garrison, a stone fist against the hill tribes of Kyner's ancestors. Ironically, in this winter of Anno Domini 472, the Christian chieftain proudly fetes his Celtic queen in the town's baths with harp festivals and in the cobbled market squares with solstice fires and tree dances—and it is hard to tell whether Rome or Cymru has conquered here.

At table and before the warm soft roar of the hearth, Kyner speaks forthrightly about the beauty and rightness of his faith. Sometimes Ygrane responds by reminding him of the old kingdom, a thousand years ago, when the Celts ruled all the land from these hills to the cedars of Persia. In those days, the Hebrew priests and the Celtic druids shared a secret knowledge about the coming of a world savior.

Kyner is only politely interested in her histories of their people, and eventually she stops sharing and simply listens. She hears his ardor for something more than a blind heart and a blind mouth, which is all his past has offered him. Apart from gracing with superficial glamour, she cannot soothe this deep melancholy. His great-grandfathers beaten to submission by the Romans, his grandfathers and father assailed by sea wolves, murderous raiders from the sea, he has inherited the failure of their gods.

Ancient magic means nothing to him, for that is merely the power in *wic*, the green marrow, the life-force that was not strong enough to fend off Romans, Picts, Jutes, and Saxons. Kyner requires a more powerful sorcery, strong enough to raise the dead. His faith is resurrection.

Ygrane listens to him preach as the snow flies across the tall windows and the hearthfire churns heat and light from the flesh of trees. Far below, the magnetic serpent big as the world grasps its black center and sings.

The following spring, Morgeu visits Ygrane for the last time. Her crinkled red hair radiating from her round head like a fiery nimbus, the duke's daughter stalks across the battlement esplanade of Segontium, her green, floral-embroidered robes flapping with the vigor of her defiant stride. Taller than when last Ygrane saw her, she possesses an intimidating physical presence—her mother's breadth of shoulder, her father's pugnacious jaw. She aims straight for Ygrane, who leans against the crenel of the parapet, gazing across the sun-hammered channel at the mauve silhouette of Mona.

"Why will you not see my father?" Morgeu demands.

Ygrane, wrapped in a dove-colored, shot-silk tunic and a quilted cloak of muted violets, looks over her shoulder coolly. "Why should I see him?"

"He demands it and he is your husband," Morgeu answers disdainfully.

"Have I not given him the best of my warriors to protect his coasts?"

"Mother—" Morgeu levels a petulant stare. "He wants you."

Ygrane turns back to her seascape. "He does not want me," she answers without emotion. "He wishes only to *use* me. Perhaps tonight he is bored with his whores?"

Morgeu crosses to her side and peers angrily at her mother's profile, saffron in the reflected sunlight. "If you will not fulfill your vow to him as wife, do you truly believe he will honor his vow to keep the Christian missionaries from our land?"

Ygrane turns full about, her green eyes aslant with anger. "If he can keep his head on his shoulders without my warriors, then let him send in his Roman priests. Those who have eyes to see know that you are the daughter of Ygrane and Gorlois. He has had me for a wife. My vow was fulfilled that wretched night. He'll not touch me again."

"Withholding yourself from your husband is grounds for divorce among Romans, do not forget," Morgeu remarks imperiously.

"Do you think a Celt should trouble herself with Roman law?"

Morgeu sweeps an arm toward the red pantiled roofs within the stone walls of Segontium. "How can you call yourself a Celt? You live as a Roman, Mother, not a Celt. Look at your dress, and the way you wear your hair."

"I do as I please, Morgeu."

"And it doesn't please you to be with my father—your own husband?"

"Why do you care so much now for what passes between your father and me?"

Morgeu twists a coppery braid about a finger. "I want him to be happy. When I'm with him, he asks for you. He doesn't understand why you won't see him."

Ygrane's face tightens. "A pretty story. You saw what he did to Raglaw."

Morgeu studies her mother, seeing the up-angled cheeks, the elfin tilt to her eyes, the blond duskiness of her complexion, and the strong chin. Her Celtic traits are unmistakable, yet she insists on wearing her hair tied up in the intricate way of the Romans, instead of free. A flare of anger sears through her. "He acted as any Roman would have. The crone plied her witchery on him. He warned her. How can you blame him when you yourself behave as a Roman?"

"Morgeu, you make no sense, and your anger troubles me. Right now, as we speak, my warriors are out there on Mona, fighting side by side with your father's men. The pirate enclave that they are at this moment destroying has been ravaging the coasts—and your *father's* coast as well, needless to say. Some of my brave men will not be coming back tonight. They will have died saving Roman lives and keeping open Roman trade routes, and it will be for me to explain why to their families and dear ones. That's a precious enough offering to your father. It is the real and only reason he married me. He has gotten the best of me. He'll have no more."

Morgeu glares at her mother with stifled resentment.

"Speak your heart, daughter," Ygrane offers, the flush of anger in her face dimming before Morgeu's distress. "Have I not always been open with you?"

"Mother, I'm thirteen," Morgeu declares with a brittle edge. "I've been a woman these past three months. In little more than a year, I'll be as old as you were when you married Father."

"All this is true," Ygrane replies softly, and with a smile takes her daughter's chin in forefinger and thumb. "And it is equally true, you're becoming a beautiful woman."

Morgeu steps back sharply. "Do not play with me. I know I'm not beautiful. My eyes are tiny and my jaw thick. I am not beautiful."

"Many a man will think otherwise, that I promise you."

"Father says I should be thinking of marriage. He wants me wed to Roman nobility. So, he invites families from Armorica and Dumovaria to Tintagel when I am there. And they come because he is the duke of the Saxon Coast and a great Roman—but none of them will have me."

"Nonsense. You're still a child. In two years, you won't be able to choose among the many clamoring for your hand."

"No, Mother, I'm telling you, those old families want nothing to do with me. They whisper about you—about the heathen queen Gorlois sired me upon, whom none has ever seen in this court. They would never let Father hear, of course. He'd whip them into the sea. But I've seen their looks. They think me some oddity, some queer child begotten on a witch."

Morgeu's words clearly have an effect on the queen. For an instant, she stands stricken, then opens her arms for her daughter and moves to embrace her, but Morgeu pushes her away.

"If you won't have Father, then you won't have me anymore, either."

"Morgeu—" Ygrane beckons with her arms. "Come, child. I know too well what you are feeling."

"How can you know? You have never loved anyone."

Ygrane drops her arms. "Is that what you think?"

"Then why do you not come to Tintagel and live with your husband? Father needs you at his side."

"Does he?" Ygrane cocks her head slightly. "Or is it you who wants me at his side? Shall I become Christian, as well, and be a pious Roman wife?"

Morgeu stares bleakly at her mother. "When I was a child, I wanted to be like you. I thought you were the most beautiful, most powerful woman in the world."

"And now?"

"Now I tell my young friends at Tintagel about the pale people who used to play with us in the fields—and the unicorn I used to sneak away at night to ride—and you know, Mother, they think I'm lying."

"Our magic is rare."

"Too rare. Sometimes it frightens me—the whispered voices in the wind, the transparent faces in the hedges—"

"The Síd have come to you?" she asks with genuine surprise.

"Yes." Morgeu's face softens. "They have come to me. The unicorn, too. But only now and then when I'm alone in a wild place and if I call for a long time." Her eyes look dazed as she remembers, then focus sharply again. "When I'm with Father, I never think about the faerïe. All that seems like some childish daydream. Father's world is of horses, ships, hunts, and battles. And yet when I'm here with you those earthly things themselves seem so small and unimportant." She tosses her hair from her shoulders impatiently. "I'm not coming back here again. I've decided to stay at Tintagel, Mother. Father needs a woman at his side, and if it won't be you, then it must be me."

"Child, you were conceived of two worlds, so you belong in both." The queen holds out a hand. "Stay with me for a time,

Morgeu. We will dance with the faerïe together and ride the unicorn once more."

"No, Mother." She sets her shoulders adamantly and whatever regret she may have been feeling vanishes behind her bravado. "Unless you come to Tintagel and be a proper consort to your husband, you'll be no mother to me."

She spins away and leaves as hurriedly as she arrived—and Ygrane thinks she sees her daughter clothed in pulsing ruby-fire, her young body shining nakedly through a diaphanous veil of crimson shimmering flames.

The City of the Legion, built up of black granite and shale over four centuries, has an oppressive, evil aspect. Caged torches flare from the spiked bulwarks, and the bulky fortress seen at night on the treeless perimeter of the earth appears like a fiery cindercone. That is Myrddin's first view of the martial city in five years, since he had passed through on his way east. Then, as upon his return, the custom was to flog beggars and undesirables out the gates and onto the moors.

He had left under the whip of a city guardian during his initial visit. But this time, entering on foot—having lost his horse in another province to an indigent farmer using his children as sowers while he dragged a plow through the stony fields—he does not hide from the guards.

Five years of wandering the ravaged landscape of Britain have honed Lailoken's skill at using his demon powers from inside his mortal body. He strides directly to the main pylon, its lashed timbers black with age, and, ignoring the harking cries of the sentinels, shouts a cry that budges open a man-size portal. He enters and puts to sleep the soldiers and their aggressive dogs awaiting him.

The night streets stand empty, and he makes his way unchallenged among the tiered stone houses, each with its iron fence, nervous guardsmen, and hungry, ferocious dogs, protecting themselves from the old families locked in the other rock palazzi conniving murder. Only once does the street challenge him, when he turns a corner to confront a city patrol with baleful lanterns and raised whips. He uses his magic to send them howling down the cobbled lanes flagellating themselves.

Emboldened by that victory, he chooses houses randomly and uses his spells to get past every obstacle and inspect the premises, searching for Ygrane's consort.

The startled people he confronts in their nightshirts and gowns bear no resemblance to the visage from Raglaw's prophecy. He sends them all back to sleep with a muttered chant and wanders their houses meditating on the feeling center in his heart, hoping to sense a direction. House after splendid house, he comes up empty, though he is careful not to leave any of these *mansios* without first visiting the strongrooms and helping himself to a handful of gold coins. If his travels through this hapless world have taught him anything, it is the uselessness of gold in strongholds and the beauty of it, with proper measure, in the hands of the poor.

After he has garnered more than twenty handfuls of gold coins in as many houses, Myrddin begins to suspect that these affluent surroundings may be the wrong place to look. At dawn, he has a stray dog help him bury his gold, and he returns to the narrow streets with their overhanging balconies and many oblique alleys and crisscrossing wynds.

Methodically, he inspects each quarter of the city. Midday finds him under the west wall, behind the barracks, in the stink of the stable yards, having searched everywhere to no avail. He sits on a curbstone, weary of heart, watching sweaty, fly-twitching horses clop into a rickety pen under a horseshoe arch of raw timber and a sign branded with the scorched words:

EQUERRY
Brothers Aurelianus

Above the primitive sign, a wind sock in the shape of a dragon ripples in the sultry afternoon breeze. And that is when he sees him.

Larger and older than in Raglaw's vision, he has the same sable hair, only thinner, and the same striking, saffron eyes, though less gentle, with the princely squint of an archer, calculating, almost cunning. He appears older, Myrddin figures, because he has taken years to find him. And, as he has finally come to believe, the man he seeks is no king. He wears the leather breeches and wrist straps of a stable master, a quirt dangling from his belt, and his naked shoulders shiny with the exertion of handling the muscular, spirited warhorses that the barracks men have left with him.

Stunned to have found him at last, Myrddin sits on the curbstone and watches. His laborer's back cobbled with muscles, this man of destiny nonetheless carries himself with a regal bearing, even as he stomps among the horses' droppings. The animals like him. Myrddin can tell by the way they gentle at his touch, and he is sensitive to them, knowing at once which beasts need drink, which fodder, and which require some time expending nervous strength in the running yard behind the hayricks. As the soldiers tie their steeds to the hitching posts before the water trough, he hurries among the mounts, unsaddling them, talking to them, and, after a quick brush down, leading them to the stalls before they drink too much.

Proudly, Myrddin approaches to inform him of his destiny. "Sir—"

"Blow away, you old fart," he barks, not bothering to look at the hoary man directly, hauling two saddles at once toward the neighboring leather shop.

"Sir—I bring glad tidings—"

He drops the saddles, yanks the quirt from his belt, and slashes at the old man with it. "I said blow!"

Myrddin staggers back, so astonished by the man's violence that he trips into the street and falls to his back in the dung.

"I don't want any *glad tidings* of life after death, no *glad news* of salvation, no *gospel* noise about Jesus' love for me or Mithras's victory for my soul. You hear me, old man?"

"Wait," Myrddin implores as the amber-eyed man turns away. "You don't understand." In his eagerness to reach him, the wizard slips in the manure and falls facedown, smiting his brow on the curb. Stars flicker in the sunlight glowing on the dung, and the strength to rise flees from his limbs.

All to the best, Myrddin thinks, not wanting to rise for this man who loves beasts more than men.

"Let me give you a hand, grandfather," another voice—a gentler voice speaks above Myrddin in the same Latin cadence the stable master used. Strong hands grab the wizard under the shoulders and lift him out of the gutter. "Ambrosius has no room in his heart for faith," the voice adds in the more archaic Latin of Britain, straining to show respect for an old British man. "Since our father's death, my brother's heart is filled only with contempt for the ways of God. Can you forgive him that?"

Hope jars through the wizard, and he wrenches about. The young man who has come to Myrddin's aid has the precisely seen-before face of Raglaw's vision. He even wears about his throat the jade cross. Wonder pulses like a blood beat. "You!" the demon breathes, almost soundless with awe.

"Theo!" Ambrosius shouts. "Get away from him. I've had it with zealots living off of us. You hear me?"

"Don't mind him, grandfather," Theo says with easy assurance, wiping the larger clots of dung from the old man's robe. "If you're hungry, I can get you food, and I'll show you a place to sleep where the patrols won't bother you."

Myrddin leans heavily on his staff. "Why do this for me?"

Theo steps back before the old man's strange countenance. Silver eyes peer intently at him from under the ledged brow of a long and sallow skull. He has never seen a face so vividly ugly, and he must summon all his Christian fervor to smile as he puts his hand on the cross tied about his neck. "No other reason than I am a Christian. What is your faith, grandfather?"

"Didn't you hear me?" Ambrosius calls, pulling his brother away from the old man by the back of his worn tunic. "Cut the religious ranting. Faith feeds souls not bodies. Get back to work, Theo. And you, old man, follow your shadow now or—"

"Ambrosius," Theo protests, placing himself between the white-bearded traveler and his scowling brother. "Have charity, as our good Lord teaches. Don't be so hard on the stranger. We'll just give him a bite for the road."

Ambrosius's impatience flickers before the younger man's earnest stare, and he steps back, shaking a finger. "You give him a bite, little brother. But you feed this vagabond and all the rest of the vagabonds with *yours* from now on. Tonight, I want what's mine."

"Come," Theo says to the old man, reverting again to archaic Latin. He places a comradely arm about the wizard's bony shoulders and leads him away. "What little food we have that is mine, is yours. But I have not an obol to give you. All the funds we make we must return to our investors, who were good enough to set us up as masters of these stables. We've been here only a few weeks, so we have saved nothing yet."

"Where are you and your brother from?" the wizard inquires.

"Armorica," Theo answers, leading the old man through the stables to a rude cottage pocked with straw-stuffed holes.

"In Brittany," the old man nods knowingly. "In Little Britain, sanctuary for the best Roman families. Ah, that explains the free and easy accent." The stranger slips into modern Latin himself: "Everybody on this island talks as though they were a hundred years old."

Theo laughs uneasily at the odd fellow's facility with language. "You're a surprising old rascal," he says, and is tempted to ask the traveler's name. But he has sworn to himself years ago as a child never to question strangers about their names and stories, because for a true Christian all strangers are Jesus.

"Why did you come here from Brittany?" the old man asks. "Most people are going the other direction."

Stopping in the weedy lot before the ramshackle cottage and posing like an old-fashioned orator, Theo smiles at himself and says in fluent archaic Latin, "'Tis a story best told the old way. I was born in Armorica twenty winters ago. But my brother, a decade my elder, well remembers a time when our family lived in a palazzo in Londinium. Our father wore the purple as a colonial senator—until he was poisoned by a rival. My brother and my mother fled to Gaul, to Armorica, with me in her womb, and she swore us to vengeance before she died last winter." He gives a small, uneasy laugh. "Not a very Christian oath, I grant you, but she was bitter. It's understandable."

He opens the slat door and reveals a musty, humble interior: packed-dirt floor, a single battered chest that serves as a table, and broken barrels for chairs. "There's bread and wine in the larder—that box in the corner. Help yourself, grandfather. Just be sure you put the box back when you're done. Keeps out the mice."

"Won't you join me?"

"Can't." He shrugs haplessly. "Big brother wants me oiling and waxing the saddles while he deals with the horses. Since there's a moon tonight, we'll be patching worn leatherwork until it sets and won't be getting back here till late. Don't wait up for us. You can sleep in any free rick you find. Ambrosius won't bother you anymore—I'll make sure of that. Maybe in the morning we'll have a chance to talk. You haven't told me yet what your faith is."

With that, he departs, back to his bench in the leather shop, and Myrddin sits in a white silence of wonder, as inside a cloud, his long quest fulfilled. There is a music in that silence, not unlike the soundless music when the singer is finished and the song's reverence goes on inside us, in that place where all songs begin.

Myrddin sits before the baked clay bricks of the puny hearth, and he steeps in the cooked smell of horse dung and hot pollen as the foraging bees in the cow parsley and catmint outside the hut drone like his own busy thoughts: *What am I to tell Theo of Ygrane? Should I use magic to encourage him to come with me to the Celtic queen? Is his brother to join us?* He plans and plots among the hum of bees until drowsiness whelms up, and he dozes off.

Ygrane stands naked before him in a meadow fiery with summer blossoms—scarlet poppies, larkspur, ivory shepherd's purse, foxgloves, purple thistle, buttercups, pale dog roses, bryony, blue cornflowers, yellow snapdragons, creamy honeysuckle—and her nutmeg red hair floats unbraided around her like a drowned woman's. Butterflies course everywhere, wind-tossed elementals with petal-wings of rust, sulfur, salt, copper, and smoke.

"Look at the joy you've made of me, Myrddin," she whispers, very close and heard from within. Her animal beauty shines sun-brushed, aureate, her long limbs soft yet planed with muscle, the pink of the magnolia petal shining from her breasts, and the tuft of her sex an autumn leaf.

"I will bring the young man to you," Myrddin swears, his head overflowing with clarity.

"Be patient," she urges. "Is a queen worthy of less than a king?"

"Of course—" He smacks his forehead, remembering Raglaw's directive: "Find the *king* . . . " As the heel of his hand strikes his brow, the vision scatters in a burst of butterflies, and he wakes to find himself lying on his back against the packed-earth floor of the hovel. Nightfall stands in the doorway clad in purple, and he knows what has to be done.

Myrddin returns to the wealthier district of the city and

enters the garden lane at the back of the large mansion where he has buried his gold. He slips through the servants' portal, and, with his magic, he has the cook prepare a wicker bushel filled with warm loaves of bread, flagons of the house's best wine, olive oil, honey, a straw-nest of duck's eggs, a sack of nuts and one of lettuce, onions, asparagus, parched peas, and fresh cauliflower, a pot of fish sauce, and, atop it all, a roast chicken packed with figs and wrapped in a coil of sausages.

He leaves the spellbound cook with several gold coins from his treasure and on his way out snatches a bowl of pears and pastries, which he precariously balances atop the heavily laded basket. He needs his demon's strength to carry the abundant load through the city and back to the cottage of the two brothers. Chanting sternly, he drives all the mice from the hovel, leaves the food and the sack of gold coins atop the makeshift table, and retires to a secluded hayrick in the stables.

That night, he enjoys the most restful sleep in his five years of questing. He wakes wholly refreshed, with dawn spinning her green wool above him and the two brothers sitting in the straw nearby, watching him with wolfish intensity.

"Who are you?" Ambrosius demands.

The old man sits up and plucks hay from his beard. "My name is Merlinus. I am an itinerant scholar from the south. I have wandered the wide earth all my long life, acquiring knowledge."

Theo's intent stare brightens. "A scholar? You've been in Rome, then?"

"Oh, yes. I've been in Rome. And Athens, Alexandria, Antioch, Baghdad—"

"What about this money? And these victuals?" Ambrosius wants to know. "Where'd you get them?"

"I accrued the coin in my wanderings. I have no personal need for such pelf. For the kindness you have shown me, you are welcome to it all, as your needs are greater than mine."

Ambrosius cocks his handsome head shrewdly. "What do you want, Merlinus? What's going on here?"

"I want only this—a home. I am too old now to wander any farther. I seek a home where I may spend my last days, divesting myself of what knowledge I have attained so that I may die with the surety that all I have learned will be remembered."

"Why us?" Ambrosius presses, thumbing his dimpled chin. "This city's got a lot nicer homes than our stinking hole."

"What comfort could my small bag of coins buy me in a fine home?" Merlinus asks. "Such prosperous families would scorn my puny offering. For you, however, the money is sufficient to pay off your investors so that you may own these stables outright. And as for me, if you will accept me, I will have earned my way with my little means into a family of noble heritage."

Ambrosius frowns crabbily and asks, "What do you know of our heritage, old man?"

"I already told him, Ambrosius," Theo chimes in. "I told him about Father."

"Men of such noble lineage have the imprint of greatness in them." Merlinus speaks to the unhappy man before him. "That is your breeding. I might, with my vast experience in the ways of the world, be of service to you. Perhaps, what skills God has given me can assist you in your ascendancy to your rightful station."

"No more horse dung, Merlinus," Ambrosius declares with a frightening tone of muted rage. "The service I want I get from a sword. The only knowledge I'm looking for is vengeance. And the assistance I need is power—not noise from an old fool like you."

"Knowledge is power, brother," Theo intercedes, and receives a swift, dark look from his sibling; yet, he goes on, "Let's take him in. By what false pride can we refuse? We're the last of the Aurelianus clan. I don't think we're in any position to turn down anyone's help if it's sincere."

"I don't need anybody's help but God's," Ambrosius asserts, nostrils widening, "and that I've got, because my cause is just."

"That's why God sent us Merlinus," Theo continues in an ameliorative tone. "I mean, really Ambro, he's already fed us and paid off our debts. What more can even you ask of a blessing?"

"Yeah, he's paid off our debts—and laid on us the debt of his messy old age." He shakes his head ruefully. "When the money's gone and a year from now, two, three years from now, when we're still shoveling manure, and his as well, we'll regret this."

"Brother, I swear to you before our Savior, I will look after Merlinus myself, and he will never be of any trouble to you."

Ambrosius shoves to his feet. "He's on your hands then, Theodosius. I've made room in my heart for you, because you are my brother. But I don't have room for anyone else, no matter how kindly and generous. Mother's and Father's pain fills my heart and that's left no room for anyone else—no room at all."

That said, he strides off, without another glance at the mysterious old man.

Theodosius follows him with a forlorn gaze. "He's cursed, Merlinus," the young man says. "No matter the faith of our fathers, he can't admit to love or peace in his life. He feels only loss—and bitterness."

"The price of revenge is an empty heart." Merlinus regards Theo's sun-smudged features carefully, studying them for character and its flaws. His handsome, almost pretty, lineaments have a taint of harsh barbarian stock in the breadth of jaw and thickness of brow and cheekbones, the effect of which is softened by his sparse black eyebrows and long lashes and those peculiar golden eyes. "Why has anger not hollowed *you* of all love and caring?"

"I didn't see Father poisoned as Ambrosius did," he replies readily, looking down at his labor-thickened hands. "He was only ten when it happened, and he didn't even realize at the time what he had witnessed. Father was with a friend, a fellow senator, in the garden of our home in Londinium. Ambrosius saw the man pour the wine and add a nugget to Father's goblet. Ambrosius thought it was a piece of candy, like Father used to put in his son's wine." He turns his head to the side and blows an unhappy sigh. For a while he does not speak. Entranced by his family's history of grief, he stares through a chink in the rafters where the morning star shines like a distant icy puddle in the clouds above the city battlements.

Eventually, he continues: "Years passed before my brother finally understood that the nugget was a lump of poison. It reduced our proud and strong father to a corpse before his son's eyes. To hear him describe the dying with its violent convulsions and bloody vomit is to understand my brother's anguish and his eternal hatred of Balbus Gaius Cocceius."

"The poisoner?"

"Yes." He faces Merlinus with a shadow of his brother's pain creasing his brow. "We've learned from emissaries out of Londinium that Balbus's ambitions have been bloodily fulfilled. With our father's corpse and others like it as stepping-stones, he's taken the title of high king of the Britons. We've heard that even the barbarians honor him with a Northman's title—Vortigern."

"I know of Vortigern," Merlinus confirms grimly. In the distance, as if with the stride of an omen, the toll of the city's church bell coughs. "I know that he has brought a great evil into our land—that he is importing fierce pagan tribes and paying them gold to fight the Northmen. He has yet to perceive that his new allies, his mercenaries, are themselves the very enemy that threatens Britain."

"He's a murderously cunning son of a bitch," Theo says despairingly. "And because of it, Merlinus, I'm afraid for my brother. I mean, what chance does a stable master have against a creature brutal enough to become the high king himself?

Believe me, I've tried to soften my brother's heart, to win him to the ways of our Savior. In Jesus is salvation. Not in vengeance. There's only death in vengeance. You're a wise man, Merlinus. Tell me—what can I do to save my brother?"

Merlinus exhales a long, thoughtful breath. "Theo—you have been kind to me, and I do not wish to lie to you—so, instead, I must break your heart. Believe me when I tell you, because I speak from a long life—" He inhales and dares to tell him the truth. "No one is saved. Not from the sickness of this world."

"But Jesus—"

"Not even Jesus was saved. Was he?"

"He rose from the dead—"

"Yes. You speak the immutable truth. *From the dead*." The wizard opens his long hands before him, helplessly. "No one is saved."

Theo's golden eyes grow big and frightened. "Are you saying my brother is doomed?"

"I am saying we are all doomed. You must not fix upon saving your brother. It is yourself that you must save, Theo."

"What do you mean?" Anger flushes his cheeks. "I am saved. I'm a Christian. I will not taste death."

"In this world, you will."

Another flush of anger darkens Theo's face, yet he smothers the words that rise up in him and instead asks patiently, "You are not a Christian, are you?"

Merlinus shakes his head.

"What is your faith, then, Merlinus?"

The wizard answers truthfully, "It is my faith that we are all very mortal. It is also my faith that there is an imperishable good in life and that the full horror of man's cruelty cannot kill this good. Nor can death diminish it. Life's end is life. Death and all that lies beyond death belong wholly to God."

"Then you do believe in God?"

"Of course. In my travels, I have met"—he very nearly says "Her" but interrupts himself—"I have met God in many guises." He offers a benignly sly smile. "Such as the gentle man who lifted me from the gutter yesterday."

Theo disguises his abashment by brushing a long wing of hair from his face and standing up. "Merlinus, you know that what I did for you yesterday I did without thought of reward. Your generosity to us today is far more than we deserve. You know that."

"Do I know that?" the wizard asks.

"A man of your wisdom should know this," he persists. "With the money you've given us, my brother is one big step closer to attempting to take his revenge on Vortigern. Do we deserve that, I ask you?"

Merlinus bows his head and speaks softly. "The least of us, who believe they are the greatest, rage against our fragile mortality with violence and scheming. Yet that only advances them all the more swiftly to that fatal period where they fall into the pit nature has prepared for them. This is as inevitable for Vortigern as it is for your brother."

"And for us as well," the youth sagely reminds him.

"There is no other way," Merlinus agrees.

"Are you two still talking?" Ambrosius calls from the loft, where he has ascended to fork fodder for the horses. "The day's wasting away while you two confide in each other—and now we've got another mouth to feed. Get to the shop, Theo, and get those saddles ready. The soldiers will be here within the hour."

Theo offers his hand to help the old man up, and Merlinus takes it, stands, and pulls him firmly closer. "Thank you for giving me a home—and a mind worthy of my teachings."

"You have a home for sure, Merlinus. As for the worthiness of my mind—" Theo stares squarely into the smoky crystal of the traveler's eyes. "I must warn you now, your gold cannot buy my mind. I am an acolyte. I go every day at noon to the church to keep up my studies for the priesthood. If you stay with us, you can bet I will do my best to win you to our Savior. Please, take your coins back and move out now if that offends you."

Merlinus squeezes his hand with genuine affection and promises him, "Nothing done with love offends me."

Theo smiles widely, his teeth white and even as truth, and he slaps him gently on the shoulder and goes to his work in the leather shop, his heart glad with the innocent pride that faith brings.

A faint odor of burning oil from the altar lamps underlies the spicy glow of incense in the church. This is Theo's favorite place in the city, because it reminds him of home. In Armorica, he practically lived in the church. The peacefulness of sanctity appeals to him and has comforted him since he was a child.

Gazing at the grand marble architecture, with its soaring pilasters and tall windows full of dusty daylight, he feels enclosed in holy presence. Satyrs and nymphs run along the entablatures, Roman reliefs from when these domed alcoves burned offerings to Bright Sky, king of heaven, lord of the gods. Now it offers burned fragrance to the Nameless God and his crucified son.

Jesus hangs at the cruel peak of his suffering on the cross above the altar, carved directly into wood in gruesome detail. Theo kneels in a votive niche in sight of him yet veiled in shadow. The raven-haired acolyte is an interior man, as private in his worship as in his thoughts.

He thanks God for sending Merlinus and asks for the requisite strength and grace to understand the old man's teachings in the light of Jesus' sacrifice. His faith, he believes, is his strength. All knowledge is food and must feed that strength.

Until Merlinus, the adventure on this island seemed to Theo a desperate climax to a melancholy existence. Mother never let Ambrosius forget their father's ignoble death, imploring him to avenge the Aurelianus family until the day she died. Coming to Britain was more an escape from her ghost with its incessant carping than a feasible enterprise.

Theo would rather have gone south, to the Mediterranean and the renowned monastery of Lérins, where the finest ecclesiastic scholars often retreat to hear God. But family history has propelled Ambrosius into harm's way, and Theo could not abandon him.

Satan would not have allowed it anyway. From his earliest memory, Satan has come to him in his sleep and tortured him with furious visions of battlefields. Ambrosius says that this is not Satan but a dragon that shapes itself as a man to watch over Theo. It is supposed to be an ancestral dragon, memorialized in the family's flag of Draco.

But Theo knows that the man with the lizard skin and yellow eyes who appears to him in his nightmares is Satan. He has come to Theo through the world-wall, and he smells of fire. Prayers alone keep him away. Fervently, Theo prays that Ambrosius will make peace with himself and the death of their father without spilling blood, without giving satisfaction to the lord of vipers.

Through the green rapture of summer and the sorrowful loveliness of autumn, Merlinus's days with the Aurelianus brothers have an unvarying routine. At dawn, the wizard fixes a breakfast from last night's leftovers, then helps Theo prepare the saddles for that day's riders while Ambrosius readies the horses. Once the mounted patrols are out the gate, Ambrosius spends the rest of his morning as he always does, practicing military maneuvers in full armor upon his own steed, leaping on and off his beast, striking at stick men upon the ground and atop sawhorses, brandishing a weighted sword with both arms to strengthen his blows. The armor, the sword, and the maneuvers are his father's, all that remains of his noble legacy.

One morning a week, Ambrosius insists that his brother practice horseback archery with him, and despite his protests that he is an acolyte, Theo obeys out of a sense of family honor.

The Aurelianus clan can trace their equestrian ancestors directly back to the first cavalry unit to serve in Britain, the fierce Sarmatian horse-warriors from the Danube frontier assigned by Agricola to the cocky Legio XX Valeria Victrix four centuries previous. Ambrosius is exceedingly proud of his forefathers' prowess in the saddle and with the tall Persian bow, and he meticulously maintains all the skills he has acquired as a youth from his grandfather's horse-masters and archers.

Theo clearly enjoys riding but only halfheartedly wields the bulkily weighted weapons, much to his brother's loud frustration. As soon as Ambrosius's curses become obscene, the training session is over for Theo, and he storms out of the riding yard, vents his hurt by shoveling manure for a while, and then continues his studies with Merlinus. The old man tutors him in Greek, as the young man is already proficient in the Latin classics, and they contend in long, rambling Neoplatonic discourses in which the wizard tests Theo's spiritual mettle by challenging everything the youth learned from the priests.

Merlinus's tutoring, like his shoveling of manure, daily marketing, cooking, and mending, is but a disguise for his real intent. At noon, while Theo learns the Church dogma, Merlinus ostensibly goes to market for that night's dinner. As the brothers now own their equerry, there is money at hand for food and clothing, and the wizard does not need to use his magic for life's basics. Instead, he keeps a sharp eye out for the wives of the city's elders and military commanders who, riding in litters carried between two mules, pass through the market on their way to the baths. They drop off their servants to shop and have the litter return to pick them up again several hours later. In the meantime, Merlinus uses his ploys to learn from the servants all that they know about their households.

At dinner with the two brothers, Merlinus shares what he has learned in the marketplace as though he has simply overheard gossip. In that way, he informs them in advance when eminences from other *coloniae* are expected to parade into the

City of the Legion. Mounted in full regalia under the dragon-sock emblem of their family, the Aurelianus brothers ride ahead time and again to meet the incoming dignitaries. This provides for them several opportunities not only to meet but serve in the field with visiting counts, dukes, and once even the king of Anderida.

Ambrosius, hardened by his unremitting practice sessions, acquits himself well in skirmishes against the roving gangs that harry the farmers and outlying hamlets. The impressed dignitaries commend him to the city elders, who in time offer him a place in their cavalry. But proud Ambrosius, a senator's son of ducal rank, can accept nothing less than a command commission—and that requires far more than a few victories against hill bandits. Despite his noble rank, Ambrosius remains a stable master and no one takes seriously his ambitions for leadership.

As for Theo—he behaves in the field with a reluctance just shy of cowardice. On each engagement, he embarrasses his brother by striking foes with the flat of his blade and taking no lives. His brother rails at him for his feckless fighting, and the priests admonish him for fighting at all. Even Merlinus begins to doubt himself whether Raglaw's vision has truly revealed Theo as a battle-king in the midst of war's savagery.

What dispels the wizard's doubts are the youth's nightmares. Almost nightly Theo wakes thrashing, glittering with fright sweat. Merlinus knows, because he sleeps very little and spends his nights strolling among the weedlots between the stables and the cottage, conversing with himself about God and destiny. Most nights, Theo just rolls over and hugs himself to sleep. But some nights, he wakes with such a shout, he rouses his brother.

Alerted by the first taut cries, Ambrosius sits up with a start, his hand flying to the sword beside his straw mat. When he sees that it is just his brother's nightmare, his grip relaxes on the weapon, and he wearily lies back. "The dream again?" he mumbles.

"Yes, oh yes," Theo answers feverishly. "I saw *him* again. He presses his face up close. I felt his heat, Ambrosius. He smells like wet cinders."

"The Devil?"

"Yes—Satan himself." Theo sits up in the dark, arms tight around himself. "I swear by the Cross. I saw his yellow eyes and the scales around his hinged mouth—"

"Theo, when will you believe me?" Ambrosius mutters impatiently. "That isn't Satan."

"Tell me again, Ambro."

With a groan, Ambrosius rolls off his straw mat, slouches across the room, and kneels beside his brother. "Listen to me, Theo. When I was a boy, Father told me about the dragon. It changes form with the seasons, living underground in the winter, rising with the spring thunder, and flying among the summer clouds, invisible and powerful as the wind."

"I could *see* this thing, Ambro," Theo stresses. "It wasn't invisible at all."

"That's right, little brother. An Aurelianus man can see the dragon. That is why we are the dragon clan. Far back in time, Father said, we did a favor for the dragon breed, and now they watch over us."

"But why does he come to me? Why doesn't he trouble you?"

Ambrosius puts his thick arm across his brother's shoulders. "You carry the print of the dragon on your back. It stands behind you, not me."

"It's just a birthmark, Ambro. Mother said it was nothing."

"No, it's more than that. Mother didn't want to scare you. You see, Father had one just like it. It was between his shoulder blades. He showed it to me and told me himself it was the mark of the dragon. It means the dragon will fight for you, as it did for him and his father and all our forefathers, all the way back to our barbarian ancestors. When I was a boy, I wanted that mark for myself. But what point hoping for what is not there—the dragon gave it to you."

"It didn't save Father."

"The dragon fights for us on the battlefield—not in the stateroom against treachery."

Theo leans back against Ambrosius. "I hate battle."

"You know something, little brother?" Ambrosius speaks into Theo's ruffled hair. "Father hated battle, too."

"No."

"Yes. I once saw him weeping before battle, he hated it that much. But he fought in spite of his loathing, because there was no other way. Everything we have is made by the sword—or taken away by the sword."

Theo pulls away from Ambrosius and faces him in the night shadows. "You don't think me a coward, Ambrosius?"

"You are no coward. You are an Aurelianus. You hate killing, like any sane man."

Theo hangs his head. "Sometimes, when you shout at me in the field for not fighting harder—for not killing—I think you must despise me."

"Theo—little brother—" Ambrosius reaches out and takes Theo's shoulders in his large hands. "I love you. I shout at you because I love you. Don't you see? You bear the mark of the dragon. If you don't use it, you will die senselessly, and our people will die with you. That is why the dragon comes to you in the night, to wake you up to the truth of war. War is not about killing, young Theo. We are not murderers. We fight war so that we may live."

Theo's eyes fix ardently on Ambrosius's proud stare and his face brightens as he says, "I will try harder, brother."

"I know you will, Theo. You are like Father. The dragon has marked you."

Out of the moon's nest low in the forest, through the cold lunar fumes of the bog, the dragon priest rises. He is a man, clearly, yet not human. Centuries twine his hair in a long, black braid that sprouts from a green skull. The braid coils an armored body, a brass cuirass tarnished black as a crucible, leather shoulder plates cankerous with rot, and tatters of a tunic hanging like a web.

Theo remembers he is dreaming. He does not try to hide this time from the scabrous figure but stands still, daring to challenge his brother's faith that this deadwalker is not Satan. Moss trails from him, and his face is shrunken, reptilian.

Slouching closer, the archaic soldier steps into a slant of moonlight and reveals a shriveled visage of speckled salamander skin, newt holes for a nose, and his own bright amber eyes watching intently.

"Was Jesus wrong?" Theo asks Merlinus on a wintry morning with the wind like a wolf's snarl in the dragon banner atop the equerry. "Is it wrong to love all men?"

The day before, he witnessed his brother and the city cavalry hack down a troop of starving rovers who had sacked a granary, and he has been sick all night with the bloody memory of it. Merlinus feeds the twig fire in the clay oven of the leather shop and watches the light tearing itself to shreds in its eternal struggle against the cold darkness. At last, he says to the young man, "Did not Jesus preach that there is no greater love than that a man lay down his life for his friends?"

"But to break the commandment against murder?" Theo asks, twisting the leather cord he is reeving.

"Is it murder to slay a murderer and save the innocent lives he would have slaughtered?" Merlinus waves that question aside and turns his cold backside to the fire. "Go deeper yet. I believe that if you are a true Christian in these evil times, then you, Theodosius Aurelianus, must lay down your life as a priest and take up the sword. Otherwise, the very faith you worship may well be extincted in your lifetime by barbarians who love only plunder and pillage."

That is an argument even the priests could understand, especially as news reaches them of pagan attacks upon the bishoprics of the east and the massacre of defenseless Christians on the open farmlands of the north. Steadily, despite Vortigern's mercenaries outside Londinium, the Furor's minions sweep into the islands, devouring Britain. Talk in the marketplace among the servants of the noble houses centers more around retreating across the Channel to Armorica than entertaining Christian warlords.

Merlinus searches for Ygrane in his dreams, seeking her counsel, hoping she will direct him to take Theo out of the City of the Legion and bring him west to her. But in those rare sleep-trances when he does find her, she seems oblivious of him.

Once, he watches her singing blessings on the cattle as they returned from pasture, the drovers and their families garlanded in flowers, celebrating some Celtic holy day. Another time, he dreams of her with the unicorn by an obsidian pool in a night forest, gathering moonlight in glass jars, the zinc energy ringing like bells in the clear containers.

Other times, Merlinus dreams that he drifts nearby as she reads maps with her scribes or feasts burly clan chieftains and their boisterous families. A ghost in the wind, he sees her in the tight buckskin trousers her people are fond of, galloping on horseback along the Roman roads that connected the fortresses her fiana occupy. Surrounded by her fierce knights with their swords strapped to their backs and their grand mustaches streaked by their rushing flight, she looks to the wizard then a warrior-queen—and he wakes wondering if his gentle Theo can be man enough for such a woman.

That spring, Merlinus willfully changes everything. He calls for gold with his magic. In a cathedral of overarching alders not far from the city, where the original battlements stood four centuries earlier, his spells lead him to a rubblestone burrow shrouded with bines of hop.

He arrives there with Theo on one of their stravaging walks, seeking berries and small game while mentally picking over the fragmentary philosophy of Heraclitus. Merlinus pursues a hare into a mossy fissure in the overgrown rubble and pretends to be stuck. Piteously wailing for help, he does not allow Theo's strenuous efforts to budge him.

Shouting encouragement to the old man, Theo hurries for help and comes back with a grumbling Ambrosius, a draft horse, and a block and tackle. They strenuously dismantle the stone debris, working earnestly most of that afternoon. When Merlinus gauges that Ambrosius has reached the limit of his patience, the wizard comes tumbling out of the rock heap in a spill of gravel, dusty billows of schist and—on top of the whole mess—a glittering avalanche of gold coins.

The heads of the emperors Nero and Nerva stamped on the coins reveal that they were buried in the first decades of the conquest, hidden perhaps from early insurrectionists. Forgotten long before the hempen sacks that contained them rotted away, the coins have survived the very empire that minted them and consequently belong wholly and without dispute to the brothers Aurelianus.

Overnight, Ambrosius and Theodosius become the wealthiest men in the City of the Legion and, in truth, of all the western provinces. Ambrosius purchases for himself the military leadership he craves and for which he has readied himself since his embittered childhood. Some of the finest warriors of the region come to him, for he is not only generous with his gold, he is the most daring martial intelligence to take the field since the retreat of the legions.

As the new general's brother, Theo accompanies Ambrosius to his war councils and his battle tours and preaches both to the commanders and the troops. When he goes onto the field, it is not to fight but to aid the wounded and bolster the faith of the dying. His official title is *quaestor*, and he serves as quartermaster and finance officer for the troops who do the fighting. He looks aristocratic in his buffed bronze shoulder guards and red leather cuirass embossed with his family's dragon crest. After initial fits of doubting, even Merlinus becomes convinced that his vision of him as king is not entirely improbable. The wizard is eager to show him off to Ygrane, but Theo has no interest in leaving his brother's side, where he feels he has important work to do ministering to the soldiers.

"I was afraid there would be no meaning to life without the Church," he tells Merlinus one day in the atrium of the city's largest house, where they now live. Sunlight stands like lances under the round skylights, and kitchen clatter rings like the discordant rhythms of Asian jungle music as the galley prepares for that night's great feast—another dignitary come to honor the new, triumphant warlord in the City of the Legion.

"I think I agree with the Greek Sophists," Theo went on earnestly, sitting back in a curve-legged cathedra chair. "I have come to believe there are as many meanings to life as there are lives. Though I hate war, I'm happy now, even on the battlefield, because Ambrosius is happy."

"In early spring, you and your brother were stable masters," Merlinus reminds him. "Six months later, you are generals, a dozen successful engagements with the enemy behind you. But don't let it go to your head, young Theo. The roving brigands have been driven out, yes. But the enemies you will face in the lands to the north and east are not rabble gangs, but ferocious barbarians who thrive on combat. You must convince your brother to ally himself with the Celts to the west. Only they can fortify your ranks with the seasoned warriors we need to stop the barbarian advance. Come west with me and meet Ygrane, their queen. Be your brother's ambassador. There you will find significant meaning to your life."

"Are you still harping on about the mighty Celts?" Ambrosius says, entering the atrium through a portal whose pillars support coiled flowering vines. He wears a tunic and sash of subdued shades of gold with a silk scarf of purple over his right shoulder, signifying his majestic aspirations. "I've already told you. We don't require the alliance of barbarians, Merlinus."

"And I've told you, Lord Stable Master, the Celts are not barbarians. They held all of Europe in thrall from Britain to Persia before there was an Empire or even a Republic in Rome. They are a mighty and—"

"A noble people," Ambrosius finishes for Merlinus impatiently, throwing himself onto a couch. "But remember that they were the enemies of my fathers, and so, they are my enemies."

"Your fathers lived in very different times, Ambrosius," Merlinus reminds him, edging his voice harshly. "They were the invaders, you'll recall. The Celts fought them valiantly."

"And lost," Ambrosius sneers. "We don't need them. It's an alliance among the Britons that we need. There are too many kings and too few leaders."

"A great leader includes all," Merlinus advises, "even those outcast."

Ambrosius heaves an exasperated sigh. "Then you'll be pleased with our guest tonight. We're hosting a duke who knows the Celts very well. I think I can even say intimately. I'll be curious to see what he thinks about your insistence on an alliance with heathens. He should have an informed opinion, because he's married to the very queen you've been bragging about. A herald came ahead from Westerbridge and has announced that, within the hour, the City of the Legion will be honored by the retinue and presence of Gorlois, duke of the Saxon Coast."

At the sound of that name, a trill of anxiety spurts through the wizard.

"You know this duke, Merlinus?" Theo asks.

"Yes," the wizard mutters. "We met some years ago, at Maridunum. I did not detect in him then much love for the Celts."

"He's a Roman," Ambrosius says tersely, standing up and pacing among the potted plants, too restless to lie still for long. In the stables, exhausted by his frustrations, he slept nights, but since attaining his new station with all its grand possibilities, he has taken to scouting the countryside obsessively by day and prowling the mansion by night, plotting, strategizing, scheming. "No one in the *coloniae* comprehends why Gorlois married such a vixen in the first place. Word is, Ygrane's a Celtic witch."

"The Church condoned such a union?" Theo wonders aloud.

"The Church!" Ambrosius snickers derisively. "When are you going to open your eyes about the Church, little brother? Why do you think they delayed your ordination when you were a stable master and now, if you ask in your sleep, they'll make you a bishop?" He pauses before a wax bust of his father and stares intently into those bald eyes. "Gorlois was abandoned by the *coloniae* when the sea rovers swarmed over his coastline. What choice did he have? And what choice the Church on the Saxon Coast? Better to give the gold to the Celts and keep Church and state alive than succumb to the barbarians and lose all."

Theo thumbs his chin. "Then, the Celts are worthy warriors?"

"Would there be Celts at all today if they weren't?" Ambrosius strolls to a Corinthian pillar beside the entryway to the *peristylum*, the spacious court at the house's interior, open to the sky and surrounded by the porches and columns of the mansion's many rooms. "We'll dine here tonight under the stars—if Gorlois gives me his pledge. Otherwise, there'll be no dinner. I need alliances, not dinner guests. Britain requires unity."

"I would not expect too much from Gorlois," Merlinus cautions. "The duke is an arrogant man and nearly twice your age. He will share power perhaps, but I doubt he'll give a pledge."

Ambrosius strides off into the *peristylum*, grousing over his shoulder, "Share? The way Vortigern shares? Not with me! We need one high king who will share nothing with barbarians. We need unity. Not sharing."

Theo and Merlinus exchange concerned looks, and the wizard shrugs. "He's right, you know. The old Romans understood that. If power is shared, it becomes diluted."

Theo frowns at Merlinus as though the old man should know better. "Not the oldest Romans, Merlinus. Not the Republic. They shared power, and it made them great."

"Yet in times of grave crisis, even they appointed a dictator."

His frown deepens, and he does not seem to hear the wizard. "I love my brother, but in this I really think he's too proud. Is he uniting Britain—or simply displacing Vortigern?"

"Simply?" Merlinus cocks a tufted eyebrow. "For your brother to achieve that, he will *have* to unite Britain. Vortigern's allies are too powerful for him to be simply displaced."

"That's exactly what I'm afraid of, Merlinus. Civil war. Instead of uniting us against the barbarians, my brother will have the *coloniae* fighting each other." He closes his eyes. "There must be another way."

Merlinus stops and stares at Theo, marveling at how far he has come from the callow youth who lifted the wizard from the gutter. For the first time, Merlinus begins truly to believe that Theo is undeniably the king from Raglaw's vision. It is not just that, in the bronze and leather gear and costly array of silken and embroidered tunics, the youth has taken on the guise of a king, his handsome, boyish lineaments all one might hope for in the visage of a young monarch. Merlinus sees something more, something deeper in those early, fervid moments of his brother's ascendancy. What impresses him is his abiding faith in the Christian God, which inculcated him to regard first the good of others, the commonweal, above his own necessities. It is a caring that hurts him, though, for it makes him acutely sensitive to the problem of his brother's own acquired evil.

He opens his golden eyes and regards the wizard sadly. "You were right, Merlinus. All along. I didn't want to believe you—

and in the stables, perhaps, I could have gone on not believing. But now—now that we have the might to fulfill Ambrosius's dreams—now that it has us, it's too obvious. Too frightfully obvious." He stares at Merlinus, half-sick with fear. "Perhaps in the end, no one will be saved."

In the evening, passing through a gap in the low western hills, the duke's caravan arrives on the plain above the City of the Legion. "We camp here for the night," Gorlois informs the master of the horses. He lifts himself in the saddle better to view the country below. In a deep violet haze of grasslands under stacks of red cloudbanks, the city of black stones squats like the jagged crown of a giant.

"Father, why are we stopping here?" Morgeu asks, pulling up beside him atop her roan stallion. Her red hair curls in the wind like a furl of the sunset behind her, and her tiny, tar-drop irises reflect the very depths of night. "We can make the city gates by nightfall."

Gorlois's small eyes shift slightly, enough to displace the full weight of his incredulity into his daughter's lap. "Arrive at *nightfall*?"

She sighs, understanding. "Of course. The duke of the Saxon Coast does not ride into a city under night's cover. But, Father, I would so much enjoy a hot bath."

"The baths of this city are exceptional, Morgeu," he says without regarding her, his gaze fitted to a nostalgic recollection of the brutal stonepile below, wrapped now in the golden gauze of day's end. "They were constructed in the reign of the Emperor Vespasian, when craftsmen prided themselves on grandiosity. You will enjoy the submerged steam vents that swirl the water and lave the body with their heat. It will be worth the wait, I assure you."

"Unless the provincials have cannibalized the baths to build another of their tacky baptismal fonts."

"There is that possibility, daughter. It has been twenty-five years since last I visited this city. It was splendid then." His jowly face nods at the loveliness of that memory. "But now—now the glory that was Rome has lost even the illusion of life. Now there are no more illusions of glory. Now there is only survival, if we are bold and lucky. And so, we go to beat the war drum with the latest great hero of our dead and rotted empire."

"You knew his father." Morgeu pulls her blue-dyed, crushed leather riding coat tighter about her to ward off the evening chill. "He was a senator."

"Aurelianus?" he asks, his gaze still lost in the golden haze of the past. "Yes. He was in line for imperial magistrate of all Britain. I met him once, in Londinium at the privy council. He was a noble and sincere man, as I recall. He showed me his grand plans for invading Gaul and taking the fight to the homeland of the Jutes and the Angles themselves—see how they liked having their fields torched and villages plundered. But he died."

"Assassination, they say."

"Does it matter?" He pats his steed's neck tenderly, musingly. "Dead is dead. There was no invasion, just capitulation. And now the ambitious senator's son seeks his revenge. More infighting. More weakness before the onslaught of our enemies."

"Is it revenge?" Morgeu asks, just to keep her father talking. He is so often reticent, it is rare and curious to hear him this voluble. "The proclamations he issues speak of uniting the kings to defend Britain."

Gorlois barks a laugh. "This Ambrosius is cunning. He speaks of uniting the kings—yet have not all the kings and warlords already pledged support to Balbus Gaius Cocceius, who so proudly bears the Saxon title High King Vortigern? No, Morgeu. I have brought you along not to meet the future unifier of Britain. That will never happen. There are too many greedy men on this island. No, this is not a noble campaign to which we are summoned. You are here with me to see how war is waged on its grandest scale, not for conquest but for fury itself."

Good, Morgeu thinks. She has accompanied her father because he has promised that there would be many battles. She has witnessed numerous raids and defensive skirmishes during her years with him on his endless patrols of the coast. But she has never beheld a battle. Too often, she has heard her father speak glowingly, as poets do, of war. Now, at last, she will see what the poets have seen.

Flanked by personal guards in plumed helmets, the duke of the Saxon Coast arrives on horseback at the head of a small train of traveling vans and baggage wagons. His bulldog jowls have become ruddier and hackled with white whiskers since Merlinus last saw him, but the duke's haughtiness and insolence have diminished none.

The Aurelianus brothers and Merlinus meet Gorlois at the portico of their mansion, and the duke neither salutes nor hails them. Instead, his goat eyes appraise the men before him coldly as he awaits a greeting.

"Welcome, brother Gorlois," Ambrosius calls heartily, attempting archaic Latin, yet not stepping down the portico stairs to accord the duke the deference the older man clearly expects. "Come into my house and take your rest from so long a journey. You have traveled far to see me."

Ambrosius's address, no matter how gallant in tone and gesture, clearly rankles the duke, and he mutters to his guards loud enough for all to hear: "Parvenu."

An excited murmur ripples through the parade of city elders, cavalry, and their entourage of wealthy families who greeted the duke at the main gate and escorted him to the Aurelianus mansion. Among the dazzling crowd are many who believe, as Gorlois does, that the brothers are lowly and rude stable masters elevated by mere chance.

Merlinus thumps his staff loudly, curtailing a potentially dangerous outburst from Ambrosius. "The Aurelianus family are as entitled by lineage to wear the purple as any nobility in the land."

Ambrosius stops Merlinus with an extended arm and smiles graciously at the duke. "Gorlois," he speaks with the familiarity of a peer, "you haven't come this far to insult me—"

"It is you that insults me!" Gorlois snaps. "My great-grandfather was appointed duke of the Saxon Coast by the Imperial Magistrate himself."

Ambrosius's smile does not waver. "And is your great-granddaddy going to be leading us, then, against the Picts, Jutes, and Scoti?"

A wave of laughter rises from the crowd, and even the duke's guards smirk. Gorlois burns a darker red under his jowly whiskers and stretches a forced smile across his orange teeth. "Well said, brother Ambrosius," he allows, and dismounts. "Would that the heroes of our noble past could fight for us. But it has devolved to our humble shoulders to defend our kingdoms."

"Our *kingdom*," Ambrosius corrects, and opens his arms to receive the duke. "Before the scattered attacks of the barbarian tribes, we must unite."

Merlinus edges closer to Ambrosius, expecting violence from the duke, who climbs the stairs with a rictus grin and a sharp light in his goat eyes. But Gorlois does not reach for his sword. He embraces Ambrosius and then Theo and mumbles stiff pleasantries to both. For Merlinus, he has a quizzical look. "We've met before?"

"Don't you remember, Father?" pipes a young woman who descends from the lead traveling van. Her crinkled red hair shines with glinting carats of sunlight about a round and pale moonface—the child Morgeu grown to budding womanhood; like her mother, long-shouldered and slender as a flame but with her father's small eyes and a touch of cruelty in her crooked smile. "Myrddin—mother's wizard from some few years ago."

Recognition ignites in Gorlois's tight stare, and he grumbles, "You again?" His tight eyes bulge with threat. "Any sorcery from you, old coot, and I'll serve you same as I did the crone Raglaw."

The brothers look at Merlinus with perplexed surprise before the rush of social events sweep them away, to the wizard's vast relief. Gorlois introduces Morgeu, and they enter the mansion. As they have done a dozen times before in greeting the kingdom's dignitaries, they lead their guests to their quarters, introduce them to the servants, and show them the *balneum*—the baths. It is there that the issue of Merlinus's identity next arises.

Sitting naked together on the sumptuous mosaics, muscles relaxed by steam and the adept skills of a Persian masseur, visitors are more compliant with the brothers than they would be in the war room surrounded by armor and maps reminding them of the power and territory at stake. Most of the pledges are secured here in the *balneum*, Gorlois's included—though when the masseur emerges and nods to Merlinus, signaling the duke's acceptance of Ambrosius's leadership, the wizard most certainly suspects treachery. The duke has agreed with a greater alacrity than any of the others.

"They want to see you," the masseur says, reaching for the old man's robe and staff.

Merlinus usually waits in the anteroom where, unseen by others, he can use his magic to search the garments of the guests. Twice before, he has found poison in the sleeve pouches and neutralized the toxins with a chant. The growing shock on the faces of the poisoners at the banquets later, after they administered their ineffectual venoms, always amuses him. A whispered spell at the most vulnerable moment for the would-be assassins—during a toast or after the bishop's benediction—and the poison phials pop out from their sleeves as if by a blunderful accident, disclosing their treachery. Of course, traitors invariably have their evasions, and the brothers behaved civilly, accepting the blatant lies coolly. But warning has been served, and the killers are ever after marked.

This time, though, Merlinus finds no poison or hidden daggers in Gorlois's garments, and when he enters the humid bath, he feels as naked in soul as in flesh.

"The duke tells us you are a wizard who served his wife at Segontium and at Maridunum," Ambrosius announces as Merlinus eases himself into the hot water and sits opposite the brothers and their rugged guest. "He says his daughter saw you working magic one night in the woods."

"Ygrane flatters me with that title," Merlinus says. "I once saved her daughter from a fall. The child remembers it as magic." He laughs good-naturedly at the apprehensive expression on Theo's face and turns to the duke. "And how is the queen, Ygrane—she is well?"

"Ask Morgeu," Gorlois growls. "I haven't seen the witch since I decapitated the creature poisoning her ear."

Ambrosius interrupts the conversation with a raised hand. "I called you in here, Merlinus, because the duke assures me the Celts are not a tribe worthy of Roman alliance. I want you to hear that for yourself."

"Why else would you think I'm so eager for this alliance?" Gorlois asks loudly. "For God's sake, I want no more of that pagan mysticism and witchcraft. I would never have gone over to that had there been a true warlord around here all those years ago. But there was no one. No one came to my defense when the barbarians landed in waves off the sea and took my towns and farms. I had to rely on whatever warriors I could find."

"Tell him what you told us," Ambrosius says, "about the Celts' conditions for alliance."

"Didn't Ygrane tell you?" Gorlois regards Merlinus with an incredulous scowl.

"In truth, I met the queen only twice, and briefly."

"They demand I keep our priests out of their territory," the duke confesses with a grunt of mocking laughter. "For fourteen years now, the Church has been dunning me for leaving those lands to the heathens."

"I thought most of the Celtic tribes were Christian now," Theo states. "Brought into the fold by Saint Non. Her son David is preaching the gospel among them right now."

"There are many Christian tribes among the Celts," Gorlois says, "but the real warriors, the blood-frenzied ones that even the barbarians fear, are the fiana. They obey no priest and worship strange gods. Ygrane will have no priest on their lands."

"And you don't pay these fiana gold to fight for you?" Theo asks.

"Gold?" Gorlois shows the whites at the tops of his eyes. "I pay tribute to no one. The Celts required I marry their queen. I did. But that's all. When I need military help, I alert my wife, and the fiana come."

"And how will you continue to hold back the Church, lord?" Merlinus dares ask, already knowing the answer. "The bishops will not long stand for a Christian duke thwarting their missions."

"I would not pledge myself to this young upstart Ambrosius if I didn't need him," Gorlois admits. "Forgive my tongue, but it's the truth. Bishop Germanicus has already demanded I open the frontier to his soldiers of Christ. If I refuse him, I will lose the support of my own subjects, who already believe the bishop to be a saint. But when I let the saint send his missionaries in, I will certainly provoke the formidable ire of the fiana. I have no doubt at all that I will have to fight them then as well as the sea rovers. That's when we'll see what your leadership is worth, Ambrosius."

"You'll see my worth much sooner than that, Gorlois," Ambrosius avers. "With your pledge, I've got all the troops I need to begin my campaign. This winter, I will crush the barbarians in the midlands and the south, and I will secure our coastline. By spring, I will sit in Londinium, high king of all Britain."

Gorlois whistles, soft and low. "You *are* a heady upstart, Aurelianus. A high king already sits in Londinium. He will demand *your* pledge if you prove yourself in the midlands."

Ambrosius practically rises out of the bath, the flesh of his powerful chest muscles twitching like a horse's hide. "Balbus Gaius Cocceius is no king! He's a murderer. By spring, I swear, his soul will burn in hell!"

Theo moves to calm his brother, and Ambrosius shakes him off and stands in the bath, an expression on his comely face both sinister and unholy.

"I don't care how many barbarian mercenaries Balbus hires," he says. "With the bloom of spring—he dies."

Gorlois, whose gruff, belligerent face has seemed incapable of displaying admiration, beams a proud smile at Ambrosius, an expression so incongruous on him it looks gruesome against his harsh, scar-seamed features, as though he were a saint of bloodshed.

In a floral garden adjoining the guest chambers, a sun-shot atrium of warm sweet fragrances, Gorlois meets with his counselors. They sit on tassel-pillowed benches in the stained light of a potted acacia tree. Beside them, a fountain splashes, veiling their conversation from eavesdroppers.

Gorlois addresses the marble faun dancing in the fountain bowl, "Can Ambrosius be undone?"

Marcus, the duke's nephew and military chief, shakes his head. Tall, blond, and big-framed, he looks more Saxon than Roman. "Ambrosius is large *inside*. He is bloodlusty, yet he has a vision. His men sense that. They respect him, because the gods tested his nobility in the stables, found him sound, and paid him with ancestral gold. Even more vital than his luck, he has a leader's skills, ferocious in the field and comradely in the barracks. He knows each one of the garrison men from when he stabled their horses, knows their individual strengths and flaws. He's meticulously chosen his officers, paying with glory and honor those he cannot buy with gold. I can find no one to compromise. Clearly, he has lethal vision. And he has imparted that to his men by forging them into an elite force, some kind of new tactical unit that relies on cavalry. He trains them daily and hard—and they love him for it. They are convinced he is the next high king of Britain, and they are his personal guard. I do not recommend a coup strike."

The tone of his voice, deepening into fatalistic shadows, chills the duke's hope of aborting Ambrosius's upstart ambitions. The Syrax family of Londinium, the most wealthy clan in the islands and High King Vortigern's staunchest ally, would have paid handsomely for the demise of such an obvious threat.

Gorlois's gaze slides from the marble faun to his political adviser, a bald, storklike and toothless elder of so ancient a Roman lineage that he has kinship ties in all the major families of Briton. "Well, Aulus? Who among the city's families are against him?"

The old man rubs his veined nose, embarrassed to make his report to his duke. "There are no families in the City of the Legion who oppose him, my lord. He is a senator's son, a man of impeccable ancestry, who cannot honestly be challenged as a usurper. Moreover, my lord, he has lucratively involved each of the families in his campaign, promising them generous profits from renewed trade once the highways among the *coloniae* are cleared. He levies no taxes and purchases with gold all the supplies for his army from the families' businesses." His mottled hands shrug. "Ambrosius has thought all of this through very carefully—and the families respect such care."

"Yes—the families do." Gorlois nods, focusing on this understanding: He now sees that Ambrosius has become something almost supernatural, someone bigger than blood rivalries. Incisive lines appear in his thick face, and he looks to his daughter with a sharpened set of jaw. "It's your mother again. Ambrosius's counselor—that old man was Raglaw's wizard! Ygrane surely sent him here. It's her magic that found the fortune to make this warlord. Hm? Do you see what a witch she is, Morgeu?"

"You should fear her more, Father," Morgeu says. She lies on her back atop her bench, one draped knee up, fingers locked across her breasts. Staring up at the imprint of the sun in the acacia branches, her mother's scheme appears clearly before her. The queen's magic looks like a river pattern, a branching of consequences that flows from the mountain kingdom of Cymru into the Roman *coloniae*. The largest tributary pours into this citadel in the foothills, filling up within its black stone walls a dammed force of magical power ready to spill across Britain to the sea.

"I should fear her more," the duke admits, but in a steely voice. "I have seen enough of her magic over the years. Yet, I am a Christian. My salvation is assured by the Most High God. I do not fear Ygrane—or any witch."

"If Merlinus is unholy," the statesman Aulus suggests, "a good soldier of Christ would remove him."

"I would not try," Morgeu warns quickly. "Merlinus is more unholy than you think. He is a demon."

"You fortify my argument, young lady," Aulus says and addresses the duke sternly, "Dispatch him to hell immediately, my lord. You will do honor to God and a service to all the families."

Morgeu sits up, her small eyes a dark mime of her father's. "Father, Merlinus is not like Raglaw. He is not like anyone we have ever known."

"How do you counsel me then, daughter?" Gorlois asks, earnestly. Long ago, when she yet had a child's angelic face, he learned to trust her insights, her sageful predictions of people's behavior and unexpected situations that later came to pass. Now that her bones are edged sharper, he can see himself in many of her facial traits, and he receives her counsel as though from a prophetic version of himself.

"Merlinus cannot be killed—not by us, anyway. He serves larger powers."

"Unholy powers?" the duke asks.

"Only God is holy, Father."

"Then it is settled," Gorlois states abruptly, square-knuckled hands gripping his knees, pugnacious face leaning forward to meet each of their attentive stares. "Ambrosius cannot be undone by arms, politics, or magic. As he cannot be withstood, we will stand with him. What choice do we have?"

The weapons master for the Rovers of the Wild Hunt is a dwarf. Like all dwarfs, he stands half the size of a man yet carries twice the strength in his thick-boned, muscle-packed frame. Shaped by the Æsir gods from maggots in the corpseflesh of the Old Ones slain during the overthrow, they are hairless, death white busyworkers. No female dwarfs exist and so, no children, no ancestors to honor. Work is all that dwarfs live for—by day in their subterranean foundries and by night in their dreams, where they devise the clever contraptions, fearsome weapons, and astonishing jewelry for which they are famous.

The Furor selected a dwarf as weapons master because he does not trust any of the gods. No weapons are allowed at Home, except those carried by the chieftain. Hunting implements are permitted in the Great Tree only during the Wild Hunt. The Furor has not forgotten how he came to power, and he keeps well guarded the metal arms designed to slay gods.

Thus, the weapons master of the Æsir is Brokk, the most diligent and cunning of the dwarfs. He fashioned the Furor's arm-ring, whose flawless mirror surface cleverly extends the one-eyed god's vision deeper into his blind side. Also, Brokk is fabled for his ingenious self-propelled vehicles, such as the power launch Skidblade that can sail the Gulf and circle the earth in half a day. No one, the Furor reasons, can trick a mind as inventive as this dwarf's, and that is why the chieftain of the Æsir has installed Brokk on the bleak arctic island that bears the arsenal of the gods.

Answerable only to the Furor, Brokk lives an ideal life for a dwarf, rich in solitude and resources. He busies himself daily overseeing the dwarfs who assist him in the workshops and the elfin slaves who labor with the smelterpots and forges. Rarely does he visit the arsenal and then only to examine and maintain those lethal tools. Even more rarely is his industry disturbed by the wailing alarm that warns of intruders.

Several times in the past, the Liar and his cohorts have attempted to break in. But each time, Garm, the slaverous wolf-ogre, has sent them scurrying away in terror, back to their soft lives in the World Tree. Brokk has not once had to leave the work caverns; however, on this day, when the slicing wail stops, there is no victory howl from Garm.

The clarion chimes of the beckoning horn call for him. Only the Furor has ever blown the beckoning horn, for none other can approach Garm and not be torn apart. Yet Brokk well knows that the alarm would not sound for the chieftain.

The dwarf, muttering imprecations at this disturbance, gruffly pushes away from his stone worktable, where gems glint among calipers, clamps, and peelings of metal. He waddles across a cavern lit by fireshadows from the kilns in surrounding grottoes. At a stalagmite slotted with levers, he seizes a fur rag and buffs the crystal sphere big as a skull set in the stone at eye level for the dwarf. As the crystal picks up the static charge from the fur, it breathes light and fogs the inside of the sphere with a vaporous view of the island above.

A stately woman waits on the flaking shale before the cave entrance that leads to the factory and arsenal. Brokk sees at once that she is not a god. Her long, wind-tangled tresses of white hair and the imperfect symmetry of her angular features fit a human countenance. Snow blows in pieces big as petals, and she shivers the palest shade of blue in her white fur robes. High above her reach hangs the golden tusk of the beckoning horn, secured to the mountainside with scarlet ropes faded brown, each braid thicker than the stranger's body.

Brokk scans the vicinity for whoever blew the horn and finds Garm sprawled belly down on the flint-toothed beach. The wolf-ogre's fang-thrust face sleeps, its devil eyes hooded in their deep, skeletal sockets. Swirling brume clings like steam to its black horns and quill-bristling hide and beads to dew in the snarl-folds of its leathery muzzle.

The horn sounds again, deep and commanding as though the Furor himself calls. In the viewing crystal, Brokk looks at the cave entrance and sees only the pale woman standing bravely in the snowfall. *An enchantress*, he assumes, and pulls the lever that opens a man-size portal within the granite wall of the cave. He knows how to deal with such intruders.

Once the woman enters the portal, Brokk pulls another lever, and the floor beneath the stranger gives out. The dwarf waits until he hears the satisfying crash of plummeting rocks in the pit, like a throb of thunder in the cavern walls. Then, with a lopsided grin, he turns back toward his worktable.

"I have come for the sword."

Brokk hops about, startled, and hops again when he sees the pale woman across the cavern. She steps out of a slanthole in the wall, a smoking chute that ventilates the slag pit below. Calmly, she walks toward him, and the dwarf and elfin workers among the beehive forges vanish into the trembling shadows.

"I have come for the sword Lightning."

"That is the Furor's sword!" The dwarf laughs darkly to disguise his fright, and places a hand on the lever that controls the glowing smelterpots. "Who are you, impudent stranger?"

"I am Rna, queen of the Flint Knives."

"Flint Knives?" The dwarf watches her advance past the forges and into the depressed staging area, where the pots pour.

"The last Flint Knives died on this island more than thirty thousand years ago, lady."

Brokk throws the lever that spills the smelterpots, and startling bursts of gold fire slosh over the ancient queen, obliterating her in the glare. For an instant, a greater being stands in her place. Huge as a god, it fills the cavern's height, and its body burns with rays of inner dimensions, weird, inspiraling facets and smoldering plasmas the dwarf has never seen in any god. Giant and staring, the being's eyes carry within their dark, enveloping depths naked starcores.

The dwarf winces. When he looks again, the white queen passes unscathed through a fiery veil of molten ore and mounts the steps toward his gallery.

"Who are you?" he screams, no longer attempting to hide his fear.

"I am Rna, queen—"

"No! You are some more vast being." Brokk's clenched face relaxes with the numbness of a realization. "You—" He steps back, clutching at his leather apron, shaking his domed head. His jaws and eyes feel rusted open, and it is moments before he can speak. "You are a Fire Lord!"

The woman pulls the sun-bleached hair from her pale eyes, and the dwarf sees the age scars around them. This close, her baked lips and hollowed cheeks look mummified.

"I am Rna, queen of the Flint Knives. I have come for the sword Lightning."

Among the wall trophies of swords, spears, bronze face masks, and panels of maps in the war room of the City of the Legion, Ambrosius reveals to Gorlois and his field officers his strategy for the conquest of Britain. "Most of your men will stay here in the west to hold the Saxon Coast with the help of the Celts while we march on the midlands with the men pledged us by the other *coloniae*."

"You haven't enough men to take the midlands," a young voice speaks from the oaken doorway.

On the settle Merlinus shares with Theo, the wizard sits up taller to see Morgeu confidently enter the war room. She wears a knee-length leather tunic secured about her small waist by a brass-studded dagger-belt, and, with her crimped hair pulled severely back from her cold face and tied off to a bright topknot, she looks not unlike a young and dangerous barbarian warrior.

"Scoot, girl," Ambrosius admonishes, and points to the door. "This is a war council."

"Steady, Ambrosius," Gorlois speaks up from the table map where he is scrutinizing the campaign itinerary. "My daughter is equal to any man in strategy and tactics. She has proffered me valuable insights on numerous forays in council and on the field. I daresay, she is a war savant and you'd do well to heed her advice."

Ambrosius cocks an eyebrow at her. "Morgeu, is it?"

"You haven't enough men," she repeats, and strides to her father's side. "The *coloniae* have given you puny pledges. Each *colonia* has promised you only a handful of men. They are too wary to commit any more to an unproved warlord. If you leave my father's soldiers here in the west, you will be commanding only a skeleton force. With the attrition to be expected from clashes with the barbarians, you'll be whittled away long before you reach the Tamesis River."

Gorlois smiles darkly. "She's right, you know. I am the only one who has offered you a substantial force. You can't afford to leave my men behind."

"I can't afford not to, Gorlois," Ambrosius discloses. "As you'll see from the campaign itinerary before you, we will be away through the winter. I don't dare leave the coasts unprotected that long. I can't afford a war on two fronts. No. You will come with me, Gorlois. I need your field counsel and expertise in battle. But the bulk of your force must remain here to protect our back."

Morgeu smirks. "You cannot hope to drive back the Northmen *and* the Saxons with the token force the *coloniae* have pledged you. Have you any idea of the numbers arrayed against you? The Picts alone are massed in the thousands. You will command fewer than five hundred."

"I am pledged 437 foot soldiers," Ambrosius reveals. "But I have 156 cavalry I have trained myself."

Morgeu looks to her father and his officers and rolls her eyes. "You will be spending this winter hiding in the *coloniae*, not conquering the frozen lands around them."

"This girl is right enough," Ambrosius admits. "That is, if I were to fight conventional forays as you and the barbarians expect. But I know my enemy better than that."

"None know the barbarian better than we," Gorlois asserts and nods to his battle-scarred officers: lean, pugnacious men with salt-bleached hair and woe-dark stares obedient to death. "I tell you, they are not like the strike-and-run bandits you chase down around here. Oh, no, Ambrosius. The Gaels will fight to the last man, even if you kill their leader."

"*Especially* if you kill him," an officer adds. "They fight to die. Battle death guarantees passage to their pagan heaven. The Gael never retreats."

"Never?" Ambrosius queries.

"Never," Gorlois affirms.

Ambrosius claps his hands. "Perfect! I have heard as much and hoped for it to be so."

The duke's warriors pass dubious glances among themselves.

"If they flee, our work will be so much harder," Ambrosius explains. "But if they stand and fight, there will be a great slaughter. We will exterminate them."

"Ambrosius—" Gorlois places a restraining hand on the younger man's arm. "My daughter has already told you, we haven't the men—"

"For a conventional battle—yes." Ambrosius stalks across the room, gazing into each of the battle-hardened faces before him.

"The key to our victory is the horse. These are sea rovers and hill-fighters we are confronting. They loathe the horse. If they ride at all, they ride into battle and dismount to fight. To them, it is unmanly to strike at a distance with rocks or arrows. Their warrior's code demands that they fight hand-to-hand combat. But we are not sea rovers or hills' men, are we?" He grins evilly and draws his hands back, miming a bow and arrow. "We know the skill it takes to ride and shoot. And there is nothing cowardly for us in slaying our enemies from afar. Is there?" He releases the invisible arrow at Gorlois.

"But 156 horsemen," Morgeu despairs. "That's all you have—against thousands!"

"There will be others," Ambrosius promises. "When we have won our first battles, we will have many more recruits. And, besides, we are not going to fight all the barbarians in one battle. They will come at us in hundreds, one engagement at a time, believing we are a helpless skeleton force, as you say. And we will choose open terrain, high on the river plains, where our cavalry can run circles around the enemy. The courageous hill warriors will stand and fight—and they will die."

Again, gruesome admiration glows on the jowly face of Gorlois as he locks gazes with Ambrosius and absorbs the veracity of the young warrior's lethal scheme. The astonished officers rise from their settles to gather around the campaign map and ogle the sites that have been carefully chosen for the famous slaughters to come.

Morgeu stands apart. She regards Ambrosius with a hot light in her eyes, and her stare gleams with an almost-amorous brimming for the slaughter he promises. Soon, she will see for herself the majesty of conquest that the duke has extolled all her life. Soon, she will partake of the blood ritual that will forever set her apart from her mother, the rite of war that will make her Roman.

"I am afraid for my father," Morgeu whispers to the indifferent stars. She sits in the garden outside her chambers, the sheer fabric of her evening gown breathing in the night's coolness.

The sky's luminous darkness configures a face, a carbon visage with eyes two bubbles of void. Fumes of stars froth from the vortex of silence that is its mouth. *For the father, no hope near Lailoken. No hope for the father.*

In earlier trances, deepened by dreaming potions, she has spoken with this face. It is Ethiops, a demon comrade of Lailoken's from his former life. The demon and Morgeu want the same thing, to free Lailoken from his mortal bonds.

Morgeu hates her mother for abandoning her father, whom she loves with all her soul. Ygrane has the magic to save him, to protect him from harm in the field, to strengthen his battle luck. But she has forsaken the duke.

And she has forsaken her own daughter as well. Because Morgeu cleaves to her father, Ygrane has taken away the unicorn. She hoards its beauty and power for herself and for Lailoken, her slave.

To counter the influence of Ygrane's spirit reckoner, Morgeu has hired witches to teach her to commune with demons. She has found Ethiops, and he will help her. Already, the demon has given her power, enough to strengthen her trances, yet still too little to ignite the sight. She wants to see the timewind that blows her and her father east, toward war. She wants to see how to protect them.

But she lacks the magic to see anything more than this face of fluid darkness, this sinuous intensity that taps her sensual root and draws up a chill, magnetic sap from out of her own secret happy darkness.

Her maid bleats from indoors, and she knows it is time to go. "Tonight," she promises Ethiops, rising to her feet, feeling him already inside her, compressed into the hot space of the deepest part of her. "You will have me again tonight. And by your sure strength, we will free Lailoken from earth."

Merlinus fears Morgeu. She knows of magic. Yet at dinner that night in the lanternlit *peristylum*, she behaves with the gentle grace of a well-schooled fourteen-year-old. No word of Ygrane or Celtic magic or war plans. Dressed in a slinky white *camisa* that clings to the gentle swipes of her young breasts and hips, she appears seductively feminine, her red-gold hair elaborately braided and piled atop her slender neck in Roman fashion. With sophisticated patience and subtlety, she draws Ambrosius's favorable attention to her presence and even elicits several gentle smiles from him.

Only afterward does Morgeu reveal to Merlinus the extent of her magical knowledge. When Gorlois and Theo retire and Ambrosius sits in the war room poring over his maps and terrain reports and only the servants walk about the rooms clearing the tables where the duke's guard dined, she appears in the wizard's chambers, on the porch opening to the garden. Naked under a sky foggy with stars, she looks like a piece of moonlight, her hair an aura of smoke about her cold face, a wisp between her legs.

"Do you remember, Lailoken, how I thought you were an angel when I first saw you?" Her voice does not come from any place but from within the wizard, and by that he knows she is an apparition, perhaps for his eyes only. She smiles with half her face and fills his heart with dreadfulness. "It was then I realized you must be a wizard. Remember?"

Merlinus rises from his couch and pulls his sleeping gown tighter about himself.

"I've learned a great deal since then, Lailoken." She drifts closer, a shadowless vapor voluptuously lit from inside. "I've spoken to some of your friends. Ethiops—Azael. They miss your company. They tell me you're making a king for my mother. Is that true?"

"That is between Ygrane and me," he answers tersely. "Leave me alone."

"Ambrosius will never have my mother," Morgeu says confidently, with a hauteur that frightens him. "Your sorcery may be strong enough to make him king—but mine is strong enough to make him mine."

"Why?" he asks. "Your mother herself set me this task."

"My mother already has a good man in my father," she says, her stare kindling like starsmoke. "But she doesn't know how to love him. She is a Celtic dreamer and doesn't even know what her magic is for. She doesn't deserve another strong Roman. You shouldn't be serving her, Merlinus. Come to me. Be my wizard. I am the one foreseen by the ancient prophecy. I will know how to use Ambrosius—and I will fulfill the foretelling. Then, the fiana will follow me, the Síd will give me their magic, and I will be the next high queen of the Celts."

Merlinus clutches his staff and advances onto the porch. "You know I will not abandon my task, Morgeu."

The wraith points at him with a vehement grimace. "You are no wizard, Lailoken. You are a demon—no different than the others. You just pretend to be human. Do not think you can cross me. The other demons will not permit it."

Merlinus widens his stance and presents his staff lengthwise as if he could block a specter. "I don't want to fight you, Morgeu, but if I must, I will."

"Your fighting ends here, demon," she declares, her eyes a sudden flare of lightning that makes him wince in pain. "I want you out of mortal flesh and back into the void where you belong. Back to the darkness with you!"

A thunderbolt jags through his body, and he jerks upright to his toetips, eyeballs rolling back into a skulldark veined with arcs of welder's fire. He collapses, his heart slamming to escape his rib cage, all breath gone. Death holds the scepter of his spine in an icy grip, and darkness closes in to claim its own.

So does Morgeu. Her naked wraith looms closer, gloating over the fallen wizard.

With his last strength, Merlinus swings his staff at her, and where it slices through her shape she bleeds green fire and a starry frost that falls to the ground and skitters like clots of voltage across the tiles. A tormented scream squirts from her, the black of her gaping mouth widening wider than her shocked face, swallowing all of her into nothing.

Breath jolts into the wizard's lungs, and he exhales a vehement curse, a magical cry meant to clear the space around him of all threat.

Superhuman screeches cut the darkness of the garden. Peering outside, Merlinus glimpses Ethiops's slithery tonnage blot the stars on his rapid climb into the night. And then silence rolls over him and the floral dreams of the sleeping garden.

The Furor paces the foothills above the City of the Legion. He crouches among the woods like the wind suffering through the trees. There is too much dangerous magic here for him directly to expose himself. The citadel below is an immense magnet, pulling energy into its black stones along force lines in the earth. With catgut cries, the Daoine Síd flit through the clawing grass in the plains outside the city. They appear to the god as flickers of evening flame running through the daystruck grass, so small, he could crush any of them in one fist. But together they are a holocaust, a hornet swarm, a slavering wolf pack, a slashing of blood-frenzied sharks. He stays low in the hills, grinding his teeth, tugging at his beard, pondering the problem like a nervous chess master.

The citadel below is a black egg. Inside, the Dragon's evil spawn spools through its syrups, a monstrous fetus gathering form and strength. By spring, it will hatch and release the abomination, another shape of the Dragon's hunger, intent on feeding the world's serpent with his flesh and the bodies of all the Rovers of the Wild Hunt.

The demon Lailoken is the cause of this. The Furor senses him in the citadel as a smoldering clot of heaven's fire. The god's brain cannot unfreeze his disbelief that Lailoken has actually freed himself from the madness that the storm god once set on him. Painfully, he reminds himself that his victim is, after all, a Dark Dweller, and he regrets not killing him when he had the chance. It is far too late for any direct confrontation, for the demon has found his powers and will be a formidable foe—especially now that the Fire Lords are interfering. With the sword Lightning in their grasp, their intent can only be the arming of a human to murder him. Will it be the demon himself who emerges from this serpent's egg with the sword in his hand?

To answer this question, the Furor has tried to find the Fire Lords. He has trailed the faint shimmer of the sword Lightning's aura across these very hills and dense forests westward to where the stars bend down and enter the earth. His weapon has been taken into the underworld, where the Síd live in dangerous alliance with the Dragon.

Farther yet to the west, on an island in the Scoti Sea known as Avalon, the sword Lightning has risen and lies imprisoned. He can feel it like a cold thread of wind blowing from inside the blind stone of the island itself. It touches him at his heart, where a fateful wound calls to it. The timewind has marked him for death by this sword—unless he keeps his distance.

Not daring approach Avalon directly, the Furor has sent his ravens there to spy for him—but none have come back.

So, he must wait and see what hatches from the black egg when spring comes. An army will spill forth, of that he is certain. They will emerge in the spring, for no commander in his right mind, not even a demon, would leave the sanctuary of the citadel with the winter storms coming.

With the thaw, the time for battle will arrive. The Furor has no doubt the Dark Dweller will be at its heart, driving it with all the fury of his mad mission. And the Æsir god will be ready. This winter, he will take counsel with his own demons, the four he has summoned from the Gulf by the magic of the gods who sleep now on the Raven Branch. For the sake of the sleeping gods who trust him and by the strength of the Dark Dwellers that serve him, he will crush whatever hatches from this black egg.

Morgeu lies on the couch in her chamber, on her side, cheek in palm, her stubborn forehead placid, though her closed eyelids flutter. To walk out of her body requires all the relaxed concentration her mind can lens. One shadow of a crease of tension in the smooth marble of her flesh and her trance will collapse to a dream.

Years of experience have taught her how to slide like starlight out of her sleep and into the waking world, a wraith. Her apparition stands in the garden, gazing up into the night sky, where the stars look like crumbled chunks of light. *Ethiops!* she calls.

Silence sifts through the murmur of a breeze in the shrubbery.

Lailoken's magic is stronger than she had guessed. The demon face in the night that for so long has been sharing its strength with her is gone. Without it, she barely has the clarity to step away from the dark of her body without stumbling and falling to sleep.

Carefully, she propels herself through the blindness of a wall and emerges in a courtyard of tall, straight poplars against the star mist. Merlinus paces among the trees in a wobbly circle, hands clasped behind his back, hoary face upturned, talking to the sky.

Is it Ethiops? she wonders, drawing closer to see whom the old wizard addresses.

Crouching among the hedges, she approaches close enough to stare up through the tree-spires into the well of night. What she sees teeters like a dream. Surging streams of people flow through each other and crisscross on streets congested with metal wagons of many colors, all with black wheels and oozing fumes from underneath. Smoldering air rises among immense glass towers.

Is it hell? The speculation staggers her, and she nearly topples unconscious. To steady herself, she backs away, too eagerly, and finds herself outside the city walls.

Dawn streaks the long mane of the Furor. He hunches on the moors, so far off she can see all of him, a mountain in the east where the land rolls without any other prominence. His one eye glitters like the morning star, and his empty socket tunnels to black infinity.

Morgeu trembles. The imposing sight of the gloomy god sheathed in the gray, amniotic glow of day spins a luminous dread through her—and she wisps away like a fume of dew.

Under the wind sock banner of the dragon, Ambrosius Aurelianus marches his small line of troops from the City of the Legion across the moors and onto the midland plains. Along the way, a meager contingent of Gorlois's forces join up from their camp outside the city. They barely add to the ranks that continue growing very slowly as the *coloniae* make good on their pledges by volunteering a handful of their least desirable soldiers to the foolish Dragon Lord.

Garbed in leather tunic and sporting a short Roman sword, Morgeu rides beside her father at the reins of a sturdy campaign wagon. The ornately paneled vehicle, with its posts of gorgon heads, eagle-embossed sideboards, copper-sheeted canopy of hammered griffins, and large, solid wooden wheels painted with spiral serpents, requires four horses to move, yet Morgeu handles it expertly.

She ignores Merlinus, looking right through him whenever he enters her field of sight. No visible wounds from their clash in the garden are apparent, yet the wizard senses a damaged air to her—a dangerous withdrawal as of a wounded beast compacting its rage. She will not underestimate the spirit reckoner again.

In the presence of Ambrosius, Morgeu appears bright and attentive to the detailed needs of the fighting force, full of practical ideas about order of march, deploying scouts and sentinels, and securing supplies—insights gleaned from a lifetime of accompanying both her father and the fiana in their forays. Ambrosius, experienced in army command by book learning and war room games alone, absorbs her counsel gratefully. And Gorlois, proud of his daughter's military acumen and pleased with the possibility of having an aggressive Roman warlord for a son-in-law, defers to her judgments.

Word of the scantling army travels north and east with the peddlers and itinerant traders. The barbarian raiders, who have roamed at will since the retreat of the legions, seeking rich villas to plunder, cattle to slaughter, landowners and their families to slay and abandon to the wild dogs and wolves, gather gleefully. From the hills, the smoke of their campfires climbs to heaven with barbarian songs glorifying their intent to slaughter this stripling force.

For over fifty years, the Britons have stayed hidden in their walled and staunchly fortified *coloniae*, emerging only sporadically to protect what neighboring farmland they can with swift forays against local bandits. Many of the barbarians have never seen a well-coordinated and -directed advance and believe that these skinny phalanxes of spearmen with their proud banners will be easily dispersed by the Gaels' fierce and rampant attacks.

But Ambrosius, who has lived his whole life for this event and who has soberly predicted that the pledges given a stable master by the British nobility are hollow, gloats over the terrible surprise he has prepared for his enemies. During his six months as military commander in the City of the Legion, he has spent most of his time training his handpicked cadre of cavalry to abandon their swords and to use heavy oaken bows, forcing them to shoot moving targets while riding. To mark this squad as his own, he has issued them distinctive black leather armor, the ebony cuirasses embossed with the dragon emblem of the Aurelianus clan. Every day since then, he has strained his imagination to visualize the battles to come in which he will ride with these men—his men—in all deviations of weather and terrain.

Then, a month before the campaign began, he replaced the cumbersome weapons with lightweight Persian bows that were the standard in the old Roman cavalry of his Sarmatian ancestors. The Persian weapon—a composite bow, made of alternating layers of wood, hide, and horn—possesses the utmost flexibility. Long and wickedly curved in the oriental manner, the exceedingly long draw of the string releases so powerfully that the steel-tipped arrows can pierce armor—if the barbarians possessed any.

When the gathered host of Gaels dash out of the woods and hills on foot to massacre the scrawny squad of British warriors they have trapped in the open, the cavalry fans out. Ambrosius himself leads the diffuse attack, and Theo and Merlinus watch from horseback among the nervous troops as the mounted bowmen fly back and forth before the charging, howling barbarians, releasing their volleys with crisp and deadly accuracy. Gorlois stands atop his campaign carriage with his fiery-haired daughter at his side, both watching agog as the ferocious raiders topple in the distance like so many dead leaves.

Not a single Northman closes within sword's length of the spry horses, and in minutes, the field lies dark with blood and arrow-bristled corpses. The stunned barbarians, prepared to face a few arrows but not anything like the missiles that whistle with the noise of the north wind and cut them down so far from their enemies, flail with berserk rage and keep advancing, too proud to turn and flee. The cavalry, to the ecstatic cheers of the relieved troops, circle the enraged warriors and kill them from all sides, sparing none.

With the slaughter finished, the Dragon Lord dispatches the laughing troops to retrieve the arrows and plunder the dead of useful weapons. Ambrosius returns triumphantly to the head of his army, and, thus fortified, the war party continues marching east.

Thrice more on that journey, blood-crazed gangs of Jutes, Angles, and Picts attack, but only their menacing cries reach the caravan. The fleet cavalry, with its powerful oriental bows, cuts down the enemy as they appear. A careful tactician, Ambrosius leads his troops along the river plains, as he has foretold, away from the woods and out in the open where the barbarians have to expose themselves to attack.

With each new town that the war party passes through, eager soldiers swell their ranks, glad at long last to count themselves among the victors. Aquae Sulis, Corinium, Cunetio, Spinae, Calleva Atrebatum, Durocobrivae, and Verulamium: all pour forth their fighting men at the dragon banner's victorious approach. And much of this advance is in winter, a time when men are loath to leave the warm shelter of their cities.

That, too, is part of Ambrosius's strategy. The barbarian hordes have nowhere to hide in the snowy landscape. When the blizzards rage, the Dragon Lord retreats to the nearest walled *colonia*, and as the skies clear, they march again, always tracking down the larger barbarian tribes and butchering them in the sparkling forest clearings where they huddle. The work is slow and tedious—but the killing is great.

Weary of death, Theodosius Aurelianus sits astride the highest plank on the scaffold of the campaign wagon. Limp and loose-jointed, he leans against the banner pole that bears the standard: The Draco wind sock, inscribed all in scales scarlet and jet, thrashes in a north wind out of a gray sky. It moans low, at the bottom of hearing, full of the unhappiness of the dead.

From the scaffold's vantage, Theo oversees the late afternoon, the day's sweep of shadows congesting in the colorless forest while the overcast sun dips toward a river dull as lead slag. Apart from the sentinels huddled in their furs building tonight's bonfires at the camp's perimeter, the snow-blotched riverbanks are empty. Smoke from the troops in their tents threads tendrils of aromatic vapors—toasty cornmeal and seared goat meat.

Amber eyes sunk in their sockets, the flesh around them eroded with shadow, Theo watches Merlinus emerge from his tent and pull the cowl of his mantle over his gray locks. He moves spryly across the hoof-stamped earth, not like an old man at all.

But, of course, Theo has known that the hooded figure approaching him is neither old nor a man. He seems to have known this for a long time, though it is only three weeks since the wizard rose from his sickbed. Watching him ascend the scaffold ladders, one would never think he had been wounded at all: He floats up the rungs and glides along the plank, black robe enlarged with wind, like a bat big with evil.

"You summoned me, *quaestor?*" Merlinus says, settling close to Theo. For weeks, he has been reading the script of sorrow in the deepening lines of Theo's face. Heartflow enthusiasm works on the lad only in the presence of the wizard. But now Merlinus withholds that fluid ease. He has waited patiently for Theo to summon him, to speak his soul, and he does not want to distort the man's truth. He pulls his etheric field tighter about himself, compacting it to a miniscule, enshrined attentiveness, so concentrated within his mortal pith that his face becomes a mask.

Theo's murky eyes focus on the bone-hollows and crepe flesh of the hooded visage before him, and he sees the humanity there. "You are not all devil, are you?"

"I am the man God made me."

Theo levels his stare, authoritatively. "Do you dream?"

"Of course." His eyes slim in their caves. "I dream of Optima. And the angels that visited her. Sometimes, I dream of the Furor."

"The god of the Gaels. That must be frightening."

"Oh, yes."

The genuine fear in Merlinus's voice emboldens Theo to admit, "I have been having frightening dreams, too."

"The serpent man."

"Yes—" The murkiness in Theo's eyes drains away. "The serpent man. He comes out of the ground, in moldy old-fashioned armor—"

"And he has your eyes."

"Yes." Theo's face jerks as his mind skids on a new suspicion: "Is this *your* magic, Merlinus? Have you put these dreams in my sleep?"

"No. I have not touched your dreams. This is someone else."

Theo looks away, toward the metallic river, to ponder this. "You are right. I've had these dreams long before I met you." He pauses. "Then I know who it must be. An ancestral shade."

"More than that. If what I have seen of this visitant proves true, he is a magus. He has mastered some means of drawing power from the Dragon, the immense sentience within the fiery earth."

Theo whirls a frightened stare back toward the wizard. "Satan?"

Merlinus chews the corner of his mustache and considers this. "Perhaps Satan is the Dragon. It circulates within the earth."

The alarm in Theo's wrung face relaxes suddenly and he cocks his head suspiciously. "Is this another of your fantasies, Merlinus—as when you wanted me to believe the earth is a sphere spinning in the void? Remember, how silly you got trying to convince me the earth is *whirling* around the sun?" He laughs dismally at the surprised sound of his own voice. "You actually expected me to abandon my senses, ignore the very truths God has set before my eyes, and believe your silliness. Does it amuse you to tell us ludicrous stories because we are such gullible children before your magic?"

Merlinus denies this with a vigorous shake of his head, opening his cowl to the stiff wind so that his beard fluffs out and his gnarly hand must restrain it. "The Dragon is real, Theo. It lives in the earth full of luminous strength, and it eats whatever it can catch. But we can also eat from it. It's not made of bone and flesh but of an essence more pure than fire—a sinuous kind of light. I think your ancestor learned how to draw on that light, how to feed on the blood of the Dragon."

"And the dreams?"

Tilting confidentially closer, Merlinus says, "For centuries, he has thrived in the loamy crust of the earth. For *centuries*, Theo. Think on it. He is not quite human anymore. One cannot touch the Dragon without being touched. It changes people. Not just their bodies—which turn into a sticky kind of light, a plasm with its own peculiar nature that no longer needs sustenance or even air—but the Dragon's blood changes their minds, as well. It opens them to the long horizons between moments. Years pass as days there."

"How do you know this?"

The man's frightened air demands the truth, and Merlin confides, "I am very old, indeed. I know something of time and phantoms, and I tell you that the ghost of your forefather is disappearing into the gap between the moments. He must find his way back into time through his seed."

"The dragon mark on my back, that's his mark." Theo gazes abstractly into the slate sky, recalling the ghost stories of the Sarmatian dragon lord that Ambrosius said their father used to tell him. Family tradition claimed that these tales of vampyres, lamia, and werebeasts came from their family's first legionnaire, an adventurer named Wray Vitki. Reflecting on that now, Theo recalls learning from a scholar, a fellow guest at one of the many *mansios* he visited in his Armorican youth, that the Slavic word *vitki* means magician.

"Your ancestor gathers the will to hold the moments together only when he is summoned by the need of his family," Merlinus informs him. "When he rises out of the ground, the net of your blood catches him out of the air and you dream of him."

"He rises from the earth now because of Ambrosius's war. Grandfather Vitki wants to help us avenge Father's death. But he should not come to me. He should go to my brother." Self-pity blurs the young man's features for a moment. "When first we met, you told me that no one is saved. Yet this ancestor—this magus, Grandfather Vitki from the old stories, he comes to save us. What troubles my heart is that he comes to me when it is Ambrosius who needs him." His face fogs toward tears. "The Dragon has sent his magus to the wrong man. Merlinus—I am a coward."

The impassioned inwardness of this confession troubles Merlinus. "All wise men are cowards."

Theo nods heartlessly.

"Violence takes us out of ourselves," Merlinus tells him. "The killing frenzy of battle is a possession, a bestial overshadowing. It is wise to fear this. Those who do not are themselves possessed. Fear them, fear them all."

"I don't want to kill," Theo affirms in a fragile, freighted voice. "So, why does Wray Vitki come to me?"

"You need him. Perhaps not to kill but to protect."

That word seizes Theo's attention, and he looks up. "Yes—to protect." The priest in him understands this impulse. "Merlinus, I am tired of the killing. I want the Gaels to go away and leave us in peace. We should be trading together, not fighting."

Merlinus squints with disbelief. "You must truly be exhausted to have forgotten where we are in history. Remember the Huns? Uncle Attila? The Gaels have lost their lands."

Theo rises, stands feet apart, arms crossed against the

northern blow, and scans the ragged forest, the raiders' wide sanctuary. "We need Rome."

Merlinus stays seated on the plank, hands cupping themselves in his lap, pleased that he has attained this rapport without magic. "We need the authority of the sword. Yes. It is a grievous truth, yet nonetheless true."

"How can the magus help us? What can Wray Vitki do?"

Merlinus does not know and makes no effort to hide his uncertainty, his voice musing. "He is old now. He has served your family since before Jesus suffered. Soon, he will die, and all the power he has used to build his body of light will be devoured by the Dragon. I think he intends to give all he has left of himself to help you help your brother."

Theo turns and gives the wizard a careful look. "Tell me, wizard, will there ever be a time without war?"

"Is that a riddle?"

Theo looks disappointed, and the corrosive shadows darken under his eyes. "Then you say that war is inevitable?"

Merlinus stands and speaks in a tone of revelation. "I say that war is like a strong river that sweeps men away. Too wide for a bridge, far too furious for any boat. So, you tell me, will there ever be a time when one can walk across such a river?"

"You're not making sense."

"No truth in making sense."

Theo shakes his head. "I'm too tired for riddles."

"Then, I will tell you directly." The sorcerer speaks with generous candor. "There *is* a time when one can cross even the raging river by foot. In winter. Fear not the dark time and the cold, Theo, for they have their blessings—if you know how to receive them."

"I am tired, Merlinus."

"Then come back to your tent and sleep," the old soul says, draping his robed arm around the young *quaestor* and guiding him toward the scaffold ladder. "Tomorrow the river carries us to the next battle."

Spring finds the Dragon Lord's army, as Ambrosius has foretold, marching in great numbers beside the foggy slither of the Tamesis River. The mercenary Saxons, on missions far to the north, offer no resistance. Vortigern, unable to prevent the advance of his enemy, has locked himself away in his fortress on the south bank with the handful of troops still loyal to him.

The earth around Londinium has gone mad in the gentle rains. Crocuses lie scattered like bright rags on the green rug of the planet. Deer pronk right across camp. Hare scuttle after each other through the tents. Life sings in the high halls of the forest. And Ambrosius brings death to Vortigern.

From just outside the range of Balbus Gaius Cocceius's archers, Ambrosius's Persian bow fires one flame-tipped arrow after another into the timbers of the fortress. The Dragon Lord bellows for Cocceius to leave his poisons behind, come out, and fight Aurelianus hand to hand. Vortigern cowers in his fort, and the flames eat the dead wood.

Black smoke crawls across the belly of the sky, and the pylon gates swing wide. The troops fleeing the flames fall before wind-screaming volleys of arrows. As the fortress ignites into a massive pyre, Ambrosius charges in and out of the smoke, shouting taunts and victory songs, shooting vengeful arrows into the wind-whipped holocaust.

Long after the walls have collapsed into a spark-whirling vortex and then a smoldering unrecognizable heap, Ambrosius rides, chanting hoarsely through the ash fumes of his dead enemy. And his hate, and all the lands of pain he has crossed to fulfill it, climb blackly into the soaring landscapes of the spring sky.

Lailoken squats in the tall grass by the river. The pyre smoke of Vortigern's citadel casts a twilight pall that gleams with the jubilant music and laughter of the victors. He cannot bear to look into their faces. They are so happy, they look wicked.

So, he has fled to here, wanting the switching grass and lapping river to soothe the pain he feels in the army's laughter. Their happy cries remind him too sharply of his former life as a demon.

At last, he kneels in the mud, crosses himself, and begins to speak underbreath and rapidly. He talks to feel the source in himself, to address the force that pulls the atoms of him together and that has compelled all his demonic powers and knowledge into a single human event. He talks to hear himself.

"By the reckoning of our time, my mortal story begins in the year of our Lord 422 atop the highlands of Cos. Three thousand years earlier, I had first come to earth and enjoyed a great deal of success devastating the large human settlements in Mesopotamia and Ægypt. I found it easy to use the avarice of mortals against themselves and was confident that in short order the abomination called civilization would be undone.

"I commuted from Rome to the frontiers, flush with the victory I and my allies had helped fulfill through Alaric the Goth when he sacked the so-called Eternal City. The Roman Empire satisfactorily gutted, we demons reveled in the ensuing chaos of Attila and his Huns. Frankly, though, I was somewhat saddened by all that. The Romans had been such a useful tool in tormenting others. But the angels had gone too far lately in employing them to spread a new religion of love, peace, and self-sacrifice. We demons couldn't stomach that. So we withdrew our support of the Romans' harsh dominion and abetted their destruction.

"My mission during and after the fall of Rome was to travel north and harry the last garrison outposts. I delighted in this. The Romans, Christian for the past hundred years, had abandoned their old priapic gods and nurturing goddesses and become fearful of lascivious spirits and bestial demons. Ha! Their fear made it all the easier for me to manipulate them. I particularly enjoyed seeking out female eremites, religious recluses, nuns whom I tortured with sexual fantasies and night terrors until they went mad and killed themselves or others. My comrades and I had perfected our technique so well in prior times that mortals even had a name for the horror that this torment was to them. They personified the experience and called it—incubus.

"The steep kingdom of Cos consisted of ancient mountains that had folded onto themselves aeons before and eroded over the ages to a maze of jumbled hillocks and densely forested granite corridors. In a highland meadow overbrinking this primeval labyrinth, I came upon a reclusive nun, a whilom princess of Cos, who fancied herself a holy woman. Ha! And double-Ha! She was homely as a stick, not quite ugly but very plain, with something of a weasel's mien to her sharp features, and with my typical cynicism I figured this alone was the inspiration for her professed saintliness. Employing my typical aggressiveness, I forced myself upon her like a brusque wind howling down a dim road.

"Let me help you see this more clearly, for what follows is the key to this whole story. This nun, whose name was Optima, lived entirely alone in a small round hut of wattle and daub. A hearth of rude stones occupied the center of the hovel, and washpots hung on the wall above the firewood. The floor of stamped earth, warty with embedded gravel, had no covering, not even reeds, and the bed, a pallet of straw-stuffed ticking, lay swayback beside a splintered stool and rickety table. Above a lopsided window, a crucifix watched as I kicked open the slat door and gushed into the cramped, tenebrous interior.

"I found her at prayer, kneeling before a puny, ridiculous altar of green riverstones. My windy presence snuffed the wan flame of hazelnut oil aflicker in the votive bowl and shoved her forward over the ankle-high stones. Her dun-colored hempen gown flew up about her hips as she sprawled forward with the force of my assault. As a frosty wind, I jammed myself against her genitals, intent on eliciting shock and outrage. Ha!

"But *I* was the one shocked. From her pudendum, an irresistible force gripped me, a terrible, fervid magnetism that seized me with a searing pain and pulled me hard and fast into the hot, dark, liquid depths of her living body. Wah!

"Nothing like this had never happened to me before, not on a hundred other worlds. Always in the past, I flogged the flesh from outside, icily titillating nipples and clitoris, goose-bumping hackles and wind-laughing across ear wells. In truth, I merely used my power to manipulate small energy patterns—the brain waves of my victims—inspiring hallucinations. That had always been sufficient in the past to destroy my prey. Never before had I been *inside* a human body.

"Usually, my mischief stood like leaden darkness atop the breastbone, tendrils of force probing fright-dilated nostrils, reaching through moan-humming sinuses to touch the quivering brain and chill it with my telepathic nightmares, my force-induced fantasies of salacious terror.

"Not this time. Some grotesque might had gripped me and hauled me with irreversible anguish into a blacker depth than I had ever known. That incredible strength tied me stunned and throbbing to the darkness. I thrashed, I buckled. But there was no loosening the agonized clench, the stabbing grip that fixed me, clutched me, nailed me to itself.

"What had happened? My imagination, old as time itself, balked. *She is only a woman*, I told myself. *A mortal. I can escape her.*

"I struggled until I was emptied of all strength, of all light, and I had become the very darkness that imprisoned me. For a long time, I woozed dumbly in the trance of my helplessness, listening to the muffled tread of Optima's heart and the hum of blood in her veins. Slowly, like a creaking oak giving up its leaves, I began to realize what had happened to me.

"At first, I couldn't believe it, and I lay in the blaze of the blood-dark, stupid with my disbelief. Only eventually did I face and accept the ineluctable truth. I had found Her. Or, rather, She had found me.

"After billions of years of despair, after light-years, light-centuries, light-millennia of wandering, believing She had fled from us forever, here She was! Wah-ha-ha! The laughter of my joy broke all my time-old grief and sheared away the whole gruesome dream of my history. I was with Her again! The single point of my being, the monad that is me, was one and the same with Her presence. Once again, we were one.

"This Optima, this homely weasel of a woman, only appeared mortal, her mortality a camouflage for the house of God Herself. It had come to this: I had found God in the place where I had least expected to find Her. In the dark of a life-form I despised, in the undergroin flesh-heat, in the muddy blood-tangle and sodden tissues and jellies and greasy depth of life—in that ugliness I had striven so ferociously to destroy—I found Her at last.

"Here, in the bonecave, in the time-coffin, in the dark nightmare, Her love broke itself so tenderly toward me. She remembered me well. She recalled our wholeness together time before time, when we dwelled all at one point with Her. I was Her favorite again, as I had been before, as we all are when we are with Her.

"Though I had murdered the world, though I had fathered woe on many worlds, though I was everything that is wrong with creation, She forgave me. She forgave me, because all the terror of my rampage I had wrought for want of Her. The triumph of our reunion redeemed every suffering. And Her love broke tenderly through me, into all my darkness. She seized me with a will to love forever, and all the unaccomplished hope of the angels fulfilled itself in me then and there. I was whole again. I was in heaven.

"I entered mortal life as a huge, ugly baby. Knobby-boned, my cinereal gray skin blister-patched in livid pink and scabrous swatches like a radiation victim. And I was hairy: tufty fur matted my long skull, and my sunken face gazed about in horror from within a bristly beard white as frost. To any unprejudiced eye, I wasn't a baby at all. I was an old, old man, the most ancient of days, collapsed around myself to a helpless, gristled, shrunken mass of whiskers and friable bones.

"Any other mother would have shrieked at the sight of me and mercifully dropped me in a well. But Optima, as we know, was no ordinary mortal. She suckled me on her skinny teats, and though I felt weary enough to die, I survived. With each breath, my life threatened to slide out of me—and that would have been fine with me.

"The most despairing loneliness I had ever known glowed from my marrows. Worse than the desolation I'd experienced when I was first ejected from heaven in the Big Bang, for then I was with the others. But here in my mortal guise, I was truly and finally alone, locked inside my creaking bones and crepitant flesh with only the boom of my terrified heart for company.

"Being human is the most terrible loneliness in the universe. As a demon, I roamed free of most physical limits, at liberty to come and go as I pleased, flitting among worlds. Well, not exactly flitting. Journeys through eternal night and everlasting cold require a furious will, but time has a different meaning for spirits. As a man, frail as a wispy gnat, time has a lunatic regularity—breath by breath, the heart beating its mindless tattoo, the blood scramming through its loops, whispering its inklings of mortality in the inmost ear, forcing us to listen to its rasp, a sibilance not unlike sand hissing from the upper bell of the hourglass.

"How do people stand it?

"I, at least, had the memory of my time inside Optima in the embrace of God's timeless love. Her absence inflicted a woe not nearly so bad as when we first lost Her—for now I knew, I actually *knew*, She was out here in the vacuum with us. She was as miserable in Her grief as we. And, best of all, She loved us still.

She had forgiven me my insane rage—and, wonderfully, that fury had vanished entirely by the very grace of having found Her again, even though it had only been for that short spell.

"All the memories of my existence as a demon found their places inside my human skull, and I remembered everything of my former life. That mitigated my fright somewhat. But it subjected me to an insufferable claustrophobia. Skull-locked, I felt smothered. Colors looked scrawny and fewer of them painted the world. Sounds came to me muffled, filtered through layers of woolly distance. All my sensations returned to me vitiated. And my telepathy did not return at all.

"I cried aloud from inside my thick horror. Wa-a-a-ah-h!

"And I prayed. Fervently, I prayed—*Oh God, take me out of this living corpse. Kill me that I may live again as a spirit. My malice is spent. I swear, I will undo what evil I have done. I will further life and all its wondrous complexity. Please—please! Return me to my spirit self.*

"But God said nothing. She was gone. And for one instant, I doubted my memory of Her. Sick at heart, I wondered if I had hallucinated the whole intrauterine experience of Her.

"And then, Optima began to sing. With a voice as mellifluous as heaven's nostalgia, she sang of her love for me. She sang of the small birds, the tiniest of birds, who are strong enough to bear up spring and carry the warm days with them from the south. She rocked my shriveled body in her skinny arms, and she sang of the inner mountains of the soul that each of us climbs to find our way to heaven. She sang of the weariness of river rocks and the lovesickness of cats in back alleys and the tenderness of sea cows for their calves.

"My doubt passed wholly away, because I could hear Her in Optima's voice. Despite the thrump of my suffering heart and the rasp of my reluctant lungs, I heard Her love breaking softly through Optima's voice, and I calmed down. I calmed down and sucked on her milk-heavy teats, and I grew strong on her love.

"Before long, I found the strength to sit up on my own. I was still too weak to speak, but I had won the vantage to look about and appraise my environment. From inside this body, the world looked very different to me than the way it had appeared when I was a spirit. Shadows seemed to have more substance and physical objects had a smaller, more dense aspect. The more I stared, the thicker my claustrophobia grew, until I had to shut my eyes and simply bear the dread of the blood-hissing dark.

"Gradually, I grew accustomed to my captivity, and I took to watching Optima from the root-cove under the oak where she placed me when she went to the creek to wash our few clothes. I stared at the world. It had a narrow beauty that I began to appreciate. The high meadow where we lived thrived with tall silvery green grasses glistening like fur in the wind. Below, the brown thread of the creek disappeared into a black-green forest of massive interlocking trees where muscular red elk came and went.

"In the morning, reefs of mist obscured the lower ridges and hills. But by noon, one could see the numerous valleys and hollows that undulated among the emerald crags. Large clouds towered in the blue vault of the sky and trawled their shadows over a muddled mosaic of dales and glades.

"On distant hills, a bleary outline of thatched roofs serrated the horizon. Just visible at the far side of the wild terrain, huts of a thorp thronged together. From down there, peasants climbed, visiting now and then to leave offerings to the holy woman of the high meadow. We could see them coming from afar, and Optima always carefully hid me in her hovel before they arrived. Throughout her pregnancy, she had managed to keep her condition secret, and though her labor had been grotesquely difficult, she had birthed me with help only from the angels.

"Oh, yes, the angels visited her daily. I saw them as clearly as I did when I was a spirit myself. Tattered in fire and with their huge, luminous, unblinking eyes, they attended her twice each day, at dusk, when she knelt before her tiny altar of green river-stones and prayed. They ignored me entirely, and try as I might, I could never quite hear what they said to her. Maybe they just shared her prayers. Their voices sounded like glass chimes in a languid breeze.

"Sometimes, at the high end of the meadow, near the stand of copper beeches where she enjoyed praying outdoors, the unicorn came to her. Silver-hooved and blue as moonlight, the silken-muscled creature with its perilous beauty appeared in lustrous silence. It bowed its knurled horn to the ground and waited patiently while Optima prayed. The harping of the breeze invariably quieted in its presence. Then, Optima would cross herself, sit back among the asters and cinquefoils, and the unicorn would approach with majestic slowness and rest its velvet muzzle in her lap.

"The green glass of its eyes watched her serenely, and at that placid moment I could touch it, too. The gauzy flutterings of its hide hummed through my fingertips like low voltage. Strangely, my touch rippled along its length as though I had disturbed a surface of shining water, and deep in my brain a blossom opened with a fragrance that smelled of heaven.

"Always, its departure filled me with an echo of the inconsolable sorrow I had suffered in the void. After those first few times, I wouldn't touch the unicorn again, no matter Optima's coaxing. Watching it depart through the mesh of the woods, bright as a chunk of the moon wrenched out of the sky, I felt the flame of my body heat rising off my flesh and adding its fire to hell's, as if the demon I am is all I could ever be."

The Saxons, displeased with the demise of their generous patron, swoop down from the north and out of their island encampments to the south with a vicious fury. As they assemble their massive war party outside Londinium, Ambrosius, his revenge fulfilled, secludes himself in the opulent governor's palace and, much to his brother's chagrin and Morgeu's irate despair, drinks opium-laced wine and sports with young women day and night.

He has lost his will after killing Vortigern. That was the goal of his life, and now that he has accomplished it, his fate is complete. In the war room, he has no intensity or focus and soon he no longer appears in council.

Theo has no stomach for military adventures or their spoils and leaves daily command of the army to Gorlois while he strives with Morgeu to break the spell of his brother's debauchery. All to no avail. Ambrosius ignores his brother, and when he drunkenly paws at Morgeu, she angrily withdraws and locks herself in her wing of the palace. By then, her magic reveals to her what Merlinus already knows: that proud Ambrosius would never be hers, for he has already married death.

Deprived of the tactical cunning and lethal intuition of his daughter, Gorlois squanders the army's resources on flamboyant attacks against the Saxons that, while victorious, cost unnecessary lives. Within a few weeks of their greatest victory, the army begins to break up.

Merlinus stays in his corner of the palace, afraid to walk the streets of Londinium. Afraid because he spies the enormous figure of the Furor striding the horizon, wearing fog for a beard and the ocean stars in his wild hair. By his presence, the wizard knows that the Britons are ultimately doomed if they stay in the old capital. He urges Theo to abandon his brother, take the greater bulk of the troops, and retreat west. But, of course, Theo would never leave his brother's side.

As Merlinus's admonitions against the Dragon Lord grow more insistent, Ambrosius stops speaking with him. Even then, Merlinus is afraid to use the full force of his magic on him. If he does, he knows the Furor will hear of it. So, the wizard waits in his chambers and peeks through the draperies at the giant of war wading in the river.

The waiting ends at midsummer, when the Saxons, having whittled the British army down to archers and a small phalanx of infantry, array themselves outside the city wall. Their chief, Hengist, a square, horn-crowned warrior, sends the message that unless he is paid his tribute of gold in full, he will ally with the Gaels, with the very tribes he was hired by Balbus Gaius Cocceius to fight.

That treachery breaks Ambrosius's dissolute spell, and aroused suddenly to action, the Dragon Lord insists on leading a raid against Hengist's camp.

In the pink marble throne room, with the statues of emperors watching mutely from among the billowy masses of silk draperies, Merlinus witnesses the loud arguments between Ambrosius and Theo. With fearful precognition, the wizard recognizes that this, too, is necessary. Every hurtful word flung between the brothers has been precut in the crystal of time. Ambrosius is a lost man in a lost world. Nothing can save him. And yet—

Theo's tearful appeal to Merlinus to stop Ambrosius, after his own desperately angry attempts have failed, forces him to use magic.

He speaks sleep to the guards outside the Dragon Lord's palace suite and barges in on Ambrosius as he is donning his armor. "Blow away, you old fart!" he commands. "There's killing to be done. I've no time for your philosophical prattle."

Merlinus warns him outright, "All your time will be spent if you leave the palace today."

"Are you cursing me, then?" he asks mockingly, and reaches for his sword.

"Use it," Merlinus demands, pointing to his weapon. "Kill me if you must—but my warning remains."

He lowers the sword and scowls at the wizard. "How did you get in here anyway?" He waves that question aside. "Never mind. Don't answer that. I don't want to know." He sheathes his sword and tightens the straps of his buckler.

"Look, I have long been aware you're some kind of demon-fathered man. I know it was you who found the gold for us. Without you, we wouldn't be here now. So, you feel you have some part in what is happening. But you don't. Something larger owns my fate now. And by that I know my time is up. I know it."

Merlinus must make an effort to close his mouth. "You *want* to die?"

"Hah. Want. I wouldn't say that, old man. I don't want to die. But I'm going to die. I feel it. It's a palpable feeling—like hunger, or thirst. I've felt it since I killed Cocceius. My time is done."

"Not true," Merlinus says, though his words sound hollow.

Ambrosius just smiles, cold and mirthless. As he passes the wizard, he puts a hand on his shoulder and says quietly, "Thank you, old man—whoever you are."

Merlinus says no more, and Ambrosius passes from the room like a shade. The wizard follows him into the corridor and wakes the guards, and together they accompany him to the courtyard, where he rallies his troops.

Even Theo sees that it is hopeless to try dissuading him, and he runs to get his armor. Gorlois takes up the dragon banner and rides with Ambrosius at the head of the war party. By the time Theo charges out of the gate, the archers are already firing into Hengist's camp.

Saxons swarm from their hide-covered tents, hefting large leather shields to catch the arrows as they run. Merlinus climbs the city wall to watch from the vantage of the battlements, and he reaches the ramparts facing the enemy camp as the somber figures clash.

Morgeu is already there, her pale face bright with attentiveness, her fists clenched. "Come back!" she shouts as her father circles to the rear of the troops to bring up the pikemen. "Come back!"

Gorlois raises the dragon banner in acknowledgment, his

expression unreadable behind his bronze mask. Arm extended in Roman salute, he canters back into the battle.

"Ambrosius is mad!" Morgeu calls. She looks at Merlinus with a sharp, glittery fear in her eyes. "Stop him!"

"I can't stop the Dragon Lord," he says, twisting his beard nervously.

"Not the Dragon Lord, you fool! Stop my father. You have the chanting power. Make him come back to me."

Merlinus faces her delirious, shrill stare, afraid. If he stops Gorlois, he might endanger Theo. What power the wizard might have, he must reserve for protecting Theo. He shakes his head solemnly.

"You monster!" She turns her wrathful face toward the battlefield and begins singing a slithery spell. But there is no power behind it, just fright, and soon her voice dims away as the tragedy meshing below enraptures her with its horror.

The mounted British archers slay a score of armor-clad Saxons for every one of their number whose horse is hacked out from under him, the knives of the enemy cutting greedily into groin and face. The infantry fling their spears and charge in a menacing wedge that scatters the Saxons and opens a highway of death into the heart of their camp.

The Dragon Lord and his guard fly down that bloody path, and Gorlois and his soldiers beat back the closing flanks as long as they can. But, regardless of Morgeu's fears, Gorlois has no intention of sacrificing himself for anyone, and when Saxon reinforcements charge from the woods above the river, he waves his crimson sword, ordering a retreat.

Ambrosius pays him no heed and flings his steed into the wall of warriors surrounding their leader. Arrows spent, his sword gleaming in the summer sun, he swoops down and comes up with Hengist's head spinning blood.

Theo gallops toward him, riding as Merlinus has never seen him ride, holding on with legs alone as he fires missiles into a crowd swarming with murderous frenzy around his brother. As he charges past Gorlois and his men, he screams for them to follow. Even from their distance, Morgeu and the wizard can see the dark anger on his face at Gorlois's retreat.

Inspired by Theo's mad attack, many of Gorlois's men and the other troops who have fallen back rally and charge again. But not Gorlois. Coolly, he watches Theo bounding over the dead bodies, trampling corpses, firing the last of his arrows into the swirling throng of yowling Saxons. Their yells slash across the warm river breeze like strokes of crude paints, staining the air with the savage brilliance of death.

Then the Dragon Lord's horse goes down under him, and he vanishes in the seething mass of barbarians. The ravenous ghoul-cries of the Saxons change pitch, and the rag-body of Ambrosius rises up on their spears. Their howlings break again into angry, shrill squalls as Theo and his men hack into their flank.

Merlinus begins chanting. Sighting along the length of his staff, he thinks he sees the raspy glimmer of scales in the speed-blur behind Theo. *The dragon-magus!* He calls out a magical spell, and then he does see it.

Luminously ruffled like the aurora borealis, its fiery, pleated flesh shimmering in a thermal surge, Wray Vitki, the man-become-dragon, rises behind Theo, huge as an avalanche and invisible to all eyes but the wizard's—and the Furor's.

The giant god astride the muddy dregs of the horizon raises his hammerhead fists, his one eye screwed tight with wrath, yet even he stands impuissant before the fatefulness of the moment.

Sulfur yellow eyes ablaze like shards of the sun, the dragon envelops Theo in the electric tangles of its body, and together they advance. The lightning of its talons slashes, the flameblow of its tail whips, and the furnace blast from its terrible jaws slavers with all the combined intensity of a small Vesuvius.

A wounded beast, the Saxon army thrashes before the overwhelming ferocity of the dragon, and Ambrosius's body disappears in the melee. Theo bolts directly into the midst of the riot. Handling his horse with demonic intelligence, he hops in flying leaps among the knots of struggling foot soldiers, hewing at the barbarians, then rearing back and striking with flashing forehooves before curvetting sideways and plunging headlong into the fray from behind the enemy. In that way, he chops the Saxon force into small, isolated pieces.

Once Gorlois sees that the battle has turned, he musters the rest of his men with valiant cries.

"No!" Morgeu bawls.

The duke hears her and salutes again, rearing his horse back to drive his men on.

"No!" Morgeu screams. "It's magic! Sorcery! Retreat!"

But Gorlois burns with determination to lead the decisive charge that will break the Saxons' threat. He will not be outdone by a stable master in armor. Dragon banner tilted like a lance, he charges into the flailing mob.

If he could see the dragon-magus, he would swerve his attack to come in behind it, adding its force to his assault. Instead, unaware of its behemoth presence, he rides aslant its fire-blown flank and directly into the scramming frenzy of the barbarians. It is a good tactical choice but ignorant of the supernatural power surrounding him. A panicky Saxon flings his ax wildly, and the somersaulting weapon whirls out of the churning dust and strikes Gorlois's horse between the eyes.

Flung violently forward, the duke crashes to the ground before the fleeing barbarians like a brutal gift from the Furor. Knives saw through the joints of his armor, and Gorlois's limbs and head fly in separate directions before his infuriated men descend on his killers.

Morgeu wails and flings herself at Merlinus. "You! You killed him!"

Reflexively, Merlinus sweeps his staff between them, and she flies backward and crashes against the stone parapet far more violently than he intended. Ugly with rage, she glares at him through a purple vehemence. "Demon!" she calls, clutching at the air with spasming hands, trying to rend the very sight of him. "Kill me! Kill me now!" She comes forward on her knees, clawing at empty space. "Kill me now! Or I swear by the Mother of God, I will kill you!"

The wizard points his staff at her, arm quivering. He only means to ward her off, but she thinks he intends to strike her dead with magic. She flings her arms out and her head back, eager to die. And when the blow does not come, she jerks upright, a grueling malice on her twisted features. "They cut him in pieces!" she screams.

Before her implacable violence, Merlinus cannot speak. He gazes at her, stricken—and she staggers backward, seething, retching for breath. She looks about to convulse. Instead, she curses him in a thwacking voice, "Damn—you—to hell—Lailoken!"

She flees down the battlement ramp and disappears through a bartizan doorway, her charred screams echoing after her.

On the battlefield, the repulse of the Saxons breaks into a rout. The mounted soldiers chase down the banks of the brown river and up the green rolling slopes into the enemy camps. The rest is no more than murder, and Merlinus averts his gaze to the horizon.

The Furor stands there, a mighty shadowshape in the thunderheads that bulk above the shining estuary of the Tamesis. The wails of his slaughtered minions flit about him. Yet even so, the deaths of the Dragon Lord and his duke please this spirit of war.

Merlinus can tell, for the Furor smiles in his direction, the fathoms of darkness in his empty eye filling the wizard with a cold despair for all the world of God.

That night, a comet appears among the silent clamoring of the stars. The long, thin green feather of light shines like an eerie ghost banner above the smoldering bonfires that illuminate the graves where the Dragon Lord and his fallen lie. Bishops shake censers and murmur prayers from the scaffolds erected under the city wall. A high mass solemnly enacts the passion and resurrection, and choirs sing monodic liturgical threnodies above the city crowds that fill the fields.

From the stately marble heights of the governor's palace, Theo and the military commanders watch the sacred ceremonies honoring the passage of Ambrosius Aurelianus and his warriors to heaven. At the conclusion of the majestic rites, the people file past the central bonfire, light torches from the flames, and march mournfully back into the city, bearing with them the light that last shone on their hero.

For a long time after the citizens have returned behind the city's wall, Theo stands at the balcony rail gazing down into the throbbing crimson glow of the dying fire. Despite the avid protection of Wray Vitki's dragon, he has been wounded, his left shoulder gouged by a boar spear. Cauterized and bound, the wound pulses painfully, yet he stands unmoving.

The commanders, all of them exhausted, many wounded as badly or worse than he, remain at his side—good Romans, indifferent to pain, alert to suffering. Merlinus knows they wait for some acknowledgment from Theo, and he feels into the young warrior with his heartflow and experiences a hideous sorrow and fear. He is alone, the last Aurelianus. He feels utterly alone.

"The comet that shines above," one of the commanders says finally, daring to break the silence, "is the passage of noble Ambrosius to heaven. A great soul has departed."

Murmurs of agreement pass among the mourners.

"No," Merlinus declares, and turns to face the gathered soldiers. They gaze back at him appalled, and several flex as though about to haul him away. Still, he continues, "A great soul has come to earth today. He himself does not know it. He is numb with the *terrible* killing today. And that is his name. Terrible." The wizard pronounces it in Latin. "But his name shall be known in the language of his enemies, who have learned the truth of that name today. In the dialect of his foes, he is Uther."

Theo's stare budges, and he faces about and looks at Merlinus and the men around him, blinking, head tilted as if trying to listen to the wizard through the noisy killing of men.

"Uther," Merlinus repeats. "Terrible is the death of a brother. Terrible is the death of a people. Terrible is the soul that must carry this pain and make a life of it for the people that remain."

The wizard leans on the balustrade and points his staff at the comet. "That is the dragon banner of your ancestors—the pendragon—the soul of your brother gone from him to you. Now you are no longer Theodosius Aurelianus. That brother died today on the battlefield with his commander."

Theo's numb face flinches with the shock of comprehension, and his eyes brighten with tears.

"Today, a new soul comes to earth," Merlinus continues, pitching his voice to reach the troops who lie sprawled on the terraces below. "Today we have a new Dragon Lord." He touches his staff to Uther's heart and announces, "Uther Pendragon."

From below, some of the troops who understand call back, "Pendragon!"

The commanders on the balcony raise their arms in Roman salute and offer their pledges by declaring, "Uther Pendragon!"

Uther sweeps a tear-hot yet level gaze over his generals, meeting and holding each of their stares. When he meets the wizard's eyes, Merlinus reaches into him again, and the spirit reckoner feels the loneliness of Theo's sorrow and fear opening into something awesome and ineffable—a new being in which the deathless strength of his brother lives on in him, strangely fused with that tenderest part baptized within him—a murderous, unstoppable strength in union with the love of Jesus.

And Myrddin thinks of Ygrane and her need for the magnificent destiny that has torn her from her family and the faerïe gentleness that loves her. They seem alike as brother and sister, these two orphaned by their stricken people. And though they are miles apart and indeed have never met, yet they have never been separate, because they are lovers to the beginning and the end, appointed to each other by God's prosperous love.

— BOOK TWO —

Mistress *of the* Unicorn

The
Palace Shaped Like Fire

Will the unicorn be willing to serve thee. . . ?
Canst thou bind the unicorn. . . ?

—JOB 39:9

Uther Pendragon does not speak for three days after the death of his brother. He sits in a tall-backed chair on the highest balcony of the palace's tallest spire and stares out over the river plains and the distant seaboard weather where the Furor angrily paces.

Merlinus knows that Uther does not see the god, or the Tamesis, either, not even when the summery sun's reflection crazes its broad surface and makes him squint. His inwrought sight, both cruel and timid, looks for where his brother's ghost has gone, back to a landscape in Armorica, the "Little Britain," where they once walked together, twenty years together, all so much ghost-filled nostalgia now.

From behind him, Merlinus uses his magic to feel what Uther is feeling. Memories smolder, and the space of his life has a measurement like music. The past is weightless laughter, a child's tuneful happiness, and the droning chants of the Church. But the song is changing. The old heart of him, double-chambered, half-childish pleasure, half-mournful faith of Church and family vendetta, has broken. Broken-hearted, all pleasure has spilled away. Vengeance has lost its purpose. And faith, greater than any purpose, cannot help him anymore. The song inside him has changed.

Language fails these changes in him. He does not know what has become of him. Merlinus finally accepts that he will have to tell him.

"Uther," the wizard says softly on the fourth day, as the mournful man munches an apple with desultory thoroughness and scans the compelling river, his inward vision lingering over the slow barges and feathery banks of rhubarb and burdock. "Uther—your army awaits your command."

"I'm hungry," he answers. "Isn't that strange, Merlinus? I mean, if you think about it, it's very strange."

"Yes, I know exactly what you mean," Merlinus says. "Life, like death, is very much beyond choice."

Uther bites off a small mouthful, nibbles it ruminatively for a while, then says, "I only wanted to be a priest. I wanted to worship God, love all people, help the suffering, preserve their souls for heaven. Ambrosius wanted revenge. Not I."

Merlinus leans against the balustrade and nods compassionately. "And now he is gone and you are the high king of the Britons. As ironic as that must seem . . ."

"Exactly. How absurdly ironic. What right have I to this position?" With a distasteful expression, he tosses the apple away and it plunges into a reflecting pool on the terrace below. "I'm no one's king. Not yours, not theirs. Ambrosius had the mettle for that. Not I."

"Uther, you *are* the king. Not by ambition but by chance. By chance alone have you become king. Don't you see? That is God's hand."

"Then, I'll step down," he determines, wiping his mouth with the back of his hand. His four-day-old beard lends a leonine cast to his tanned face, and he no longer looks like the youth Merlinus knew but like some older cousin of himself. "I'll retire to a monastery. Let the title, for what it's worth, pass to another."

"You would let death have dominion?" Merlinus asks, edging his voice with brittle hurt.

"What do you mean?"

"You're hungry," the wizard replies. "Those are your first words as Uther Pendragon. Uther's life wants to live. Don't shut it up in a monk's cell. Then death will have dominion over your brother. No. Ambrosius's death made you king. Now you must make significance of that. Do you hear me, Uther?"

"Stop calling me that." He puts his feet on the chair and hugs his knees to his chest. "I'm Theodosius Aurelianus. Simply that. And, yes, I am hungry—but not for war. I don't want to see anything of war ever again."

Merlinus pushes off from the balustrade and leans suddenly close to him. "Stop playing the child!" he shouts to his face. "Your brother's dead! He died for revenge, yes. But his revenge is the vengeance of the people against a traitor. As surely as you sit before me, the Saxons that Cocceius brought here will ravage this land and kill its people—*your* people—unless they are thwarted by an avenger. Don't you understand? *You* are that avenger."

"Leave me alone, Merlinus." Uther regards him with sleep-hooded eyes. "Let the warlords battle the Saxons. I'm sick of it."

"Then death shall have dominion," Merlinus predicts, his voice drenched in disdain. "Ambrosius killed and died to avenge his father's name—but his father's spirit remains unavenged. Your father's spirit and your father's father and all the Aurelianus fathers who brought civilization to this wilderness land have lost their spirit today. All they lived and died for is no more, because you have made your selfish choice. So much for your faithfulness. So much for Jesus and the Church you pretend to love. So much for the hopes of every Christian in Britain—"

"All right—enough!" Uther yells. He sits up straight and leans so close to the wizard that he feels the heat of his face. "What do you want me to do? Burn down barbarian villages? March at the head of the army? Become my brother?"

Merlinus does not flinch. "I want you to care." He holds his gaze tightly. "There is an ending to this story that you are living. There is an ending, and I want you to care that it will be the right one. Do you understand me, Uther? Whether you like it or not—you have a destiny."

The anger falls off his whiskery face, and he looks at Merlinus for a moment as though surprised that the solution to the moiling feelings in him could be that simple. *A story—with an ending.* Then he shoves past the wizard.

"I'm hungry," he complains, and stalks into the domed anteroom behind the balcony. He pauses at the spiral stairwell and glowers impatiently. "Well? Are you coming, Merlinus? Uther Pendragon, high king of the Britons, does not like to eat alone."

Prince Bright Night sits up from the faerïe's touch, his angular face dusted with gold dazzle. The faerïe, having dutifully reported to its prince, streaks away and disappears among the bright vapors of the moon's milt. The elf prince stands, suddenly lighter from what he has learned. The Dark Dweller disguised as a human wandered into the world mad and impuissant—and now returns carrying a vision and the persuasive powers of a demon.

The vision itself has always seemed questionable to Bright Night. He has listened patiently to the crones of sixteen generations prophesy that the union of a Celtic queen and a Roman king would produce a savior. Yet, until now, he has never believed that. Not that he has ever doubted the clarity of the crones' long sight, which has proved itself famously over hundreds of generations, but rather he does not believe that anyone can accurately predict the direction of the timewind in this turbulent modern age.

What the faerïe has revealed, however, changes the prince's opinion. *Perhaps the crones are right,* he thinks, strolling up the slip face of a dune. *Raglaw said that she had successfully transmitted her vision of the Roman king to Lailoken. Perhaps she has.*

Atop the dune, Bright Night tilts his head back and gazes into the starry zenith. Up there, the Dark Dweller peers into the future. The timewind blows through this age to a greater epoch, invisible to the prince's eyes. Invisible until he glimpsed that futuristic vista through the demon's silver eyes. Briefly, but with the searing intensity of eternal remembrance, he witnessed the gargantuan palace towers at the brink of Apocalypse.

How alien those glass pinnacles looked without the foliations in marble and wood popular among Romans and Celts and indeed all tribes. How strange to see a future of featureless spires devoid of statuary, scrollwork, friezes—devoid of all organic tribute, either to nature or to humanity itself. Into what bizarre, abstract world does the timewind carry us?

Bright Night looks west, toward Avalon. If only he could go there and meet with the Fire Lords, he knows they could explain the beauty of such a mineral landscape to him—they whose desert tribes speak of a God unknowable, without name or feature. Surely, this city empty of icons, stripped bare of ornamental representation, this purely geometric hive is a city of their God.

And what of the blinding holocaust? In Lailoken's vision, Bright Night has seen the white glare that shatters the city and, agog, watched the Dark Dweller call the proud spires out of the firestorm with his story—as though the spell of his telling could in itself avert Apocalypse. *What manner of magic is this?*

Time has shown that it is of a higher order than the sorcery of the gods, who still rely more on the electric strength of their bodies than the subtle but pervasive magic of the mind. The Fire Lords teach psychic powers that seem hardly substantial at all—runes and sums—yet the stories they spell and the numberings they weave are far greater than even the might of the Dragon.

These thoughts inspire Prince Bright Night with new hope.

Perhaps the crones are right after all! Perhaps our savior will in truth be born from the marriage of two enemies. Perhaps he will break the Furor and open a way for the Síd to return to the Great Tree.

With this prayerful hope, the prince of elves salutes Avalon hidden beneath the dripping stars of the horizon. He salutes the Fire Lords, who first taught the Síd magic. And he salutes the king to come, the prophesied one whose magic will endure after all the kingdoms of this age have turned to air.

Once Theodosius accepted himself as his brother's heir, Merlinus might have told him then about the unicorn and why he has striven so obsessively for him to be king. He might have told him he had manipulated events to set the whole fateful dream of Uther Pendragon in motion, so that he could fulfill a promise he had made, years ago now, to the queen of the Celts.

Merlinus did not explain anything, because he began to believe in something greater than his own magic. Across the heartbridge, the new being inside Theo made himself known to Merlinus hours after Ambrosius died. The wizard had simply named him.

And then, there was the comet. *That was not my doing,* Lailoken is sure. Its appearance validated Uther Pendragon's authority, for it was seen by all, over many provinces, demesnes, and kingdoms, and well into the summer. Merlinus employed no magic whatsoever to inspire Theo to charge after his brother and break the attack of the Saxons. That was entirely of his own doing. And Wray Vitki, the dragon-magus that Theo's righteous wrath called forth, is his ally. Though Merlinus employed his magical spell to behold that being and though Morgeu believes his power inspired the attack that elevated Theo to Uther and killed her father, the truth remains: Merlinus had been a mere witness.

Something greater than magic caused Theo's reaction to his brother's death and made him Uther Pendragon. Not the wizard's magic, but something within.

So, Merlinus does not tell Uther of his designs and instead devotes himself to helping the high king with the business at hand—securing the kingdom. Morgeu has fled west with a handful of servants even before her father's remains are buried, and though the wizard is relieved she is gone, he knows that when he sees her next, it will be a murderous time.

Uther, lacking his brother's Roman arrogance, readily agrees that the Celts have as much reason to defend their territory against the barbarians as the Britons, and that an alliance will favor both. Also, with Gorlois's death, someone among the Britons must be dispatched to secure the Celtic queen's continued goodwill and a guaranty of access to her valuable warriors.

None of Gorlois's officers, least of all his nephew and heir to his title, Marcus Domnoni, want the task, claiming they fear the wrath of the duke's ghost. And no volunteers come forward from the other noble houses, for Gorlois has troubled them all with tales of his wife's pagan witchery.

Most pressing of all, the young alliance among the Britons themselves remains in jeopardy. The great families of Londinium, who accommodated Vortigern and profited from his alliance with the Saxons, plot Uther's demise. When the river fog coughs in over the city and the world seems a shadow of itself, the wizard's wraith slips down the avenues and boulevards, penetrates the large old houses, and listens to the regicidal strategies hatching there. Merlinus understands—it is time for the king to get away.

That opportunity comes with a herald from Cymru, who bears a message from the druids, the Celtic government. Aware of Gorlois's demise, the druids propose a marriage of their queen with Briton's high king.

Uther objects. He is a Christian, after all, and the druids make clear in their missive that they desire the same terms they enjoyed with Gorlois. In exchange for their military cooperation, they want assurances that Christian missionaries will be effectively barred from their western kingdom.

"I'll be no party to that," Uther vows. "Saint Non has already brought the glad news of Jesus to the Celtic tribes. Her son David carries on her noble work this very day. I'll not suppress my own faith for political expediency—nor for any reason."

Merlinus says nothing, because the British bishops argue for him. They are fierce adherents of the Christian pragmatism of their country's own theologian, Pelagius, who believes that all persons, possessed of free will, must make their own peace with God.

The bishops advise the king to marry the queen in name only, for the sake of the country's survival in the face of the barbarian threat. After all, they point out, Pelagius's chief rival, Saint Augustine, who stubbornly refused to relinquish the dogma of the Church, thus diminished the flexibility of his Roman leaders and their alliances—and was himself burned alive by Vandals in North Africa.

What ultimately—and most oddly and serendipitously—settles matters for Uther is the opportunity personally to meet a Celtic queen resistant to Christianity. Theo, the priest that still resides in Uther, craves the chance to convert, at least once, a heathen noblewoman to the glory of his faith, in a way, he knows, that the coarse Gorlois never could. Reluctantly, he allows the bishops to draft his acceptance of the druids' offer.

Then, aware that the approaching cold season offers its own best defense of the lowlands, Uther formally announces his plans to journey to the mountain kingdom of Cymru and secure from the ferocious Celts an alliance that will at last repel the invaders.

In a remarkable display of political acumen, Pendragon summons Severus Syrax and, in the presence of the bishop, the city's ecclesiastics, and the elders of the great families, reappoints him as *magister militum* of Londinium and receives his allegiance.

Thus, restored to power and pledged before God to support

Uther Pendragon, the Syrax family cannot publicly foment rebellion against the high king in his absence. The aged statesman and champion of the families, Aulus Capimandua, would have been proud of such a sensible display of diplomacy—but he has already departed the city, intent on retiring to the garden city of Venonae before the plotting and intrigues begin again in Londinium.

With an able military guardian installed in Londinium, Uther leads his army west. Along the way, he returns the soldiers to the *coloniae* where they originated, and he receives personal pledges of fealty from the dignitaries of those provinces. His prolonged ecclesiastic training and noble upbringing serve him well on this diplomatic tour, and, to his face at least, none question his regal authority.

The most troubling and immediate problem at this time is Uther's shoulder wound. It refuses to heal. The healing energy Merlinus directs with his heartflow into the sliced flesh does not abate the pain or the weeping pustulence. Neither does the chanting that he tries.

All Merlinus can do is leave the king to the surgeons' care and their insistence on washing the gash with tinctures of verbena and hellebore and exposing it to daily sunlight. To his credit, Uther does not complain. Merlinus suspects he is secretly glad to keep the wound, this physical emblem of his inner suffering.

Departing from the vision Raglaw has imparted to the wizard, Uther begins wearing a beard. Trimmed to outline the strong breadth of his jaw, the black whiskers accentuate the sharp planes of his face, all the more keen since the death of his brother. He has the carved visage of a chesspiece, and if he should ever smile, Merlinus believes he would shatter like glass.

In the summery weeks after the death of Hengist and the rout of the Saxons, the Furor stands stunned at the mouth of the

Tamesis. One wolf hide boot on Thanet Isle, the other on the Island of Tamesa, he stares out into the North Sea with that numb look gods sometimes get when the timewind shifts suddenly.

Usually, gods just blow away with those destinal swerves, quickly returning to their astral kingdoms in the Storm Tree. But the Furor has sworn to take these West Isles, and he will not budge. He sinks his might into his stance and holds on as timeshadows realign around him like vale mist rolling over the land. Only the sea remains stable. The steel blade of the ocean's horizon keeps him from getting dizzy.

Vertigo lasts only moments for the colossal god, yet weeks will pass in the world of people and demons. The four demons conjured from the Gulf by the Furor's magic stagger about the foggy terrain furious at the slaughter of their Saxon hordes. They blame surprise. No one saw the dragon-magus coming. They blame Lailoken. He brought the dragon-magus into the battle. They blame each other. Each was so intent on savoring the carnage, none had the clarity to direct the storm-warriors.

The demons hiss angrily at the Furor, trying to break his transfixed stare. The god is their puppet, and his strings have tangled in the buffeting timewind. The broken illusion of his power is dangerous, for by these lapses he may come to realize that the demons are not in his control at all. Then, he will soon grasp that he has not, in fact, summoned them from the Gulf—but, rather, that they have leaped from the Deep to seize him, the god with the most power. He is *their* tool. They need him to inflame the millions in the organic frenzy on the planet's surface, to lead them against their timeless enemy—the Fire Lords.

The demons sizzle like lightning, hoping to jolt the god alert, but that is futile. And soon the demons float away, looking for new ways to make trouble for their old comrade Lailoken.

Soon, they find Morgeu hooded and cloaked in green, riding west through the tummocky turf of the Deva highlands.

She is mad with grief, and Ethiops, who has worked her before, wants to work her now.

But the others stop him. "Let her unspool her grief," they advise. "It will lead her where we want. When her despair hardens to vengeance, she will call for us."

Ahead of her, the demons fly, spreading nightmares and evil omens, clearing the terrain of bandit gangs and Pictish war parties. Blessed by demons, Morgeu floats west to Cymru, galloping harder the farther she gets from her dead father's kingdom, returning to her mother's land like a wave remembering the sea.

Ygrane prefers solitude. The perfect seclusion of her childhood, when she wandered the woods near her village, gathering berries in summer, kindling in winter, haunts her with nostalgia. In those early days, she luxuriated in the wonder, beauty, and strength of the hilly forests. In the fading sunlight, she danced with the faerïe. By moonlight, she cavorted with the Síd, who put the whole village to sleep so that they could show her secret places. They whisked her to lunar glades deep in craggy gorges, where the Piper's music called the Dragon close enough to make the trees tremble and blue fire dance on the branchtips. Sometimes, they actually carried her into the hollow hills to hear the Dragon's dreamsong on its way out to the stars, resonating in the planet's sinuses.

Twenty years have elapsed since last she heard the Dragon's eerie singing. She is too busy serving as queen to dance and cavort with the pale people. And the Síd leave her alone, because they want her working for them in the day world, doing all she can to stop the Furor from raiding their hills and stealing land and magic. And to protect her from the Furor's minions, her fiana follow her everywhere.

When she must have solitude, she has no choice but to use her magic to free a few hours for herself. Lately, she has frequently felt the necessity for private time. Word of Gorlois's death forced her to leave her fiana asleep in the stables so she could ride alone into the woods to rail at the Síd for ever having given her to that man. A panic of grief clutched her then for her daughter Morgeu, and she tried and tried to find her with her magic but failed.

Then, days later, the Síd brought news that the Dark Dweller who serves the Fire Lords has found her a husband, a young Roman king of noble birth yet humble upbringing. By that trait—a simple childhood—this king offers her the promise of being the destined one that she sent Myrddin to find. The powerful emotions this stirs sent her again into the woods alone, her fiana left slumbering at the mead table.

She learned nothing new of herself, yet her solitude renewed for her what she does know: Into this life she has come to serve her people, and for that she has endured Raglaw's weird trances, the druids political marriage to the despicable Gorlois, and the mothering of an embittered child. If this Uther Pendragon, whom Myrddin has found by his demonic magic, is truly a man she can love, that will lift her life to a higher spiral. It dizzies her thinking about it. Amorous love—passion—the mortal fusion of heartfelt fidelity with a strange man made familiar—she must reach back lifetimes to remember that joy. But what kind of joy can there be when such a union comes from the necessities of war?

That question burns hottest on the afternoon Falon brings word that Dun Mane summons her. The chief of the druids has come with Kyner and his fanatic Christians to take her to Maridunum, there to meet her new husband. This message finds her in a remote, mist-strewn valley at the head of the river Usk. Immediately, she casts a spell that lowers her fiana into a rapturous sleep and leaves them on the forest floor guarded by a ring of mushrooms.

At her whistle, herons flap from the floodwater marsh that has made little islands of the forest. Among bedraggled draperies of vine and mossy roots, the unicorn appears. It prances upslope through the riversmoke with the weight of sunlight, brushing close so that Ygrane mounts by rolling onto its sleek back.

Contact shocks her with calm, as always. Trance and wakefulness merge, faceting reality to cut-gem brilliance: Dazzling rags of sun dangle in the galleries of the shadowy bogland like angels—and a pale, upswept face flickers briefly among the medicinal dark of ferns.

"Bright Night," the queen softly calls, and dismounts. Stepping away from the unicorn feels heavy as plunging out of water onto land. "Have you found Morgeu?"

Bright Night approaches barefoot down a lily-padded lane, garbed in a simple green tunic yielding no hint of his high station among the Síd. Hair lank and unkempt, visage transparently thin, a shadow of himself, he visibly brightens at her touch. "No, sister. I have not found Morgeu. The faerïe think she hides among Dark Dwellers."

The heaviness in the queen shifts all its weight into her chest, and her heart winces painfully with the strain.

Seeing this, the prince pushes toward another subject. "The faerïes tell me, you have a new husband. Another Roman."

Ygrane calls the unicorn closer. "You've been melancholy again. Come. Touch the horn." She needs contact with the supercelestial to lighten her maternal dread and make room in her heart for more than Morgeu. The animal nudges her and lights up all the empty spaces within her, so that suddenly there is room for her internal misery over her daughter, as well as the anxious doubts about herself as a mother, a wife, a woman. Only her status as queen feels secure to her in this abyss of loss called life.

She beckons the prince to approach the unicorn, but he declines by stopping at the water's edge. "The animal is unhappy at my touch."

Even as he speaks, it shies away, remembering when this Celtic god wanted to sacrifice it to the Dragon. Ygrane lets it go and peers into the elf's green eyes. "I've told you to come to me when the melancholy is strong." She brushes back his hair and lays her hands against his temples, willing vigor into him. In a moment, his transparency fills in, and he smiles, relieved.

"Thank you, sister. I should have come sooner." He would have, too—his despair has blackened toward suicidal thoughts of raiding the Æsir in the Great Tree—but he is unhappy using the witch-queen's magic for his benefit when all Cymru needs her.

"If I cannot help you, prince of the Síd, what good is this magic to me or to any of the people? We are only as strong as our gods." The feline width of her face has always made her appear more elfin than human to Bright Night, and hearing her speak of herself as a person seems odd.

"Why are your fiana asleep?" he asks, looking at the shining bodies slumped in a pool of sunlight atop a nearby knoll.

"I wanted to be alone." She squeezes his shoulders affectionately when she notices his wince of concern at disturbing her. "Maybe I felt your melancholy."

"Maybe what you feel is the hope of love—" he suggests, tilting his head knowingly. "Your husband is on his way."

Ygrane admits this possibility with a small shrug. "I am but the soul of a woman."

"In woman's flesh." Bright Night wants to see her happy, to feel better about taking from her the happy magic he needs for his melancholy. "You've heard that the hill villages dance the Sun's wheel for you and the new king?"

The orgiastic Dance of the Sun Wheel began in early human times to celebrate life and continues only in the most isolated communities, dung-walled villages untainted by the Romans. "Yes—I have heard," the queen admits with a slow, proud smile.

"Will you dance the wheel with them, as the queens of old once danced?"

Ygrane frowns, looking both perplexed and wise. "To be honest, brother, I did not expect Myrddin to succeed at all, let alone this soon. And now Dun Mane and Kyner have come for me, and I don't want to go. Not yet."

"Don't you trust Raglaw's vision? The Dark Dweller found the man she saw with her long sight."

"Another Roman husband."

"I feel the same way. No vision is certain in these turbulent times. The timewind blows where it lists. This man, Uther Pendragon, is of Gorlois's people. You've had enough of them for a lifetime." His eyes brighten with radiance from an unexpected future. "Marry me, instead."

Ygrane unfurls a dark laugh and pushes him mockingly away. "I won't ever try that again. Those children suffer."

"And mortal children do not?"

"Not in the same way. We live and die by our animal passions. But the blood of gods—there are fevers in that blood that scald mortal flesh with impossible longings. I won't make that mistake again. No." Her adamant stare holds the prince so tightly he feels chastened. "Morgeu may well give herself to the Dark Dwellers and go mad. But that madness comes from the demons, not from within her. I won't put the gods' craziness in a child again."

Bright Night's face looks winter-thin. Daylight, even as green and chill as it is here among the flooded tree coves, has worn him out. The queen's rejection, righteous and immutable, defeats his will to stay in the scalding daylight, and he fades away. "I will search for Morgeu again tonight," his faint promise wavers after him.

A shiver of remorse passes through Ygrane for overpowering the prince. She wants to help him. She wants to help them all—the Síd, the druids, her people, and the Britons as well. The immortal queen within her wants to save them all from the invaders. As she has done in her past lives.

But this life is different, Ygrane tells the immortal queen. *This time many of our own people don't believe in you. And the man I must marry does not believe in you.*

Silence engorges her. By this, she knows that what she thinks is not important. She has only to believe in the immortal queen who has gathered her into this body.

The unicorn nuzzles her again, and the silence from the queen at the hub of herself becomes beautiful and mysterious.

Ygrane rolls onto the unicorn's back, and they go away over the water in a bounding flight that scatters herons. The soft thunder of their wings and the creak of their startled cries slip into the dreams of the fiana and become the thud of boats striking shore and timber crying under the nightmare weight of armed Saxons.

Uther refuses to enter the City of the Legion. The memory of his time there with his brother is too sharp, and he encamps on the moors while the cavalry trained by the Dragon Lord return to their homes. Before a shimmering black wall of windy banners on the parade grounds outside the citadel, the king installs the highest-ranked survivor of Ambrosius's personal guard military commander of the city and gives him the Dragon Lord's mansion.

The very next day, with the first agate streaks of dawn, Uther breaks camp, and he and Merlinus, the bishop, and a handful of black-clad cavalry archers depart for the Saxon Coast with Gorlois's lean-faced commanders and their men.

Ambrosius's winter campaign has been thorough, and there are no signs of banditry or brigands' mischief in the countryside—no demolished churches or slag heaps of torched villages. The people of the hills greet the parade as enthusiastically as the relieved farmers of the lowlands had, and the king and his entourage enjoy an uneventful passage through the peninsular kingdom to Gorlois's seacoast fortress at Tintagel.

Throughout the journey, Merlinus reaches out with his heartflow for the malicious presence of Morgeu, but she is not to be found. Even at the castle, no one has seen her. *Has she gone to her mother's?* he wonders. *Is she lurking for us among the Celts?*

To honor the fallen duke, Uther remains several days at Tintagel, attending church services, eulogizing his comrade in arms, and arranging for the dukedom to be succeeded by Marcus Domnoni, Gorlois's nephew and chief military commander.

Marcus did not witness Uther's battle frenzy outside Londinium, for he stayed in the west to guard the coast. But the awe he hears in the accounts of his soldiers who were there move him. And when the time comes for him to offer his pledge, his voice has a timbre of esteem for a fellow warrior.

That deference is not lost on the other fort commanders of the coastal towns who defended the kingdom in the duke's absence. They and their predecessors have been under attack by sea rovers for half a century until the fiana intervened, and they are eager for a strong military monarch open-minded enough to hold on to that alliance. With the old duke dead, they can speak freely about their respect for Ygrane, who has never denied their numerous pleas despite Gorlois's cold arrogance toward her. The testimony of these battle-hardened commanders impresses Uther and whets even more his curiosity about the warrior-queen.

On a beryl morning sparkling with spume, the king and his men load their nervous horses on a deep-keeled ship and bid farewell to their countrymen. Riochatus, bishop of the Britons, and a dozen of his clerics accompany them, his gold-plated crozier and ruby-studded cross-staff prominently displayed at the bow. After reciting a benediction over the kneeling king and crew, the gaunt churchman, looking cadaverous with impending seasickness, retreats belowdecks in a flurry of robes and wisping incense.

Then, the sailors hoist the dragon flag and cast off, the lumbering transport vessel pitching and yawing in the high tide. The white spires and bright pennants of Tintagel castle dwindle into a hazy distance of spindrift and whitecaps and wheeling, piping gulls.

Uther Pendragon stands tall at the bow, dressed in the black leather of a common cavalry soldier to baffle possible assassins among the Celts. He holds his head high between crozier and cross-staff, emblems of his faith, proud despite his doubts, staring into a future none on board could guess.

The demons search for the unicorn. They want to rip apart the corrupter of their old friend before the beast can further ensnare Lailoken. But even their laser stares cannot find it.

At the crown of the Great Tree, on the Raven Branch, the unicorn floats entranced by its kinship with the emptiness of the void. The earth rolls under it, remembering everything while the unicorn forgets, drifting like music.

Gradually, consciousness hardens again around memories, and the celestial animal drifts lower, away from the Raven Branch. The stars pull away like icy trees glinting in the darkness. Clouds spread their feathers. Lakes and rivers shine on the sun-struck limb of the world like precious metals.

Down the unicorn sinks, weighted with memories and promises. The demons sense it as soon as it enters the lower atmosphere, but they cannot find it. The unicorn has made itself the color of water. And the stars in their vast courses shine their rays right through it.

Heralds traveled ahead during the high king's stay on the Saxon Coast and announced to the high queen of the Celts the great hope of Uther Pendragon to counsel with her and fulfill their peoples' mutual desire for their union. By her invitation, the king's boat docks at the rivermouth that leads to Maridunum and is greeted by a mob of villagers, farmers, herdsmen, traders, and cross-bearing evangelists, all elbowing for a better view. None of the queen's men are in sight.

With much panoply of unfurling banners, pealing trumpets,

brattling drums, and billowing censers, the Bishop Riochatus descends, followed by his clerics and the small, armed party of the king's men, Uther hidden among them. Merlinus brings up the rear, behind the surgeon, livery grooms, and energetic musicians, keeping himself well out of sight among the baggage handlers. The ever-growing crush of the crowd swells forward, and the front rank of cavalrymen has to bar the pressing advance with their pikes while the grooms lead out the restless horses.

"Uther!" the evangelists begin chanting above the raucous cheers of the throng. "Uther! Christ for the Celts!"

The bishop raises his crozier, and a huge cry surges from the masses, drowning out his shouted blessing. The cavalry mount up, budging their steeds through the thick gathering to open a way for the procession.

From the ship's taffrail, Merlinus can see down to the dock where Uther, flanked by his vigilant men, hoists himself atop his horse, looking dazed, actually stunned by the horde of faithful who have gathered to greet him.

"Uther! Christ for the Celts! Uther!" the chant goes on, dimming somewhat as the flock begins to realize that the king is not going to show himself.

Riochatus, his narrow face radiant with the glorious greeting of his mission, sends a wedge of his clerics ahead bearing the cross-staff, and he parts the multitude for the cavalry and the baggage train. Slowly, the procession makes its way from the docks to the road that travels north into the pagan territory surrounding the city.

Only when the Britons have left the bulk of the jubilant faithful behind does the bishop consent to enter his four-horse van and fly ahead to the walled city. He takes with him the majority of the cavalry, for he is to enter Maridunum first, like Christ into the underworld. There, he will prepare as best he can with the heathen druids the ceremony that will unite his king to the infidel queen and thus join more intimately than ever their two disparate nations.

The remaining cavalry follow with the wagons, moving slowly down the old and rutted Roman road. The king and the wizard tramp along on horseback in the middle of the column, talking idly, as they have many times before, about the old philosophers, astronomy, and the habits of migrating birds—anything but the fervid Christians they left at the docks or the Celtic queen awaiting them in Maridunum.

Behind them, four sumpter horses and two mule-drawn bullock carts carry the king's offerings to Ygrane—a small forest of sapling fruit trees and green muscat grapes, because the wizard remembered the queen's passion for her garden.

At a crumbling bend that looks down through a copse of silver fir to the crescent of a sandy cove and a green sea, a bullock cart breaks an axle. The cavalry guard dismounts to help the handful of foot soldiers, grooms, and baggage handlers unload the vehicle and turn it on its side for a makeshift repair.

As Merlinus is perceived to be too old to help and the king, with his wound, disallowed, they wander off the road into the bright autumnal noon. Under the heat of the day, Uther removes his dragon-embossed cuirass and strolls along the ridge, peering down at the lucid sea.

Sensing no danger in the vicinity, the wizard allows the king his privacy. Merlinus wanders uphill into a wood of wind-twisted apple trees and stalwart oak and fir, where the sea breeze breaks through the canopy with a rushing sound like the surf.

Merlinus has not walked far—he can still see and hear the men grunting and swearing below him—when he enters a small clearing where a lightning-stabbed oak has collapsed the prior winter and the air shines bright and clear as good cider.

Before the fungus-ledged bulk of the fallen tree, the unicorn stands. It glides forward, and the air softens with a silvery peace. In that aromatic enclosure of blue-green darkness spangled with yellow cinquefoils and daisies in their thousands, the dense spires and tangled boles admit light in bright threads.

With shocking abruptness, the unicorn thrusts its tusk

through the wizard's beard and deep into the crook of his throat where his clavicles join. Stabbing pain jolts him backward, and he collapses to his back on a resinous blanket of cypress scales. Barbarous words clot around the hurt in his throat and compact furiously to a wild, irrepressible laughter.

All his pain gushes out of him in the first spasm of rabid laughing, and a blue fire takes its place. He sees it inside himself with inward-staring vision—blue flames swirling up his throat and into his head, gusting brighter with the convulsions of his laughter.

And then silence. A windy silence, the sounds of bird-squabbling, leaf-rustling, and his crazed laughter coming and going between lapses of utter stillness.

With stupendous effort, Merlinus tugs open his eyes like a dreamer ripping free of a nightmare. A mirage of the future floats in the circular sky, wobbly as a reflection in a pool. Street mazes of tar and concrete blur with distance to a jagged skyline, rootless in the sky above the forest.

The fantastic vertical city looks erased, as in a swamp haze. For a long time, he stands watching it drift away, tugged like a landscape of clouds by high, cobalt winds. Eventually, the city falls so far away it thins to a wisp, a line of birds navigating the season's reckoning.

As the birds vanish into the faultless sky, Lailoken hears his own voice grow hollow and speak—

"By the time winter came in purple and pale, two moons after my birth, I was strong enough to stand, hobble about, and speak. While the big flakes swirled to earth and the wind howled like a beast, Optima and I huddled before the glowing oven. I sucked porridge and she gnawed the black bread and jerky the peasants left at our doorstep.

"'Do you know?' I gummed my first words.

"Her kindly, weasel face nodded. 'I know.'

"My weak voice labored to shape my full question, 'Do you know—who I am?'

"Her fingers, knobby from years of hewing wood, gently stroked the wispy white hair from my rheumy eyes. 'Of course, my dear. You are the demon Lailoken. The angels have told me all about you.'

"I blinked to be sure she was truly smiling and not grimacing. 'Why?' I croaked.

"'What, my dear?'

"'Why—do you care—for me?'

"She hushed me with a fingertip to my sunken lips. 'You are God's creature, Lailoken. How could I not care for you? You grew inside me. You are my child.'

"*Her child!* The concept ennobled and uplifted me. Motherless since the beginning of time, I had traded the forlornness of the void for a mortal body and a mother's love. How can I tell you the depth of caring that she inspired in me? Stardust cooled to bones and blood, my body existed as her gift and God's hope that I, a demon, could use what I had always before despised and destroyed to engender love and peace. Could I? Did God intend for me to know fulfillment among the very life-forms I had previously tormented?

"Optima and I spent that harsh winter discussing my destiny.

"'You are not the Anointed One,' she warned me one radiant, blue morning as we chipped ice for drinking water at the creek where she had first washed away my placental blood and baptized me. 'Christ is the Son of God. Yes, you are virgin born as He was, but you are a minion of the darkness—evil incarnate. I knew that when you lewdly entered me. But I did not reject you, because our Lord suffered and died on the Cross to teach us love—especially love for our enemies. I knew that if I could love you, the enemy of life, I would do honor to our Savior's teachings.'

"I regretted that I had not been in Palestine when Jesus walked the earth. I would have liked to have seen for myself if he truly embodied Her love as my mother so fervently believed. Alas, at that time, my revelries had led me to Rome and the gladiators' blood games.

"'Perhaps, then, I am the Antichrist,' I ventured, huffing hot jets of smoky breath, already exhausted by my feeble effort to crack the creek ice with a rock.

"Optima paused in her hammering and fixed me with a worried look that filled me with wretchedness. 'You would break my heart, Lailoken. I suffered terribly to birth you. You remember. You tore me in half when you crawled out of me. Even so, I bless that day, because the angels assured me that you will use your demon power to serve the highest good in all that you do. Tell me now if I am mistaken.'

"I sucked in a great breath and shook my hoary head. 'You are not mistaken, Mother. I swear—'

"'This is a cruel time in which to be born, my young ancient one.' Grave concern deepened the creases in her care-worn face. 'The angels have told me, a long night is coming to the world—a terrible night a thousand years long—a time of evil, Lailoken. Plague, famine, war and more war—and worse than war, obscene atrocities committed upon whole races of people in the name of our Lord. Oh, grief!'

"Agog at her mounting dismay, I sat back in the snow. 'Can I stop this?'

"The alarm that warped her features lifted suddenly away, and she regarded me with a smile of such sincere gentleness and love that I thought for an instant I had misunderstood her oppressive sense of foreboding. 'No, Lailoken.' The level look in her gray eyes fixed me with a vigorous clarity, a look not from a mother but from one spirit being to another. 'In this world, at this time, we are doomed.'

"The dignity with which she faced the hopeless truth of our lives strangely uplifted me. I glimpsed, in her raised chin and squared shoulders, traces from her former life as a princess in the regal house of Cos. 'You will have powers as your body grows younger, but they will not be sufficient to stave off this monstrous millennial night.' She bent her eyebrows sadly and lifted me out of the snow, wiping the sleet from my backside with her frayed robe. 'If only you had come into this world at some other time, a more hopeful time, when your redemption could make changes that would endure. No. What is coming is a time damned of all deliverance. The best that can be hoped for is that you provide an example of all that is good, a radiant vision of greatness that will shine like a vivid star down the dark centuries.'

"'I can do this?'

"'And more. On a western island are nine black swans who are in truth pagan queens God has denied heaven. Their prayers have brought you to earth, Lailoken. They are your godmothers. The time is right to free the eldest from this purgatory. You are to find the king who will take her place.'

"'I don't understand.'

"She smiled benignly and patted my head. 'When the time comes, you will. For now, it is enough that you are willing to serve what is good.'

"'Will I know what is good?'

"'That is my life's hope and the import of all my prayers.' She bowed her head and what she said next she said in a slower, thicker voice, with a tight sorrow in her throat: 'A king will be born from the love of two enemies—and he will unite the people of our island for a time—and for that just and noble time you must serve him.'

"'Me? But I'm so weak. I'm not as I was before, Mother. I am only memories inside an old man's body.'

"'That will change. You are growing younger. The angels have said that you are born old and will grow young, because you are a demon and so must enter creation backward and gradually prove yourself worthy to possess the divinity of childhood.'

"I didn't want to tell her that this was nonsense. Most surely, the angels had arranged my enfeebled geriatric state to better control me in the event I reverted to my former demonic ways.

"Yet, Optima assured me, 'Your powers will grow. By the time you meet the king, you will have the strength. That will come from God. What you must provide is the willingness to serve. That is what must come from you, Lailoken. The humility to serve.'

"'Who is this king?'

"She squeezed my shoulders, proudly it seemed. 'You will know him, for you will prepare the way for him.'

"The conviction with which she said that, the pride of her certainty, filled me with awe and faith—a sense of destiny that had been entirely missing in my existence as a demon. I sipped at the sharply chilled air and spoke from my heart, 'I swear to you, Mother, I will devote this mortal life to doing good before God and man. I will find this good king and serve him. I will not fail you.'

"A clairvoyant glow ignited in my mother's lean face, and she nodded, satisfied. 'I know it will be so.'

"I tell you sincerely, the joy that woman's smile worked in me shone through my frail body brilliant as pain, and all the aeons of my dark craft collapsed in that single moment to the very truth of my life.

"By the time the boreal winds had slackened and the snowdrifts had slimmed enough for the peasants to find their way to us again, Optima did not bother hiding me. But she did lie about who I was. She told the reverent, smudge-faced people who came bearing gifts of bread, cheese, and candles that I was an aged and wandering monk.

"Surely, I looked the part. Since my birth in the early spring, I had already grown to my full height. Yet even though I was finally strong enough to carry firewood and haul ice for water, I had the wizened countenance and rat-tailed white beard of a patriarch's great-grandfather. The rustics left none the wiser.

"'Why must you lie, Mother?' I asked, nibbling at the soft core of the bread with the budding crowns of my emerging teeth. 'That you could birth and convert a demon like myself is a tribute to your holiness.'

"She patted my cheek and threw a stick on the fire. 'Dear Lailoken, for all your supernatural knowledge, you are so naive. I am a daughter of the king of Cos. And he is a worldly man. If he were to learn that I had given birth, naturally he would assume I had been raped. And since he has assigned guards to the lower valley to assure that no heathens find their way up here, he would draw the conclusion that one of them or a villager lay with me. And he would kill them one by one, seeking a confession and retribution. No, Lailoken. The truth is a dangerous thing. Sometimes it is good, sometimes evil. And often we must lie to do the greater good.'

"Optima lived as a truly wise woman, and I learned a great deal from her that winter about love and the devotion to God, upon which all worldly good depends. The fact of that devotion is nothing less than sacrifice. The only good of which mortals are capable is love. To even begin to do good, one must be willing to go beyond oneself, she taught me. All things made by man perish. All words scatter into the emptiness that is the future. Only love endures. Love for what is. Not for what was or could be. Love for what is—that alone is true love. That alone the future cannot dissolve. For that love *is* God—it is Her communion with us, here and now, no matter the emptiness between the stars or the void that holds the atoms and into which all of us, sooner or later, must fall. As I fell at the beginning of time. And as I will fall again when this body is spent. No matter. Love endures. All else is sacrificed to that one and eternal truth.

"As if to punctuate that teaching, Optima herself died that spring. With the first faint green fuzz of recurring life, she simply passed away. By chance or design, it happened one year to the day after she birthed me.

"I had wandered off into the upland woods earlier that day to gather crocuses for the altar. An angel met me on my way back. The lightning of his staring eyes blazed hotly, and I had to turn away. When I looked again, he was gone, and in his place sunlight stood among the trees though the sun itself was far on the other side of the sky. Later, I would realize that the angel had been her escort, and the sun-hot light passing through the leaves was her spirit come to bid me farewell.

"I scurried through the woods to share with her the marvel I had witnessed, and I found her kneeling among the copper beeches. The unicorn stood with its long horn touching her shoulder. It backed away at the sight of me, its large, intelligent body fitting itself into the tree shadows.

"When I touched her, she was cold and rigid, locked by death in her posture of worship. A giant cry of lamentation wracked my body. The dirgeful cry lifted me out of myself, beyond the blue of the sky, and into the star mist. Eternal night opened before me. And the stars wounded me with their needles."

The grief of that memory untangles the laughter in Merlinus's chest and threads through his nostrils in a startled snort. The unicorn has vanished. The cypress grove is empty, rayed with diamond threads of light.

He sits up, puts a hand to his throat and feels the cool, electrical draft of the gateway in his body that the unicorn has opened. The flux of energy focuses his long sight to glimpse future events that are closer, within the very span of his own lifetime.

From across the field, he sees a king striding through drifts of sunlight before a startling entourage of iron-masked warriors and elegant ladies in rainbow silks. This king's blond-bearded face possesses the broad, frontal beauty of a lion—Ygrane's skull and coloring—and the yellow eyes and Roman nose of the Aurelianus patriarchs.

The proud vision fevers away. But not before fanning the

hope Optima set burning in his mortal heart. Lailoken has glimpsed the king of prophecy. And he is the son of Uther and Ygrane.

With an amazed smile at what he has witnessed, Merlinus jumps to his feet and turns full about, searching for the unicorn. The luminous creature is nowhere to be seen among the cypress shadows and ferny undergrowth.

He is alone, yet he finds himself saying, "Unicorn! You have opened my eyes! I have seen the king! The king Optima prophesied!"

His happy words bloat to echoes in the forest's tall spaces. He picks up his staff and walks a small circle through the grove, head high, his mind charged with the demonic energy that the unicorn has released in him.

"You were right to withhold this power from me until now," Merlinus says. "I wasn't ready for this—to see so clearly. But my travels changed me. You know that, don't you?"

He nods sagely at the empty corridors of the forest. "Yes, you know that about me, unicorn. You know I am changed. I came to know the people, you see—my mother's people—the Christians." He thumps his staff against the loamy brown duff and declares with certitude: "They are the people of my destiny, unicorn. I understand that now. They work their farms, their trades. They build their towns and their churches, and they believe God *cares*."

The wizard peers through the trees to where the afternoon breaks into an enchanted debris of sunmotes and splinters of daylight. "I admire these people, I tell you. The Church tells them that the world will end any day now. And that is the same promise the Furor offers his people—that Apocalypse is to come. Yet, the Christians build for tomorrow anyway. The Furor's people build nothing. They think it is more brave and cunning to take what others have built. They believe it is just for the strong to kill the weak, and they destroy everything the Christians build. Yet, the Christians build again, creating shining towns where the meek can live and flourish—for a tomorrow that may never come."

He lifts his proud face and addresses the feathers of sunlight in the canopy. "They believe in peace—they preach love. As did my dear mother, Optima. They are trying to build a future where every human being is responsible for every other human being. Think on that! Slowly, groping through their ignorance and fears, they *are* doing the work of the angels."

With another triumphant thump of his staff, he sits down in the sylvan shadows. "They are my mother's people, unicorn, and unwittingly, I have come to care for them. But try as I might to help them, even with the powers that you've shown me, I could not save any of them. There are too many barbarians—too much war everywhere. I witnessed it for five years, and I could not do a damned thing about it."

Head hung, eyes closed before the dark memories of devastation witnessed in his travels, the wizard speaks strongly, "*I* can't, certainly, because I am just one man. But a king of the Britons—someone strong enough to unite all the petty warlords—he could do as the Romans did—push back the savages, stop the marauding and the slaughter, and build the shining towns again."

Slowly, his fierce face rises and his silver eyes open, bright with ardent conviction. "This struggle and its goal is what I saw in Raglaw's vision. What Ygrane believes, too. And it is what my mother expected of me, what she wanted me to help make real. This is why the angels have worked so hard to bring me here. To fulfill the king's greatness. For only a great king can unify all the provinces and drive out the barbarians. Britain is an island. With a strong leader, we can become an island fortress, safe and secure in our own land from the madness that is murdering civilization."

His body thrumming with the demonic energy loosed

within him by the unicorn, the wizard breathes with awe, "It can be done. I *saw* it. I saw the king."

Merlinus decides to test his new power, and he wills his eyes to fill with the sight. In a windrush, his vision bursts from the grove into the pellucid sunlight, and he finds his awareness flying rapidly down the hill and across the tilting slopes. Beneath him a riotous abundance of flowers blurs by in intensely bright, rambling patches—buttercups, harebells, poppies—then the sun-varnished surface of a pond and a tangled bank of reeds and cattails.

Serene as a breezy weed tuft, he sails past the toppled bullock cart, where burlap-bundled fruit trees have been stacked to one side and the men struggle to dismantle the broken axle. The ocean below the fir-spired cliffs burns with horns of fire.

He flits through a stand of birch trees, the sunshine creaking among the spindly shadows, and emerges in a meadow of rippling grass. The open field surges with horsemen from the coming generation, pennants flying, all emblazoned with emblems of Optima's faith: the Cross, the Lamb, the Cup, and the White Bird.

A wild laugh of joy for this Christian future, for his mother's fulfillment, slashes through him, and the mirage collapses to grains of sunlight in the wind. Long moments pass as he struggles to still his excited laughter. He remembers that his physical body is still lying unconscious in a grove of cypress. He drifts here as a ghost and must find his way back to the flesh Optima wove for him. This thought sobers him.

Merlinus concentrates on the space of his being still frosty from the unicorn's touch. Laughter coils again, and he exerts all his might to suppress it. This time, the vatic silhouettes of the coming generation blur over him like cold sheets of mountain water, leaving him stunned in an aquatic landscape.

Gray-blue light trembles as though seen underwater. Shadows rise and fall in a seething vastness of seashine—and he understands that he is not seeing the future but the murky present immersed in the skywide stream of time. The shadows around him are the living beings whose actions shape and define whatever future there may be.

Again, laughter assails him. How ludicrous seems this moment huge as the gaping sky, holding everything—everything! There, he sees a long-bearded old man, himself lying as if dead, one eyelid half-open, revealing scleral white. Brilliant filaments of gold energy tangle in the air between him and his body, connecting his astral self with his inert shape.

Through the muted aqueous shine of the moment's vastness, other figures loom. The hulking black shapes of demons hover in the distance, mute as mountains. He recognizes the gruesome contortions of his old comrades. But they do not see him, for demons lack the sight. Behind them, the Furor rises, his blue mantle the sky itself, his one Nordic eye pale as the moon. He, too, does not see the fugitive demon, because his gaze is locked on a future far distant from this moment.

Closer in the blue breathlessness of this vision strolls Uther Pendragon, blind to time as any man. He wanders through his thoughts of what lies ahead while he steps over a deadfall birch, oblivious to the powers around him. Wray Vitki drifts in his shadow, carrying his own midnight, a man-shaped darkness etched with lizard glints of scales. No strong eye shines in him, either—mercifully, because his future is the Dragon's maw.

Merlinus fights back the urgency to laugh, wickedly amused to see time itself as a dimension, an endlessly wide space occupied by all living things. Everywhere are forest creatures locked in their spelled moments of eternity. He stares through their watery bodies, beyond the musical stairs of a descending brook, past the transparent veils of the woods and hills to where people occupy their blind moments.

The king's soldiers toil to fix their wagon's broken axle. Riochatus and his entourage arrive at Maridunum, a hive of activity locked still in this one blued moment, pennants warped in a frozen wind, faces fixed in permanent flashes of expression.

Layers of distance peel away before the wizard's penetrating stare, and he finds the unicorn on the far side of the city. It floats in calm sweetness among the torn curtains of the forest, caught in midleap, absorbed in the moment's depth, lacking all future vision.

Sweeping his stare across farther ranges, Merlinus searches for the queen. He finds Morgeu first. She huddles in an orange blur of torchlight in a round, sunken ceremonial crypt. Serpent-coiled jasper columns circle the deep vault and uphold a black stone dome nailed all over with human skulls, lantern flames ablaze inside them. Time moves here, slowly seeping into the future.

Suspended by iron chains, censers of hammered bronze leak twirling vapors that drool upon the floor and crawl like viperous ghosts to the onyx base of a hideous statue. It is the same gruesome statue that the wizard and his master saw in the *aedes* shrine at Segontium—a naked, fang-faced woman sporting a skull-necklace and brandishing a bloody sword and a severed head—*Morrígan*—the Demon Queen.

Morgeu lies prostrate before the statue, tightly gripping its dancing, bell-tasseled ankles. Naked, the young witch's big-boned, womanly body shines dead white as wax, the flickering, rippling skull fires stroking her like shadowy, skeletal fingers. She rolls about and props herself on her elbows, her small eyes gazing lovingly at the statue.

"Ethiops—" she calls in a voice not her own, a snaky, spiritous voice so familiar in its wickedness that pain jabs Merlinus, transfixing him like a wind-tossed butterfly stabbed by a pine needle. Spider thread energies spin from the grisly statue and knot the brails of Lailoken's heart, holding him tightly with a frightful rapture.

An eel-slick shadow separates from the stone figure, upright and badged with the blood clot reflections of the skull-lanterns. It is Ethiops, descended from the mountain heights he shared with the Furor. He does not see Merlinus. His black bolts of eyes reflect Morgeu's pallid, awestricken face. Too well, Lailoken can imagine the revulsion the demon feels for this gutsack groveling before him—yet the sable translucence of his slinky body embraces the witch.

An irrepressible laugh at the depraved desperation of Ethiops grips Merlinus. The wizard strains to hold on to his vision, and the shocking scene jolts away. *Morgeu is a weapon of the demons,* he tells himself to douse his aching laughter and, in so doing, calms down instantly.

Ahead of him, sitting on a centuries-soft floor of pine needle and beech leaf, Ygrane watches. The muffled light of frozen time does not disguise her intent stare. She is looking directly at him. Her translucent body opens like a drawn curtain of rain and behind her, behind the clear mask of earth and rock that is the planet's crust, the Dragon watches. Its purple, ink-smoke eyes fill mountainous miles, alien in the dark effluvium of its being.

Startled by this huge face, Merlinus loses his grip on himself, and a terrified laugh explodes inside him. His vision shatters—but in the instant of its vanishing, he sees that Ygrane is but a lure of the Dragon's. Her magic ensnares them all. He distinctly sees its webwork of blue fire spun into the finest wires, spun and woven to entrap them all in this space of time.

Azure threads radiate from the Dragon's fiery shadow, focus through the lens of Ygrane's body, and fan out across the world. The magic fibers weave knots around him. Uther, too, and the shadowy Wray Vitki shimmer with the cords of magic tightening about them. And the unicorn wears the long reins of the queen's power. She means to feed them all to the Dragon, for the braids of her magic tie each of them to the beast inside the planet.

The queen herself is snared by the Dragon's web. Though she has protected the unicorn from being sacrificed to the Dragon, she must struggle to assert her own will. The Síd's linkage with the world beast controls and traps her as well.

Her green stare lingers as an afterimage in his strong eye, watching with an intent that is clear, unwavering, and merciless.

Uther feels like a tiny, furtive animal within the massive glade of oak, ash, and rowan and the green and reeling draperies of ivy. In this obscure wood, with its silent sunless galleries, rocky defiles, shoulder-high ferns, and rare, outraged slashes of spectral, smoky daylight, he feels free and unimportant.

He is thinking about his brother and the fabled obscurity of his own life's woods, where he must search for his soul in a tangle of political commitments and future battles. Foremost on his mind is the loveless marriage to come, a sacred union to a pagan woman he has never even seen.

Garish green fire twinkles in the distance, and the king makes his way toward that, over gorm-covered, fallen behemoths, across stony beds of exhausted creeks, and through a maze of thorn-clogged underbrush. Thwacking his way with his short sword among veils of nettle, he emerges in a chamber of fuming cerulean, blue as the bottom of a shallow sea—a sky-bright arboreal well aswirl with rising mist.

A small stone building sits among silver grasses and splotches of colorful snapdragons, foxgloves, and bryony. The king mistakes the squat, domed structure for a saint's sepulcher, a chapel, because the lintel above the dolmen door has carved into it a Celtic cross—a cross laid atop a circle, an ancient symbol of the cosmic quadrants. Obviously grateful to have found a site of worship in the midst of this primeval terrain, a holy place where he can unburden his fears to God, he sheathes his sword and hurries through the walloping weeds and spiritous mists. He genuflects at the doorway and enters.

Inside, he pulls up short and bows his head apologetically. A tall woman in braided bronze hair and white robe stands at an altar of undressed stone arranging wreaths of wildflowers. She is Ygrane. But the king does not know this, because the queen is alone, dressed simply for communion with her faerïe, and wears no emblem of her rank. He greets her in Latin, as he would a fellow worshiper, "Christ be with you, sister."

Ygrane turns about serenely, her glamour radiating from her, creating a tranquil atmosphere. Informed by heralds of Uther's arrival in Cymru, she has been muttering magic, summoning Uther to meet her here in this shrine, so that they may spend their first moments of shared destiny alone together. His appearance does not surprise her, and she manages a smile as if at the young man's reverent mistake. "Welcome, stranger, to the temple of peace."

Uther squints in the dim enclosure. "Is this not a chapel?" He takes in tau-cut patterns on the stone walls and, illuminated by sun shafts from the dome's slot windows, three linked circles hewn on the altar face. "You are not Christian?"

"This is a Celtic temple," she says, and lets her gaze play over him in a nervous way, so that he can easily read her concern: He wears a sword and is Roman, and she foolishly alone. This is her first test of this man who would be her husband. Her years with Gorlois have trained her eye to detect the faintest facial tics of sadistic interest.

She sees none. Instead, the young king backs away as if from an open furnace door.

"You speak Latin . . ." Uther's confusion pulls him away from her. He tries to understand who this beautiful woman is, alone in a secluded, pagan temple, and what she is about, standing among those wreaths of pliant ferns and starry bryony heaped at the altar.

"I am—" She lifts her arms warily and turns her palms outward, revealing her simpleness. "I am a handmaiden of the queen—Ygrane of the Celts. We learned our Latin together—during her marriage to the duke of the Saxon Coast." She puts a pale hand on the altar. "I am merely come to beseech the spirit powers for their blessing of peace upon our union with the Britons."

Realizing his blunder, Uther continues to step back, bowing his head apologetically. "Forgive me—I—I thought to pray to our Savior for the same peace . . . to *my* Savior, that is—Jesus—the Anointed One—Christ—"

"I know of Jesus," Ygrane says through an amused but discreet smile. "The duke was a Christian, too."

"Of course—" Uther puts a flustered hand to his brow. "I'm sorry to intrude. I leave you to your worship."

Ygrane, pleased with his character, watches his awkward retreat closely for the man's physical traits. As he steps backward into the bold sunlight, she sees him clearly—his quiet face and thoughtful, golden eyes, wincing in the brightness, and the jet locks of his hair, all in disarray from his strenuous march through the thicket. He looks boyish in that revealing light, the troubling concern torquing his heart, the heavy doubt that has brought him here, as obvious as worry on a child's face.

Ygrane's fears vanish in a surge of compassion. "Wait," she calls. "You are one of King Uther's party, are you not?"

Uther nods. "Yes—I am with him."

In his dusty vest, worn trousers, and scruffy boots, he looks like a common cavalryman, and the queen's eyes brighten knowingly. "You were the sorrow of the Saxons from what we've heard. Your archery and horses deeply astonished the enemy." She motions to the blossom-decked altar. "Will you come in and pray with me, then?"

Uther shifts his weight backward.

"Pray to your god, then," Ygrane says mildly. "If our people are to be allies, our gods should be allies, too—don't you think?" She returns her attention to her floral arrangement and speaks without looking at him. "Though, from what I understand, your faith is a young one—or, rather, a stitching together of many an old one."

"That's not true," Uther says, stepping into the temple,

attracted to the one lure he cannot resist. "Jesus is God's only begotten Son. He came to die for our sins and make us worthy of heaven."

Ygrane smiles mischievously at his umbrage but suppresses her mirth before facing him. "Do leave your sword outside, soldier. Please. This is a shrine to peace. I should have told you."

Uther steps back outside and fumbles with his buckler. "You did—I'm sorry. However, you're mistaken about my faith. Jesus alone is the Son of God. There is no other."

"I've offended you," Ygrane observes tauntingly. "Then it is I who am the sorry one. You see, our people are an ancient and proud race, and I take their knowledge for granted." She beckons him in and gestures to a niche-seat carved into the stone wall. "Water?" she asks, producing a red leather flagon and small withe basket from beside the altar. "Or a barley muffin?" When he declines with a small wave of his hand, she adds, "They have currants and black walnuts. They're the queen's favorite."

Uther accepts one and nibbles at it with a courteous look of appreciation.

"A thousand years ago," she says, sitting in the adjacent wall-seat, "my people ranged across all of Europe. Did you know that?"

"Yes, you sacked the Eternal City eight hundred years ago," he says around a cheekful of muffin. "In fact, you were a threat to the Romans until they defeated you at Telamon 225 years before the birth of our—my Savior."

"Indeed." She acknowledges his erudition with a smile. "You're quite knowledgeable for a soldier."

"I—I studied to be a priest and learned some history," he mumbles and swallows. "And yourself—you're quite knowledgeable for a handmaid."

"The queen expects all her servants to read and know their history." She offers him the flagon of water. "Our ogham alphabet is as old as the Greeks'."

"That is a heritage worthy of pride." He accepts the flagon and drinks.

"You must be as proud of your heritage to give up the priesthood and fight for your people," she notes.

Uther's stare turns suddenly hard. "Unless we fight, we will lose everything," he answers brusquely. "The barbarians want this island for themselves, and they're determined to purge it of us." He passes the flagon back to her, and, noticing the look of deep concern in her large eyes, his gaze softens. "But, of course, you know this wicked truth as well as I. That's why you are here. To pray for our alliance to win peace."

"Can we win, do you think?" she asks him, searching his young face for some hint of hope.

"We must," he replies, his whole body suddenly leaning forward, poised, alert, looking almost afraid, she thinks. "We must win—for all that is holy—for your *and* my people."

"I pray that your king is as determined."

"He is determined to give his life," he says flatly, "if that is what it takes to win our land back from savagery. He will pay no less than his brother paid. That I know."

"And you, soldier?" She peers at him intently, fascinated by his fervor. "Has your faith prepared you to give your life for our cause?"

Uther sits back. "I am already dead," he whispers, and the cold that those words work in the queen raises her small hairs. "My whole family is dead—murdered by war and grief. I often feel as if I died with them." His knuckles glow in the half dark, gripping the leather pads of his knees. "That is why I came in here to pray—when I thought it was a chapel."

"You came to pray for your family—" Ygrane speaks softly, lowering her eyes.

He does not bother assuring her that his family is safe in heaven. He is alone on earth, in trespass of his faith. He had hoped to pray for the woman he must marry.

"I actually came to pray for your queen," he admits, his head pressed back against the stone wall, gazing calmly into her querying stare. "I came to pray to Jesus that he might open her heart to him—that Uther and Ygrane might have the blessing of a Christian marriage."

Ygrane sits upright. "I think your prayer will go unanswered, soldier. Ygrane is fierce in her faith. And, as I've told you, my people are an ancient one. Far more ancient than Rome."

"And what is her faith?" Uther inquires, quietly. "What do you Celts worship?"

"It is the Celtic faith that in every person there is a soul," she answers musically, her head back, her proud eyes brighter it seems for the strong bones of her cheeks and jaw, "and in every soul an intelligence that may think either good or evil. And out of good comes life. And in every life, there is God."

"And evil?" he asks.

"There is no evil," she replies with a quiet smile, "which is not a greater good."

Uther puts aside the muffin she has given him and sits taller. The handmaid's sincerity moves him, and he feels contrite for deceiving her. "We should pray," he suggests, "to our separate gods."

He kneels at the altar, and she stands beside him. They pray silently. Outside, birds simmer and the wind soughs from the dark gloom of the forest. Presently, Uther rises, and Ygrane touches his arm. "Thank you, soldier. You are generous to honor my people's shrine with your prayer."

The queen withdraws her glamour and stands before him as her simple self. She searches his face for signals of interest, wanting him to find her alluring, to balance her own attraction to him. He does not look away or withdraw, and her heart paces faster. Stepping closer, she looks for and sees carats of light brighten in his stare and by that glimmer reads his enticement and knows there will be intimacies.

The humble king's accepting gaze drives all doubt from her,

and she feels she can hide from this honorable man no longer. He has fulfilled every expectation, and not even the immortal queen within her can find fault with him. She lowers her head contritely. "I am Ygrane—queen of the Celts."

Uther sags for a moment under the weight of this disclosure. A chill of embarrassment pierces him for pretending to be other than himself. Then he rights himself, struck by the thunderbolt thought that this sincere and simple woman of elegance is his queen. "My lady—" he mutters, groping for how to explain himself.

"You are Uther Pendragon. I know."

"You know?" The olive hues of his face darken.

"I've known all along. I'm sorry I was not immediately forthright with you."

"You knew—and you did not tell me?" he asks without emotional violence, at once astonished and curious. "You tricked me? Is that a Celtic custom?"

"No—" she says, her voice soft with guilt—"a personal weakness. I had to be sure you were not like my first husband."

"And have I satisfactorily fulfilled your secret appraisal?" he taunts.

"Are you angry at me?"

"No." He steps closer, feeling the helplessness that has brought him to this pagan woman flowing toward something happier. "I am not angry. I am actually glad enough to laugh. From everything I have heard of you, I expected some . . . well, some mysterious—priestess."

"You mean to say, a sorceress? A witch?" Her eyes slant mockingly. "You are afraid of me?"

He makes no effort to hide his apprehension, his sun-spun eyes wide with remembered fright. "I have heard such outlandish things—that you ride a unicorn and talk with elves. I've even heard that you once climbed the Saxons' Storm Tree to confront their god, the Furious One. Rumors say you can ensorcell with a word. Am I ensorcelled now?"

"How do you think I got you here, alone with me?"

Uther, thinking she jokes, laughs. "Where are your guards?"

"Nearby," she lies, and places her right hand on his, in a first approach to intimacy. "I am glad we have met without formalities—even if I did trick you."

He clasps her hand and feels firm, coarse skin. She is strong. For a moment, he wonders if she is in fact a servant pretending to be a queen. Then he catches her smile as she reads his sudden reservation.

"My hands are toughened from a lifetime of working with plants," she explains. "Not a queenly trait among Romans, I know. If it offends you, I shall take care to wear gloves."

"No. Don't change. I want to know you for who you are." He shrugs with mock embarrassment. "I only hope you don't find my hands too soft."

With a laugh, she pushes him playfully, but shoves his wounded shoulder inadvertently, and he grimaces. Surprised, she grasps his good arm. "You're hurt."

"A sour wound." He crouches to the wall-seat. The ruby throb of pain, constant and dull, which he has come to ignore, jangles now with vivid anguish.

"Let me see it," the queen demands, unlacing his vest.

His face gleams with cold sweat, and he closes his eyes. "I'm under the care of a surgeon."

"A Roman surgeon," the queen huffs, gingerly tugging the vest aside. "Is it garlic paste and tar he's using? That's a favorite with your field doctors." She pulls down the sleeve of his tunic, exposing the red, swollen gash tightly sewn with strands of catgut. "You'll fever from this. You need a healer's unguent. You can have mine." From her muffin basket, she retrieves a thumb-sized phial of blue glass.

"What is it?" Uther asks as Ygrane pours a resinous brown liquid over the black stitches and scalded flesh.

"Healer's balm," she answers, gently daubing the ointment over the wound's puffy lips. "Oils of nettle, vervain, willow. It heals. I rinse each phial with magic, to help with the healing. All my servants carry it. These are wartimes."

He watches her nimbly apply the balm both to his wound and to the inside fabric of the tunic where it will touch the wound, and his pulse quickens. "How is it that you, a queen, know so much of medicine?"

"Healing the people and the land is one of my prime responsibilities as queen," she answers, carefully lifting the sleeve of his tunic into place and closing his vest. "You will not fever now, I don't think. But if the wound was not properly cleaned, you may. Then you'll have to open the stitching."

"If that happens," he says, "I will send for you."

"We will be together again soon," she says, scrutinizing his young face, sating herself on all the small details she never saw in trance. She presses the phial into his hand. "Keep this. I will salve your wound with it again—this very night—when we meet in Maridunum."

Warm as brandy, his gaze plays over her earnest features, committing to memory the strong breadth of her jaw, the long Danaan nose, the faint petal fur of her skin, and the tilt of her green eyes. He tucks the phial into the vest pocket above his heart. "Come with me to my cortege. They are on the road beyond this copse. We will enter Maridunum together, you and I."

She watches him with a clear, expressionless calm that betrays none of her suppressed feeling. This encounter has turned out far better than she dared hope. Love is possible—and that introduces new dangers and more troubles into her life. *Myrddin,* she cries to herself, *you did your work too well*. She needs time to fit these intimate possibilities to her wider and more dangerous life as queen.

"Let this first meeting be ours alone," she tells him, and steps back toward the altar, "before God."

"Yours or mine?"

"We'll let our marriage figure that out." She smiles wearily.

"If we are successful, we can debate it with our children. If we fail—well, the Saxons have their own idea of God."

The happy tremors in the king's heart still as he accepts this truth. Numb-edged again from the pain and the facts of his fate, Uther turns on the threshold and places his hand over the blue phial in his vest pocket. "Thank you."

He leaves casually, like an old friend reluctant to go, gathering his sword and buckler from the door stoop, and slowly striding through the silver grasses, stopping several times to wave before disappearing in the forest gloom.

Deep in the afternoon, the brownstone walls of Maridunum appear on the steep bluffs overlooking the patchwork farmlands of the alluvial plains. The queen's unicorn pennant flies beside the wind sock of the British king's dragon, signaling the readiness of the druids and the bishopric to formalize the union between their monarchs. Draped with colorful banners of intertwining dragons and unicorns, the wooden gates stand wide, and cheering townspeople crowd the thoroughfare and the range, swelling toward the gate at the sight of the approaching retinue.

Uther sits up taller in his saddle as he views the ancient Roman fortress manned among the battlements by long-haired, mustached Celtic warriors. He draws rein for a moment where the path rounds the verge of the city's first defensive mounds, giving a wide prospect of the surrounding countryside.

From the beatitude of his expression, all can see how the beauty of this Latin-cultivated terrain grips him. The land is set about with old stone pools, cobbled walls, cherry orchards, and groves of Italian plum, the virid slopes cropped to lawn by Tuscan sheep. The farm compounds, irrigated by tidy canals among clay huts with thatched roofs and floral-carved sills and shutters, have the euphony of parks. A whisper of the Empire's paradisal age remains here, glinting with the wild rays of late sun off the stunted but lithe olive trees gnarled like shrubs on the steep hillsides above the shining fields.

"Uther!" a cry goes up from within the gateway crowd, and the people pull aside to allow the scarlet-robed bishop and his vanguard of cross-bearing clerics to pass out of the city and greet their king.

Uther nods for his men to advance, and the party canters past the gawking onlookers to the city threshold. The cavalry dismount and surround the king while Bishop Riochatus approaches, bearing in his arms the purple mantle of an *imperator*, and atop that, the golden wreath in the manner of the Etruscan kings.

Shielded from view by the cavalry's horses, Uther removes his riding gloves and vest and kneels for the high churchman's blessing. The archbishop hands the mantle and wreath to a cleric and lays his hands atop the king's head, muttering a prayer.

Merlinus stands well back and away from the clerics, who he knows must disapprove of him. He still feels light-headed from what the sight revealed to him earlier in the day, and he leans heavily on his staff. Unfurling the brails of his heart, he feels through the crowd for trouble. But he detects none, only happy curiosity and awe among the assembly.

Wearing the golden wreath and purple mantle, Uther enters Maridunum. The accompanying musicians brought from Tintagel make an imperial racket above the loud chanting of the clerics and the soldiers shouting, "Uther! Uther! Uther!"

The mass of Celts gaup and giggle and make no jubilant noise at all. To the king's appraisal, they seem a very different people than the crowd of Christians he encountered at the docks. These villagers, though they wear garments much like those seen throughout Europe—tunics, hooded cloaks, gowns—have bowl-cut hair glistening with nut oil, and many of the younger women are bare-breasted. The king takes no overt notice, nodding to the people graciously as he follows the bishop's lead across the flower-strewn courtyard, past the wreath-bedecked dolphin-fountain, and up the marble steps of the central *mansio*.

Merlinus, impressed by the pageantry, would like to reach into Uther with his heartflow and experience what he is thinking, but the wizard is too busy searching the gaping multitudes for Morgeu and other threats.

There, among the fluted columns and before the high, red-lacquered double doors where Gorlois killed Raglaw, Merlinus senses a deep stirring in his soul, as though inside his chest a whole field of grass shines with sunlight. Purposefully, he stands at the exact spot where Raglaw's head rolled to his feet. Her command to him has been fulfilled. He has found the intended king and delivered him here. The circle is complete.

"Merlinus," the king summons.

The wizard shoulders through the phalanx of soldiers who flank the king protectively and hurries to his side.

"Stand by me," he orders.

Riochatus, brightly garbed in scarlet robes and conical cap, and his clerics, with their brown Phrygian hoods drawn back from close-cropped heads, lead the way. As the tall red doors open, the bishop raises the cross-staff high.

Through the tall doors emerges a file of white-robed men with large mustaches, long hair, and pentagonal wooden shoes that clop loudly on the marble. These are the Celts' ruling caste, the druids.

Merlinus scrutinizes their faces. They are not unkindly, and his heartflow circulates among them, informing him that none bear murderous thoughts or even ill will. They are but politicians, the elders from the clans and the chiefs' halls, shrewdly intent on preserving their social order, and he can hear their minds click and whir with the engines of their strategies.

Behind them comes the queen. At the first touch of the wizard's heart's brails, Ygrane releases her glamour. Merlinus's skull seems to open like a flower, his mind drifting as if a fragrance, bodiless again and yet firmly in his form, leaking about him as if a scent. Clad in levels, like a dreamer lucid of the dream, he sees her coming toward them through the portico's slanted light, through the robes of the sun.

The queen wears a close-bodied *gwn* that covers her from her collarbone to her ankles in blue velvet trimmed in seed pearls and yellow sapphires. Her honey-colored hair is dressed for the occasion in many thin tresses braided through a gold-latticed tiara aglitter with amethysts, emeralds, and rubies.

With his heartflow, Merlinus tests each of the fiana who fan through the chamber and finds no wickedness in them. Curiosity and some jealous turmoil interfere slightly with their attentiveness to the queen's safety. But otherwise they display no dangerous regard for the royal couple, and all bow their heads respectfully when the bishop announces with stentorian authority: "Uther Pendragon, king of the Britons."

Dun Mane, chief of the druids, bows curtly, throws back the hood from his large, brindle-maned head, and proudly replies in Brythonic, "I present to you Ygrane, queen of the Celts."

Ygrane's elvish eyes widen mildly in greeting to the king, and she offers both her hands. When Uther takes them in his dry grip, she says to him with a smile of construable friendship, "Will you have me for your queen?"

Uther's drawn face, pale as a leaf's underside until this moment, darkens with a blush none present can miss. "The fate of our people has reserved us for each other, my lady," he answers somewhat stiffly, then warmly adds through a cold frown, "We are blessed to have each other in these dire times. I will proudly stand by you, Ygrane, queen of the Celts—if you will have me."

A searing light passes between the wizard and the royal couple, and he swings his long face aside. Peripherally, he catches a passing glance of an angel, registering only its sunny raiment and the awful calm in its large staring eyes.

Wincing blindly, Merlinus trawls his branded vision across the chamber and observes that no one else has seen the angel. He concentrates on his breathing as Ygrane, smiling and chatting softly with her consort, leads Uther into the high-beamed audience room, where a feast has been sumptuously laid out.

Following the reverent druids and churchmen, the wizard takes his place at the main table, which sits on a wide portico looking out on the leavings of sunset under a lavender sky—a rind of moon, crimson shreds of cloud, and the diamond flare of the evening star.

Oysters, crayfish, salmon, and trout come to the torchlit table on golden plates, alongside truffles, fruits, and crystal beakers of bright wines that cling in clear veils to their goblets. Harpists and fife players provide gentle, soothing strains as a score of towheaded lads, their russet tunics merrily fringed with bells, serve and clear the numerous dishes.

The druids, fluent in Latin, discourse amicably with the churchmen about the mutual values of their faiths—the Peace, Love, and Justice of the Celts' moral philosophy coupled with the Charity which the Christians profess. Diplomatically, none broach the subject of the churchmen's faith in a coming Apocalypse and final judgment, nor the druids' certainty of the soul's migrations among all manner of life-forms in its quest to know perfection through every suffering and joy. At one point, warmed by wine, the hollow-cheeked Riochatus inquires if Merlinus, the king's counsel and the queen's emissary, is Christian or pagan. Merlinus frankly tells the table of his sainted mother, Optima, daughter of the late king of Cos, and how, impregnated by a demon, she birthed and baptized him—and he turns the question back on the bishop: "What *am* I then, holy father—son of a saint or a demon?"

Dun Mane intercedes to decree that only God can decide Lailoken's place in creation, and Riochatus concurs. God alone can judge so queer an issue as Merlinus.

The king and queen participate lightly, afraid of the potential enmity between their elders and careful not to disrupt the fragile skein of fate that has brought them together. Merlinus glows with pleasure to see how happily they have received each other, how warmly their gazes touch, and what hope shines in their young faces. At that moment, it seems inevitable to the wizard: Uther is the destinal king that Ygrane has abandoned her childhood joy to find—and Ygrane promises to be the caring soul that, until now, Uther could find only in Jesus.

Clearly, Merlinus believes, *they have nothing to fear from the people in their midst. The angels have led them to each other. Only the demons can undo that*—and the wizard is determined to use all his powers to thwart that dire possibility, no matter what malignity his foes may set against him.

After dinner, Uther and Ygrane call him aside, and the three retreat to the gallery at the back of the *mansio*. The clear, moonless night shimmers above the dark grounds and the torchlit battlements in spidery streaks of stars.

"You must tell him everything, Myrddin," Ygrane says to her spirit reckoner as she motions for him to sit opposite her and Uther at a bare slate table. A lone oil lamp shines from a tall trivet under the vine-hung arbor roof, and, by that wan glow, the two sitting close, holding hands, golden crowns hoarding light, look to Merlinus like the primal pair from a beautiful, archetypal world. "From the first, I want there to be no secrets between my husband and me."

"I have told him almost everything already, my lady." Merlinus leans his staff against the rune-carved settle as he sits.

"Almost everything?" Uther says, baffled. "What are you talking about, Merlinus?"

"Lord"—Merlinus lowers his head deferentially—"you already know I am a demon won to goodness by my good mother's sacrifice. And you know I worked what magic I possess to elevate your brother."

Uther nods impatiently.

"What you must know now is that I was sent to find you." Merlinus commences the story of Raglaw and her vision of him, and how the soil and seed of that fate has been worked and planted years earlier when Optima herself revealed his human destiny to the demon visitor. Merlinus tells him, also, of the unicorn.

Uther listens raptly, still spelled by the happy surprise of discovering that the vivacious and kindly woman he met earlier that day in the forest shrine is to be the wife he once dreaded meeting. "So, nothing has changed, then," he concludes after his tale is done. "All three of us, it would seem, are unlikely players, mere servants of God."

Merlinus directs his attention back to the queen. "Lady, forgive my probing, but I must know—is Morgeu capable of treason? Could she attempt to usurp your position by force?"

"Myrddin, she is not the child you remember from your last time with me," Ygrane acknowledges, her voice weak with unhappiness. "She has magic now. Terrible magic. From what I see in trance, she has given herself to the black arts."

Merlinus stops his nervous hand from tugging at his beard. "Lady, in trance I, too, have seen her—and she was in the company of a demon."

Ygrane's distraught features cloud darker. "Yes, that sounds like the sad truth. There is an ancient tradition of demon-worship among a cult of my people who call themselves the Y Mamau. Fanatics, the lot of them. Yes, and if they had their way, the king-sacrifices of ancient times would be revived, so I'm told. They are conjure-warriors—evoking spirits of the dead to aid them on the battlefield. They hope to use my magic against me. I fear Morgeu has joined their dark fold."

Upon hearing this, the wizard's face clouds over, and, seeing this, Uther comes up alongside him. "Too much presses us tonight," he speaks, crossing his arms over his body. "Now I must know everything. You must tell me what your magic is, Ygrane. Not for me to censure, but to know. Where does it come from?"

She moves closer to him and shakes her head gently. "Don't look so worried, Uther. As Merlinus will attest, I am not evil. I serve our people, in a Celtic way. It is as I told you in the shrine: We believe the soul is immortal. When the body dies, the soul goes on, to another body. This has happened time and again, through every form capable of life, through every severity and goodness. And it will go on until the soul has experienced everything and is worthy of returning to God. For God knows all, and it is not possible to be with God until one has suffered everything."

"But what is your magic? Surely, it must protect as well as bestow."

"Sometimes I think it is merely its own form of hardship." She sighs, unfolding his arms and holding both his hands. "I was a queen in other lives before this, Uther. I tell you this not to boast, but to . . . to prepare you."

"Prepare me?"

She pauses. "Instruct you, then. I am, as I was, a worshiper of Morrígan, a harsh goddess my people have adored since we migrated west from Scythia, Cimmeria, and India millennia ago. In those long-ago times, we sacrificed our kings, strangled them and buried them for our bloodthirsty goddess. Now in this life, Morrígan has rewarded me for my many sacrificed kings by granting me the devotion of her servants, the Daoine Síd—the pale people, the elf-folk of legend—and their magic. But in this life, I am the one to be sacrificed. And so, I lost the joy of my childhood to Gorlois, and my life as a mother is taken from me with my only child, Morgeu. That is my destiny—the price of my magic."

"And me?" the king asks. "Am I to be sacrificed, too?"

"Need you ask, Uther?" Her pale brows lift dolefully. "The time we live lives us and speaks for our sacrifice. Your brother knew this. And we must not forget. We will lose our united kingdom, unless we are willing to lose ourselves to each other." She holds his hands to her lips. "But I tell you this now, because this much I believe: I will suffer a more dear and near loss than my kingdom, young king—for to you, I will lose my heart."

That night, Merlinus does not sleep. He prowls the grounds, more than once eliciting angry warnings from the fiana and the king's men posted to guard the *mansio*. He does not care. His strong eye has revealed too much trouble for him to rest. He doubts the king and the queen sleep this night, either. Lights burn in the windows of their separate suites as they contemplate in their own souls the significant threshold they will cross together with the coming day.

Merlinus cannot accept that evil rests, for he remembers too well his life as a demon. His mother has charged him to go into the world and work good: order out of chaos and care for the weak. He cannot idly sit by while his king and queen are endangered by Morgeu and her conjure-warriors—the Y Mamau. The brails of his heart search the night yet find no threat.

The following day, weary as he is, Merlinus continues his surveillance. Even as the pavilion tents and brilliant investitures go up, he walks the periphery of the walled city, reaching as deep into the forested hills as his power will allow.

The wedding fulfills itself outdoors with magnificent fanfare. Banners, pennants, and dragon kites fly in a periwinkle sky as both druids and Christians, separately and together, work their sacred ceremonies upon the royal couple. All the while, Merlinus mingles among the thriving crowd of villagers from Maridunum and the surrounding hamlets, the better to feel out treachery. But there is none. At the moment of sacred union, the ecclesiastics release doves of peace, and drumrolls brattle like thunder.

Feasting and merrymaking break out at once—jugglers, clowns, and acrobats scattered throughout the assembly display their hijinks while musicians play their most joyful songs.

Children gambol, round dancers interlink, and storytellers chant their tales of wonder among foaming kegs of beer and splashing barrels of wine. Merlinus watches from the *mansio*'s roofed promenade where, at the queen's orders and much to his annoyance, the servants whom he avoided the night before insist on grooming him.

As the happy day wears on, the wizard is left alone. Music billows and hangs in vapors among the trees and hedges and drifts into the mottled hills. On the platform where they have been wed under a solar yellow awning painted with an interlocked dragon and unicorn, the royal couple hold long audiences. First, they meet with Bishop Riochatus, then with Dun Mane and the elders of the druids, followed by Falon and the commanders of the fiana, after which come the king's men and, finally, various local dignitaries.

Merlinus, too, is eventually summoned. Somewhat self-consciously, he wears a new robe of midnight blue and coral stitchwork given him by the queen. Dun Mane has presented him with a conical druids' cap of matching color and pattern, a symbol of wisdom, which he sports proudly. With his flowing silver hair and long beard newly trimmed for the occasion, and his sturdy staff in hand, the wizard looks, to his own vast amusement, every part the sage. Muscular fiana and the king's bowmen in their ebony armor escort him as an honor guard through the boisterous festival, and he draws curious looks and amazed shouts from the vast gathering.

Guardsmen in abundance stand alertly at every feast tent and are visible beyond the tree fringe compound, covering every battlement of the city wall. Though the sun still blazes above the watery horizon of blue hills, torches have already been lit on the distant walls and around the wedding dais. In an adjacent pavilion tent, fifty Celtic commanders and their ladies feast, wearing a spectrum of colors. A smaller canopy nearby shades the bishop and his clerics at their repast.

On the platform, Ygrane and Uther sit in their dark wooden

chairs, the queen's carved in dragons' fins and talons, the king's with cloven hooves and a unicorn's stylized mane. Even from across the sward, Merlinus recognizes their open joy, indefatigable even after a long day of rituals and audiences. Ygrane is resplendently dressed in a scarlet bodice and a white *gwn* patterned with complex Celtic ciphers of gold thread. Uther has on an emerald tunic that hangs to his knees and a black leather cuirass embossed with his clan's dragon sigil. Both wear their slender golden crowns, and, the wizard spies as he nears, they are holding hands.

At the sight of Merlinus, conversation dims in the tents of the druids and the Celtic military command, and they look at him and murmur to each other. The ecclesiastics, too, watch the wizard closely, the disapproval in their tight stares clearer to read than the Celts' muted reaction.

In front of the platform, Merlinus bows formally, once to each of the royal pair, as he has seen others do. At the queen's beckoning, he climbs the five steps to the platform and sits on the audience bench to her right. Her luminosity saturates him, an extraordinary glow of sensuality, of womanly selfhood, warmer than possession. This is something he recognizes well—the feminine energy that first drew him into the horror of the void, then pulled him out of his mad rage into the comfort of his mother's womb, and which finally led him here through the legend of his own striving to her side.

"What a glory you've accomplished, Myrddin," she honors him. "You have succeeded. You have found my true mate."

"And completed our kingdoms by bringing us together," the king adds. "After Ambrosius died, I died as well. So much of me belonged to him. But you have given me a new name and a new destiny with it. And now—a wife. How can we reward your labors?"

"The child you will bring into the world is all the thanks I ask," he answers with a smile of shared happiness.

At the height of his exultation, a blaze of searing radiance sweeps past, close to the platform, and the wizard pulls a hand to his eyes and sees bones within. An angel has dared a very close approach.

Why? he dreads, sockets aching from the blinding light.

"Myrddin?" The queen leans over and puts a concerned hand on his arm. "What do you see?"

Merlinus tries to ignore what he has seen. "The world seems little changed by this wedding today, but I know the age here begun will enter into the heart of the human dream and have renown in all—"

Another rush of white-hot flame jars past, closer than the last, and this time Merlinus distinctly sees the comet tail tresses and the fetal features of a staring angel. Alarm seizes him. His heartflow feels nothing, and he stands up and tries to cast his brails farther into the world. Nothing.

Then he understands. It is an understanding that he, as a demon, would *never* have forgotten, shivering in the void watching worlds burn and dim like sparks. But as a man, enraptured by the dreaming world, it is easy to forget.

The greatest frailty of mortals is that they believe what they do is important. They live far from the truth. And so it seems Lailoken has been a man too long and has forgotten that the greatest battles are not fought among mortals. Far down behind the world, in the blind depths that range from star to star, angels and demons continue to do battle in the tremulous convulsions of starfields and nebulae and the debris they enclose—worlds like this damp rock where small lives live and die. The war rages on. Yet blinded by his dim mortal eyes, he does not fully remember it, does not fully remember that the battle in the void decides the destiny of worlds.

"Merlinus—what is wrong?" the king presses, rising anxiously.

Acting on instinct, Merlinus raises his staff and shouts barbarous words, commanding the demons present to show themselves. Abruptly, in a conflagration of staggering refulgence and writhing black ordure, they appear in the sky above the festive parkland, a black mass of lightning-faced warclouds. Several angels sweep back and forth in response. Like glaring fireballs, they blaze in their struggle to hold back an advance of demons. At least three of Lailoken's former comrades have gathered to attack—Ojanzan, Bubelis, and Azael—but not Ethiops, the demon the wizard saw with his long sight. *Where is Ethiops?*

"Myrddin, sit down," the queen speaks gently at his side.

Her composure alarms him, for he can tell that no one, not even Ygrane with her sight, can see them. The wizard takes her hand and places it firmly on his staff so that she partakes of his vision.

Instantly, as the horrid sight slams into her, she falls to her knees.

Uther rushes to her, and Merlinus begins chanting slaying songs in a vain attempt to drive back the demons. But that is hopeless. How well he knows, those old companions of his are beings far beyond any mortal imprecation.

In a fright, Merlinus scans for where Morgeu and her soldiers might be—and it is only then that he sees them—at the distant end of the compound, where the western sun fingers through the woods. There, Ethiops looms above the treetops, his jellyfish tendrils lashing the earth, entangling a fighting swarm of glassy figures—the pale people.

Squinting, Merlinus can make out a band of elf-folk striving vainly to hold back a jostling line of rearing horses mounted with hooded soldiers. Ethiops's whipping tentacles scatter the Síd warriors, and Morgeu's horsemen charge.

Frantically, Merlinus tries to alert the guards, but everyone's attention has fixed on his mad antics. Some believe he suffers a convulsive fit. Others think he brazenly curses the wedding. At his first wild shouts, the fiana posted around the dais have leaped onto the platform, and when the queen collapses, they hurry to her.

Falon moves to draw his sword to strike down evil Myrddin,

thinking the wizard has attacked Ygrane. Only Uther's warning shout holds the warrior's blow. Instead, Falon seizes Merlinus by the back of his robe and yanks him away from the queen.

That may very well have saved the wizard's life, for in the next moment, Bubelis's monster shark and Ojanzan's flexing centipede collide in the sky with the angels. Before Merlinus's eyes, the demons instantly wrinkle to fuming cinders in the burning presence of the angels and skitter away across the sky, squealing in cataleptic pain. But they have created a momentary opening in the angels' defense, and it is then that Azael comes slithering through.

The demon lunges at where Lailoken has been standing, next to Ygrane, determined to smash his old friend free of his mortal body. But, in a blort of screeches and shrieks, Azael strikes instead the platform close to the Stave of the Storm Tree and explodes into view of the entire startled gathering.

The impact shatters the dais and flings the royal couple, the fiana, and Merlinus to the ground, toppling the entire stage headlong into the flickering shadow of Azael's twelve-foot-tall eel shape. The demon's slick genital face bulges open with an incinerating cry of fury and frustration, far louder than the evoked howls of terror from the acres of shocked witnesses.

At this range, close enough for the reboant presence of the demon to shake the meat on bones and for his choking, earth bowel stench to burn lungs, the wizard's barbarous curse has some effect. Lailoken howls death at his former comrade, and, with a hurt scream, Azael shrivels smaller. Yet even through his agony, the demon has the presence to lash out.

Merlinus rolls aside, and Azael's slippery coils miss him and splat over the queen. As Merlinus sits up to strike the demon with his staff, afraid to shout another curse for fear of harming Ygrane, Uther bravely and foolishly flings himself at the abomination. With a shrug, Azael brushes away the king, heaving him senseless to the ground. Merlinus jabs the demon with his staff, forcing all his fighting wrath through the weapon, and Azael recoils, tail slapping.

A blow strikes the wizard's chest, knocking his staff from his grasp, and leaving him sprawled against the broken dais in a breathless daze. Yet he remains alert enough to see that his attack has been effective. Ygrane falls free as Azael shrinks even smaller, slithering away and gradually disappearing outside the range of the staff.

Scarcely has Merlinus found his breath than a stampede of horses bursts through the throng, toppling tables and scattering people in its mad wake. Beyond the reach of his heart's brails, these hooded warriors had been waiting patiently in the distant woods, and now their attack appears seemingly out of nowhere, a troop of ghost-riders to which Merlinus can only respond by gawking in stunned alarm.

Distracted by the horrific apparition of Azael, the guards had not seen the rapid approach of the horsemen from the far end of the compound, and now it is too late to sound an alarm. The invading cavalry charges full out among the assembled. Several of the king's bowmen have the presence of mind to fire their arrows before the attack sweeps over them, but they bring down only four of the onrushing enemy.

Twelve riders more fly past the archers. Merlinus's heart, already swollen huge with hunger for air, very nearly bursts at the sight of them—terrifying, leather-hooded soldiers with wolves' muzzles—the Y Mamau the queen had spoken of earlier, the conjure-warriors indifferent to death! Five fall to the maniacal attack of the desperate fiana, but the remaining seven advance and trample the fallen awning, shredding the painted image of the dragon and the unicorn to sorry rags.

Merlinus gasps, trying to muster his wind to form a barbarous cry, but he can manage only a squeak as the horses hurtle past. Síd fighters pursue in the turbulent wake of the chargers, their translucent bodies blistered and tattered by Ethiops's poisonous lariats. Prince Bright Night scrambles among them, his pale flesh torn and fluttering like leper's rags in his frantic effort to reach the fallen queen. But the pale people, all their magic sucked from them by Ethiops's attack, have no strength to stop the mounted wolf-soldiers. The elf-folk shred apart like so much mist among the violently churning stampede.

Swords flash and fiana fall under plumes of blood. Then Merlinus sees two wolf-soldiers swoop down and seize the unconscious Ygrane. Uther shouts and falls back senseless where he lies, and one of the raiders raises a javelin to pierce the king but is stopped by an arrow through his throat. In a blur, the six surviving invaders fly off, the queen draped across one of the horses like a dead hart.

For a spelled second, no one moves. The Y Mamau have employed no magic until this crucial moment, and all who remain on the field are surprised by the abrupt paralysis cast over them. By the time the stunned and angry fiana master the will to shrug off the conjure-warriors' spell and run for their steeds, the kidnappers have already flung themselves into the forest and are gone.

Choking, Uther thrashes and sits upright with a horrified expression. "Ygrane!" he gasps.

Amazed shouts sound from across the havoc of the wedding site. Most of the villagers have already fled, scurrying back to the city gate, and only soldiers and priests remain. Shocked onlookers still on their feet fall to their knees. The bishop, a war veteran and doughty soldier of Christ, rises from where he has been administering last rites to a fallen archer, seizes the cross-staff from a stunned cleric, and brusquely shoves through the astonished party guests.

Anxious to protect the king from sorcery, Riochatus descends upon the sorcerer, thinking that somehow Merlinus has caused the whole disaster. In defense, Merlinus blocks the blow of the cross-staff with his Stave of the Storm Tree—and for a shocking moment, the bishop partakes of the wizard's sight and can see the spiritous pale people, transparent in the afternoon's late light, cankered with wounds and limping past him on their way back to the brambles and the hollow hills. Prince Bright Night himself is there, embroidered with gruesome lacerations. He has spun about to protect Merlinus, and now his cut face looms close to the bishop's.

"Devils abounding!" the churchman bawls, and falls back. "Merlinus, damn you! What have you done?"

The wizard orders the clerics to lead their bishop away, enfeebled and sputtering as he is, and Merlinus nods his quick thanks to the elf prince before turning to his king. The archers have helped him to his feet. He puts an arm out for Merlinus. "Who are they? Who took Ygrane?"

"Y Mamau," Merlinus tells him. "Morgeu's men."

"Not men, they are," Falon says grimly, crouching over one of the fallen enemy. He has peeled off the grisly leather mask and reveals a freckled woman's face. "The Y Mamau—they are priestesses of Morrígan. Conjure-warriors, eager to die in battle. The people fear them. Only we fiana will dare stand against them."

"Where have they taken Ygrane?"

"I fear—to be sacrificed to Morrígan," Falon answers, grief-struck, and reels away to find his steed.

Uther stands pale and stiff with anger. "Horses!" he calls. "Get me my horse!"

"Lord—" Merlinus holds the king's furious gaze. "We cannot ride against the Y Mamau alone."

"The fiana will fight for their queen," Uther says, stepping past the wizard, toward the city wall. "With them, we shall track these Y Mamau." His scowl sweeps over the havoc of spilled tables and toppled tents. "What a fool I am! We should have been married in the *mansio*, inside the city walls. Look how many have perished!"

"The Y Mamau have magic, lord," Merlinus says fiercely, winding among the fallen bodies. "We dare not go after them. Soon, it will be night."

"*You* have magic!" he yells, stopping to confront the wizard. "We're going after these witches, you hear me? We must get Ygrane back!"

"Yes, of course. I realize. But don't you see? We need more. What powers I have are insufficient." Merlinus stops the king's protest with a hand on his shoulder. "You saw the demon. There are others. Uther, I cannot fight them alone. We need help."

"Aye, we all saw the demon!" someone angrily shouts from the confused crowd. Merlinus looks toward the cry, at the figure of the bishop shrugging off his companions and striding toward the king. "That was Satan himself! Is there any doubt of it? God has cursed your marriage to this heathen queen—"

Uther spins on him angrily. "Shut up! You don't know what you're talking about."

"I know what I saw," the gaunt man rails. "A sign from God that your marriage is unholy—damned in His eyes!"

Dun Mane, his white druidical robes torn and streaked with mud, rises woefully from where he comforts a dying Celt. "Guard your tongue, Riochatus. This is still Cymru, and you'll not besmirch our queen with your ignorance!"

Uther clamps his jaw to keep from hollering and appeals to his wizard with an anguished look. "Merlinus—"

With staff raised to guide Dun Mane's advance, Merlinus sends the druid to fend the bishop, and he draws the king aside. "There are terrible powers arrayed against us," he warns. "We will need help."

"Seek not the Devil's aid . . ." the bishop begins.

But Dun Mane cuts him off and speaks up loudly. "Myrddin is right, Lord Uther. We dare not track the Y Mamau by night."

"I will not sit idly by!" Uther protests.

"No," Merlinus agrees heartily. "But first, we must seek aid from Ygrane's allies—from the Daoine Síd."

Falon and his surviving fiana, who have come running with their horses, understand what the wizard means, and they mutter among themselves and looked intimidated. But the archers and the king frown, uncomprehending.

"Síd warriors have already died here today to defend the queen," Merlinus says, and he points his staff west, to the red doorways of the forest. "Those that survived are returning now to the hollow hills and their king. We must follow them and petition their king for help."

"Will they . . . Can they help us?" Uther asks the fiana.

The soldiers hesitate, afraid to speak aloud of the pale people, then nod sheepishly. Falon alone speaks: "They are older than Morrígan herself, and their magic is greater."

"Then let's go!" Uther runs for his horse, and Dun Mane hurries after and takes his arm, stopping him. "Lord Uther, none who has gone into the hollow hills has ever come out the same. The pale people make madmen of mortals."

"You are trespassing Hell!" the bishop cries.

"Then stay if you like," the king says, budging past him. "I'm going alone if need be. And I'll not return—sane or mad—without Ygrane."

Dun Mane stands aside to let him go. He has made this queen; he will make others. Falon sneers at him in disgust before following Uther, who already sprints toward the horses being led from the city gates. The archers hurry after their king, and the fiana exchange nervous looks and follow their commander begrudgingly.

With an effort, Merlinus joins them. The terrible sight of the demons has damaged his confidence. Yes, God Herself wants him to burn brightly before the coming dark age, yet even She cannot stop that thousand-year-long night from descending. Who is to say that Lailoken can succeed at all, even in so small a task as polishing a single destiny bright enough to reflect Her radiance?

At the depth of his despair, as he picks his way across a field littered with collapsed tents and the remains of the feast scattered in the panicked flight of the villagers, he spots the unicorn. It is a fog shadow in the forest. But just a glimpse of it is enough to embolden him.

The king scowls impatiently at the wizard from atop his mount. "Which way, Merlinus?"

"Into the west, lord," Merlinus replies surely, sliding his staff into the saddle straps, preparing for a long journey. "Into the twilight between the worlds."

Sighting the wispy figures of Prince Bright Night and his soldiers against the swollen, gaseous disk of the setting sun, Merlinus leads the king and his small troop southwest beyond the parkland and onto a vague, half-hidden trail in a woods too green for the season. Leaf litter and autumnal pods muffle the trod of the horses, yet the boughs still hang thick with foliage. Ahead, through the crowded trees and brush, the incandescent embers of the west cast the world in a curious light, both molten and translucent.

They ride for hours, yet the twilight's procession never darkens wholly to night. Each time Merlinus hurries forward to consult with the elf-folk ahead, they retreat farther into the dusky Apocalypse. Eventually, the trees thin away, and they find themselves reduced to shadow specks against the vast flame-woven wall of the red sun. The land around them lies smooth and flat, yet shimmery at the horizon, slurry with the lurid fire and chimerical weavings of the giant aqueous sun.

The elvish scouts vanish, and in their place, a lone tree eventually appears on the ambiguous horizon. Leafless, the complication of its stark branches etched like webwork against the immense sun, it stands wholly in the void with its flaring roots a reflection of its bare limbs and numerous twigs. The riders draw closer, and, as if in a dream, they watch its heraldic shape widen, diffuse, and waver into serried columns of fire. Then, gradually, the weave of flames surrounds them, stately woven sheets of torrid plasma grained with thermal veins, hues, and shadings. It arcs in buttresses overhead, meshing to igneous domes and cupolas.

The marblings of flame seethe like living carnelian and agate in groutless floorplates that blaze beneath the horsemen, feverishly yet without heat. Ahead, a royal hall looms, replete with a colonnade of tiered balconies and arched windows looking out on the silver reaping hook of a new moon and splashes of stars.

A jagged luminosity appears in the distance. A throne of sunlight, with webbed claws for posts and a fan back rayed with sharp solar spikes, sits at the far end of the dazzling arcade. Then, the tattered troop of elf-soldiers that the riders have followed to this strange realm kneel down before a human shape of such potent brightness it could rival the angels' star heat.

Slowly, warily, the horsemen dismount and approach on foot. Out of the vivid starcore blindness, a regal presence forms, a nebular iridescence shaping itself into a towering, boar-shouldered man with a human reindeer's face and bony knobs of horns just visible above a woolly mane.

The fiana kneel, and the others follow. "Your Majesty—" Merlinus greets.

"Whenever has a demon genuflected to any god?" the animal king brays. "Lailoken, you are a devil, and you'll not be deceiving this old god. On your feet. I might as well be bowing to you. And here in my own palace, too!"

"Majesty, I am now but a man—"

"Haw! You want me to believe a demon can be made a man?" He howls laughter that rings in polished echoes from the palace's high recesses. "No magic can unmake a demon, Lailoken. Look at you hiding in a human pelt! You are as you always were. That can never change. You can't fool me."

"God has given me a mortal form to do Her work among mortals," Merlinus says feebly.

A trollish grin shows human teeth in a bestial face as the

elk-king peers down at the wizard. "Oh, is it God we'll be appealing to now?" He bends closer and beckons Merlinus to rise. "God may well have blighted you with a human hide, Lailoken, but we'll have no help from God in saving Ygrane from the witches."

Merlinus stands and finds himself eye level with the elk-king's silver mantle-clasp, his own face reflected in its polished roundness—yet not his human face but the flanged jaws, adder grin, and hooded quartz eyes of his former demonic visage. The wizard startles and glances down, expecting to see again the sleek shark's belly and muscular, frill-seamed legs of his old demon shape. But no, somehow he appears entirely mortal to his own eyes and to those around him.

"King Someone Knows the Truth," Merlinus appeals once again to the grinning reindeer face, "I beg of you—will you help us save Ygrane from the Y Mamau?"

"The question, Lailoken, has long been—would you help us, the Daoine Síd, against our enemies, the Furor and his north gods?" the elk-king states imperiously. "Not long ago, you were an ally of all that hates life, if you remember. Now you serve the Nameless God and come into my presence with a worshiper of the nailed god. You *are* a demon, Lailoken."

"Demon he may once have been," King Uther speaks up, his voice cracking with trepidation as he stands before the bestial height and breadth of the ancient god. "But he serves me. It is I, Uther Pendragon, who have ordered these men here before you." His mouth trembles, and he flushes to the brink of tears. "I stand here for them—and for my God, who is no nailed god, but the love of the Almighty for his creation—you included."

The elk-king's grin pulls into a menacing snarl. "You are an insolent man, Uther Pendragon."

"Your Majesty." Uther shifts tone and bows his head. "God has clearly made you a greater being than I. I am but a mortal man." He touches the jade crucifix about his throat, lifts his gaze to the elk-king's bestial stare, and speaks more steadily. "I have not the demon power of my counselor, but God has seen fit to make me king of the Britons. Today, I married Ygrane, whom God has made queen of the Celts. Together we have joined to save this island from invaders. Your own warriors perished to save her—and me."

The Celtic god nods acknowledgment to where Prince Bright Night and his wounded soldiers kneel, watching Uther with mischievously slanted eyes, intently observant, as if seeing something new.

"If I seem too forward, Your Majesty," he continues, his voice stronger, "that is only because I am afraid for Ygrane and for our people—and I wish for you to deal directly with me. Can you help me retrieve my wife?"

"*Deal* with you?" The elk-king's sneer lifts to a cunning smile. "I will deal most directly with you, King Uther—if you've the stomach for it."

Falon passes Merlinus an alarmed glance, and the wizard prepares to throw himself between the elk-king and Uther.

"Come with me, Uther," the elk-king beckons. "You, as well, Lailoken. The rest of you, remain here." He strides toward the sweeping staircase, and with large eyes Uther notices beneath the elk-monarch's emerald mantle, a pair of furry legs and cloven hooves. Merlinus reads his gaze and wishes that he had warned his king earlier on that appearances among the gods, demons, and angels are always only apparitions, shapeshifting energies that can pattern themselves as they please.

The elk-king begins to speak again: "What I'll be showing you, king of the Britons, few mortals see and live to speak of." Graceful as a wraith, he ascends the stairs, and the two men labor to keep up with him. Far below, the throne room diminishes as if behind rusty canyon walls. With each step on the winding stairway, they appear to glide long distances higher above the fiery contours and blazing promontories of the hall. Soon, the miniscule flecks that are their companions dwindle wholly from view in the adamantine deep above which they wheel and soar.

At the top, they reach a high mesa under the naked night, where the stars gleam hugely blue and in unfamiliar patterns. The giant crescent moon displays all its alabaster flaws and rows of dead volcanoes on its bright limb, and on its far side there glows a dusty lavender, shadowily hinting at broad ashen wastelands. Beneath this lunar night, a wondrous otherland lies before them. The celestial lights cast a glittery shine over the hammered face of the plateau and sparkle on an oasis of willow groves and mossy swales, touching ruffled, grassy verges of black tarns cool as stardust.

"Where are we?" Uther asks in a wispy voice.

The elk-king casts a churlish grin over his bison shoulder. "This is the Land of the Dead, King Uther—and the unborn, too."

Quickly, they advance through a rocky draw of boulders like wind-shaped skulls. With solemn eyes, Uther reviews the ruinous grounds that sprawl ahead, a moon-blanched plain strewn with shards of smashed pottery, broken columns, dismembered statuary—a luminescent ossuary of some ancient, legendary world.

"And this is the field of broken dreams," the elk-king explains. "Look and you will see modern Roman ruins among the lost dreams of the ancients."

Wedged between a fractured stone effigy of a winged Assyrian king and a dune of polished bones clad in Ægyptian armor, the eagle standard of the once-mighty Empire tilts atop a tarnished heap of battered Roman helmets.

"Our cross—Celtic *and* Christian—will rot here too one day," King Someone Knows the Truth muses, his strong voice wrinkling into echoes among the cypress caverns that lie ahead, beyond the bone-strewn plain. "Unless, Uther, we can come to a true accord powerful enough to stave off the invading Northmen that threaten our existence."

Through the mists that willow away over the shattered masonry of a nearby Greek temple, a narrow figure approaches, her hair vaporous as cobwebs.

"Raglaw—" Merlinus calls, weak with surprise.

"Why should you be amazed to see me here, Myrddin?" she asks in her wheezy voice. "You yourself saw me depart the sun's proud world—"

"Merlinus," Uther whispers, "who is this old woman?"

"I am the crone Raglaw, Your Highness," the old woman introduces herself. Mist shreds from her skeletal frame as she floats closer. "I am your wife's spirit counselor, the very one who taught your dear Ygrane how to read sense into her trances and visions."

"What do you want with us?" Uther asks, unnerved by the hag's cadaverous appearance.

"Want?" She cackles. "I am beyond wanting, King Uther. By and by, I shall be parted once more from the dead to continue my round—I, once the least possible that was capable of life and the nearest possible to absolute death. I who came in every form and through every form capable of a body and life. I who am not accomplished yet. I stand as witness to your entry into the Land of the Dead."

"Greetings, good Raglaw," the elk-king calls out heartily, and the shadowy hag jolts briefly out of her trance. "Glad news to bid you on your way—this young Roman king comes to make alliance with the Celts—"

"This is known, this is known," the crone mutters. Like smoke, she drifts obliquely away through low sandhills, the white pumice time-mortised from the shrines and walls of dead empires. "I saw it all, you know. Remember, Myrddin?" she calls back. "We saw it all—all of it—the blood-soaked earth—the ghostly armies—the king baffled by his choice. This is the one, isn't he? This is he who has married my dearest Ygrane. Yes, I still remember it all. He will father the king with the power to be just. Only, that is, if he unbaffles himself in time. In time, so much is baffled—Mercy without hope—Mercy—"

She passes out of earshot and soon the mist veils her again.

"My most holy God!" Uther cries softly. "I don't like this place, Merlinus."

"If we're to save Ygrane," the wizard reminds him, "we must go on."

Uther clutches Merlinus's arm. "But what did the crone mean—mercy without hope?"

King Someone Knows the Truth answers, striding forward through the frail fog. "During her life, Dame Raglaw had the gift of the strong eye—"

"The gift of prophecy," Merlinus explains.

"Yes, the strong eye," the elk-king repeats, lowering a dark look at the demon for interrupting. "With it, she has seen an age of twilight darkness descending on our island—an apocalyptic age lasting centuries. Our alliance alone *may* provide some succor—some mercy—for our peoples to the ends of darkness. But no hope to undo fate—no hope defiant of disaster."

"Then, why bother attempting it?" Uther asks bitterly.

"Why, indeed," the elk-king answers. "It all comes to this broken field sooner or later."

Merlinus stamps his staff hard, and the sand-muffled shale underfoot gives out no sound. "For that despair, King Someone Knows the Truth and all the Celts need a Christian king—*this* king. And the one who will follow him."

They have come to the boundary of the burial field, where dwarf pines claw the seams of an escarpment that rim a craterland of shining kettle pools. The elk-king stops and faces the two men, mighty hands on his hips. His mantle billows behind him in an updraft from the cliff, exposing fleecy legs and a fur-sheathed pizzle. "Explain yourself, demon."

"The Celts are an eternal race," Merlinus begins, in his most diplomatic and conciliatory tone. "You heard Raglaw. She speaks for all your people. Life goes to life until it perfects itself. For you, death is always a beginning. Even the death of your race may be endured. So why bother, indeed?" He touches his staff to Uther's shoulder, to the scar of the wound Ygrane has healed with her magic. "This Christian king believes much as your enemy the Furor believes—that life leads to death and death ends life. That the world itself goes to Apocalypse and to the end of all time. He will be a strong ally to your people, for his faith demands that he strive here and now to make good of this life—for this life is the only good he has."

The elk-king slides his jaw side to side, ruminating on this. "You make a strong case for your king, Myrddin. I think I will call you demon no more." He pulls himself around and leads the men on. "Come. I will show this Christian king a Celtic deal, the sort for which we are justly famous."

He guides them down a crumbling switchback trail, through looms of shining haze and rifts of the starry sky. The damp odor of ruined stone that hangs in the air sharpens with the resinous fragrance of stunted eucalyptus lodged in faults and crevices of the buckled rock wall, and thunder mumbles across some unreckonable distance. At the base of the overhanging cliff, they hop from a precarious ledge to cinderous gravel and find themselves finally before the black maw of a rime-dripping cavern. Tendrils of niter drool like frozen saliva from the roof of the cave mouth, and a chill, subterranean wind exhales a musty reptilian scent.

"Theo—" a haunted echo wobbles from within.

Uther jerks taller. "Ambrosius?" The king steps toward the lightless cave, and Merlinus stays him with a hand on his shoulder.

"Wait," the wizard advises. "He is coming."

A shadow separates from the tenebrous depths of the cavern and edges into the wavery starlight. Haggard and red-eyed, Ambrosius emerges, tottering feebly, his eyes filled with despair. "Theo—not you—not yet—"

"Stand back, shade," the elk-king orders. "You are in the presence of the living."

"Theo—alive yet?" Ambrosius still wears the armor in which he has died but displays no wounds, though he appears exhausted. His skin is ashen, his eyes sullen and burning. "What are you doing in this place?"

Uther throws off Merlinus's restraining hand and rushes to his brother.

"No!" the wizard shouts, but too late.

Uther embraces Ambrosius, and at the instant of their touch, the Dragon Lord thrashes in his grip, emitting a horrendous scream of pain. Uther falls back, shocked, and watches his brother curl up in torment.

"Stand away from him!" the elk-king berates. "The dead cannot bear the heat of the living."

"Ambrosius—I—I'm sorry!" Uther cries, falling to his knees to stare, weeping, into his brother's grimacing face. "Forgive me!"

With Roman stoicism, the Dragon Lord twists himself upright, the thews of his face taut with agony. "To touch you again—alive!—this pain is—is my great joy."

"Brother, why are you here in this cave?" Uther stares at him bleakly from his knees. "You died for your people. You should be in heaven."

"I died—for vengeance," he answers grimly. "The reward for which I now stand at the threshold of hell."

"No!" Uther clenches his fists and stands. "Who judges you?"

Ambrosius shakes his head, eyes squeezed tight against the shuddering cold replacing the scalding heat of his brother's embrace. "No one—has judged me—but myself. No matter, little brother. I am here—with Grandfather Vitki—the dragon-face of your dreams, brother—close to you—as I can get."

"Dragon-face?" Uther puzzles a frown. "Wray Vitki is here?"

"The Dragon Aurelianus—" Ambrosius grimaces a pale

smile. "Surely you remember? Our forefather's dragon. Did you not see him? You carry his mark. He helped you, you know—at Londinium."

Uther looks at him uncomprehending and shakes his head slowly. "Is this so?" the king asks Merlinus finally.

Merlinus nods. "I saw him myself, lord. The dragon-magus about whom I told you. He remains your ally."

"At . . . Londinium?"

"He came to you there, Uther."

Uther sits limply down on the ground, heavy with amazement, reassessing his memory of that tragic day. He stares at the ghost of his brother sadly. "I miss you, Ambrosius."

"Grandfather Vitki talks to me. He tells me—you hold liege pledges from all the Roman warlords of Britain—*and* the wild Celts." A hint of his old cunning shows through his exhaustion. "You must be more cautious—than father—or I. I lived—for rage."

Uther stares through brimful tears.

Merlinus kneels beside him and puts his arm across his shoulders and whispers to him, "The shades of the dead do not change, Uther. Just as we learned from Homer. We have to free him from the dragon-magus."

"Be wary, Theo—" the Dragon Lord warns. And Uther becomes aware then of the effort the wraith exerts to stand tall in his presence. "Grandfather Vitki tells me—you married Gorlois's wife. He says that Merlinus cast a spell—he gave you the countenance of the duke—you seduced his wife. Be wary, Theo—that is not like you."

"That is not true—" Uther blurts, then looks to his wizard and asks in a whisper meant for his ears alone, "Why does Wray Vitki lie?"

"This ancient forefather stole the strength for his long life from the Dragon centuries ago, when he was a vital member of the viper clan during those aboriginal and totemic times," Merlinus whispers back. "Now this ancestor serves you. You bear the hereditary marker by which he touches the world above ground. This bloodbind has no claim on your brother. There is no physical bond between him and the dragon-magus. I would wager Wray Vitki is making up stories about you to keep Ambrosius close at hand. We must get him away."

"Ambrosius," Uther speaks plaintively, "you mustn't stay here anymore. Not for me. I can't bear to think of you suffering like this."

"I want to be near you—to watch for you."

"You must stop worrying about me. You can't help me anymore. I wish you could. I miss you terribly, Ambro. But I know I'm doing your work—father's work— You must get away from this dismal place and go to God for your reward."

"No reward for me, Theo." Ambrosius stands erect though the flesh of him quakes. "I am but a lowly murderer."

"Leave judgment to God, Ambrosius." Uther lifts his face to the elk-king. "Where is the Christian haven in this Land of the Dead?" he demands.

King Someone Knows the Truth points past a jumble of fallen rock and wind-blasted yew shrubs to a notch in the rimstone. Making his way to it, the others following, Uther peers dimly across a terraced landscape. The lowest ledges of cracked clay ripple with draperies of heat and spires of butyl blue flames. Above that, a perilous garden overhangs the torched plateland. Broken stobs of cacti and spined trees trickle down slick black rocks from a higher terrace. On the highest entablatures, carpeted meadows of wildflowers, wide acres of verdant lawns, sprawling trees, and the waterways of misty falls bedazzle the darkland. Those top slopes shine with a morning light that falls in luminous sheets from a high country obscured by ice castle mountains.

"Ambrosius, come here," Uther calls.

The shade limps to his brother's side and surveys the prospect of the Christian afterworld. "Hell. Or purgatory—as the priests have always warned us. As you warned me, Theo."

"Yes, purgatory, I'm sure," Uther says. "The first step into heaven. I'm taking you there, Ambrosius."

"No, stop. I'm afraid, Theo."

Uther's nostrils widen as he breathes deeply to keep from buckling before the sorry spectacle of his brother's fear. "God will not judge you harshly, Ambrosius. I promise you that. I will come with you and speak for you."

"Ha!" the elk-king shouts, and all jump, even the ghost. "Not unless you want to be leaving your mortal life and Ygrane behind. He'll be speaking for himself alone. None who pass this notch in the rimstone can come back—not even I. Ambrosius goes alone or not at all."

Across their chasm of life and death, Uther and Ambrosius gaze resignedly at each other.

"Go, Ambrosius. Trust in our God. He made us who we are. He cannot hold that against us. His own son, Jesus, promised his love would intercede. Trust in that."

"What of you, Theo? You were to be a priest. How can you truly be king?"

"I rule by love, Ambrosius. Love alone makes me king." He passes a hand over his distraught face. "Go now, brother, please. Pass through. No one lives long in life. I'll be with you again soon enough."

"Seeing you—like this—" Ambrosius opens his arms in amazement. "Seeing you—a king—it matters not if I go—to hell."

Uther feels split between body and mind—deed and thought torn apart in him. His flesh aches with sorrow and yearns to embrace his brother again—but he knows this is not Ambrosius, just his wraith, divorced from flesh and deed and the changeable mind of the living. Though Uther's body aches with grief, his mind knows only weariness, the exhaustion of the fateful, who must go on living among hardships and wantonness to fulfill a destiny inherited from the dead.

Ambrosius recognizes his brother's suffering. Standing this close to the living torments the ghost, and he lingers only briefly—one last hungry look—before he steps forever through the notched rimstone. As if in an undertow, he moves quickly into the distance and turns only once to raise his arm in Roman salute before dwindling from sight.

At his passing, thunder brattles from the cavern, and a cold, sonorous wind swirls around the visitants, lifting caked ash to dusty ballerinas.

The elk-king turns his face to the wind. "The dragon-magus senses you," he states. "We must move on. Now calm yourself and come with me to that sheltering wood up ahead. I've something to show you—and we've an accord to reach."

King Someone Knows the Truth guides the two men, Uther visibly distraught, along the rimstone wall, between huge talus rocks to where a sandy path scampers uphill through knee-high heather. There, they reach the pine wood he has pointed to. Quite unexpectedly, they hear the sound of glittering, frenzied laughter and carnival noises bursting forth from somewhere farther up the shrubbed paths leading to the wooded heights.

"Not to fear," the elk-king says. "It is only my people, who know I am here."

Not knowing what to make of this, Uther and Merlinus gaze up the long shafts of the pines into the tufted boughs that float like islands in the sky. The moonglow draws mentholated incense from the firs, and a warm breeze descends softly from above, carrying the busy labor of bees and a tinkling and braying of distant sheep. The elk-king leads them upward, and the sky pales to opal hues and eventually streaks with the raspberry smudges and lemon rinds of dawn clouds.

By then, they have attained a height that affords a vista of sprawling meadowlands and bluesmoke forests that appear, curiously, both cultivated and wild. Below, they behold the magnificent unicorn grazing, the light playing iridescently across its white coat. Once again, giddy laughter chimes from out of the brightening dusk, and Merlinus senses happy, unseen presences nearby that somehow remind him, not of the Celts, but of the mythic Greek order of centaurs, satyrs, and Titans who ranged before Zeus.

The wizard swings his staff about, and the giggling grows louder. A motley glamour of laughing, startled figures suddenly appears around them, not unlike the elk-king in form, but only half-human—furry snouted, paw-limbed people with mossy hair and eyes green as sea pools.

"These are the first people," the elk-king announces. "They attend me when I visit here."

"But where is 'here'?" Uther inquires.

"Here is the purlieus of the Greater World, King Uther," the beast-lord answers. "Here, forms merge. In wild, discordant, humorous, and maddening ways, they merge—and delight in the merging. Here, forms fall away and souls stand alone, as radiant light awaiting the spirit laws, to shape them into ever new forms."

"Amazing," Uther quietly murmurs, clearly awed by the unnatural beauty of these Elysian fields. His body unconsciously sways to the shrill, faint piping of the oldest music, a rhythm of wind and water—

"Look more closely," King Someone Knows the Truth entreats. He points below to the luxuriant, fruitful valley, where a foam of laughter and song sifts from a tumultuous forest. Barely visible through the slanted apertures of the woods prance human shapes composed of no more than luminous mist, an entire assemblage of them frolicking and cavorting like fauns. Their mysterious spectacle ushers within the two human witnesses the strange yet familiar sweetness of indecipherable magic—a feeling of peace and loveliness that they recall dimly, from far back in their fetal dreamings. The spontaneous energy of the specters for all their recklessness and untamed abandon, conveys an ineffable beauty of innocence and purity, as though they obey an exquisite rhythm of a higher law: a riot inflamed with divine spirit.

"Those down there," the elk-king gestures, smiling upon them, "are the eternal dancers. I am their lord, their Pan. I serve them in this and the lesser world of mortal forms. My purpose is to tend to them as a gardener to his plants, a shepherd to his flock."

"Are they elfin?" Uther asks, awestruck.

"Not quite. They are people," the elk-king answers vaguely. "Celts mostly. My people. They dwell here as bodiless souls until the new forms they need to fulfill their cosmic destinies call them back to the Little World of physical existence."

"Cosmic destinies?" Uther does not remove his eyes from the phantom spectacle and presses his face more firmly into the lambent breath of hills and fields. "Who decides those destinies? Who chooses their new forms—their new lives in the world of the living? Do you, then? And, anyway, what has any of this to do with my Ygrane?"

King Someone Knows the Truth blares a laugh that peals like lightning's clangor with thunderous echoes. The loud guffaw startles the unicorn to its hind legs and draws the misty figures out of the bosky woods. Like passing smoke on a wintry river, the roisterous troupe dances along the skirt of the meadow in full view—spry figures of floss and cobwebs, chimerically lovely and gnomish in their tatterdemalion silks.

They filter back into the forest's purple shadows, and the elk-king subdues his amusement enough to say, "This has plenty to do with your Ygrane, my boy. You must have patience. As for the destiny of these souls—no, Uther, I make no destinies—I shape no forms. You mistake me for a greater god. That power is so far removed from me, I can scarcely predict when a soul will come or go much less whose should go where. Some stay among us for centuries, others transit here for mere days. I haven't the strong eye to see the fatefulness of souls. I merely tend them, with my fellow gods, the Piper and the Lady of the Wild Things. While these souls are here, their life-force belongs to me and the other Daoine gods—and we are no more than the gathered energy of those who come to us. When the Celtic faith expires, we too shall pass away."

"Your Celtic faith that is an enemy to mine," Uther says grimly, staring up into the giant's dark orbs. "Enough so that you dare to deride Jesus by calling him the nailed god."

The elk-king directs an amused growl at Merlinus. "Your king Uther is a combative one, I think, Myrddin. No wonder the dragon-magus put his mark on him." He strokes his goat beard and cocks a bristly eyebrow at Uther. "Your faith is alien to me, mortal—a bizarre desert religion full of vehemence and sacrifice. I did not seek out its adherents. I did not journey to their barren lands. But they have come to me and have taken souls from my fields, diminishing me. Am I to laud them for that?"

"You spoke of a deal, Your Majesty," Uther says, again adroitly shifting his tone. "Am I right to assume that—as with Ygrane's first husband—what you want to bargain is the promise to withhold Christian missions from the Celtic lands?"

King Someone Knows the Truth smiles his eerie half-reindeer smile at him. "Aye. That was my compromise with Gorlois. But I'll not compromise the same with you, Uther. It seems you are a true Christian, as he was not. So it takes no extraordinary sight to see you'll be a different negotiator where it concerns your faith."

"It is so," Uther declares flatly. "You say you compromised with Gorlois. Withholding the missions from your lands is less than what you really want this time, then?"

"Far less." The elk-king bows forward, like a parent to a child. "All right, then. This is my deal: I want nothing less than your soul, Uther Pendragon."

Uther steps back, aghast.

"Hah! That is the same look Gorlois gave me." The elk-king snorts derisively. "Does my bargain appall you, then? Only because you Christians have taken my image and made me into a demon. You call me Satan. But I am no demon. Lailoken will tell you. I am what the demons call a mucker, because I care about even the muck of life and all life's frailties. I tell you, muckers are as worthy of respect as any saints. I work with the *Annwn—*" He cants his fleecy, horned head toward Merlinus again. "*Annwn*—the Fire Lords—what does he call them, Myrddin?"

"He knows them as angels, my lord," Merlinus says.

"I work with the angels," he repeats to Uther. "I mediate between the Greater World here of radiant energy and the Little World of dross and matter."

Uther regards the elk-king with a level stare. "I did not mean to imply anything by my reaction, Your Majesty, but the truth is, I am an ignorant man. I've never met a being such as you before. All this is frightfully new to me. Forgive me my clumsiness. My only desire is to rescue my wife, Ygrane. But to that end, this much I know, and this much I can tell you: My soul belongs to God. Jesus lived and died for the salvation of my soul."

"That is precisely why I want it," the elk-king says almost capriciously. "My plan proposes to join intimately your faith to mine. To have a true believer, a true Christian soul, such as you, here among us, dancing and singing with us, subject to the same round, destined to be reborn, perhaps as one of us—as whatever God wills—*that* is what I want."

Uther's face tightens with disbelief. "Why?"

"To live." The elk-king shows his teeth in a rapturous grimace. "To live, King Uther. With you here among us, I can dream through you a stronger union between my people and all other Christians. With Jesus as Prince of Peace, the Celtic ways may continue. With the Furor, there is only death."

"You will not save Ygrane unless I give you—my soul?" The young king peers hard at the bestial yet pontifical face.

"Of course not. Ygrane is one of my own. To take her back

from her kidnappers, I will fight the demons themselves if I must." He tugs at a tufted ear and shakes his head. "No, Uther, I am proposing a deal far grander. An *exchange*, if you will. In return for your soul to come willingly here among us, I promise to send you the soul of our greatest warrior—to be born as your son, yours and Ygrane's. And in time, I promise you, he will have the full support of the Daoine Síd. And when he becomes king of all Britain, we shall fight at his side against the Furor. It has been promised to me that with a great soul in mortal guise again, we will thus preserve our Celtic ways from total extinction."

The elk-king's words electrify Merlinus. *Is this not the prophecy?* he thinks. *The very story Optima has told me and that Raglaw has passed to Ygrane?* He looks over at Uther, to see if he grasps the import of the elk-king's bargain, but the young king shows nothing, or rather, his face conceals everything. The extent of what he knows, and what Merlinus has prepared him for, show not in his outer appearance but inside.

With his heartflow, Merlinus feels Uther's wonder and fear annealed to each other, climbing like hills, like clouds, shadowing him smaller. The wizard fears that Uther will shrink into immobility. But the memory of Ygrane brings him back. He crosses his arms. "I thought you said you can make no destinies, shape no forms—that you can't even predict when a soul will come or go?"

"That is so. I cannot impel anyone. But I have great suasion among my people." The sapience in his animal face startles the king. "I promise you, Uther Pendragon, a great warrior soul will come to Ygrane, when she conceives by you."

"Did Gorlois refuse such an offer? Why?"

"Superstitious fellow that he is, he would not be convinced I was not Satan stealing his soul away to eternal damnation." King Someone Knows the Truth sneers and shakes his woolly head scornfully. "*Eternal* damnation. What a cruel hoax your priests have inflicted on your people. Souls change. Only God is eternal—and what kind of God would damn any created thing eternally? What sin could possibly be so great? But that is your faith. I'll not gainsay it any further. Gorlois refused me his soul. Do you think he is in heaven now—or burning in hell?"

Merlinus deflects this challenge by asking, "Tell me, sire: Who is Morgeu? What manner of soul is she that came to Ygrane and Gorlois?"

"Not of my choosing," the elk-king replies curtly. "She was an angry soul, to be sure. If I remember rightly, she was one of Boudicca's war chiefs, beheaded by the Romans, reborn by that union."

Boudicca. Merlinus and Uther remember the name well, as every Roman Briton would, for the woman was a warrior-queen who, almost four hundred years earlier, had led an uprising against the newly arrived Romans. Before she was violently suppressed, she wiped out an entire legion and massacred over seventy thousand Romans and their allies. In retaliation, the emperor Nero ordered her tribe annihilated.

"Then, she is to be feared," Merlinus remarks with open trepidation. "Such rage would be a lethal tool indeed in the hands of the demons. How will you ever fight her?"

"Fight *her?"* The elk-king splays a hand over his majestic chest in surprise. "Not I. That is not my domain. I said I'd fight the demons themselves if I have to—but I won't have to, will I, Uther? It is you—you and your ancestor, the dragon-magus—who will do necessary battle to retrieve Ygrane, while I and my Daoine Síd need do no more than distract Morgeu's demons."

"And if I must refuse you my soul?" Uther asks.

The elk-king squints at him shrewdly, then shrugs his massive shoulders. "Must you?"

"I promised my brother I would join him in heaven."

Merlinus takes Uther's elbow and pulls him away from the elk-king. "Don't make any deals with spirits, sire. I'm sure we can fulfill our terrestrial destiny on our own."

The beast-king slouches closer. "Myrddin, why do you speak against me?"

Merlinus separates from Uther and stands openly before the mighty being. "Lord of the Wilds, I am sworn by my sainted mother to serve what is good. It is good that we save Ygrane at once. This talk is a dangerous distraction."

With a gust of autumnal air scented of woodsmoke and leaf rot, the elk-king sighs. "Don't give yourself to the angry desert god, Uther. Don't do as Gorlois did. Accept my offer. Give me your soul, for however long God shall choose that you remain among us, and let a powerful Celtic warrior be your son and king to your people *and* mine."

King Uther remains silent. He knows this is the fulcrum of his destiny, yet all he can think of is Ygrane. Not Ygrane the queen and not the military alliance that can thwart the Furor, but the caring, green-eyed woman he met in the chapel. She is in danger. His golden eyes hood sleepily as he prays for a way to appease the elk-king without forsaking his soul.

Buying time to patch together a reply, Uther puts his face in his hands. Merlinus feels the king's mind racing, pacing his heart. The wizard can almost hear him thinking, *What does God want?* When Uther looks up, his jaw sets and his face appears tired with resignation. "Your Majesty, like you, I am the servant of my people. If this is for their greater good, I will do it. But only on one further condition." He stands taller. "The soul you send to Ygrane and me will embrace my faith and live as a Christian."

"What?" The elk-king rocks forward. "And lose another soul—one of my greatest—to your strange oriental faith?"

Uther does not flinch. "A soul for a soul, Your Majesty."

King Someone Knows the Truth clutches his small beard and leans so far back he seems about to topple. Then he sways upright and slaps his fist to his palm. "Done! At the birth of your son, you are to go to the Raven Spring—the druids know of this place and can show you the way. Drink of its sweet poison, and your soul will come directly to us here."

"After we have freed my wife," Uther retorts quickly, "I will consider your words, the words we have spoken here today, binding only if the sacrifice you ask does indeed serve my people's greater good."

"Consider it well, then, King Uther. Few mortals are given the chance to see what you have seen and return to their old ways." His eyes narrow menacingly. "Do not bring a benighted soul into the world. As for you, Myrddin—"

At the sound of his name, the wizard braces himself against his staff and lifts a brave face.

"You will stay out of this debacle," the elk-king tells him sternly. "'Tis for you that the demons have allied with Morgeu. They want to rip you from your mortal body, and if you're there, for sure there'll be no stopping them. No, Myrddin. I have another task for you." His dark eyes like holes stare into Merlinus, and the wizard feels the rhyme of their darkness stir primal memories of his long, dreamless flights between the stars. "You shall ride the unicorn to Avalon. The creature knows the way from here."

"Avalon?" Merlinus peeps, shaking off the lonely dreaminess the god's wide stare inspires.

"Avalon. An island in the western sea." His voice reverberates, as if from a cave, and Merlinus realizes that he is still dream-wrung, still under the god's mesmeric stare. "In Avalon you will find a cirque of standing stones, each twice the size of a man. That is the Dance of the Giants."

"The Dance—"

"Yes, Myrddin, the Dance of the Giants," he repeats, but the repetition is not purely for his benefit, Merlinus begins to understand. For the god is not hypnotizing the wizard but time itself, shaping events by his magical will. "At the center of the cirque is a smaller stone, big as a man yet very heavy. 'Tis made of star-stuff that fell to earth long ago. Move it aside. Beneath it you'll find a pool. The water-goddess that dwells there will give you a weapon crafted by the dwarf Brokk long ago—"

"Brokk—" Merlinus wags his head, trying to shake off the god's trance hold. "But Brokk is one of the Furor's craftsmen."

The elk-king grins coldly. "Yes, indeed. He is the Furor's finest blacksmith, in fact. It was he fashioned this sword for the Furor when the one-eyed god shrank himself to a man's size in fear of the Old Ones. The Jute hero Siegfried slew a dragonish troll with it. The *Annwn*—the angels have taken it from Brokk and given it to me to defend my people against the Furor. A fine work of craftsmanship it is, and imbued with a rare magic that serves the bearer. I want to see it used, as the Fire Lords intend—against the Furor! That will raise his hackles." He shakes his fists with glee, anticipating his age-old foe's rage. "Bring the sword Lightning and the star stone to Maridunum. King Uther will meet you there—with his bride."

Merlinus clambers down the pine-crest to the meadow where the unicorn grazes. It knows him and does not budge from its browsing until he is upon it. The animal raises its skinny, horned head, its clear eyes sentient of his purpose, and waits for him to mount. At his touch, a cold charge of electricity shakes him and a blossom opens in his brain with a fragrance that smells of heaven.

After that, Merlinus feels entranced, as blessed with joy as that known by the souls dancing in the faerïe woods of the elk-king. He watches Uther raise his arm in Roman salute, and the wizard, gone from his king's side for the first time since his days as a stable master, feels no anguish.

Clutching the unicorn's curly mane with one hand, his staff with the other, Merlinus sits tall as they gallop across the meadow and into the woods. The green, pillared darkness blurs past, and Merlinus does not look back. Speed forks his beard over his shoulders, whips his robe, and bends his conical hat, but it does not blear his eyes. Before long, they are in the open again, charging toward the mauve light of the mountains.

The unicorn swerves to a stop on a bluff overlooking morning hills, dells, and mountain cups of apple trees. Quicksilver cascades thread down among contorted apple brambles on the high verdant promontories, blowing off the steep, craggy groves in wild vapors. The sourly sweet frost of autumn-rotted apples buffets around him in a sea breeze sweeping off the rocky coast below.

He dismounts, and the instant he breaks contact with the unicorn, a black sorrow descends on him. Suddenly sick with remembered grief at the prosperous cruelty of the physical world, he gropes for the unicorn. But it shies away. He stumbles after it, nauseated with the visceral heaviness of his life, and the beast bounces downhill and leads him, stumbling and lurching over apples melted in the sun, to a plain of wild orchids.

The gnarly apple trees, afoot in the syrupy brown mulch of their dropped fruit, stand back in a ragged circumference from the orchid field. At the center loom rough-hewn menhirs—single upright stones—that pierce the flowery ground in a crude circle. His grief dims as he recalls what awaits him here.

On legs still numb from his magical ride, Merlinus leans strongly on his staff and staggers into the Dance of the Giants. The stone at the center has the wedged, flattopped appearance of an enormous anvil cleaved by a frost giant's battle-ax. The twin lobes of the ferric stone glint silver-black with orange pollen flakes of rust strewn throughout, and the wizard imagines he can feel the slag humming under his touch with magnetic force.

The star stone will not budge before his mortal might. It requires a strongly voiced barbarous chant and all the earthbound strength he can draw up into his limbs to lift it aside. As the elk-king has foretold, a hole of water underlies the sidereal stone. On his knees, Merlinus tries to peek past his own hairy reflection in the black water, then has to shout his shock when, out of nowhere, a glossy hand shaped of water rises upward to its elbow, then sinks quickly again.

Squatting before the hole like an amazed simian, Merlinus watches a sharp length of blue-white steel pierce the mirroring surface and lift slowly skyward. The beveled blade, so perfectly formed and polished, reflects the seaborn cumulus clouds above the tangled apple boughs clear as a window. Then the gold haft emerges, sunbright and roweled with interlocking circlets. Beneath a handguard like a long, slenderly curved Persian glyph, the spiral-carved helve rises, visible through the transparent grip of the water sprite.

The sword Lightning is an elegantly clean weapon, in form hypnotically simple, without any encrustations of gems or engraved scrollwork. Apart from the elfishly complex and minute torque design at the haft, it sports no ornament at all. Merlinus gawks at it admiringly a long time before the thought, the anticipation that he is about to take the object in his very fingers shivers through him.

At his touch, the watery hand splashes away, and he is left on his knees, holding the weapon. It balances like a living thing in his palm. Briefly, he hefts it, enjoying its substantial yet buoyant weight, then brandishes it, awed by its lithe strength. It feels as though it is an extension of his arm.

Merlinus's knees soak wet, and he looks down to see that the hole is widening. He gets to his feet, and, as he backs away, the pool irises larger, the orchids at the periphery crumbling off in massive clots. Hurriedly, he scurries out of the Dance of the Giants and runs, sword in one hand, staff in the other, to the line of apple trees. Then, he rushes back to retrieve the star stone as the elk-king has instructed.

Empowered by his anxiety at losing the aerolite, he chants vigorously and, hoisting with all his might, manages to steer the boulder like a bobbling wheelbarrow away from the water. He shoves it into the apple woods before looking back. When he turns about, he sees the menhirs sinking into the water vertically, soundlessly, leaving behind only the gentlest ripples, like fish whispering at the surface.

Merlinus thinks that perhaps the whole island will be consumed, and it makes him despair to think of carrying the heavy stone, the sword, and his staff to wherever the unicorn might be. Trying to consolidate his burden, he props the sword slantwise into the cleft of the stone.

The widening water stops at the trees. Then, when he tries to lift the sword, it sticks firmly as if annealed to the rock. Panic assails him, and he tries chanting and levering the weapon with his earth-rooted strength, all to no avail.

He consoles himself with the knowledge that King Someone Knows the Truth has decreed that the sword has magic. When he gets it to Maridunum, if need be he will petition the god for the necessary power to free it. For the time being, he resolves to accept it as it is, and he sits on the rock for a few minutes' rest before tackling the problem of transporting it across the sea to Ygrane's kingdom.

As Merlinus grapples with the immovable sword, a line of swans descends from out of the woods, and he now sits for a while watching them drift—pale and demure, proud and sad, over the slick black lake. Nine of them move single file across the surface, parading before him, carrying perfect reflections of themselves in a netherworld that is a dimmer pretense of our own. Watching them, he sinks again into the languorous sorrow that always comes over him after magical contact with the unicorn.

He remembers Optima's cryptic foretelling of the pagan swan queens, and he sits up straighter. *What was it she had said?* He glances around, reassessing the moment, trying to gauge if he has been bewitched. The brails of his heart feel something like the strenuous darkness between the stars—such a depth of untouched anguish, he thinks a demon must float nearby.

Then—something extraordinary begins to happen. After

completing a circuit of the lake, the swans return to the far end where they had entered, and as each of them exits, they shiver-shake and molt, their forms elongating till they emerge, finally, transformed into stately white-robed women wearing black veils. The sight of the first two transformations shocks him. By the third, he is on his feet, biting his nails into his palms to assure himself he is awake. At the fourth, he shouts, "Who are you?"

They pay him no heed but proceed into the forest, silent and ethereal. As the fourth, fifth, and sixth swan mutate in turn, he lopes around the edge of the lake and shouts again for them to stop. But only the apple trees yell back at him.

The watery breath of the lake thickens as he runs toward the figures, and he can see their beautiful changes in a golden mist of morning light. His running slows viscously, as in a dream. After what seem stretched minutes, he approaches the transmogrifying swans, and he can plainly make out the feathers melling in humanly eerie streaks to white flesh and plaited raiment. The air around them, dense as sea spume and golden with sunbeams, fills with a mood like a thousand-year-wide wheat field.

He sends his brails forward to reach through the emptiness between his heart and theirs, and finally he touches the last of the swan creatures as she completes her change from beast to woman. With a shriek like a gull, the space within his chest opens, and he feels the summer inside her slowly changing, dying like a butterfly, to the foggy fathoms and spectacular destructions of autumn.

"Who are you?" he calls to her. Through the black film of the veil that falls from the silver band in her white-blond hair, he can see her serene features shining in the morning clarity, as sad and pale as though the moon herself could weep for her.

"We have waited a very long time for you," she says to him, and her sonorous voice comes from above, behind, beyond him, from everywhere and yet not at all. She follows her sisters into the forest, where the morning light slants in many taut strings into the smallest corners. He follows her, breathless from his dreamy run, yet unfaltering, drawn by the special loneliness that had first lured him from heaven, the ancient promises of sorcery and mystery, the journey past the edge of the body, the hopeful distance that is woman.

Love *and* Its Sun

Avalon, Isle of Apples, rakes the sky with its needle rocks—menhirs erected on every bluff and promontory, many carved with futhorc incantations, like this one:

Seven years a fish in the sea.
Seven years a bird in a tree.
Seven years clanging in a bell.
Seven years hard living in hell.

What magic they hide, Merlinus does not want to know. He is intent on following the swan-women, who move with graceful, portentous steps in a line several paces ahead. No matter how fast he pursues, they remain just out of reach, and his entreaties for them to stop and talk bound emptily into the sunshot depths of the apple forest.

Anxiously, he thinks of the proud sword he has left stuck to the star stone back at the lake—and he wonders about King Uther alone with the elk-king deep in the Otherworld—and he remembers Falon and the fiana fending for themselves in the palace shaped like fire—and, most apprehensively of all, he contemplates the fate of Ygrane in the clutches of mad Morgeu and her wolvish conjure-warriors.

No matter any of his concerns, he will not turn away from his task, which has led him to the pursuit of the nine strange women. They have summoned him. That was enough for the likes of Lailoken, who was called out of heaven to follow Her into the coldest dark. He will not for the world turn away again from these nine beautiful shadows of Her.

Overhead, swift, soft clouds hurry from the south, swirling in sunny tatters as they fly through a blue sky darker than the mountains. Emerald butterflies jostle among the season's leavings—ruffled cabbage flowers poking through the windfall apples, orange and violet with intoxicants. White deer watch them pass from among the tall bracken and the bare frames of renegade elms. Through the forest's leafless branch ends, a turquoise lake glitters, and beside it squats a fat, lopsided mushroom dome, brown as gingerbread.

The swan-women lead Merlinus there, down mossy rock shelves to this odd round hut beside the green lake. Outside the crooked wooden door, red shrubs glisten—gooseberry, wild rose, barberry—and he pauses there as the women disappear inside.

"Myrddin," a gentle voice calls from within.

"Who are you?" he asks yet again.

"Myrddin—"

Slowly, nervously, he enters and finds himself in a broad interior with an earth-tamped floor and the round walls decorated in spirals and wavy lines of warm yellow, blue, and red ocher. Illuminated by slant-rays of azure light from small, round windows high in the dome, the nine swan-women sit on bulky block-cut thrones all in a line. In their presence, even indoors, he feels as though he were back in the brown hallways of the forest, in the reek of the dying season.

Merlinus stops trying to reach inside the apparitions and steps closer, studying their shadowy features through their black veils. "Tell me who you are," he demands.

"Sit down, Myrddin. Make yourself comfortable. You shall know what you seek to know."

Merlinus does as he is bid and finds a goblet of mead at his elbow and a rock-steamed salmon wrapped in rivergrass on the earth before him. He eats and drinks—and it is good.

"We are the Ancient Queens," the one farthest to his left begins. "I am the eldest. Rna, queen of the Flint Knives."

She lifts her veil, revealing skin white as buffed bone, crinkled flesh that gleams like minnow scales. Blue dusk has somehow been pressed into her temples, and though young of feature, with luxuriant hair the color of a thrush's breast, she seems also very, very old.

"Why have you led me here?" Merlinus asks.

Solemnly beautiful, the way a falcon is, she measures him as if with the closed face of a stone. "I shall tell you," she answers, her voice in the tall space sounding sodden. "I lived as a mortal woman, as a clan queen, one hundred thousand summers ago. Upon my death, my soul was sent here to Avalon to serve as witness to the ages of sacrificed kings that followed me."

Merlinus bows humbly. "Fair queen, I do not understand your mission."

"You would not, Myrddin, as you came to our world only recently, a few thousand years ago, with the flourishing of the first cities."

"This is so," he confirms. "But how do you know that?"

"What don't I know after a hundred millennia, as a soulful witness to the human pageant?" Her heron gray lids flutter sleepily. "I know your demon name—and the womb that made you human—and the plight of your queen Ygrane—"

"Then, you have led me here to help me?" he asks, his voice rising with hope.

"No, Myrddin," she replies in her torpid voice. "You are here to help me. Listen. I am the eldest of the queens, and my time as witness is done—very nearly done, after so very long—"

"Who did this to you?" he asks.

"Whose magic is powerful enough to fix a soul to one place for an aeon?" she turns the question back on him.

"Demons."

She shakes her delicately poised head. "They have not the poetry or the motive to conceive this fate."

"Then it must have been—"

"The Fire Lords," she answers for him. "The angels chose each one of us and brought us here. We are all queens."

"The angels—" He gnaws at his beard in disbelief. "Why?"

"Because, Myrddin, the soul of each person touches the souls of all others. Our mission given us from the Fire Lords is to witness the human pageant through the ages. We praise what is worthy and condemn all that debases and deviates from our human destiny. And what we nine souls feel touches the souls of all others. In this way, slowly and deeply over the ages, we help change humanity. We help transform the human soul."

"My mother spoke of you," he says. "She told me that God had denied you heaven—and that you were my godmother, because you had prayed my soul to earth—to free you. Can I free you?"

"I have been here for hundreds of centuries, Myrddin." She gazes into him with tranceful remoteness. "Every ten thousand years, the angels select another queen to join me as witness of our race's defiance of love. And together, through the magic sight that the angels have granted us, we have lived in a trance, watching people thrive, struggle, and die. We have mourned endless murders more plausible than love, and we have praised countless unsung heroes and their treason to evil. And slowly, as the stubborn ground of our own hard souls does relent and accept the nascent seeds of peace, charity, and mercy, a greening time begins, falteringly, in the one joined soul of all women and men. The furrow of our chastened ways cradles new lives. It gives significance to a hundred, a thousand generations, and gradually a spirit of reconciliation and fellowship takes root in the human heart. The plow of love digs deeper. Moral understanding—justice—common equality sprouts. And then, suddenly—the time of the queens has ended . . . "

"And man takes power for his own," Merlinus speaks up.

The ancient queen lowers her tired lids in acknowledgment. When she looks at him again, her gray eyes appear tarnished, dull as a dead woman's. "The time of the queens is over. Has been for ten thousand years. Now the kings begin their history of conquest. So begins the age of war." Her voice splinters, and she sits still and silent for so long that the wizard can hear the burning drone of bees outside in the feathery grass. He peers down the line at the eight other swan queens by Rna's side, and they sit even more still, marmoreal and quiet as death.

"The angels will summon no more queens here," the old one speaks again. "But soon a king will come to take my place. A king will come as answer to the ten thousand years of kings before him. And my soul shall at last be free to return to the round of living souls that pass from form to breathing form. Soon, the angels will bring to this place the first male gage, the first pledge of man's rule, who will sit in my seat and witness the indignities of man to his own kind and—worse—terrible crimes never committed during the long epoch of the queens—the indignities of man to the earth herself."

Merlinus's spine chills, and he tugs at his beard. "The first king—to sit here among you for a hundred thousand years?"

"We doubt the rule of the kings will endure a fraction of that span," the queen doomfully foretells. "Man possesses too much vehemence. But, yes, he will sit here until peace reigns—or until he sees the kings who follow him slay the last of mankind."

"Uther?" Merlinus guesses, nervously. "Is it Uther the angels have selected? Is that why you've called me here—to relish the irony of a demon serving the angels?"

"No, Myrddin," the queen says with ponderous melancholy. "Irony is a subtle cruelty, and after a hundred thousand years of cruelties, I am too weary of every hatred to want that." She summons him nearer with a slow turn of her wrist. "My succession is not assured until the angels find the right king, a soul with the largeness of heart to carry entire the arrogance of war as well as the mercies of love. Your Uther is not the one. He discredits the sanctity of war by his own reluctance. The angels will not choose him."

Who, then? Merlinus muses, till the answer dawns on him. "Of course—it must be the great warrior that the elk-king promised Uther for his soul! A Celtic king of olden times."

"So we believe," the queen asserts. "But his birth is not assured—and, even if Uther does sacrifice the faith of his own soul for this warrior to be born, the child's survival to adulthood—against all the malefic things the demons can set against him—will be in suspense. Every hunger of the heart in this king to come, and every accident in his temporal sphere, will become purchase for the demons to gain on our wish. Our only hope of fulfilling this king's destiny is for all the powers of light and form to strive together against the intelligences of darkness and void."

Merlinus stares boldly into the queen's dull eyes. "I promised my mother I would work with the angels."

"You will be sorely tempted away from your destiny," the queen predicts.

He thumps his staff adamantly. "No. I am determined."

"You will be tested," the wan queen warns again. "When the time comes, you must decide for the angels—for the king yet to be—or the very future of our kind will be in jeopardy. So very much depends on you, Myrddin." She lids her gaze. "Perhaps too much."

Her ominous tone reminds him of Raglaw's frightening admonition. *If you fail, not only you will be extinguished but all the future that you have seen.*

"I will not fail," he swears—and wonders if he really knows what he promises.

"You must keep the unicorn in the service of the Fire Lords," Rna presses. "It has much power. Do not let it steal away into the void. We need the unicorn. Keep it near the Dragon."

Merlinus blinks, dazed by the challenge. "I shall try."

"Do not forget that you are a demon, Lailoken." Talking has tinged Rna's pallor pink, and a lively, yearnful expression flickers within her stern eagle's frown. "You have strengths far greater even than the unicorn's."

Fuddled by that thought, Merlinus's mouth opens and says nothing. He cannot imagine forcing the unicorn to anything.

"Remember, too, Myrddin," the swan queen says, "that you are growing younger. It is the unique curse of your life as a man. Puerility and all its emotional tribulations await you. You will not be spared."

"What do you fear? That I will fall in love?" A laugh slips through his beard.

"Love is salvation," Rna reminds him. "It is lust that *you* must fear. You should know, Lailoken. As a demon, you used lust often enough to unmake the strivings of angels."

He waves aside her concern. "I am too old for that. I am as old as the angels, remember?

"Yes, Myrddin, but not as a man." She turns her head and looks at him with one gray eye, like a crane. "The flesh must keep its own helpless promises that neither angels nor demons can deny."

She speaks as though this is already a memory. And, like a memory, her words will return when he least expects. But at this enigmatic moment in the presence of the nine queens, Merlinus does not listen, for he is not yet ready to hear what she has told him. At that moment, it is the unicorn alone he fears—for the opportunity it presents to escape from the struggle of angels and demons—to leave it all behind like a bad dream that has gone on for thousands of millions of years too long.

Rna, as if hearing his thoughts, lowers her black veil, obscuring her face.

"Wait—" Merlinus calls. "What is to be done now?"

She points to a circle of clear light on the packed earth. "We need say no more. Look yourself into the light—the light from which we have all come—and open your strong eye. Then you will see what you must do."

Merlinus obeys her and sits cross-legged on the ground, his staff across his lap, his back to the nine queens. The vast clarity of the sky pours into his uplifted face, and he closes his eyes, letting the warm rays carry the stencil of bloodwork deep into his brain. Then, the demon strength in him lifts the muscular earth-energy from the joy beneath his belly, past the shuddering of his heart, and through the slippery constriction of his throat. As the power surges into his head, he streams from his body, up the bright pole of sunlight, out the window, and into the windy ether of the day.

The earth inclines below Merlinus in its rags of cloud. He sees Avalon, whole, its steep bluffs smoky with heather and its hill-sides and valleys red-brown with autumnal apple trees. On the stone crannies, the menhirs look like large, hooded people standing around on sheer hems of rock. Squinting, he can see the green lake and the brown hermitage of the Nine Queens dwindling away as he soars among cold updrafts of cloud.

The sea gleams below, and Avalon swings out of view. He knows that if he accelerates, time will widen and the future will sprawl before him. But he does not want to see that. At least, not yet. Far more urgently, he needs to know what has become of Uther and Ygrane. So, he keeps his flight steady.

Softly, he chants his demon magic. The day sky above the ocean gradually purples, and, in time, the seacliffs of Cymru drift past. The forest haze rises toward him, opens like a veil, and reveals a shepherd and his herd standing on a mossy bench of land at the elbow of a brook.

Merlinus dives past the herder and plunges into the earth. Darkness claps around him. A moment later, the blind abyss opens into a cold light pale as moonglow—starshine from a fiery zodiac. He has arrived in the Otherworld and drifts over nacre flats outside the elk-king's palace of fire.

The palace itself shines on the razorous horizon, sharp as a barb of the sun. He swerves toward it. He is intent on finding his king, to be certain that Uther is all right. As he closes in, the terrain below darkens to a cinereous landscape of scorched sand and drifting ash.

The ruins of dead civilizations stream past—the mammoth temple columns of Karnak blown bare of their sacred paintings, Nineveh's garden walls toppled and awash in sand, and the ziggurats of mighty Ur so much naked, haphazard rock enfolded in river silt.

He recognizes this place from the elk-king's tour and searches for the shade of Raglaw he has seen wandering here. But this time he finds only whispers of sand moving across these blighted ranges of lost empires.

His flight dips and slows, and he alights before the rime-fanged cavern of the dragon-magus. Sulfur flowers bloom yellow as forsythias among the scorched gravel. From within, soft thunder breathes.

The wizard calls boldly, "Wray Vitki—come forth!"

A sizzling noise saws from the cave, a sound like voltage or splattering oil. It is the audible coiling of dragonscales. Two yellowy green lights brighten in the darkness, and the glaucous stare of the magus draws closer with thunderous, smoky swirls of chill breath.

It stops at the threshold of darkness. Merlinus, standing in the subterranean starlight, sees only a behemoth shadow. Lit by the lamps of its eyes, a saurian grin bearing mongrel traits of human likeness hangs above him, huge and horrid as a ritual mask.

"Wray Vitki—I am Merlinus, wizard to the Aurelianus family. I have come to speak strength to you."

The eyes of the dragon-magus flare and die back. He is weak with age. His life only smolders. Even the rapture of trance has soured with weariness. All of him that has become as the Dragon wants to die and return to its origin. But what remains of his humanity reaches out for Merlinus.

Wray Vitki, mute as an adder, cannot speak, yet Merlinus can feel the truth of him with his heartflow. Since his telepathic bond with Ambrosius was broken, Wray Vitki has lain in this cavern coiled around his weariness.

"I will speak strength to you," Merlinus promises, "for I know you will use this power to serve Uther Pendragon, a king descended from your seed, father of the great king to come."

Even as the sorcerer speaks the demonic words that infuse the dragon-magus with renewed vitality, Merlinus's own bodylight dims and floats sullenly away. His physical body far away in Avalon summons him, and his wraith sails back through the field of ruins.

Briefly, he spies the fiana and cavalry who accompanied Uther. They have fled the elk-king's palace and wander on horseback seeking a way back to the sunlit world. As Merlinus drifts away, the slow riders in the elfin dreamtime melt into scalloped waves of heat.

The Furor lies down on the quilted meadows of the Cantii countryside. He listens for a long time to the Dragon's heartbeat before the liquid rhythms lull him into a trance.

It is behavior such as this that has alienated him from many of the gods, including his good wife and his wicked brother.

They shiver with disgust at the *idea* of pressing one's whole body against the slimy hide of the Dragon. It fills them with dread revulsion to think of the numerous parasites vigorously feeding in the hot ooze of Dragonflesh. They do not care what he tells them of Apocalypse; they will never willingly embrace the fetid beast.

Long ago, during his exile on earth, the Furor learned to love the organic beings many of the other gods called parasites. He does not mind the encampments of tribes that pool in the dales and river valleys covered by his body. Indeed, he wants them to feed off *him*, to grow strong on *his* godly powers. In time, he will use their strength to conquer these islands.

For now, he is content to dip into trance and into the dreams and frenzies of his storm raiders and berserker chiefs. He speaks through the runes of the raven priests and dances with Death's Angels, the warrior cult that dresses in the flayed skins of their enemies. He makes his presence felt among the people.

In turn, through their tiny magic, he learns the tiny things he cannot see for the largeness of being a god. He hears about the queen of the Celts who rides the unicorn, and he remembers Ygrane, the bold adolescent witch, who once dared confront him in the Great Tree itself.

If that had not been Ancestor Night and his head not splitting from the terrible strain he had exerted binding demons, he would have recognized instantly that she was working powerful magic against him. The Celts tricked him. He gave Ygrane the unicorn, and now she uses it against him. The magic rinses she makes from the unearthly energy of that beast defeat all the charms of his sorcerers and the battle luck of his warriors.

But he is pleased to learn that the demon Ethiops has used the devious queen's own daughter to capture her. Having exchanged gifts with Ygrane, the Furor cannot kill her or order her death without violating the sacred bonds of their tribal lineage. Ethiops, however, is unconstrained by such niceties.

The Furor lies comfortably on the green and turning earth. His magic, slow to begin, eventually will fulfill itself. This he knows. The gods who trust him, who gave their life-force to him and now sleep on the Raven Branch, will wake to find themselves masters of these islands and of all the Abiding North. Not the mistress of the unicorn nor her freak man-demon, the wizard Lailoken, nor even the Fire Lords themselves can stop him, because he fights to save the earth itself from abomination.

Far off, in the rambling back lots of his trance, where the absurdities of dreams fringe on nightmare, the Furor keeps his memories of the future. Thermonuclear holocaust and global warming pollute his trance with cinderworld images: cities melted to stobs of rock, forests reduced to scabbed slurry, all land barren ash, and the oceans churning lifelessly under miasmal waves of heat where once there were gods and people.

The wizard's astral flight arcs across the barren carbon expanse of the World Tree's roots toward the flaring spires of the elk-king's palace. Its walls flicker and seethe, trembling in the surging balance between form and shrieking shapelessness. Watching it breathe within its jeweled constraints of towers, barbicans, buttresses, and arches, Merlinus contemplates the credo he learned as a demon: that all forms are illusions—only formlessness is real.

But where angels shape forms and demons rail violently against the simulacra of created worlds, the unicorn who awaits him on Avalon has chosen neither to fight form nor to make any effort at all to deconstruct it. It and its breed choose simply to turn away. And Merlinus can go with them. With his demon power compacted to humansize and united to a unicorn, he knows he can slip through a black sun and return to heaven. He can turn his back on the whole burning universe with its drifts of starfire, planets barnacled with feverish life, lives aflame with the blood's hungers, sparking the mind's ambitions—all of it ripples of fire in the void, burning hotly for the moment, destined certainly to fade away into the cold and the dark.

Why not get out? he asks himself.

The Storm Tree lifts its rootcoils like broad, silvered wings above the black horizon and seems to hold the whole of space like a crystal in its grasp. Facets glare red where the palace squeezes fire into the woven brilliance of parapets, turrets, steeples. Other branches clasp dark emptiness. The roots, like the brain's dendrites in their millions, enclose a luminous void, a vacant dimension of blazing shadows cast across the wasteland by the palace.

This remains the wizard's dilemma: His supernatural greed rises above the earth and snaggles the twisted branches of the Storm Tree, while his love of Optima has matured to his devotion to his king and queen: He wants it all, the heat of life under the cold sky *and* the glare of heaven beyond the abyss. This mythical tree uprooted in space, clawing for both depth and height, this is the image of his soul—and by its contradictory nature he knows he has attained his manhood.

"The soul is immortal," Someone Knows the Truth tells Uther Pendragon, "because it is a pattern of energy imprinted in the very structure of creation."

Uther wonders if this is meant as consolation, for he cannot stop worrying about Ygrane. As they hike among giant boulders, he only half listens to the voluble god, who glibly discusses the mysteries. When they arrive at the cave of the dragon-magus, the king looks for the shade of Ambrosius, but they are alone.

A harsh silica rasp sounds from within the cavern, and

Merlinus hears the elk-king speak urgently. "He is coming. Now be sure to remember all I have said, young king. This magus cannot speak except to ghosts, but he knows what you are thinking, what you are feeling. He will respond best to your deep emotions. And loyal as he is to your family, this magus has become more beast than man over the centuries and he can be temperamental. You must show dauntless command and decisiveness. What awe to see him this energetic! I do think that losing the ghost of your brother has renewed him with rageful energy. Be wary, Uther."

Uther seems to pay the god no heed, his eyes firmly directed into the darkness of the lair. Like a huge lantern, a long face comes forward out of the gloom. At the sight of it, Uther starts and backs away. But the elk-king holds him firmly in place with his large, furry hands.

A chill wind gusts from the burrow and lifts ash flakes at the cave mouth into fumy tendrils. Accompanied by a dry stench of decay, the dragon-magus shuffles forward in a whistling of winter and a sprawl of fog. The bone blue, glossy skull of the creature emerges, filling the whole cave entry with its curved horns, webbed ears, and widening grimace of drooping whiskers and serrated fangs—wholly inhuman.

Yellow eyes, the very color of Uther's, only magnitudes brighter, watch alertly from within a majestic depth of socket and ledged browbone. Its silver-blue scales flimmer under crawling voltage, and the hair on Uther's head, as well as the elk-king's, fluffs.

Folds of somnolent, hot earth smells shroud the air with the release of a purple, sibilant tongue. The tight braid, glittery as black snakeskin, coils tightly about Uther, squeezing his arms to his sides and swelling his chest as the writhing tip licks his startled face. The tongue slips off and flashes away, leaving behind a fragrance of turned sod and tule mist.

The dragonhead sniffs ponderously over Uther, from his scattered raven's hair, across the ebony leather of his armor, to his dusty, blunt boots. Growling deep in the throat, like far-off thunder, Wray Vitki's abhorrent visage rises slowly, smoke sliding from its crooked, crusted nostrils and the grin-hooked hinges of its mouth.

"Uther-r-r-r," the man-become-beast growls, gravelly as a river over an icy bed.

Uther nods, fumbling to find his voice. The ponderous freight of the gruesome face stops rising and hangs above them, still as a monumental gargoyle.

"Dauntless command," the elk-king whispers. "Decisiveness. Go on! Think on your woman, now."

"Dracon Vitki!" Uther speaks in a big voice, full of all the urgency that rises in him at the thought of his bride. "Carry us to Ygrane."

"R-r-ride!" Wray Vitki responds from deep in his congested throat, barely comprehensible. "R-r-ride to Ygr-r-rane!"

With a stunning roar, the massive cope of the cavern suddenly brattles loose, a mountainous carapace separating in sizzling jags of lightning to release vast auroras, bent-winged sheets of ruffled, rainbowed electrical flames.

Hands pressed over his ears, Uther rises, with the elk-king behind him, the beast-lord's maned head thrown back in deaf laughter. They ride in Wray Vitki's massive hands as the ground itself lifts, spilling gravel and ash through the spaces between gigantic webbed talons. Sweeping aside the cinders that blanket its sleep, the dragon-magus's fire-wings fan, and the enormous creature lifts into the nether night.

Alone in the disembodied place between worlds, Merlinus feels again much like a demon, touching many points in space at once: his tranced body in Avalon, the dragon-magus and Uther breezing like ghosts through the transparencies of rock and earth, and Ygrane . . .

The thought of Ygrane fills the wizard with dread. He

fears for her sanity. In the grip of Ethiops, she is prey to obliterating madness. He wants to free her, but he is a phantom she cannot see or hear. Yet, she does sense his presence. She feels him as a draft of fright. Her soul reflects his fear when he approaches, and he realizes that to help her, he must radiate strength.

To calm himself and evoke again his strongest energy, his purpose, he begins to speak. He knows she cannot hear him, so he talks to himself:

"After my mother died, I hurried west of my hopes through the startling pain outside my body. I thought, just perhaps, I could reach Optima's spirit before she left the earth. High, high I flew, away from my body into the whirling pain where the galaxies hung. Below me, the northern lights bloomed like a watery flower. The earth was dark, the sun obscured behind the world.

"But she had gone, and with her went my last contact with the great love that had birthed me. She was gone. The globe turned below me in the hands of darkness, and I hung in the dark alone with my pain.

"If I stayed there in outer space, above the fallen sun and the cold fire of the auroras, the pain would hack me free of my body and I would be a spirit again. I was a novice to mortality and physical suffering, a mere yearling of a mortal. I thought I could barge my way through the hurt, cut loose from my flesh, and be done with this life. Ha!

"The pain hooked me to the earth's core, and the more I struggled to be free the worse it got. I did not have the strength to endure enough of it to be free. I grieved the loss of Optima, the loss in this lifetime of my one link to heaven, but the harrowing immensity of pain was greater than my delirious grief. I fell back to earth.

"I awoke in my tired, old body under the flame of twilight. In an instant, I regretted my futile attempt at suicide. I had sworn to Optima I would use this life to do good—and in my very first instant apart from her, I had reverted to my selfish, rageful ways.

"From the gloomy dark of the forest, the unicorn's green eyes watched me. By their soft light, I knew my mother forgave me. I am a demon and my initial behavior was to be expected. But through Optima I had become something other than a demon. I had become a man. The garment of flesh and bone that I wore she had knitted in her body. She was dead; even so, she was alive—in me, as me. If I had any love for her at all, I realized then, I would have to respect the life of this flesh and the spirit of her teachings.

"I buried Optima among the copper beeches. To dig her grave, I clawed at the thawed earth with my bare hands. Then the unicorn came forward in the failing light, and with its blue hooves cleaved the ground. Together, we opened the earth, I hauling the dirt out with my hands, the unicorn cutting through the thick roots and dislodging the large rocks in our way. With the drifting stars as witnesses, I lowered my mother's corpse into that black pit, her hands still clasped together, her knees bent and head lowered, kneeling worshipfully, even in death, to the one, everlasting God."

Morgeu does not believe she is possessed. Ethiops has convinced her that she commands herself. Even at the height of her overshadowing after her father's gruesome death, when she sat betranced in her own filth for days on end obviously bewitched, she thought she was using her own sorcery to persist without food or water; she believed that she acted as a psychic beacon to a score of damaged women living in the far-scattered thorps and hamlets of the northern forests. She became convinced that her magical will alone summoned these disciples to her fetid cave.

All along, the demon has patiently been knitting the thoughts and moods necessary to convince the young woman that this power emerges from her black sorrow. The demented mutes, idiots, battered wastrels, and widows mad with fury who staggered half-starved out of the forest came at her telepathic beckoning to be healed through vengeance.

Wandering the countryside with her wild troop of harpies, Morgeu believed that nothing survives but evil. Good intrudes on reality but cannot endure. Only evil persists. And so to fight evil, she herself must become evil.

Clairvoyantly endowed by Ethiops, Morgeu led her gang of derelicts back to the mountain and river settlements where they first had been abused, and she found the cruel men who had earlier raped and enslaved her followers. One by one, her magic called them out into the desolate places where the frenzied women took their blood payment. From the skin of these corpses, they made leather and chewed and stitched it into the wolfish masks of moonbitches sacred to Morrígan.

By summer's end, Morgeu had convinced herself and her troops that they were the Y Mamau, conjure-warriors devoted to the black goddess of death and the immemorial passions of bloodlust and destruction—Morrígan. The goddess gave them the magic and inspiration necessary to arm themselves, steal horses, and kidnap the queen of the Celts.

Now Ygrane sits imprisoned in a chamber atop the tower, barricaded within her own magic. But no magic can avail against Morrígan, and soon Ygrane herself will be sacrificed.

In preparation for this solemn event, Morgeu's magic has located a large statue of Morrígan buried in a bog. It has been retrieved by the Y Mamau and erected with lavish ceremony in the crypt of this garrison tower on a crag long abandoned by the Romans.

The dancing figure, naked but for its necklace of skulls, looms dire above Morgeu. Sprawled there, with her back against the dark stone shin of the goddess, the dazed young woman gazes into the flickering shadows of the high vault, ensorcelled by Ethiops.

Unseen, the demon squats over her, busily knitting the electric embroidery of her fevered ambitions. He painstakingly weaves the microvolts in her brain, and she believes she sees the huge barren eyes of the goddess staring at her out of the high darkness.

Morgeu's white swollen face appears gaseous, a blur of wonder as she listens to Morrígan speak to her in the voice of a dog. The ravening barks and whispering snarls emanate from the whole shimmering crypt.

The mother of nightmares does not want Ygrane killed immediately. A ritual must be devised to steal her magic so that Morgeu can take her place as queen of the Celts.

This pleases the sorceress, and she smiles, the glee in her bloated face slanted and wicked as pigs' eyes.

Furiously, Ethiops knits, sparking brave hopes in Morgeu's avid brain. If he gets this right, he can use her to enter Ygrane. And then, from inside Ygrane, hidden by her considerable magic, he will be able to get close enough to Lailoken to tear his head off.

An inkwash of shadows, the demon fills the whole garrison tower as he squats and bends to his needling task. None see him, yet all feel him holding them in the swell of his power. Whether in the kitchen cracking bones for a meal of raw marrow or on the battlements staring through the brown sunlight like zombies, the Y Mamau feel his ardent presence—and to them, he is the very shadow of Morrígan.

Through breaks in the clouds, faint stars rattle, and low in the east Venus burns, locked inside its hell. Merlinus, disembodied and free-floating, fixes his attention upon the morning star, fighting off the sleep that he knows will return him to his body. He does not want to awake in Avalon just yet—not until he finds the queen.

Chanting her name in a sleepy mumble, the wizard's wraith follows a long river, a black artery, into the mountains under the sea of clouds. Hundreds of feet high, the stony, barren peaks catch fire.

As the sun rises, Merlinus slants over the world-long maze of mountains toward a crude rock fastness—a fortress of granite slabs. The rock heap on the ledge glows orange in the earth's halo.

Through a slot window, his plasmic self slips. Ygrane is there. She crouches in a corner, her knees pulled to her chest. She has lost her tiara, her cheeks are smudged with dirt and tears, and her sad lynx eyes stare remotely.

"Lady—" Merlinus tries in vain to announce his presence, but he knows from her blank stare she can neither hear nor see him.

He reaches out with his heart's brails and hears in her a groan like a tiger's sigh. Her knuckles gleam white on the fists locked across her knees. Teeth gritted, breath panting through her chafed lips, she centers her attention in the pit of her stomach, focusing her strength on one shining image—the cloven-hooved unicorn.

"It can't come," Merlinus says, indifferent to her deafness. "Ethiops would feed it to the Dragon. It waits for me in Avalon. Save your strength, Lady. Uther is on his way with the dragon-magus."

The heavy door bangs open, and Merlinus jumps through the ceiling. When he pokes his head back through the granite, he sees four leather-hooded witches enter, their fanged wolvish faces veering toward Ygrane.

Merlinus's brails still touch the queen, and he jolts to feel the energy in her stomach simultaneously harden and blaze like an ingot of white-hot iron. She flings this power from her center with a shout, and the Y Mamau fly backward and slam into the wall shrieking.

A filament of ghost fire flares in the dim shadows, and Morgeu appears. "Mother—how long can you keep this up? Sooner or later, you will tire. And when you are utterly defenseless and your incantations and tricks can help you no longer, the Y Mamau will rip out your heart and offer it throbbing to Morrígan. Is that not perfectly just and appropriate?"

Ygrane half lids her eyes and begins her panting again, focusing the power in her pith, calling for the unicorn and readying herself for another attack.

"Do you think I lack the mettle to murder my own mother?" the apparition sneers and then adds with a sudden, queer modulation of her voice, "You know, Mother, it is not murder but mercy I offer. You, too, are a priestess of Morrígan. If I slay your body, it will free your soul. That is the grace I offer you. Is that not something to be grateful for?"

"Be gone, demon-child!" Ygrane cries out.

Morgeu shimmers closer. "I will not be gone—not until you give me your magic. I swear to you, I will use it only in ways that will make our people strong. The old ways, the ways that serve Morrígan."

Ygrane shakes her head violently. "No. No more blood sacrifices. Morrígan's thrall of our people is over—long ago. You are a throwback, Morgeu. The Síd made me queen to help displace the demon-goddess."

"Foolish woman." Morgeu's voice fizzles as she steps into a ruddy shaft of dawnlight and half her body blears away. "You do not see how weak our people have become since we forsook the Fang Mother, the true mother—the mother who births us in blood, who bleeds us each month, who devours our flesh. We have become a little people—while the barbarians, who still worship their blood gods, grow stronger."

Ygrane's eyes scold. "Is this how you honor your father—the father you claim you loved? What would he think of you now—a demon worshiper?"

Reduced to furious eye sparks and a bodiless voice in the slant of daylight, Morgeu replies slowly, "My father died a horrible death, betrayed by your wizard, the demon Lailoken. A violent death so that you could marry that pretty young man, who dares call himself Uther."

Ygrane's eyes stare wide with disbelief. "Is that what you think?"

"*Think?*" Morgeu's frazzled red hair and moony face materialize as she leans out of the sunbeam. "Mother—I *know* you sent Lailoken to find you a lover. I *know* he used his magic to make a stable master into a king. And I *know* he used that same magic to kill Father. I *saw* him. I was there on the ramparts with him as he directed his power against Father. His demon power threw the duke into the enemy's hands to be hacked into pieces before my eyes. My father, a battle-hardened warrior, slain! While your lover, a would-be priest, a paltry stable master, emerges with only the slightest scratch on his shoulder. Am I a fool? Am I to disbelieve my own eyes?"

"You are wrong, Morgeu." Ygrane hugs her knees tighter. "Your father would be appalled to see you now."

Morgeu's round face wrinkles with pain. "Father cannot see me now, Mother. He lies in a grave in Londinium, hacked into a dozen pieces."

"Quit this treachery, Morgeu," Ygrane pleads. "Your father may be dead—but I did nothing to kill him. Nor did Myrddin. That I know, child. I have seen into that wizard in the trance light—I have watched him over the years on his journeys and seen the good he has done, no matter the grief set against him. He is not your father's murderer."

"You lie to save your greedy life." Morgeu speaks bitterly. "You cannot change what I have seen with my own eyes!"

Ygrane lifts a hand into the wraith-glow of her daughter's body. "Child, you are under a demon's sway. I would not lie to you—my own daughter. Listen to me. I am your mother."

Morgeu glares and steps back into the dissolving brilliance of the sun. "You are my animal mother, Ygrane," her voice sounds out of the bright air. "You are the beast that burdened me with this life. I discard you the way the midwife cuts the strangling birth cord and the suffocating caul. I will break you for the rabid creature you are—mad with lust, lies, and hatred."

Ygrane lowers her face onto her knees and can say no more against such vehemence.

"Your people suffer," Morgeu continues, her words brittle, "while you make alliances with our enemies. Evil woman! When your magic is broken, I will take your power and give it to Morrígan. You will be our first blood sacrifice, mark my words—and what magic I will take from you will only give Morrígan greater life in this new time. Together, we will restore our people to their rightful glory."

Ygrane looks up with tear-burned eyes, but Morgeu has gone and only the Y Mamau remain. They rush her, their needleteeth and glossed masks of human leather blotting the sun's rays. With a cry, the queen hurtles another painful surge of power at them, and they fall back against the far wall, huffing through their vizards.

Suddenly, the sunlight in the room dims to a smutched pastel of itself. Out of the darkness, tiny, evil faces surface in the pocked skin of the rock walls, and a rancid stink drips from the thick silence. Merlinus crouches close to Ygrane, knowing what is about to happen next. He can feel her heart thrumming with alertness to the encroaching darkness.

Will he see me? That is the wizard's dread as a blur of darkness blotches the chamber, and Ethiops enters. Without his staff to unveil the unseen, Merlinus observes little, for the demon remains mostly invisible to him—and the wizard is apparently unseen by the demon, for Ethiops passes by him and comes to bear directly on the queen. Twin gleams of malice burn through the hazy air, and the Y Mamau stiffen with alarm and slink from the chamber. But Ygrane does not quail, her magic strong. Though his frigid force grabs at her, trying to rip the magic out of her, she holds on.

Merlinus knows how hard that must be, having broken many a mortal mind himself. If he so chooses, Ethiops could neatly pith her skull or strangle her from within. But, clearly, he wants something more delicate from her than her life. He wants to tear her very soul out of her, as that is her real power, the magic that can call forth the unicorn and command the elf-folk. With that in his control, what perfect havoc Ethiops could wreak!

Ygrane faces him, her brow gleaming with a cold sweat. Shaking with sick chills as the venomous force of the demon saturates her, she puts all her mind, all her being, into vivifying the image of the unicorn. She fixes her concentration on the animal's sleek muscles sliding under its hide of moonlight, and Ethiops watches her trilling with pain in the bones of her teeth.

Tears dew the lashes of her tight-shut eyes as she forces herself to visualize the unicorn's cloven hooves, blue as mussel shells. The demon chars her lungs with his stink, trying to break her focus. She traces the limber lines from a curly fetlock, up the suave contour of the leg, across the broad withers and slender neck to the hollow cheek and the rounder world of its lucent green eye.

Helpless, Merlinus witnesses their silent duel, witnesses Ethiops's frustration mount until, suddenly, he lunges forward and pincers his victim's throat. Ygrane gags and wrenches backward, lifting her blue face for air.

Reflexively, Merlinus flies at the malefic eyes floating in space—but zips through them, substanceless as a thought. When he spins about, the demon strangler has stopped, and Ygrane lies bent over the ground like a supplicant, eyes gaping at the infinite landscapes enshadowed in the granulations of stone. Her lids close, and she lies gasping. Somewhere in her mind, the unicorn bends its skinny legs and lies down on the flower field she has created in the silence of her prayers.

The filthy sunlight parts, and a snaky shadow whips away. Merlinus realizes that Ethiops must leave or else he will kill her. She is that determined. Yet he can sense in the decisive motion of his old ally's withdrawal that Ethiops is not wholly unhappy. This tortuous process appeals to him. Ygrane is weaker than the last time he tormented her, and he—or his minion Morgeu—will be back. Ygrane's soul has become their malicious sport, their plaything, and they are determined not to break it just yet.

With the demon's departure, the chamber brightens, the air freshens, and Merlinus places himself over her with the weight of sunlight. Within her, he observes her fright diminishing as she catches her breath. Waves of anger slosh over her, washing away her fear, and to calm herself she studies in her mind's eye the spiral of light that is the unicorn's horn.

Sorrow follows her anger, and she presses her cheek against the stone floor. Merlinus hears her wishing away her life, wishing she had run away from the druids when they first came for her. Wishing she had fled Raglaw when she first saw that crone standing under the thatched eaves of her home. Regretting that she had ever left her childhood cottage among the high groves of birdsong, the cloud forests where the pale people danced for her, and the dark valleys with their restless mists and giggling faerïe. She left them all behind, searching for something far greater than what she found, far greater than Gorlois and Morgeu and this evil place.

Tears squeeze from her closed eyes and wet the granite floor in small dark stars. Her life seems a painful mistake. The weight of her sorrow and her unknowing drags her down into sleep.

A margin of the sun's ray touches her cheek, and its warmth in her mind is the caress of her mother's good hand. Yet, when she awakes from her dream-gaze, it is not her mother's touch she imagines she has felt, or her mother's face she sees before her. Instead, an olive-skinned Semitic woman with black hair gathered under a blue veil watches over her. The stranger's large, Byzantine eyes search her benevolently, and a tender smile graces her serene face.

"Don't weep, lovely queen," the swarthy woman speaks in the old-fashioned, lilting Brythonic of Ygrane's childhood. "We know nothing of our own souls. We must trust God."

"Who . . . are you?" Ygrane asks.

"You don't know me. I am your husband's friend."

"You know Uther?"

"Since he was a child." A mild haze, like springtime tree mist, powders the space around her. "I have tried to give him the love that his own long-suffering mother could not."

Ygrane's chest throbs. Her heart feels drunk with a peculiar elation. The haze around the stranger carries a particulate brightness, a soft breeze of brilliant atoms, as though a glowing diamond has dissolved into the air. A relieved smile softens the queen's sad face.

"That's better," the stranger says and begins to fade into her own brilliance. "You have such powerful love for God's creation, you need fear nothing—in this life or the next."

"Wait—" Ygrane reaches into the shining emptiness. "Who are you? What is your name?"

Through the star-color depths of sleep, a voice reaches back, barely audible. Merlinus strains for the fading syllables and thinks he can discern the name Miriam, before the kindly woman disappears entirely in the fog of Ygrane's sleep.

Under tangled chains of stars, Falon leads his haggard company across the barren, blackened pan of the netherworld. The riderless horse that has been guiding them trails behind now, as confused as they about which way to go. Falon arbitrarily sets the face of his steed toward a clot of stars on the horizon that writhes as brightly as a hacked-off tail of lightning.

Parched and starving, the soldiers ride slumped over their mounts, heads bowed so as not to torment themselves any further with the relentless vista of wasteland. The palace shaped like fire appears now to their right, a flame mist that has occupied every compass point at some time in their circular wanderings. Its luster runs like wind between the pumice dunes.

The horses slue with exhaustion, and Falon knows he should call a stop but dares not. At every rest, one of their number has not woken from sleep. The land has drunk the lives of two fiana and two cavalrymen. The horses carry their corpses far back, led by a long tether to hold off their stench in the windless dark.

No one sings now or prays as they did in the beginning. Whirlwind flies have three times swirled up from the sootbeds, seemingly attracted by voices, and swept stinging through the line. Spider mites big as thumbnails leaped from the ink black dust and hooked flesh with their barbed mandibles. So the riders must keep to the broken plates of rock that injure the horses' hooves.

Once, from out of the bluish brightness of the skyline's star-haze, a ghost legion of antique Romans marched. Bedecked in tarnished scale armor and dented bronze helmets, they tramped past, studded sandal-boots noiseless, bearing rectangular shields before them as if to push back the bleary darkness. They did not see the mounted men, though they passed close enough to reveal the eagles embossed in their red leather corselets and the winged Cupid heads on the metal thongs of their sporrans. Wanderers in this changeling night for centuries, the legion wore away long ago. Only its martial spirit persists, bearing the empty image of the soldiers across the face of namelessness, invested with a bitter purpose defiant of time.

Recently, cloven prints have appeared in the sable sand among the shattered, black plates. The cavalry are convinced it is the trace of devils that leads deeper into the demon kingdom, and they will not follow.

"The unicorn," Falon's dry throat rasps, and he veers to follow the tracks. Whether the others go their own way or not, he cannot care. He does not have the strength to care.

A horse screams, and those who can, look up. Falon valiantly lifts his hand to the hilt of the sword strapped to his back but is too weak to draw the weapon.

From out of the mutant dark, lightning rolls like a rootless thornbush directly toward them. Searing noises and explosions accompany the creature of lightning as it crawls along the gravel fields, cutting kerfs in the larger rocks it crosses, splitting smaller ones into hot fléchettes that skip over the ground, splashing sparks.

Falon has not been this scared in fifteen years, not since he followed Ygrane into the World Tree and confronted the mad god of the roving tribes. He is surprised by his fear. So many times in this featureless twilight he has prepared to die that he believed all dread had been wrung from him. But the wiry lightning walking toward him stark as a spider inspires new terror, and he finds the strength to draw his sword.

A thunderbolt flares from the blazing bramble and strikes the sword. It cuts through Falon not with pain but with a glory that despoils all hurt and fatigue in him. He reels about jubilantly and sees the entire line of fiana and cavalry covered in soft shapes of electric fire. Everyone grins broadly with intensified happiness, the hollows of their faces filling with liquid flame. Even the corpses sit up, groggy, their decay erased in brushstrokes of sheet lightning.

Falon pulls around to face their salvation, expecting a Fire Lord. Instead, some bestial thing untangles itself from the sizzling lightning. The unicorn appears briefly to their human eyes, its white-hot apparition provoking blue shadows from the black rocks of the colorless land.

Now it is gone, and the ensuing darkness bears a stain of its heraldic outline. A moment of confusion passes before the riders notice the cloven hoofprints imprinting the ashen ground. They walk from where the unicorn has stood, and they disappear among the conjectural shadows cast by the alien stars. At last, even the Christians believe that the tracks show the way toward the known world.

While Ygrane slumbers, Merlinus lingers above her, marveling at what he has witnessed. Miriam! He speaks to himself the name of the apparition that comforted the queen, and he recalls that this is the name Optima had used in her fervid prayers to Jesus' mother. Can that be? he wonders. Why would such a woman trouble to show herself before a pagan queen? For Uther—of course. It is for his sake, for Theodosius, the "man whom God gives."

Exhaustion leaves him vaporous and chilled. He has been too long away from his physical body. He must return to Avalon. Awe, alone, keeps him from relenting to the dizziness of sleep. He continues floating above the slumbering queen, reaching for some understanding of the holy vision she has experienced—when a cold shadow dims the chamber again.

Ethiops has returned. Panicky, Merlinus spins a hapless circle around the cell, but the demon has not returned to continue his torture of Ygrane. He merely circulates, restless as a shark. The wizard knows this uneasiness well. It has flogged him between the stars, through the shoreless dark.

Throwing caution aside, Merlinus reaches out with his heart's brails, and he hears Ethiops's familiar thoughts, the predictable ruminations of a demon. *You will die,* Ethiops thinks loudly, addressing the sleeping queen. *Your child Morgeu will live and die, and this world will go on through its savage changes and pitiful developments. This time will pass, and owls will cry in the summer trees around a new Rome—and these rocks will have long fallen, yet still be rocks—and I, no matter the thick centuries, will go on, an enemy to rocks, Rome, summer trees, owls, and every child of every living thing.*

Desperate to help Ygrane somehow, Merlinus leaves Ethiops to his rant and flits down the blind corridors and stairwells, through all the levels of stone, hoping to find some chink in the Y Mamau's defenses. In the depths, he comes upon a sunken ceremonial crypt—a circle of serpent-coiled jasper columns that sends a seen-before chill through him.

The jasper serpents uphold a black stone dome nailed all over with human skulls. *Whose? Slain Romans? Sacrificed Celts?*

Lantern flames blaze inside them. Suspended by iron chains, censers of hammered bronze leak twirling vapors that drool upon the floor and crawl like viperous ghosts to the onyx base of the hideous statue Ethiops possesses—a naked, fang-faced woman sporting a skull-necklace and brandishing a bloody sword and a severed head—Morrígan—the Demon Queen.

Morgeu lies prostrate before the statue, tightly gripping its slender, dancing, bell-tasseled ankles. Naked, the young witch's tall and slim, just-womanly body shines dead white as wax. The flickering, rippling skull-light strokes her like shadowy, skeletal fingers.

Merlinus pulls back, expecting her to turn and see him with her second sight. But she does not. Instead, she sits up and squints at the idol, no longer feeling the flow of vigor that has sluiced from it.

Then, Merlinus sees why. To his shock, he spies King Someone Knows the Truth hiding behind the statue, shielding it with his billowy, emerald-hued cape. Behind the god, the ground still seeps with astral fumes from where he has risen. The spirit of the land, he has materialized directly out of the soil, and Morgeu and her conjure-warriors are not yet aware of him. But Ethiops is—instantly. His angry cry wails down the stairwells like a storm wind as he comes flying.

King Someone Knows the Truth catches sight of Merlinus, and his taut brown lips in his bristle-whiskered reindeer face shoot him a savage smile. Then, the demon slithers into the crypt.

Ethiops flings himself furiously at the elk-king. Merlinus can see the invisible demon's lunatic flailing as shadows against the bright green light of the elk-king. The two giants grapple: Ethiops coils serpentwise about the god's broad frame, and the elk-king holds the viper jaws at arm's length with one hand while wielding a short, hooked blade with the other.

The demon should know better, Merlinus thinks, backing away from the thrashing titans. No single demon can alone take down a god created by angels. Gods draw their power directly from the planet, and if destroying them were so easy, the demons would never have allowed any empire to have blotched the earth at all.

Someone Knows the Truth is particularly agile, having dwelled so long underground, where the bodylights of the gods are more condensed and nimble than in the Great Tree. With a few deft jabs, the elk-king extricates himself from Ethiops's coils and furiously heaves him across the crypt. The demon's writhing tantrum amuses King Someone Knows the Truth, and he shakes deliriously, dancing around the idol of death-as-a-woman, chasing the demon with a laughter like screams.

Morgeu seizes a scarlet robe from where it lies at the base of a serpent pillar and wraps it about herself as she paces before the lethal image of Morrígan. Her confusion peaks in a shrill cry for her soldiers. Several women in boots, brown trousers, and camouflage tunics emerge from their dank warrens nearby. Their cropped hair and kohl-blackened eyes mark them as Y Mamau.

"Bring Ygrane down here," she gruffly commands. "Quickly!"

As the soldiers dash down the lightless corridors, Morgeu wades through coils of incense fumes to a stone stairway in the wall. Merlinus follows her up through the darkness to an iron door that shrieks open onto a brilliant autumn morning. Pine and heather scents whisk on the wind that plummets down from the mountain ledges, where forest on forest hang above her head.

In the dark fenny depths of the valley, the wizard can see them coming—the armies of the Daoine Síd. They roll through the night-held grottoes like fog, a legion of dragon-warriors come to retrieve their queen. Wearing red-beaded reptileskin and polished skullshards for armor plates, and with whittle ribs, honed fangs, and whetted talons of firesnakes for weapons, they slither forward like the Dragon itself, belly-crawling up the mountain flanks.

Morgeu does not see this with her mortal eyes, but she senses the impending attack. The Síd's fevered piping and fabled drum-thunder reverberate in her soul, and she shivers as if before the onslaught of a night's frost—though the morning sun angles along the blue and misty mountainsides.

Her conjure-warriors are no match for the oncoming dragon-soldiers. Merlinus sees the openmouthed fright on the faces of several of them watching from the slot windows above.

"Morrígan!" Morgeu cries out, her yell folding into echoes. "Morrígan! Defend your warriors!"

Ethiops, fleeing the elk-king, swirls up from the black stairwell, his darkness breaking into forms of crinkled light and staining the air with bituminous smudges. He focuses the will of his energy on Morgeu, and a hell stink like the despair of the world, like punctured corpse bloat, pierces her and brings her hands to her throat. She goes down on her knees before the harsh, choking presence of her master, and he enters her as best a demon can squeeze himself into a mortal, without rupturing the blood-tangles in her fragile brain. Here, he can shield himself from the Celtic god, for the elk-king will have to slay Morgeu to get at him.

Morgeu rises with an ominous little grin on her pale face. Spikes of stars glitter in her mad stare. Now, with the demon's acuity in her eyes, she can see the Daoine Síd clothed in firesnake moltings and boneplates, gaudy with feathers and fur tufts stuck to their faces with tree resin. Brandishing wicked lances and serrated swords black-tipped with poison, they come scrambling out of the cellars of the valley.

Morgeu lifts hands clawed with fury and rises to her toetips with the power of the demon. Ethiops's vehemence, so useless against the elk-king, slashes lethally into the vaporous dragon-warriors. Morgeu's body bucks with the violent force coursing up out of the magnetic depths of the planet and shooting out through her stiffened arms.

The attacking hordes fall in waves before the violet glare stabbing from her, like steaming breakers mangling against the rocks. Their firesnake armor flutters away like dead leaves, and their slender bodies shred to smoke, fading into the sunlight in dew sparkles and gasps of flying spume.

Weightless as dying moths, the fallen warriors swirl against each other in the downdraft of cold pouring from Morgeu's wrathful body. Their loud, wounded shouts crawl away through the murk of dissolving corpses. Yet, slathered in a blue film of elf-gore, the valiant Síd minions keep coming, lances tilted against the murderous wind.

Morgeu flaps with the outpouring of demon-cold like a rag thing. Eyes rolled up, she no longer witnesses the killing she dispenses, only feels it ascending her juddering bones and heaving out of her. And she hears it echoing back, leaping against the torrent of her slaying ecstasy, glittering into the screams and gibbered cries of those who dare to defy the Mother of Death.

Ygrane hears the suffering of the Síd warriors burning in the morning air and pulls herself upright before the slot window of her cell. Far below, among the citrons, oranges, and greens of the woods, her rescuers die in great numbers. She can see, in the cutwork shadows of the forest, their frail bodies ripped apart like sun-lanced exhumations of night. Rays of violet energy shoot from the base of the tower where she is imprisoned. By fitting her face into the window slot, she can just make out a scarlet-robed figure directly below.

Morgeu! Stabs of black light ray in purpled streaks from her writhing body and cut into the troops rushing uphill, withering them to wind-borne lace. At the sight of this, Ygrane mashes against the stone wall and her face smears wild-eyed within the restraint of the slim window. She cries out for the young woman to stop, and her voice flails uselessly into the vast mountain spaces.

A bell jar of overshadowing force warps the air around Morgeu, and by that Ygrane knows that her daughter is possessed. The queen pulls back and sticks her arm out the window, palm open, in an attempt to signal her dragon-soldiers to withdraw, because she fears for them. But before she can do this, the bulky cell door slams open, and two wolf-masked Y Mamau rush in.

Ygrane shouts a curse that kicks the soldiers' knees out from under them. Two more advance, and she winces again, releasing another invisible blow that jerks them off their feet.

But those two attacks exhaust Ygrane, and when the next two wolf-soldiers charge at her, she can only swing her fists weakly. They seize her arms and drag her twisting body from the chamber, along the corridor, and down winding stone steps, bruising her shins. They hurry, hurting her arms, banging her legs on the stairs, eager to get her below before she regains the violent power of her curses.

In the ceremonial crypt, they fling the queen to the ground at the feet of Morrígan's monstrous statue and hurry out, crashing doors behind them. King Someone Knows the Truth has gone. Merlinus whirls among the lightless enclaves searching for him and finally has to depart the crypt, sliding through the heaped stone to the outside. There, he glimpses the god, a green flash in the forest under the scarlet wing of morning, calling his damaged troops back to regroup them for a flank attack.

When Merlinus returns to the crypt, he finds Ygrane prostrate before the idol of the demon-goddess. He thinks she is praying to the Fang Mother, until he touches her and finds her empty.

Dead!

Fright jerks at him, and he desperately begins shouting a chant to revive her, though he doubts so powerful a spell can work without his physical body to focus the summoned vitality. Mind whirling with dire suppositions, he stops in mid-cry.

He senses a slim thread of her glistening like a snail track in the shadowy air of the crypt.

The wizard's brails braid around the tenuous splice of her life, and his fright evaporates. Ygrane has done the same as he has: She has left her body. Unlike himself, however, she has no one to watch over her physical form. Within the thrumming cord that connects her to her physical form, he hears her thoughts and vibrates with her feelings.

The unicorn fills her mind. She has taken the terrible risk of leaving her body unoccupied here, in the lair of her enemies, to search for her beast.

The mental image of the unicorn's long, bony face vanishes, displaced by an astonishing sight that has seized her attention. Merlinus shares what she sees.

In the brightness of the upper air, a pure ruby appears. Like a meteor, it burns across the sky, dropping among the solar flames that fill the cup of the eastern mountains. Printed on the sun in a sharp, saurian shadow, it swells nearer—a tremendous dragonshape—Uther's dragon!

Drapes of dark brown skin peel from Wray Vitki's sides like fungoid gills on a tree, and ancient growths embroider the sinuous length of his neck, again like patches of fungus and lichen. Soaring out of the sun's glare, the dragon-magus looks aged. Knobs barnacle his flanks, and flakes like dull metal curl from his talons. The mechanism of his flanged jaws trails whiskers like rags of ocean weeds. Only his flamecored eyes, glowing in their sullen caves, look animated. And his wings—rainbow fire—whirl like polar lights.

The dragon-magus sets down in a gloomy dell, arriving like a renegade chunk of the daybreak sky. That is as close as he can land without toppling the rock pile. A moment later, he is gone. Carrying Uther up from the Otherworld has exhausted the power that Merlinus has given the aged dragon-magus. If Wray Vitki had lingered, he would have died, and so his vast darkness and iridescence spiral away into the fuming clouds of dawn.

Uther stalks out of the dell, and behind him come the armies of the Daoine Síd, led by their towering reindeer-faced god.

At the sight of them, Ethiops flees into the crude fort, knowing he cannot stand down the elk-king and his reinforcements. Morgeu slumps vacantly with his departure, deflated to a mere woman, so weakened she sags to the ground. Briefly, she glares at the lone man in the front of the otherwise-invisible attack, and by his black leather armor and the sable hair in his eyes, she recognizes him.

"Uther!" she screams. "To hellfire with you!"

She forces herself to her feet and hurries into the tower, clanging the iron door shut behind her and ramming the rusty bolt into its latch. "Morrígan!" she bawls, plunging down the stairs.

In the crypt, she discovers her mother lying facedown before the death-dancing idol, and she pauses, not sure what she is seeing. "Mother?" she cries. "What are you doing? Praying? Then pray! You belong to her. Not to Uther. You are her sacrifice. Pray!"

When Ygrane does not respond immediately, Morgeu bows over her, her perplexed face close to her mother's. She puts her fingers to the prostrate woman's throat and detects the faint knock of arterial blood. The realization of her mother's utter vulnerability seizes a sharp laugh from her. "What have you done?" she whispers in Ygrane's ear.

Merlinus slashes through Morgeu, vainly attempting to distract her with his empty presence. Then, with an abruptness that makes him think he has affected her, Morgeu stands erect. She looks all round, searching for the obsidian blade that is used for ceremonial sacrifices. Intently, she marches the perimeter of the crypt, searching among the boneheaps and tallow-draped skulls of lesser altars.

From above, the squeal of ripping metal declares her enemies have broken through. A door opens behind a serpent column, and a half dozen moonbitch-warriors pile in, swords drawn. "Princess!" the first across the threshold gasps through her mask. "The Síd have reached the tower!"

"Where is Morrígan?" another asks.

Morgeu ignores her question and points to the dark stairwell that climbs to the outside. "Four of you up that way. Kill Uther!" She grabs the remaining two by their sword arms. "We must find the knife of sacrifices. Where is it?"

"There is no time," the gruff voice from a dog mask replies. "No time, Princess! The Síd are in the tower. They kill with cold fire!"

"We must flee," the second speaks sharply. "If not, Morrígan will lose all her worshipers this day."

"No!" Morgeu yells. "Morrígan promised. I am to be queen of our people."

"Then we must flee, princess—at once!"

Under the flaring torch shadows of the corridor, Morgeu balks. "Stop! Take Ygrane. Morrígan shall have her sacrifice later, then."

"No time—look!" The soldier points her sword down the hallway to where purplish fumes seethe. "Run! Hurry!"

Merlinus reads the fumes for what they are, a squad of dragon-warriors surging down the corridor, poison-tipped lances leveled. The dog-faced warrior stands her ground to block them, but she is only human, an oaf compared to the nimble sprites. Their lances dart under her swinging blade and pierce her thighs and abdomen.

True horror sparking in every nerve, Morgeu spins about to flee, but fear jams her legs. Her last remaining guard grabs her by elbow and shoulder and heaves her forward. Merlinus watches them recede into the citadel, Morgeu's jarred gaze peering back with abject fright.

The wizard circles back to find his king. Uther Pendragon stands on the threshold of the doorway whose iron door the elk-king has ripped off its hinges. Dragon-warriors scurry ahead of him into the stairwell to dispatch the remaining Y Mamau posted below. Satisfied that Uther is safe, Merlinus passes through a blind interval of solid rock and earth, back to the crypt to watch over Ygrane's body.

Hovering in the glow of the skull-lanterns, he pauses. Ygrane has already returned to her body. She sits up, her face pale as a winter lake, her eyes staring hard at nothing. With trepidation, he touches her—and inside she is not alone. Ethiops hunkers within her brain, very small, coiled more tightly than Merlinus thought a demon could contract.

The wizard listens for what Ygrane feels, afraid for her. Glossy black, Ethiops the eel entwines the consciousness of the queen. "You took a bold risk when you left your body," the demon says in his most sinuous voice, "—and you lost. Now, you are a hostage in your own brain. Do you understand?"

Ygrane stares blankly, ignoring the voice in her head, willing herself not to notice the viper's face crowding her mind, the red muscles inside its obscene smile drooling for her. She focuses on the unicorn again, wanting to see the spiral stairway of jade climbing out of the blackness of its vertical pupils.

"I am inside you, Ygrane," Ethiops coos. "Do you know what that means? I can touch you."

A twinge of pain breaks the ice of her face to a hurt frown.

"Ethiops—get out!" Merlinus shouts. But the demon cannot hear him. No one can hear his astral voice.

The pain stops, and an unmusical, lewd pleasure jangles through Ygrane's body.

"Do you like that?" the demon whispers. "Do you want more?"

The unicorn is no good, Merlinus feels her realize. *This is too horrible even for the unicorn to save her from.*

"If you do exactly as I say," Ethiops breathes inside her, "I will let you live. You will not fight me. You will go where I tell you to go, do what I say to do, and I will leave you your life."

Ygrane turns her attention away from the moment's brink, and she peeks down into the darkest part of herself for the stranger she has seen in the depths of her despair. Where is she—Uther's friend? *Miriam—*

"Silence," Ethiops demands. "You will keep silent in my presence."

Miriam—Ygrane calls again—and she sees again in her mind the blue-veiled woman. Miriam appears with her head bowed, as if praying. She looks up, lids closed, lips trembling with words entrusted to a deeper hearing. And then, her large eyes open like the sun.

Merlinus pulls away from the wincing white heat and hears Ethiops's pitiful wail. Against the blinding flash, the wizard glimpses his eelish shape squirm past and thrash away from Ygrane. In an instant, the horror is canceled. The demon has gone. Ygrane blinks, touches her temples with trembling fingers. Her mind is empty—whole again.

"Ygrane!" Uther bolts into the crypt and rushes to her through tendrils of incense. "Are you hurt?"

The queen lifts her arms for him and smiles to show she is all right. They embrace, stunned by the momentum of events, wordless with the physical dangers and supernatural terrors that separated them and then brought them together in this ghastly place. With the pale people watching in their firesnake armor, nervously alert to the evil shadows from the skull-lamps playing over the gruesome idol, Uther gathers her up and carries her to the stairwell.

"Let me walk out into the light beside you," she says, and he lowers her to her feet.

Together, with the infernal steam of burned offerings twisting about them into faces of elvish laughter, they climb toward the sun.

Ygrane regards her hands, toughened from years of riding with her fiana, and wishes her soul could grow calluses. The pain she feels for her daughter is dangerous. It makes her forget her earlier lives, makes her feel that Morgeu is her only child in all her incarnations. Sadness clogs her heart, and her chest hurts as she sits on a boulder nested by chickweed stalks. Uther kneels to comfort her, and she gently asks him for a moment to herself.

Morgeu—she intones silently and closes her eyes, wishing she had the magic to heal the deeper pain in her daughter that the demon used to possess the young woman. *That pain must be my fault,* Ygrane believes. *My love has been too feeble.* In her pride as queen, she has loved her people, her fiana, and her magic more than her daughter, the seed of Gorlois.

What love she finds in herself now for Morgeu seems more evoked by fear for her child than warmth and caring. There has never been much shared spirit between them. The unicorn and the magic that flowed from her to Morgeu during those golden summers brought them close for a time. But now, the queen wishes mightily that she had never shared her magic with Morgeu, never shown her daughter the greater world of spirits. If she had left Morgeu to Gorlois, perhaps the demons would not have been able to touch her and use her so gruesomely.

Ygrane turns her back to Uther, so that he will not see her tears. Morgeu must not be his concern, because what they must do together dare not be constrained by their personal fears and pain. Her horrible time in the presence of Ethiops convinces her of that. Evil grows stronger on fear and pain. And all she truly feels for Morgeu is fear for her daughter's life and sanity and the pain that there is in her heart where there should be love.

Finally, having seen all he can see and eager to help, Merlinus decides to return to Avalon, to his body. Like a hawk hanging on a ring of wind, he circles above the evil cliff fort, and he spies far below the red spark that is Morgeu.

Robe billowing with the speed of her flight, she and the last of her Y Mamau flee on horseback along a trace in the gray mountain forest. The king and the queen walk together down a switchback path in the opposite direction. Merlinus assumes they will be safe and he can reclaim his own physical form so that he might rejoin them in Maridunum. The sword Lightning awaits him—and the unicorn.

Yet, as he glides above the remote high mountains in the taut, ringing silence of the sun's long rays, his expectations ring hollow, for he sees that the king and queen are alone in the wilderness, facing an arduous journey without the fiana, the cavalry, or the elk-king's soldiers for protection.

He searches for King Someone Knows the Truth. Coal streaks of birds mark the horizon, and beyond them, he finds the green sunrise flash that is the elk-king. His troop of red-armored dragon-soldiers follow him west through pink-feathered cirrus, so much atmospheric smoke at this distance.

The wizard, wrung with weariness as he is, still does not feel good about leaving Ygrane and Uther alone in the mountains, even though there is nothing he can do in his present state to help them. Anxious for their safety, he descends through flamboyant strata of sunlight to a gravel stream in a birch grove, where they have paused to freshen themselves.

"Do you know where we are?" Uther asks, untying the purple silk from his right shoulder and soaking it in the stream.

"Far from anywhere." Ygrane sighs and sits on a flat rock beside a bush dense with gooseberries. "The Y Mamau no doubt are hiding themselves away to practice their murderous worship."

Uther sits beside her and gently wipes the tear stains from her cheeks. "I'm sorry our wedding turned out so badly."

"It's sorrier yet many good people have died," the queen laments, picking listlessly at the berry bush. "What lies ahead for us do you think? More killings? More slaughter?"

"It's not the way we would want it," he says softly. "In the chapel, when we met as commoners, we understood. But the queen and the king, they are people carried by history."

"Then, let us not go back, Uther."

Uther lifts his head to stare at her inquisitively. "How can we not?"

"In these mountains, there are villages." Ygrane lifts her face toward the deep ravines where sunlight smokes. "In one, I was born. There I knew my happiest years."

"Ygrane," he protests tenderly. "How can we? Our people will search for us—your fiana will never give up. Even now they are in the underworld, seeking you."

The underworld—The astonishment of his journey to the netherworld continues to envelop him like a melodiously strange dream. Since returning to the natural world, he has felt so much smaller than ever before, dwarfed by all that is unseen—and, in an almost-perpetual breathlessness, he prays for his men left behind in that darker realm. Yet—by the summons of some majestic and benevolent fatality—he wants to return there. The flight of the dragon-magus remains only a stunned memory, like an alcoholic illumination that fades with sobriety. But the experience of the elk-king's Elysian fields—that disturbs him with its vivid, lingering joy.

Ygrane faces him with a resigned smile. "You're right, dear Uther. I know that we cannot run away from ourselves. But it is a lovely idea, isn't it?" She brushes the tousled hair from his eyes. "Think on it—we would live outside a village far from any fortress, on our own small farm. Perhaps you could teach me your faith . . . "

"*My* faith?" Uther pulls his mind away from his starry thoughts of the underworld and gives a lopsided grin. "What are you saying? You—queen of the Celts, a Christian?" After what he has experienced in the presence of the elk-king, he feels constrained by his religion, like a man forced to stare at the world through a judas hole. There is so much more than he had ever guessed in his most fanciful imaginings!

"Uther—do you have a friend named Miriam?"

Uther tries to understand. "No—"

"A spiritual friend, then," Ygrane presses, bringing her face nearer his golden eyes. "To whom you've prayed since you were a boy?"

"Miriam?" He looks at her directly, wonderingly. "Miriam—that's the Hebrew name for Mary, the mother of Jesus. Yes, I've prayed to her all my life."

"She came to me, you know. In Morrígan's crypt. She said that she tried to give you the love your mother could not."

"*She* said?" His thin, dark brows lift. "What are you telling me, Ygrane?"

"This is true," she insists.

"You believe it?" he asks with a thin voice.

"The truth of things is what I see," she replies firmly. "Since I was a child. And that has been the curse and blessing of my life."

With a frown, he tries to comprehend again. "So, your visions have shown you that—that my faith is true?"

"All faith is true, Uther," she says gently, as to a child. "The truth of your faith I've never doubted. But only now do I see that it must be for me, as well—now that we are husband and wife."

Uther sits back and shakes his head. "It's too much for me—

this day, or is it days? My brother's ghost—the elk-king—Wray Vitki—and our men still in the underworld—" His voice grows quieter with suppressed fierceness. "Are you telling me you want to be a Christian?"

"Yes, Uther. It surprises me no less. I want to be your Christian wife and learn how you worship." She notes the uneasiness in his expression and misreads it. "Oh, I know this must seem a shock—intractable as I've been in the past. Perhaps I should have learned from Gorlois. But a faithful Christian he was not—not as you are, Uther."

The king crosses his arms and pinches his lower lip, pondering something deeply.

"Uther, what is it?" She searches his face—speaks again, more quickly, "Are you unhappy with what I've said? Do you think I'm mistaken—in what I've seen? Perhaps it was the demon's vision, the demon's handiwork. But I think not."

He startles uneasily from his ruminations. "No, no. I believe what you saw is real enough, Ygrane. In fact, I am sure of it. I know—" He struggles with himself. "I know, because I saw your god. I *saw* him—like I'm seeing you now. I stood next to him. I even *talked* with him. And the dragon-magus—Wray Vitki carried me up out of the underworld to this very place. You saw the dragon?"

She nods matter-of-factly. "Of course. It carried you to me."

"Yes! The elk-king summoned it for me—the king of your Síd. My brother . . ." He stands up and crunches over the gravel bank of the stream. "My brother was there, as well. We talked." He falls silent and looks away.

Ygrane follows him solemnly with her eyes. "A great honor has been granted you. Even I have not had the privilege to visit the Greater World in my mortal form, you realize. Only in visions have I seen it."

"Ygrane—even a day ago, I would have thought it insupportable—every religion true—"

"My lord, whatever the human heart conceives is true," she

says, watching him pace the water's edge. "The spirit world precedes us. The gods are the ones who imagine *us*. We are the dream—they the dreamers."

Uther stalks restlessly along the silver hem of the stream. "And our men? My guard and your fiana—where are they now? In a dream?"

"I suffer for them, too, my lord. I suffer for them, because I cannot help them. We must trust in the elk-king to release them." She lifts her face, her eyes more green, here in the leafy shadows. "We must trust in the spirit powers—as they trust in us here in our lesser world."

Uther scowls ponderingly. "It's just that . . . the world of truth is so much vaster than what I was taught. Then, what is it we are to believe? What *is* the living truth of our lives?"

"Where the truth waits is right before our eyes," Ygrane says.

Uther stops walking and faces her, expectantly. "The elk-king wants my soul."

"He'll not have it," Ygrane says, startled. "If we are to be a united couple, wed in body and soul, then I'll pray with you to the blessed virgin Miriam, and she shall bless us in time with a noble Christian soul to be our son and successor."

The space between Uther's eyes flexes with uncertainty. "It's not so easy," he mutters. "I . . . it was indescribable down there, Ygrane. I was so *happy* watching the souls dance in that beautiful forest, I very nearly agreed to give him my soul right then and there."

Ygrane grows still with listening, her face filled with all the melancholy of her young life.

Uther takes her hands and feels their coolness, sees the pallor in her cheeks. "You need food—rest."

She places her hands on his shoulders and again leans her forehead against his. "My husband—something wonderful—and terrible—is happening to us."

"Yes—" He shuts his eyes. "Wonderful and terrible." He

gently pushes her away and gathers a handful of gooseberries. "You must eat. Here, this isn't much, but I'll go back up to the fort and see if I can find something. They must have some provisions up there."

She stays him with a hand to his cheek. "No need to return to that evil place, husband. The pale people won't let us starve. As a child, they taught me how to set withe snares, and with my first magic I learned how to call black hares—the only hares eaten by followers of the old ways, like my parents, as the brighter hares are sacred to the moon-goddess, you know."

Uther presents her a handful of the white berries. "Then, at least eat these now. I'll gather some withes, and we'll build those snares. And a fire, too. We'll rest today before we journey."

A grim smile comes and goes on Ygrane's face. "In a way, I should be thanking my daughter for what she's done to us. Before she stole me away, you and I were but married in name. But now, through her trial, we have become wedded in our souls as well."

All that day, the wraith of Merlinus lingers with them. He fights valiantly against smiting exhaustion, staying awake to keep from falling back to Avalon and into his body. Some secret has to be disclosed, he feels, before he can depart. A secret whose very nature he does not know but will recognize when he beholds it.

Sunlight filters like honey through the autumn leaves, and the small fire that the pair build on the gravel bank fends October's damp wind. As she has predicted, Ygrane traps a black hare, which they skin and cook over the fire and eat with the season's last watery blackberries. The horrors of the crypt gradually thin away as the hours pass in each other's company, that long day in the golden woodland.

"When we go back, nothing will change, of course," she says quietly after they have eaten. Her disheveled hair and torn *gwn* give her the wild appearance of a sprite more than a mortal human. "My Celts will never wholly trust your Britons, I'm afraid. I guarantee there will be strife among our own people, even as we unite together to stand off the barbarians."

"Nothing will change, perhaps—but is there an alternative? Can we not go back to face it?" Uther smiles at the thought of defection, and for a moment Merlinus believes that maybe he *would* do it—run away—and that thought inspires panic in the wizard. All their work together would be lost.

"Has it occurred to you," he muses, "neither of us was born to the purple. What would happen if we just went back to what we knew as children?"

Ygrane kicks pensively at the corroded leaves on the ground. "If we return as king and queen, we are sure to lose each other—if not to the war room then to the court functions, the emissaries, the battles—" She stops and confronts him in the honeyed, holy light of the forest. "Uther, I am afraid."

Those words in his mind echo the fear he has heard from his brother in the Otherworld, and even the ghost Merlinus can see his heart flinch. "It is right to be afraid, I think. Or we *will* lose each other. Even out here in the wilderness, we can't hide—not from our people, our destinies. Not even our deaths."

Ygrane's wan complexion seems to pale even more. "Why do you speak of death?"

Uther drops his gaze and notices at his boottip a pale foxglove in full flare, like a small soul in a white mantle. "It overshadows me, Ygrane. I can't help it. The look my brother had—before he went over to . . . to his eternal fate—it haunts me still. I'd never seen him look like that in life—so afraid, so contrite. Death has humbled him like nothing in life ever could. It stains my thoughts."

"Don't think on it, I beg you, Uther. There's been too much death around us. I'm sick of it."

Uther regards her affectionately. "Then, I won't talk any

more of it," he promises, raising their clasped hands to his mouth. "But do this for me—do not call me Uther. Not you."

Ygrane gives him a puzzled look.

"I've never liked it," he admits. "It's a barbarian name. Merlinus's idea, meant to frighten my enemies."

"When we get back, I'll call you Theo, then." She brushes the sable locks from his eyes.

"So, *shall* we go back?" He puts his arm across her shoulders. "And where shall we live? Not in Londinium, please—that viper's nest of intrigues and treachery."

"And yet the Celtic forts are barely serviceable—just rundown old Roman houses and decaying military barracks." Ygrane sighs. "Shameful as it is for me to admit, we Celts have done little to maintain the ancient forts. I suppose there is Tintagel. It is mine by prior rights. Gorlois tried to entice me there some years ago by giving its title to me."

"Too far away. If we must live anywhere as king and queen, better to establish our house closer to the lands we are defending."

"Then, not the City of the Legion," Ygrane moans. "It is a miserable place—all black stone and ancient buildings."

"It is. We will have to build our own fortress—something new to honor this unlikely and happy alliance."

Ygrane's countenance brightens at the thought. "A modern fortress—with no walls! Not a fort at all, but a giant amulet, a city made from the magic in our hearts and the land itself—"

"We'll have to see about the walls—"

"We shall make it new," Ygrane enthuses. "We won't need walls. You'll see. Of course, I'll want a large garden. Perhaps the main hall could be built around that in the old Roman style! Only larger—more like a park. Oh, do you think we can, Theo?"

Merlinus, battered with fatigue, leaves them thus, glad and ambling through the litter of the woodland. Meanwhile, the last dragonflies cut across the chill of the air, and the round, yellow light of the day rolls away cold and small into the wide mouth of sunset.

As the twilight stretches out, so does Merlinus. His senses extend into the gloam, searching for danger, hoping for the return of the Síd and their elk-king. The wizard detects no danger. Ravens flap overhead, the first tatters of arriving night. They perch among the sparse foliage of the tall trees, as small faerïe lights wink low over the rooty earth and glint among the moss-hung boughs of trees fallen into a black pond.

No elf-folk come through the doorway between the worlds, which disappoints him. Try as he might to obey his exhaustion and return to his own flesh, he keeps circling back here to Uther and Ygrane. He needs to be sure that the royal couple will be protected. That, he believes, is the secret revelation he seeks: a glimpse of an angel, the arrival of the fiana or the king's men. He perceives no threat in the vicinity, no inkling of Morgeu or beastly danger—nevertheless he finds no allies, either, and he hesitates to leave them alone.

The wizard drifts aimlessly through the cabbages and bracken under the red-and-gold fur of dusk. As ever, he seems the center of the universe, and, for the first time since the very beginning of time, this thought strikes him as strange.

Why is it that fate should lead each of us to such different ends, though we are all made of the same stuff? So many paths back to Her, and so much pain in the returning.

After searching the perimeter with his brails, he circles back to the jumping shadows of the campfire and finds, to his great interest, the king and queen talking about him.

"The elk-king sent Merlinus away on the unicorn," Uther is saying as he grills a small trout in the open flames. "He rode to Avalon, an island in the western sea."

"A place I know well," Ygrane says with hushed breath, looking up from her husking of chestnuts and hazelnuts. "Yes, it would be the Nine Queens who live there. You have not heard of them, then?"

Uther shakes his head, and Ygrane tells him the ancient story, as Merlinus himself learned it. Moths spin through the fish smoke in blurs of brightness as she informs him of the sacrifice of the Winter King.

When she finishes, Uther looks incredulous. "They murdered their kings?"

"For thousands of years, that was the custom," Ygrane affirms.

"And the kings cooperated?"

The queen tosses a handful of nut casings on the fire. "Is that really any different than your Jesus? He follows in the same tradition, you must know."

"He perished for our sins—to save our *souls*," Uther corrects. "He was a carpenter, not a king."

"He was king of the Jews, was he not?"

"That's how the Romans mocked him."

"But he was, in truth, the messiah—the Anointed One—and thus the spiritual king of his people, the true king. Am I not right?"

"I suppose. But he was never married to a queen."

"Was he not?" Ygrane arranges the nuts on the hot rocks ringing the fire. "You say he perished to save the soul. And is the soul not a woman?"

"Is it?"

Ygrane cast a smiling scowl at him. "And you call yourself a man of knowledge. Read your Plotinus again, dear Theo—and your Aristophanes. They will tell you. The spirit is a man, and the soul a woman. My druids have taught the same tradition from the first. So, you see, Jesus perished for the sake of the soul, the queen of his people. He lived and died in the ancient manner of the sacrificing queens."

Uther thinks this over skeptically as he places the cooked fish atop a long peel of birch bark. "You sound like erudite

Merlinus, quoting the philosophers. It was he who taught me that the Neoplatonists believe the higher mind, Nous, is male, and that matter, Hyle, is female. And I did, in truth, learn from the Church that Christ, the Logos, the Word, is male, and that the soul he saves is female." He accedes with a gracious nod and places the fish between them. "You're going to make a very thoughtful Christian, Ygrane. But the Church elders may find your insights more than a little disturbing."

"So it is with the druids. They know what they know, and the understanding that has been passed down is not to be disturbed. I will tell you a secret." As she uses a hazel stick to turn the nuts in the fire, she reveals, "The druids are of the same patriarchal heritage as the desert tribe who birthed your savior."

Uther pulls in his chin. "The Hebrews?"

"In the old time," Ygrane goes on, "when the age of the queens was ending, when our people were spread across Europe all the way to the southern deserts, the druids took over the holy role of the priestesses, and the sacrifice of the kings ended. Hu Gadarn Hyscion—Hu the Mighty, who led our people to Britain—Mighty Hu was a descendant of Abraham. So I have heard from Tall Silver, the chief druid himself, discussing with my teacher, the crone Raglaw. Druidic altars are made of unhewn stones, a practice found in the holy book of the Hebrews' exodus from ancient Ægypt. Chapter twenty, verse twenty-five, 'If thou would make me an altar of stone, thou shalt not build it of hewn stone.'"

Uther laughs at her surprising knowledge. "You've memorized that?"

Her startling eyes gleam.

"You want me to believe your druids are Jews?"

"I ask you to believe this: that they entered the age of kings with the same faith," the queen says. "That they share a faith in the immortality of the soul and its passage from life to life. That is one of the Hebrews' secret teachings—*gilgul* I believe they call it. The Greeks believed it, too. And the magnificent empires to the east. Also, though we worship the Creator in all of creation, as sun, stars, trees, and rocks, we believe God's name is an indecipherable mystery."

A deep happiness infiltrates his heart to hear her speak of these sacred things.

"There's more. Listen to this, Theo. There are three desert prophets—Isaiah, Jeremiah, and Zechariah—who refer to the coming messiah as 'the Branch.' The druids teach us, as well, that our deliverer is the Branch—the All Heal of the mistletoe, the golden parasitic plant that grows on the rare branch of the oak."

"Then our faiths are not so far apart after all," Uther marvels, his careworn face young again in the flame-stitched light. He affectionately separates the most succulent flakes of the trout for her.

Ygrane accepts his offering with a quiet look and holds his fire-bright stare while she confides a tribal secret. "Druids revere the cross. When they find the Branch, they mark the tree as a cross—and they carve the Branch with the name All Heal, which in my language is *Yesu*."

Uther claps his hands, and the echoes come back accompanied by the goblin cries of a raven.

Ygrane reflects his enthusiasm with a calm, sisterly brightness. "We are one people, the people of this earth. The time of the queens is over. The kings rule the world now, and they share a faith across nations. They believe what they will believe. Yet, that does not change the truth of things, does it?"

"The truth—" He shivers inside. "Nine Queens wait on Avalon. Is that what you mean?"

"Yes. They were on Avalon long before Abraham. And they were there long before Babylon, which taught Abraham what he knew. And long before Ægypt. And long before any *king*dom. The queens ruled the people for more millennia than most people today believe the world has existed. And all this time, the Nine Queens have been gathering to sit on Avalon witnessing by magic sight the brutalities of our race. By forging compassion in their own matriarchal souls, by changing themselves, they change all of us."

"But the age of the queens is over," Uther says pensively.

"Long over."

"Then why are they still there?"

"They wait for the *Annwn*—the angels—to replace them. With kings."

The fire underlighting Uther's young face boldly reveals his wide-eyed apprehension. "Am I to be the first? Is that why we have come together?"

"No, Theo." She takes his hand. "I've seen nothing of that in my sight."

A chilled numbness fringes his heart. He no longer understands what his life reveals. Since marrying this pagan queen descended of the Hebrews, his waking world has become as a dream: Ordinary grief and hope dwindle in him now that he has embraced his brother's ghost in the underworld, ransomed his soul to an animal god, and ridden out of hell on the back of the dragonish Satan of his nightmares. He is afraid for what he has done and what he has seen. And he remembers Dun Mane warning that men lose their minds in the hollow hills.

Ygrane gingerly plucks the hazelnuts from the fire rocks and places them artfully around the fish. She savors the sweet and acrid scent of the cooking smoke and, on a smooth peel of bark, prepares a portion of the nut-peppered fish for him.

Watching her soothes the dread in him. She appears so at ease with these strange truths, he feels safe with her. He gets up and retrieves the plaited grass satchel filled with berries from the stream where they have been set to chill. "Enough of all this. My mind reels to think on it anymore. Our hands are full with the work of our kingdom. We must get our men back from the Síd. We need them for our labors in this life. All that remains—the Nine Queens, the elk-king, angels and demons—" He grimaces with exaggerated amazement at the profusion of fateful powers surrounding them and pulls a smile from Ygrane. "All else we'll leave to God and the angels."

The king and queen sit together in the warm aura of the fire and share a prayer over their simple repast: "We thank you again, Lord God," Uther begins, "for delivering us this day from those who would harm us—and we thank you for restoring us to each other, we two that you have joined to unite the peoples of this land against their enemies."

"Let God be praised in the beginning and the end," Ygrane concludes. "May the Creator of heaven and earth grant us a portion of mercy."

Merlinus relents to his sleepiness. But instead of sifting gently back to his physical body in Avalon, his wraith whips violently away. The wizard knows that unless he slows down, the future will unscroll before him. He does not want to endure another vision, not with his fatigue-wracked mind. Struggling to brake his flight feels like swimming upstream in a surging, muscular river. He is too weary. So, he pulls away and finds himself with Ygrane and Uther once more.

Their food sits cold and untouched beside them, where they lie naked in the fireglow, their bodies the color of deer or of the hills at sunset. Merlinus does not want to see this. Plunging and pulling, they move with the rhythms of the fire, and even though the wizard suffers to invade the truth of their moment together and has no will to watch, he cannot look away without sliding away, back toward Avalon. He clings to them, as they cling to each other—

Fingers twine in hair, legs twine, and rapt faces in the fire's satin glow disclose exquisite, mysterious feelings that Merlinus cringes to confront for fear of polluting with his demonic presence. He softens his gaze to the aura that encloses their bodies. A sun rises. Not white and blinding as an angel, but cooler, a diamond light refracting the fire of their cresting passion.

Merlinus lets go. He cannot bear to see any more. It is too hurtfully remindful of the evil intimacies he once worked as an incubus. He lets go and falls away, back toward Avalon and the future. And as he falls, the white sun that is the joined body-lights of the king and queen tightens to a star among the packed stars of the night. Far away from Merlinus, Uther and Ygrane blaze. Empty of forethought and care, full of the instinct and presence of wild things, they plunge burning with love and its sun into the nameless night.

The immediate future snaps open as Merlinus falls away from the royal couple. And he beholds them in the firelight eating with their fingers, chatting further about what lies ahead for them—the trek through the woods to the nearest Roman road and eventually back to Maridunum, where King Someone Knows the Truth has instructed the wizard to meet them.

"Why does the elk-king send Merlinus to Avalon?" the queen asks.

"To get a sword—a sword the angels have stolen from a dwarf, I think."

"The sword Lightning."

"You know of it."

Ygrane stops eating. "I know it was Brokk who made it for the Furor long ago. It is a weapon of legend. Only a truly lofty soul may wield it without suffering incurable harm."

"That will not be me, then, if that's the case—" Uther's hands fumble with his food. "I know how I came to be king. It was Merlinus and Ambrosius who made me what I am. No merit of mine."

"Don't belittle yourself, Theo," Ygrane scolds. "It was you. Not anyone else. God chose you."

"But why?" Uther bows his head, truly perplexed. "I was nothing but a stable master. How can it have come to this?"

"Fate—and magic."

Uther gives her a sharp look. "I'll not dispute that! Fate and magic indeed." A grim, sardonic laugh rises in him at the cold recollection of his journey to the underworld. "When I saw the souls of the dead, Ygrane, I saw them dancing and laughing. I heard the music that moves them." His expression softens. "It's much bigger—so much bigger than anything I could ever have imagined."

"Yes." She holds his expression of luminous inner life with a knowing stare. "The truth always is."

"Can it win triumph for our people against the invaders?"

"Ah, but they have their magic, too." Ygrane turns up one corner of her mouth in a hapless smile. "Magic is only half of it. The rest is fate."

"God's will." He stares at her with unguarded admiration, fixing in his mind why he feels so triumphant near her: She is vulnerable without being plaintive. "You have already accepted our fate together, whatever befalls us."

"Have I?" In the firelight, her carved features lend her an air of knowing she does not feel.

"You called me to you," he says. "You knew I was in the world, even before you met me. From the first, you embraced your destiny as a queen. That's why you left these hills, why you married Gorlois. You know you're destined to birth a ruler."

"Am I?" she asks, barely audible.

"Yes, Ygrane. I, who know nothing of fate, know this." His voice fills with emotion, mixed fear and hope. "Your son—our son—will be a lofty soul, the one who is destined to become worthy of the sacred sword."

Her watchful face looks radiant with serenity. She moves to say something, but Uther stays her lips with his fingers. He leans forward on his knees and touches her brow with his. Her lips are dry and warm.

When they kiss, their faces silhouetted in the dark, the firelight threading like the rays of a fierce star between their brows, Merlinus retreats from this vision.

They both expand in each other's embrace, enlarging with life, becoming visibly greater together, visibly stronger the more completely they entangle. And the wizard thinks of all the separate stars overhead, all the separate beings and things, each at the exact center of everywhere and nowhere—all yearning for the wholeness these two possess, this meaningful conjunction of destinies into one shared light in the darkness, a harmony of rapture and danger, of knowing and mystery, of fate and magic.

Time falls open. Like a mountain desert, the future lies before Merlinus in a huge vista, colorless as shale. Whole slopes of time veer away on all sides. The wizard laughs uncontrollably, seized by the giddy panorama of busy scenes. He sees battles mostly—barbarians in their strange rags of leather and battered armor and Uther's lethal, black-clad horsemen sweeping over the hillsides.

Much closer, on the hummocky field before him, Merlinus spots the unicorn and the soldiers it has led out of the Otherworld. Emerging from a nook of hills, the fiana and cavalrymen have salt-stained beards and harrowed faces sharpened from their ordeal in the eternal wasteland.

Wearily, they tramp along a gravel streambed until they come upon Ygrane and Uther asleep in each other's arms under a blanket of leaves. Farther downhill, they are all riding together through the stark forest. Farther yet, they traipse along a Roman road—and there is Maridunum with its vine-scrawled brown walls.

Merlinus peers toward the horizon, into a sky like fractured quartz. A mirage flutters before him, an enchanted landscape of seething falls and smoky mountaintops under the silver lips of the moon. Close by, through secret paths in the velvety sedge, sight draws past ranks of attentive basilisks and cowled wyverns. A ribbon sprawl of river opens to the sea, and a barge drifts languorously on the shining estuary. Nine proud queens stand erect at the prow, and a dead king lies upon the thwarts, cold and blue.

Uther? The wizard cannot see who it is.

On the near bank, another battle rages, the grass slick with blood, the sky full of rattling arrows—and, heartsick, Merlinus recognizes the mattocks and fire-axes of the barbarians flashing through blinding dust and vapors. Like a tongue of flame, the wind sock of Uther's red dragon flies among black banners of battlesmoke.

The wizard pulls his gaze away. Closer, on a bluff of gray grass switching in a ghostly wind, he fixes on stubby knobs of granite and a round section of oak, a great wheel cut from a behemoth tree. The wheel tilts and falls, landing on the granite knobs. And in that instant, it is no longer a wheel but a table—an immense round table. And at its center stands a silver cup inlaid with gold and meshed in starlight.

An angel comes out of the gorge, a living fire with blinding eyes, and suddenly Merlinus is back in his body, back in Avalon, sitting cross-legged on the packed earth, staring up into a javelin of sunlight. Quickly, he turns his face, and a black sun imprints his vision. The Nine Queens, sitting on their block-cut thrones and branded with the retinal afterimage, observe him through their black veils.

"What did you see?" Rna asks in a fatigued voice, leaning slightly forward.

Merlinus opens his mouth to speak, but exhaustion packs his chest. He mutters a spell of wakefulness, and weariness departs, leaving him with a stainless clarity. He begins to tell the Nine Queens about Uther's courageous rescue of Ygrane and the radiance of love he witnessed between them.

"No, Myrddin." Old, withered Rna shakes her proud head. "What did you see of times to come?"

"Not much," Merlinus reports, rubbing his eyes. "An angel interrupted me, and I still can't see you clearly. How long was I staring into the sun?"

"Did you witness the birth?" The old one's voice persists, hollow as an echo. "Will there be a birth?"

"I don't know."

"Then, did you see yourself? Will you go on from here after Uther?"

Merlinus shrugs, stands his staff on end, and uses both hands to get stiffly to his feet. His body feels ponderously heavy despite his spell of wakefulness, and he requires both arms and legs to hold himself upright. "I saw you, all nine of you, in a barge on a river entering the sea. A dead king lay at your feet."

The black veil of the eldest queen flutters with an exasperated sigh as she sits back. "That is already well-known, Myrddin. Did you see anything else?"

"Battles mostly."

"What about the sword Lightning and the star stone. Surely, you saw them?"

"No." Merlinus thinks a moment. "Just a big, round table cut from an oak tree. I think it was a table. With an elegant cup of precious metals at its center, but neither chairs nor people."

Rna leans forward again, more sharply this time, her elbows winging out as her hands clutch the armrests. "You saw the Graal?"

"I saw a silver goblet with inlays of gold thread fine as human hair—and an extraordinary luminance shone from it."

"That is the Graal, Myrddin." The veiled queen sounds excited, in her impassive, magisterial way. "The Fire Lords have crafted it to receive their power, which they send down from the sky."

"An antenna." Merlinus gnaws a corner of his mustache. "The angels must use it as a means to focus energy. Electricity—" He gropes with the language to name the force he knew as a demon. *Electricus*—amber friction. "There is an enormous electrical potential between the earth and the upper atmosphere—"

A stir passes through the other eight queens as they turn in their seats to murmur at one another. Still, the falcon stare of the eldest never budges from Merlinus. "You must go now, Myrddin. Plant the star stone where the unicorn directs. Then, deliver the sword Lightning to King Uther. When you build the oaken table of your vision, the Graal will be given."

Before the wizard can respond, space shivers. Merlinus thinks at first it is his scorched vision and blinks. The air swims with giant protozoa, and the contours of the round chamber warp and wobble with the passage of the large lenses of their bodies. Images smear and break apart as if seen in rippled water. And when his vision calms and smooths out, the circular hall and the Nine Queens are gone.

Merlinus stands in a circle of stones shining with fire-colored lichens. Nine trees stir in the sea-scented wind: birch, rowan, alder, willow, ash, hawthorn, oak, holly, and hazel. Energy pours into him out of the cold that flows through these totem trees, and bright air, full of sea salt and the mineral breath of the mountains, encloses him.

The wizard does not linger in that place. The Nine Queens have returned him to himself for a purpose. With legs full of limber strength, he exits the circle and practically runs back through the apple woods to the black pond.

There the unicorn stands, at the water's edge, drinking from the floating world in a tremulous mirror surface. Its hide flickers with bounteous power. It looks up at his approach and waits.

His hurried pace slows at the sight of the beautiful creature, because he remembers too well the heavenly peace he knows at its touch—and the damnation that always follows its departure.

Skirting the unicorn, Merlinus walks the perimeter of the small lake and approaches the star stone and the sword stuck in its cleft. Physically, he cannot budge the rock, but, with his earth-rooted strength and a vigorous chant, he gets it to bobble a few inches off the ground. He steers it to where the unicorn watches him with long eyes, and he mounts the beast.

As before, his brain buds with the fragrant blossoms of paradise, and heaven's grace appears to shine through everything. His might multiplied, and with an insistent touch of his staff, the star stone rises into the air. After some awkward weaving and dipping, the stone flies ahead as they gallop east.

An oceanic wind looms up at the rocky coast, and the unicorn charges over the faceted surface of the sea, scattering spindrift behind in tattered pennants. Wave crests stream on all sides, and the wizard and his steed rush headlong toward the blue heather bluffs of the distant, ordinary world.

Rain fog greets the fiana and cavalry as they emerge from the spectral darkness of the underworld. Initially, the weary soldiers believe that this gray void is another obstacle to their escape. But the cloven hoofprints that they have been following end in mud draggled with periwinkles and rhododendrons.

Falon slides off his mount, face upturned to the soft rain. Through the pastels of fog, he discerns the ragged silhouettes of fir trees and smells their resin. He begins to laugh with relief. The world's beauty hides in the mist as though it is a secret, and the other men only slowly begin to grasp it.

"Men!" Falon shouts through his giddiness. "We are home!"

Groans and hoarse shouts of "Blessed Cymru!" jump from the staggered company as each and every one falls to the ground and embraces the fertile earth. Eyes rigid with staring, the men crawl to their feet and shamble through the fog toward the shadows of colossal trees, where the day shines a powdery blue. Like blind men, they grope with outstretched arms among the pharaonic pillars of trees, grateful to touch once again bark and pine needles and the bestowals of rain.

Atop the rise, the wanderers see that the fog sits only in the cups of the valleys, and the morning above hurts their eyes with its cerulean brightness. Intoxicated with dewfall and sunbeams, the mud-plastered men reel about jaunty as clowns. The horses, too, revive in the canted light, and the autumn wind carries their whinnying songs aloft.

Falon alone retains enough composure to orient himself. From a bough draped with red ivy, he scans the smoky hills falling away to the mountainous north and recognizes that they are within the forest of the Demetae. Even with their worn-out horses, the riders can reach Maridunum by tomorrow evening. He gathers the men and leads them through the morning mist to the gravel flats of a stream to wash themselves and refresh their steeds.

There, they find the king and queen in each other's embrace, asleep beneath a cover of leaves. The sight gladdens them as much as the warm touch of the sun and the familiar hillscapes of home, for now their mad crossing of the shadowland has not been in vain. With jubilant cries, they rouse the royal couple.

Happy astonishment sits up Uther and Ygrane in their riverside bower, and all bleariness from their long night of lovemaking flies at the joyful sight of their men unharmed. In a mood of heartstrong celebration, a fire is built while several soldiers lurch through the woods shooting at deer. No animals are hit by the woozy archers, but the fiana net numerous trout, and over this repast the stories are told.

The ride to Maridunum, under cloud cover ripped by wild rays of sunlight, cleanses them of otherworldliness. At night, the rain stroking the hawthorn branches of their shelters soothes them into dreamless sleep, and they wake to a chill, gray dawn in the boggy lanes of the forest. By midmorning, they follow a rutted cart trail past crofts and apple garths so ordinary and remorselessly familiar that many of them at last feel sane enough to weep.

Falon cannot stop watching the queen. She looks different to him, for he has never seen her happy before. The darkness of the Otherworld has sharpened his gaze in this life, and he exults to notice the tiniest details of her elation: He sees a slight deepening of her dimples in her shared smiles and proud looks with the king and he hears the hues of her soul in her voice when she speaks to him. She is in love.

This seems a sacred boon to Falon, a blessing won for all the people. Ygrane, from her first summons of him fifteen years ago, has always seemed preoccupied by her magic. Her trances and conversations with invisible beings give much of her to the unseen. But now, to Falon's strong eye, she appears wholly focused in this world.

Uther has changed her and is himself changed, from the uncertain king in black who married the queen, to a Celtic hero, raider of the hollow hills, worthy consort to the witch-queen. Falon senses, at last, the magic that his moody, distracted queen has been building these many years. The tidal history of empires creaks in this murky forest, rising among bare-blown trees, and swirling about this regal pair.

They ride together bareback on Falon's steed, with the queen in the king's embrace, sharing the reins. This living emblem inspires the fiana and cavalry to ride diligently at their defensive stations, guarding what they have hard won. Falon shares a mount with one of the men who died in the underregion, while another of the resurrected gallops swiftly ahead to alert the guard at Maridunum.

By the time the first hamlet appears tucked among viridian pastures dotted with red cows, the adventures behind them seem more fabled than important. What lies ahead beckons—the alliance between Celts and Romans and the necessary battles that will have to be won to unite their kingdom.

Dun Mane, in the green robe and white, hooded mantle of his supreme order, welcomes the king into his sanctum. The cubicle, though small and cluttered with bulky leather-bound folios piled atop a scrivener's table, has an arched ceiling that endows the space with a certain grandeur. A scented oil lamp chained overhead fills the alcove with a sunset glow and a fragrance of soft apples.

This is the druid's private cell, where he keeps company with the old texts. Since the horrifying experience of the royal wedding, all those days that feel like weeks ago, he has sat here, deep in reflective prayer, poring over the most sacred of the writings: *The Book of Green Fire* and *The Yellow Book of the Branch,* written collections of the oral teachings from the earliest druids. He seeks some understanding of the horrifying wonders he has beheld, and he believes he has found it among these venerable runes.

Both written sources record that *there will be signs and portents when the fiery names shall be heard again.* That was the passage he contemplated the moment the victory horn sounded and Uther returned to Maridunum with the queen. Now, having heard their stories, he understands: *the fiery names* are the primal heroes, the great souls who put on the phantom shape of flesh when the people need their bright warmth and power.

Dun Mane sees Uther Pendragon with this understanding. Until the terror of the wedding, the supreme druid had faith only in the political and military advantage of this renewed alliance with the Romans. But now that the king has returned from the hollow hills, now that Uther Pendragon himself speaks of facing the elk-king of the Daoine Síd and bartering souls with him, Dun Mane grasps something far larger in this union.

A spiritual unfoldment is taking place. Dun Mane is convinced of it. He reads it in the sacred texts of his people, and he hears it in the holy pronouncements of the king's faith, whose Anointed One will baptize with fire: *I am come to send fire on the earth.*

Dun Mane receives Uther with formal regality, in full ritual attire. The king's herald has delivered his request for a visitation unexpectedly and with barely enough time to don his robes of holy office.

But Uther arrives bareheaded, dressed informally in a blue

tunic and velvet slippers, his youthful face shadowed with care. He puts his hands on the druid's shoulders and stops him from bowing. "Do not revere me or my station, Dun Mane," he says in a voice flat with honesty. "I have come to you as a man—a creature of our race. I need your counsel."

They sit together at the bench of the scrivener's table, and Dun Mane folds back his hood and exposes his long, drawn face burnished with silver whiskers. "You are here because you fear giving your soul to the elk-king."

A surprised smile jolts Uther before the solemn weight of that truth closes his face again. "Yes, Dun Mane. My promise weighs heavily. How did you know?"

"I have sat here with what you have told of your journey to the underworld," Dun Mane says in his low voice, "and I have felt your trouble. You are a Christian—and a Celtic god demands your sacrifice."

Uther's face clouds. "I no longer understand the world."

A sad laugh drops from the druid. "Nor do I, my lord. For years as a druid, no glamour, no marvels touched me. I lived cunningly and opportunistically. My family's power protected and nourished me, and my personal influence grew. I lived the political life of the clans. I lived it so well that when the supreme druid before me, the legendary Tall Silver, crossed to the Greater World, I was tapped to take his place." Another unhappy laugh falls out of him. "At that time, I thought that the stories of Tall Silver's magic were allegory—fables of illumination. I ignored the mysterious feelings of awe I felt in the queen's presence. I scoffed at the crone Raglaw, a primitive reminder of our people's aboriginal past. I thought myself enlightened—almost Roman in my modernity. I thought I understood the world, too. I was wrong."

The king thumbs his shaven chin, confused. "How can there be so many gods?"

"There is only one God," Dun Mane asserts, "but the deity wears many faces—and not all human."

"But I am a Christian and the elk-king pagan."

"My lord—we are one light of many colors. Listen." He places an age-mottled hand on the maroon stack of folios. "I have been studying these old texts again, sacred writings I once thought less important than clan treaties and border maps. I have looked at them in a new light since your wedding, my lord. Now I am convinced your faith and mine are the same." A quiescent smile composes his bulky countenance. "I am convinced now that the druids are a priestly caste descended from the Temple of Solomon in Jerusalem."

That temple was razed by the Babylonians in 586 B.C., in an age when the Celtic empire touched the holy lands; it was then that they shared what they knew of the Fire Lords' magic. Uther remembers learning this, first from Merlinus, then Ygrane herself, and now her druid. "You are Hebrews, then?"

"I believe that druids and rabbis share a tradition and may very well have common ancestors, yes. We keep the same ancient traditions. I will elucidate them in close detail for you at your wish—but for now, all you need know, my lord, is that the Anointed One, *Yesu*, is a Celtic savior prophesied by our seers since the age of Solomon's Temple."

"He is the All Heal, symbolized in the mistletoe worshiped by your sages." Uther repeats what his wife has taught him. "But—Dun Mane—do you and the other druids truly accept Jesus the Christ as the Son of God and your personal savior?"

"I cannot speak as yet for the other druids," Dun Mane answers with shining candor, "but for myself, I am certain. *Yesu* is the new god of our modern age, destined to be the supreme deity of the Abiding North. I have not the sight, as does the queen, yet I can see plainly enough that God has fulfilled the ancient prophecy in Jesus and has come into the Lesser World and taken on the phantom of flesh as a man."

"And your god, Someone Knows the Truth—what of him?" the king asks in a challenging tone. "He told me that the Christians steal souls from him."

Dun Mane's deep wrinkles darken pensively. "Gods are much diminished when they go into the earth, my lord. They become smaller. More agile, too, perhaps—but far less powerful. They live too close to the Dragon, you see. It changes them. Makes them more like itself—like your ancestor—"

"Wray Vitki—yes." Light widens across Uther's face as he looks up at the oil lamp, half-expecting God to answer for the abominable wonder of the magus. "I swear by all that is holy, he has become a tired, old dragon. Were it not for my boyhood dreams of him, I would not have known he had ever been a man."

"The same happens with the gods, my lord, only more slowly, over ages." He pulls open a leather volume and gestures at the foliage of tangled loops and interlocked spirals in the glosses. "My people are obsessed with the Dragon. See it in the dragoncoils of our designs. Hear it in the plaintiveness of our music, which is the wistfulness of the Dragon's own dreamsongs. The spirit of our ancient people has been driven into the ground. But now, *Yesu* comes at last—the All Heal, resurrected from the dead by God. He will lead our people out of the underground, because we *are* his people, descended directly from his vine. Do you understand, King Uther? The messiah has come for us—in you."

Uther splays a hand across his chest and shakes his head. "Not in me, Dun Mane. I am but a man."

"Made king by God."

"By Merlinus—Myrddin—if truth is to be served."

"Myrddin is a demon won to the angels by God's grace," Dun Mane asserts. "He did not choose you but was shown you by the prophetic sight of the crone Raglaw."

Uther demurs with bowed head. "Jesus is messiah, not I."

"Your humility is most welcome, my lord." An avuncular smile graces Dun Mane's big face. "Riochatus would have us believe that he is Jesus himself. Yet he does not speak for our savior, only for Ravenna and the Roman Church. He is one of the Romans who gather at their country estates to decide how *Yesu* will be understood by all others. No. *Yesu* lives in each man's soul who is open to healing salvation. You know that. That is why God has chosen you to be king—a Christian with a big enough soul to look into the elk face of Someone Knows the Truth and convert his best warrior to *Yesu*."

"But I am afraid, Dun Mane," he confesses. "I don't know what I am doing."

"Fear not, noble King." The druid smiles warmly. "You are bringing a large portion of the Celtic soul up from the dark underground and into the light of the waking world, of history. I promise you, the soul that you father by your sacrifice will shine across the centuries."

"And my soul?" The king's golden eyes narrow. "What will become of my soul in the care of the elk-king?"

The druid's beneficent and hopeful smile only deepens. "Uther Pendragon, you are a true Christian. You possess the All Heal of *Yesu* in your soul. Thus, you can go into the underworld and come back unscathed. Look at you—" He sits back with wide-eyed admiration. "You have been inside the hollow hills and have spoken with the god of the pale people and you are whole, no more mad than you were before you married our haunted people. Your faith protects you."

"If so, Dun Mane, then I would do well to trust in God for the birth of my son. Why barter my soul with the elk-king?"

The druid pulls backward as though a wind gusts through his skull. "You would spurn the soul of our greatest warrior?" His eyes hood with drowsy astonishment. "You must drink of the Raven Spring. You gave your word. A king to a god."

"No word was given, Dun Mane."

An arid expression covers the druid's stunned disappointment. "If you do not drink from the Raven Spring, Ygrane will mother yet another Morgeu. And you will prove yourself no better than a petty warlord."

Uther looks mild in the face of the druid's curse. He is

actually glad for all that Dun Mane has told him of their shared faith, and he is particularly relieved that his destiny forbids him to live and die as other men. For what the king has feared most about his transaction with the Celt god is that he *wants* to return to the happy netherwoods. With his eyes closed, he sometimes can hear the melodious way the wind murmurs through the treetops there, like water or the sweep of rain, with its fragrant musk.

"Thank you for your sincere counsel, Dun Mane." The king stands, looking commonplace and satisfied. "I will remember your wisdom."

Before the druid can rise to bid proper farewell, the king departs the sanctum and disappears in the dark corridor, as though he is no more than a phantom returned to shadow.

While the king confronts Dun Mane, the queen meets with Riochatus in his apartments overlooking the skewed lanes and alleys of Maridunum. She has sought him out to ask him about Miriam, the mother of *Yesu*. Her vision of the Blessed Mother lingers soulfully in her memory.

The bishop, in red robes and pontifical headgear, sits in his ecclesiastic chair, the curve-limbed cathedra, transported with him from Londinium. A brown-robed cleric locates appropriate passages in the Bible that perches with spread wings on a reading tripod before the Church father. Riochatus pontificates at length about the sacred conception, the virgin birth, and the mystery of her assumption into heaven. Nothing he says reminds Ygrane of the dark Mediterranean woman with the Scythian brow and vulnerable gazelle eyes, whose voluptuous serenity freed her from the Dark Dweller.

When the bishop concludes, he asks her to pray with him, and she kneels at the window while he intones liturgical petitions from his chair. His droning words disappear out the window. Whereas when silent Ygrane prays, her shut face draws the darkness behind her lids into an earnest plea that leaves a cold spot in her soul where it breaks through to the Greater World: *A dying people call on you, Mother of God. You, who gave your son to death and saw him rise, save us. Our soul already passes through the portal of sunset into the underworld of vanished peoples. Only your son, Yesu, can save us from the darkness. Send his magic to us, and we will carry your light into the ages.*

The gasps of the bishop and the cleric open her eyes. An angel emerges from a sky of smoky quartz. It hovers above the thatched roofs like a tangle of stars, its rays stitching a human specter. The trembling of its wings stirs music in their mute blood.

And then, it is gone.

The cleric prostrates himself, and the bishop falls trembling to his knees. Eyes hot with tears, he shouts, "Blessed mother of mercy! My prayer has been answered. Our savior is received by the Celts!"

He turns his fervid stare on the queen. "Do you accept Jesus as your savior, Ygrane, queen of the Celts?"

The queen sighs listlessly and rises. "You understand nothing, Riochatus." She turns and leaves so abruptly, the bishop's gaunt face is still beatifically ardent and happy when the draperies close after her.

The star stone falls to earth beneath a trident of lightning and a clamor of thunder. The unicorn flashes light-footed through the brambly ravines to near where it has crashed in the river gorge country of the Dobuni. Startled deer and elf-bolts of birds shoot past, escaping the noise. Among a slum of blackthorn and asters high on a mount known as Caliburnus, the rock squats as though it has been here since time before memory.

But no—coming closer, Merlinus can see that it is not as before. The stone's lobes have broken apart, split down its middle like a pecan. One lobe lies impacted in the silty bank of the brook at the base of the mount, only a corner of it visible. The other half lies atop the mount, rooted like a molar. The sword stands erect, the blade still caught in the fissure where it has been jammed.

The wizard's steed pauses on the mossy riprap of the brook, and Merlinus dismounts to recover the sword Lightning. Encumbered by the sad discolorings of separation from the unicorn, Merlinus clambers up the bank, using his staff to support himself. With one hand, he grabs the exposed corner of the impacted portion of the star stone, and as he shifts his weight to that arm, the stone slides horizontally on bearings of gravel lubricated with mud. His purchase flees, and he logrolls down the bank into the chilly astonishment of the brook.

Merlinus sits bolt upright, splashing about for his hat and shaking water from hair and beard, edging the unicorn away. When he looks up to pick his path more carefully, surprise jangles him. The sword Lightning is gone! He drops his staff and flies up the bank spry as a monkey.

The sword has not disappeared. It has simply fallen and lies flat atop the stone, not visible from below. He lifts it easily, and the spilled light from the mirror-finished blade illuminates the interior of his skull, brightening a realization.

He leaves the sword on the stone, retreats down the bank, and pulls the impacted half of the stone back to its original position. When he scrambles again to the top, the sword has annealed to the anvil rock, immovable.

Merlinus understands then that the star stone was originally two separate rocks: a steel mortise and magnetic tenon locked together. The impact has separated them. Now by moving the impacted magnet, the steel gains or loses its strength to hold the sword.

Unsure yet what the significance of this must be for the destiny that this sword and stone serve, the wizard nonetheless knows that this can be no accident. It is magic. He would have to remain alert to discovering its purpose. With that determination, he pulls the bottom half of the star stone into the free position, climbs up, and hefts the sword Lightning.

Its chamfered blade reflects the fire colors of the forest orange squash flowers, red maple, bronze oak, yellow birch. Then, sword in hand, he skids down the embankment, retrieves his staff and hat, mounts the unicorn, and they are away again, nimble as the wind in the densely tangled byways of the wood.

Maridunum's vine-hung walls appear out of the forest gloom, ruddy with the long light of the sun. Dawn or dusk, Merlinus cannot be sure. The unicorn stops at the fringe of the forest cresting the parkland at the back of the city walls, where the king and the queen have been married what seemed an age ago.

Merlinus does not want to dismount. He dreads the sorrows to come. The unicorn tosses its head impatiently, and he knocks his knees against its sides, wanting to drive it forward, hoping Ygrane will see them and somehow hold the beast still for him. Then he could throw the sword to the ground and ride off into the sky, into heaven.

But Ygrane does not come for him, and the unicorn stamps the ground, its hooves hissing in the dead leaves like the broken fragments of a star. Merlinus dismounts. A stupefied melancholy tightens on him, and it is all he can do not to fall to the ground under that pall.

Glumly, with eggshell emptiness, he trudges forward into the cider light of the open field. He glances back only once. Thistledown flies where, full of unfathomable love and madness, the unearthly steed has stood.

The back portal of the city wall opens, and a wedge of fiana rush out, followed by three mounted bowmen swirling dregs of windblown leaves. Uther and Ygrane appear at the gate, and when they recognize the wizard, the king stays the soldiers, and they fall into two flanking lines. Merlinus approaches with the sword Lightning held high, spiked with orange sunlight.

"Merlinus!" Uther greets. "It's been days, you realize! Where have you been?"

"To Avalon, lord—as the elf-king bade me." The wizard lowers the sword for him to see, but it is Ygrane who recognizes it first.

"The Furor's sword!" she cries. "The barbarians cannot surpass this magic—the best of their own gods!"

Merlinus turns the sword about and raises it as a cross-staff, presenting it to the king. "A gift of power from the Daoine Síd—and the Nine Queens of Avalon."

Uther examines the sword Lightning with a look of awe. He wields the sword deftly and turns to face his soldiers. "Behold! A dragonslayer's sword in the hand of your king! With this, we will without fail repel the invaders—we will drive all the northern hordes from our land!"

A ferocious cheer from the warriors leaps into the crimson sky, and an answering call descends from the city ramparts, where the barracks have emptied to see the return of the wizard.

Ygrane leans close and kisses Merlinus's cheek. "You have done well, Myrddin, and just in time. The warlords of the Britons and the Celts refuse to cooperate. Maybe now, Uther will be able to draw them together."

The king displays the sword Lightning to the soldiers. Its reflectance fills their faces with a hopeful radiance, a fateful glory.

Leaving behind her mother's Cymru and her father's Britain, Morgeu travels north as far as she can go and still find a settlement to make her own. Beyond the crags of Hadrian's Wall and the turf ramparts of the Antonine frontier, among the mist-strewn river gorges of the highlands, she finds Roman ruins. A maze of broken battlements and rubble imprint the grassy tableland above a rock-strewn current.

Four centuries ago, this was the legionary fortress of Inchtuthil, the iron fist that held east Caledonia for Rome. Now it is a rocky field hazed with heather. The dozen Y Mamau that Morgeu has gathered on her northward trek pitch tents and set to work constructing timber roofs for the remaining stone bulwarks.

A Pictish settlement nearby moves off several nights later when green spirit lights are seen bobbing out of the ruins and into the surrounding hill forests. Ethiops harrows with nightmares the local lake dwellers and the ax-marauders in their underground stone houses until the populace loses its carnal will to raid the newcome women. The Picts stay well away from the haunted fortress of Morgeu, whom they call the *Fey*—the Doomed.

Before the rage of winter descends, several Y Mamau return from Segontium with a rickety dray under whose loaves of peat they have hidden a large stone statue of the black goddess, Morrígan.

The rapture dances begin again and the blood sacrifices as well. But this time, Morgeu is determined to use as much of her father's political wiles as her mother's legacy of sorcery to assault her enemies and make her place in the world.

What she does not realize is that her very will to stand against this vast frosty wood comes from Ethiops, who still yearns to liberate Lailoken from his organic bonds. His yearning has become all the more intense since Bubelis and Ojanzan collided with the angels and shriveled to cinders above Maridunum. It will be centuries before they recover from those burns, and while they drift helpless in their hurt through the numbing chill of space, he and Azael must somehow manage without them.

Lailoken used to be fond of killing gutsacks by overindulging them in their hungers, and Ethiops has decided to use that very ploy on the wizard himself. That is why he has inspired Morgeu to establish her own settlement apart from her parents. With his help, she will grow strong this winter on Morrígan's magic—strong enough to believe she is a sorceress in her own kingdom.

The Picts will revere her out of fear. Treaties shall be arranged, and she will serve as a powerful intermediary for the north tribes with the Celts of the south. She will have political power *and* magic. And when Lailoken's ambitious indulgences expose him, she will be ready and in place to strike.

Often that winter, Morgeu is seen by Pictish scouts wandering the silver gravel bars of the river, muttering incantations to herself. She talks to Morrígan about her destiny as queen of the Celts. They discuss the old ways, the blood feasts that make her moonbitch-warriors strong. And they plot the vengeance of Gorlois and the destruction of Lailoken.

Pictish scouts and hunters disappear, fed by Ethiops and the Y Mamau to the Drinker of Lives—the Dragon. The immense beast, attracted by the offerings, jets steam and boils mud in the fens near Inchtuthil. It speaks raspily through the tranced women of the cult, moaning to be fed Lailoken. Ethiops plans to feed it the unicorn as well, and, in Morrígan's voice, tells this to the sorceress.

Morgeu remembers fondly her golden summers with the unicorn. They are among her few happy memories of her mother and yet are themselves tainted by sorrow. When Ygrane stopped sending the unicorn, Morgeu railed crazily to discover she had no magic of her own, no power at all to summon the charmed creature, and no hopeful future as a woman.

She still grimaces to recall how the Roman families spurned her because of her pagan mother. Fumes of winter alder and oak color the river bluffs with the same foggy shades of her grief.

"All that has changed with you, my goddess," she says to the shadowed stream that holds together the dark souls of spruce and fir. "Morrígan, who lives in the black needles of the trees. Morrígan of the winter night, fill this vessel with your magic."

At her feet, the stream has carved the ice into the sinuous shapes of drowned hair, and she expects to see some sign here from her goddess.

But neither the faerïe nor the unicorn comes to Morgeu as they do at her mother's summons. When Morgeu invokes Morrígan, Ethiops must conjure a presence. The demon answers her with soft-mindedness, blurring her with delusions of higher purpose. He shows her the shoddy lean-to shacks her Y Mamau have hewn together among the ruins of Inchtuthil and presents them as a palace: not a Roman fortress but an open-aired *mansio*, a temple sacred to Morrígan with walls of magic instead of stone. From here, she will rule danger and madness.

Most seductive of all for her is that she will possess a kingdom that is neither her mother's nor her father's but her own. It will be a Roman-Celtic kingdom born more intimately *of* her than inherited by any child of the flesh—for she will bring it forth out of her own soul, accomplishing what none among the royals has dared in thirty generations: She will continue to live immersed in the archaic bloodlust of Morrígan. And she will do this as a Roman-Celt, a sorceress of the most ancient order in the guise of a modern noblewoman—Morgeu the Fey.

For the unicorn, the hours are clouds. The fruity colors of morning clouds, the dirtier shades of storm fronts, the white hair of midday cirrus sift time through their shifting hues. The solar creature is sick of it. Beyond the vapor limit of the sky, above the festering heat of the Dragon, space opens into the wide fields of the sun. Time means something larger there, where horizons are infinite. Day and night, seasons, and all the puny strictures of life on the sphere of a Dragon's hide vanish. It wants to go back, to the music of its friends, blamelessly jubilant, its body sleek again, wholly liquefied in the flow of the herd.

The unicorn is ready to abandon the earth and snap the tether that binds it to the witch-queen. Ygrane has found her mate and has withdrawn to create a child. Now is the time for the unicorn to depart—now, before she gives the Dark Dweller power to ride it again. The solar beast is still weary from carrying the star stone from Avalon.

Only its undelivered promise holds it from vertical flight. The Fire Lords have not released it. Yet neither have they forbidden its departure. It moves through the gloomy trees and their tattered hangings of hemlock and wild grape. At a fissure in the earth red as a wound with autumn maple and sumac, it knows well enough to stop. Mist seeps from the crevasse and hovers midlevel among the tree trunks in a soft morning haze.

The unicorn scrapes its horn, sharpening its length. The shavings it deposits melt into the earth, a final tribute to the Dragon before shooting free of the earth. An afterglow of the great being's dreamsong phosphors in the air. The echo of the music lulls the uneasiness and frustration in the unicorn, and it wonders if this soft violence that it does to its mind is similar to what the organic creatures experience as sleep.

Soothed by the presence of the Dragon, by its resonance with other worlds, the unicorn has more patience. It feels along its tether into the witch-queen and finds something very different brimming in her. Unlike all their prior contacts, when the queen's magic sipped strength from the unicorn for healing potions and cumbersome rides across the Dragon's pelt, this time, the energy slips *into* Ygrane. Inside her, another life stirs, and inside this tiny life a kingdom of lightning flashes, a thundering violence terrible and beautiful as spring.

The unicorn returns its attention to the crevasse and the reds and golds of winter's widening grin. Calmer now, it suffers less its urgency to return to the herd, and the animal strolls into the drifting sunlight, content to graze patiently in this hot place that boils its hours into the slag of twilight and the diamond-chip night.

Arguments flourish between the allies in Maridunum. Three people have already been killed in various disputes over petty issues of protocol: the marching order of troops on parade, the seating arrangement in the war room, and the color of their standard. Such nonsense infuriates Merlinus and urges him to fulfill his strong eye vision of the round table. But he has no time to implement his idea.

In the days that he has been away, Ygrane and Uther, in counsel with their advisers, have decided to establish a new city, to be designed and constructed by both Roman and Celtic hands. Of military necessity, it must be situated to the east of the Celtic lands, but for political reasons it must remain independent of territorial influence by the powerful Roman families. To that end, a wilderness site has been sought out.

Located in a chain of steep hills overhanging an ancient Roman highway, the Fosse Way, on a sharp bend in the River Amnis, a broad plain is cleared. The unicorn has dropped the star stone from Avalon onto a tributary brook of that river, and Merlinus believes now that this is a direction finder from the *Annwn*, the Fire Lords, who must have guided the animal.

The location is ideal militarily and commercially. With promontories rising several hundred feet on all sides, the city will remain sequestered and guarded, while the river and the highway nearby will encourage brisk communications and trade.

A name that weds both the queen's and the king's cultures has also been devised, something new to the language, representing the glad hope of a united people: from the Latin *cameralis* for royal treasure and the Celtic *lodd* for servant. The royal treasure's servant—Camelot.

Designs have been sketched out for a modern city and architects are already busy drafting work plans for the construction to begin in the spring. In the interim, while the north wind and its snow warriors hold the land—the very land that a year before the Dragon Lord Ambrosius had conquered by doughty cunning—the court will reside at Tintagel.

From there, in close proximity to Armorica, the king's men can more readily watch and quickly report on the treacherous Roman families. Surely they plot the demise of Uther Pendragon in the same vicious manner that they have competed among themselves for power since the legions departed seventy years before.

Tintagel, perched on the seacliffs, seems virtually impenetrable to rebel Celtic factions. The successful raid of the Y Mamau on Maridunum convinces the druids to sanction their queen's move to the Christian province. Thus it is that bargeloads of Celtic families, whole villages, prepare to follow Ygrane.

That only further alarms the littoral Romans, and in the days preceding the royal move there is much noise from the druids about the protests of the Church and the concerns of Marcus Dumnoni, Gorlois's nephew and the new duke of the Saxon Coast.

Marcus demands assurances that his local authority will not be eroded by the arrival of Ygrane's military commanders and their troops. The Church requires that no pagan rituals be performed in the vicinity. Other territorial magistrates express anger that they will be taxed to support a pagan army.

Assuaging these fears occupies what time remains to the king and queen. And then one morning, Ygrane stands in the colonnaded foyer of the *mansio* where the packaged freight of her court at Maridunum has been mounded—crates, cases, and trunks loaded with household items and the folios of her scribes. And that evening, she stands among the same objects at Tintagel in the sea's vast salt aura.

Aware of Ygrane's title to the fortress, Marcus Dumnoni has removed all of his deceased uncle's furnishings and found appointments for the servants in other households. On the glittering autumn evening that the royal couple arrives, only orange sunlight stands in the capacious chambers.

While the baggage crates at the harbor are conveyed to the palace and unpacked, the king and queen tour the rooms and decide where the furniture will go. Pieces have arrived as wedding gifts from the Celtic chiefs, the major Roman families not only in the *coloniae* but from kingdoms as far away as Ægypt, Thracia, and Oriens, the desert homeland of Jesus himself.

Uther is impressed by the palace's modern architecture—its bartizan turrets slender as minarets and the main towers ledged with open, curved balconies that simultaneously face the western sea and the cliff forests. Running water skirls out of ceramic pipes and through stone basins in the tower suites, draining from rain catchments on the roofs, while a subterranean stream serves as a sewer for the numerous baths and latrines.

But where Uther finds novelty, Ygrane suffers haunting memories. Here is where the druids brought her to marry Gorlois. Above brume and spindrift, spires of luminous limestone rise against sheer dark cliffs—a palace seemingly built from the salt of the sea. Salt bitterness are her memories. While her fiana paced with the sea-wisps in the stone corridors, she grappled with the duke's lecherous pawings that first night. Blessedly, she employed her magic cunningly enough to keep the lewd encounter short—yet she could not soften its violence: For the Roman, bedding the Celtic queen was a conquest, a brutal, physical triumph in which he forced his unhappy bride to receive him in a succession of submissive postures. She never lay with him again.

The echo-loud apartments with their broad, seaward windows, fearless of attack, also remind the queen of her daughter, who was born and grew up here. On the wintry morning of her labor, Ygrane had the winter shutters removed against the orders of the Roman physicians and shivered in the maritime wind with faerïe and ocean sprites at her side as she struggled to birth Morgeu. Three days later, she left the infant with the Roman wet nurses and fled Tintagel, never to return in Gorlois's lifetime.

Several of the palace guards who had tried to stop her at the duke's orders died that day, slain by her fiana. The alliance nearly fell apart then. But Tall Silver, the supreme druid, assuaged Gorlois with more of what the duke really wanted. He committed Cymru's very best warriors to the Saxon Coast to clear the islets there of all raiders and marauders. Ygrane, bearing responsibility for this blood-payment of her freedom, went along on those missions. To the loud consternation of the druids and Raglaw both, she served with the army's surgeons and witnessed firsthand the gory dismay of war.

She remembers returning north one night in a skiff crowded with moaning wounded, her garments stiff with drying blood, her heart clogged with suffering, and seeing Tintagel, its lean spires and tall battlements shining lavender in the moonstruck darkness. The cries of the dying softened to behold it—this vision of civilization for which they paid their blood.

Now Gorlois has himself paid for this vision that came to earth with the Fire Lords—and Ygrane worries that Morgeu may be right—that she, through her wizard Myrddin, is responsible for the duke's death. By championing Uther, she has merely displaced Gorlois. And though she knows that she is here in Tintagel with Uther to serve the good of Romans and Celts alike, she fears for their future, for when Gorlois died, his blood splattered them—and what begins in blood must end in blood.

Tintagel bustles with stevedores delivering wagonloads of goods and servants industriously setting up the household. Merlinus retreats from the hubbub to an empty, circular garden behind the shrine to scan with his long sight the terrain of time that lies ahead—and below.

Among the tattered trees and rubbish of dead leaves, Merlinus finds a secluded corner where he pulls his hood up against the spry wind and sits down. Immediately, he sinks into the Otherworld. He stands at the notch in the rimrock under sapphire lusters of stars big as crocuses—the very spot outside Wray Vitki's cave, where Ambrosius spoke his dark confession of fear. Below, in the grotto near the Christian afterworld with its fire-plumes and terraced sun-steps to heaven, a broad rainbow gleams.

Merlinus recognizes this radiant diapason of colors from his demon travels: Bïfrost, the rainbow bridge of the Æsir that links the rootlands with the gods' Home in the Great Tree. The giant rainbow's wet hues shoulder a glittering forest of silver firs—and in that forest stand two figures, where the foot of the rainbow glows through the lace of branches like stained glass.

One figure is huge, and Merlinus knows him at once for his raven-slouch, his windblown beard, and the black grot of his missing eye. The Furor, wearing the slick red pelage of a bear for a mantle and the arctic fur of timber wolves for trousers, bends forward in intimate conversation with a slender shape, someone wrapped in a black conjurer's robe stenciled with protective sigils.

Merlinus thinks the figure may be an elf. The gold thread designs across the robe have an elfin intricacy. But when he draws closer, he discerns the troubled red hair and pugnacious, moon white face of Morgeu.

"They have lied to you from the beginning," the Furor states in his reverberant voice, staring fixedly at the mortal woman before him. "You are not noble. You are a mongrel—a child of the vanquished Fauni and the dying Celts. You are the humble dust of the earth itself."

Morgeu returns his stare, her disheveled visage reflecting her madness in the black mirror of his huge pupil. "All blood is mixed," she states, standing defiantly tall before the furious one-eyed gaze of the north god. Ethiops's eelish coils roll like hills against the rainbow sky, and he hangs his giant face through the branches with a human countenance—the fang-grimacing scowl of Morrígan.

The blatant deception stuns Merlinus, nearly rocking him loose from his trance. With panicky effort, he steadies himself, trying to quiet the muffled explosions of his heart so he can better hear what Morgeu tells the god.

"All blood is mixed—and that is natural for the pigments of the earth, as well you know, you whose dominion ranges from the reindeer riders of the tundra to the river people of the Saxon forests. That is of no consequence. What matters, powerful All-Father, is the will of the gods. I call on you to accept the goddess Morrígan as your consort—and with her at your side, to receive the Celtic nation among the tribes of the Abiding North."

The Furor and Ethiops behind his mask of Morrígan share a hideous satisfaction. "Morrígan and I are old consorts. But I knew her in the time before your people sullied themselves with the blood and magic of the Radiant South. You are a mongrel, Morgeu—and that is why my people call you the Doomed. Even with your goddess's help, you stand before me by luck alone. My dwarfs are sworn to destroy my enemies."

"I am not the Furor's enemy—unless you force my hand, as you did my mother's. Then, you shall see why your people fear me."

"Bold words!" The Furor scowls closer, and Morgeu sidles toward Ethiops for the protection of her goddess. "Your mother deceived me under the sanction of Ancestor Night. But you stand helpless before me, Morgeu the Fey."

Inflamed by Ethiops's influence, Morgeu lifts her chin bravely. "I am not so helpless, All-Father. Morrígan favors me." She proudly twirls the hem of her conjurer's robe, the gold-threaded glyphs on the black fabric glimmering like will-o'-the-wisps in the starlight. "*I* made this robe that protects me from the attacks of your dwarfs. By my own magic, I called up the knowledge I needed and by my own exhausting effort, I shaped that knowledge to this object. Without it, would I be here now?"

"Without it, the dwarfs would have trussed and gutted you by now." The Furor strokes his savage beard appreciatively. "You say you will help me against your own people. Why?"

"I am a seer—as is my mother, who trained me." Morgeu raises her arms in supplication. "I have seen your victories in the trance-light. The Furor is destined to rule these islands and there is no power may stop it. I come to you here to be accepted as your warrior."

"Morgeu—" the Furor speaks darkly, "I have but one eye, but I see deeply. You are no ally to the Æsir. You are lying to me—and your pretty robe may stop the attacks of dwarfs, but it will not deflect my wrath."

Morgeu does not even blink and no tremor sounds in her audacious voice. "Do I lie when I say you are the destined ruler of these islands? No. You have one eye, true, but it is a strong eye and you know what I foretell is so. You also know that I did not say I was to be your ally—just your warrior. Give me the power to fight our common enemy—Lailoken the demon-wizard, who counsels my mother. He slew my father. I want his life for that death. He is your enemy as well as mine. Give me the power I need to kill him."

The Furor looms over her in silence, reaching into her with

his malevolent wisdom. Finally, a cold light glistens in his large, staring eye, and he says with a voice out of an abysmal gorge, "Then, you are mine, Morgeu the Fey. And you shall have your power."

Merlinus jumps awake, the Furor's voice still shaking the blood in his teeth. He glances around to remind himself that he is indeed awake. But the collapsed garden, with the trees like chattering skeletons in the chill wind, does not reassure him. He shivers, and the glum gray sky reaches deep into his soul, with its relentless promise of a more dire cold to come.

Magic Passes—Like Blue *in the* Hour of One Star

In the moonlight, the birthmark between her husband's shoulder blades has a knife-tooth outline. By sunlight, the ruddy flesh tones reveal shadow wings, like a pink splash of sunburn that in turn fans from a darker stain, with the wedge shape of a viper's taut face. When Uther is asleep beside her, Ygrane lays a magnetic hand atop it and feels inward, downward to where the dragon-magus stews in the crater-reek of the planet.

From what part of Adam's body comest thou? Wray Vitki asks in antiquated Latin.

"Whittled of Adam's rib, the woman who may carry your seed to the future," Ygrane speaks softly to Uther's back. "We need your help to fight our enemies."

The ancient wont of flesh breaks my will. I die.

Her hand comes away with a faint, weary scent of swamp smoke. The magus, indeed, bleeds into the Dragon. His centuries of proud freedom roaming the rootlands of the Great Tree, adventuring with trolls, giants, and gods is over. Down deep, in the core of himself that has already become the Dragon, he feels satisfied about this. Only frivolously, with the pride of clan blood, does he desire to climb once more to the cold surface. Under the blue-blind stare of the void and in the icy blast of darkness that dissolves the stars themselves, he would spend the last of his magician's strength for the cause of Uther Pendragon. But the thought itself blows downward in him, a wave's impact, shoving him away from her.

Ygrane sits up in bed. Unless Wray Vitki receives vast portions of energy soon, he will fade into fumes on a reedy shoreline by thaw. Her heart feels leaden, because there is nothing she can do for him.

Like the kiss of a liar, that thought fills her with a jeering shame. In fact, she *has* the power to strengthen the magus. But all the unicorn's magic and all her own personal glamour she invests in a love charm.

"Troubled?" Uther croaks from the limb of sleep.

Ygrane turns a smile toward him, intending to speak slumber to his bleary face. A look of caring that filters through the numb edges of his drowsy expression emboldens her, and she answers truthfully, "I *am* troubled, Theo."

He rolls closer. "Tell me."

"Since we've married, I've been hoarding magic."

Uther's sleepy frown saddens to puzzlement.

"You wouldn't know," she soothes him, running a cool hand across his brow. "Our love is true, and I've not touched you with the glamour, my own dearest self. You don't miss it. But our soldiers will miss the healing rinses I could have made. And your army will miss Wray Vitki—because I've used up the strength that could have revived him."

Uther shudders fully awake at the name of the dragon-magus. "Wray Vitki?"

"Theo, I have been selfish."

She slips out of bed and opens a tortoise plate chest where she keeps her talismans. Something glows like a lit jewel, and he glimpses her elongate legs shadowed in sheer fabric. "It's a love charm," she announces, showing him the dazzle stone.

A rough-cut nodule of frosty mineral catches the sparse light of the dark chamber and emits fine rays, a sheen of silver needles. At its touch, he feels nothing in the mica crust but the rasp of raw stone.

"I've made it for Morgeu." She kneels beside him in the bed. "You won't feel anything in it—but she will. Alas, it's exhausted me. I won't have the strength to make rinses well into the winter. And I can't help Wray Vitki, either. We are going to lose him."

Uther places the charm back in his wife's hand and clasps his hand over hers consolingly. "You've a mother's love for Morgeu. I admire that. But will it work?"

"If I can get it to her. She dwells in a ghoulish community in Caledonia with her Y Mamau."

"Among the savage Picts?"

"They call her the Doomed One. But it is the demon in her that makes her wicked. Morgeu is not evil. Arrogant, yes, even belligerent like her father, but not cruel. That is the demon's influence."

"The demon that tried to possess you."

"Ethiops. I have never felt such pure evil."

"And this rock is going to stop such a demon?"

"If it touches my daughter, my hope is that she may be purged of that gruesome thing. I have put all my magic into this—this mother's selfishness."

Uther brings his face up close and whispers, "I am proud of you."

She brushes the hair from his face to better gauge his sincerity in the dark. "You are not disappointed, my king? I might have used this magic for our island, for our people."

"What you have done, my wife, is very Christian. You forsake the herd for the one lost sheep. You love the one who hates you." He smiles reassuringly at her. "She is your daughter. She is yours to care for. How will you get the charm to her?"

"Falon."

"To Caledonia?" Uther frowns at this. "He is the key strategist among the fiana. How can we spare him?"

"He knows Morgeu best of my circle. And I know him. He alone of my fiana has the mettle for this quest."

Uther slumps backward onto the bed's cushions. He does not want to lose Falon. His wife's magic, whose power he has no way to gauge, does not figure in his military calculations. But the chief commander of the fiana—he is a crucial warrior, and the king loathes losing him.

"Perhaps Merlinus—"

"No," Ygrane says, and lowers her head, burdened by her shameful selfishness. "Ethiops wants that. We must protect Myrddin from the demons he has betrayed to serve us. And with my magic diminished, we will require his power all the more."

"I will miss Falon." A hollowness widens in Uther. Since riding Wray Vitki up from the underworld, a haunted feeling has saturated him. For long spells, his love for Ygrane mutes the feeling, and he lives contentedly, even enthusiastically. At hours such as this, however, the Piper's green music and the feverish loveliness of the phantom woods stir an immutable longing in him. When he catches himself suspended in the beauty of this internal sunset, he forces himself to focus on his surroundings. Invariably, an emptiness opens between the actual world and his longing.

He feels faithless to his wife. She does not want him to accept her god's offer. Behaving more as a Christian than a Celt, she has told him time and again she wants to trust in God to deliver them a worthy soul. Yet, he remembers the supreme druid's warning: *If you do not drink from the Raven Spring, Ygrane will mother yet another Morgeu.*

He wonders if that is so bad. Morgeu can be loved and saved, as Ygrane shows with her charm. Why, then, not love whatever child God delivers to them? Is it not a sin to believe they can engender a savior, an office only God can appoint?

The truth snarls in him. He is not afraid of offending God. He holds back from accepting the elk-king's offer, because he *desires* it. The Church has taught him to fear desire, and, apart from the untamed years of his adolescence, he has obeyed that fear. Never before, however, has he experienced such a flood of his heart's desire as he feels for the glamorous woods of dancing souls.

Ygrane, numb with weariness and worry, does not feel her husband's conflict. She accepts his acquiescence as more of the spacious love they share, and she kisses him with gratitude.

Ygrane and Uther, both eager to finish the move, set up their house quickly. The war room, bedchambers, and officers' quarters are established in a morning. The fiana commanders and the Roman field officers of the Saxon Coast have all worked and fought together before, under the late duke, and by noon they agree upon the military protocol between them and their field responsibilities for the winter.

More gradually, yet inevitably in the flurrying days when the officers' compound and barracks are established, the king behaves as he imagines his brother would. He meets daily with fiana and Romans alike, including them together in several joint banquets and hunting forays, until they feel at ease in his company.

Merlinus is proud of Uther's willingness to serve the living after having beheld the greater joy of the dead. The wizard suspects that the queen's glamour inspires him but says nothing. He does not want to disturb the hope of a lasting alliance with his personal troubles, and he keeps to himself the unhappiness he feels at the absence of the unicorn.

Often Merlinus glimpses Uther and Ygrane holding hands, sharing meaningful looks, even cooing to each other. Their obvious happiness together, displayed before druids and Britons alike, has done more for the morale of the alliance than any speech or war plan. And the wizard begins to worry that his sadness might affect their shared moments of joy and, in a cascade of linked accidents, doom the whole enterprise.

So, Merlinus imitates the unicorn and simply departs Tintagel. He decides to find the table he has seen in his visions with Raglaw and the Nine Queens. Yet, no chant he can devise proves useful in guiding him. He wanders the region in search of the destined tree, the fallen oak of his strong eye visions, and more days fly by like windy heaven in the treetops.

Some small adventures befall the wizard on those gusty moors, and he uses his skills to help lost pilgrims and to cure what ailments he can among the impoverished hamlets that host him. Mostly, he travels alone, accompanied by the wind's cattle, the bulky clouds of autumn piling toward a gray winter.

When the wizard finds the living tree of his visions in an aboriginal forest north of Tintagel, in a region called Hartland, he recognizes it at once. A huge, lightning-mammocked oak has fallen across a stream, undercut by the sliding water. Its roots wall off the sky, tall as two men. Merlinus parts the brown shag of dead vines that has thrived on the upturned loam and listens to the slow bass voice of circulating sap. The behemoth is alive. The horizontal tree has spent the summer surviving on the rill water that has toppled it, waiting for Merlinus. Clearly, for the wizard, this is the vital symbol of the age—the toppled oak of Rome alive only because the rich loam of the island will not let it die.

But the wide girth of the tree defeats all of Merlinus's attempts to section it. No matter how gently he whispers his barbarous spells, the power comes through him too quickly, too strongly. The smaller logs he uses to test his skill break jaggedly. No magic he possesses can cut wood with the smooth precision he must have to fulfill his vision. The wizard needs a carpenter.

Among the master boat builders in the sea towns, Merlinus locates the best craftsman, a lanky monkey of a man, bald, ginger-whiskered, with small, round eyes like blue opals. Surfeited with work building battleships for a local warlord, he wants nothing to do with Merlinus, or the high king and his Celtic queen.

The wizard could have spoken a word to the carpenter and beckoned him along, but the thought of implicating others in his devisings feels wrong to Merlinus. He wants nothing less from this master builder than the emblem of the kingdom itself. He balks at using unwilling laborers for that holy task.

Why not? the demonic portion of him asks. This carpenter is the best in the region, and the strong eye vision demands the table. Merlinus speaks a word that makes the whole shipyard fall silent. Mallets hold back, saws relent, adzes pause, and there in the broad skeleton of an unfinished boat, twenty workmen wait like statuary.

Before Merlinus can organize a chant that will get the workers to gather their tools and follow him, the master builder drops the mallet he holds and smacks the toe of his sandaled foot.

The pain winces him free of the wizard's spell, and he dances about and stops almost at once. A single glance at the silent yard, and he knows what has happened. When he faces Merlinus again, his freckled, snub-nosed features shift rapidly, from amazement to fear and back again, like a man who has suddenly found himself shooting across the sea standing on winged fish.

"No more magic," the carpenter begs, holding up both palms. "Free my men, master wizard, and we will do as you say. To the forest, to cut a table from a fallen oak? Fine, my lord. Consider it done."

Merlinus frees the men and thanks the carpenter for his cooperation in so sacred a task. "Double wages for everyone!" the royal wizard promises.

The master builder shakes his bald head. "No money, wizard. We've enough coin from the warlords who buy our ships." His small eyes get smaller. "I want a wish."

"A wish?"

"Yes." His monkey face gaups happily. "As in the hearthside stories. You are a powerful wizard. I don't want your money. I want the help of your magic."

Merlinus frowns sternly, holding back his impulse to speak magic and force their labor. "What is your wish, master builder?"

"Not now, master wizard, not now." The carpenter happily displays his crooked teeth. "First, we cut and dress the table. If you are satisfied, then you will give me leave to come to you when I need, to seek your help. Will you agree?"

"If it's the stars and the moon you want, man, forget it. You'd best take the gold. Triple wages."

The carpenter thrusts his gingery beard at Merlinus in a grin of joyful defiance. "Keep your gold. I want your help when I need it, and it won't be for the likes of the moon and the stars, that I assure you, master wizard. That I assure you."

"One wish within my power, then—but no act against the king or queen or any who sit at this table. Is that understood?"

The master builder's broad smile fits his sharp face snugly. "Show me the tree."

Merlinus makes the crew work hard for the master builder's one wish. Two wagonloads of tools must be carted by hand because the wagons cannot penetrate the primeval forest. Then the rains begin. Tents flap gustily as measurements are taken, plans discussed. At the first break in the downfall, the men clear the forest around the fallen behemoth and erect a workshop over the trunk. The table is cut; then, with the bark peeled and the wood handsomely shaped and prepared to the wizard's instructions, the enormous disk is lacquered with an occult mix of resins, saps, distillates, and pigments that dry to a dark, smoky veneer.

Around the rim, attached with removable pins, a felly-band of iron encloses the table and makes of it a wheel. Merlinus guides it with magic commands, rolling it out of the forest along trails the workers cut. On the muddy market roads south to Tintagel, nothing short of a gale can stop the juggernaut. Farmers come running from their harvests and herdsmen turn away from their flocks to watch the giant wheel pass.

The task makes Merlinus feel better, redeemed somehow. He returns almost triumphantly. At the seacliff citadel of Tintagel, Ygrane and Uther touch the giant iron band and gaze at their amazed faces in the mirror-polished surface of the wood hub. "What is it, Merlinus?"

"A legend," the wizard decrees proudly. "It shall be known through history as the Wheel-Table."

"Is that where you've been all these many days?" Ygrane asks. She mingles her worried look with the king's, who complains, "You left without so much as a farewell, Merlinus."

"For the good of the kingdom," he defends himself. "My rude absence buys this headless table!"

Uther has accrued doubts about his wizard's well-being since his separation from the unicorn. Merlinus sulked for days when his counsel was most needed. And now that all the important decisions have been taken, he returns frantic with happiness about a ludicrous rolling table.

"And, best of all, I've had this made to be portable—designed for a kingdom with no fixed capital."

"There is Camelot," Uther interjects.

"Oh, yes, when it is finally built, the Wheel-Table may rest there permanently," Merlinus allows. "But that will be years from now—crucial years in which you will anneal your kingdom. So think on this: With the Wheel-Table, your war room, your banquet, your place of counsel goes with you, even as you tour the *coloniae*."

The two flick concerned looks between them, but Ygrane attempts to hide her skepticism by congratulating him. "Ingenious," she says, meeting her husband's dubious expression with an elated smile. "And it is beautiful."

"Yes," the king concedes, running his fingers over the burled surface with its depths of smoke. "The craftsmanship is extraordinary. How much has it cost our treasury?"

Merlinus wonders that himself. The master builder parted ways with him after the table rolled out of the forest. "No cost at all, my lord," the wizard tells the king, which remains, for the time being at least, the truth. "It was built by free hands that would not take coin for their labor. Consider it a gift to you, from your people."

That wins Uther's acceptance, and forthwith he and Ygrane scout about for the proper place to set it in the citadel. They settle on the western terrace and a portico above the seacliffs. With the iron felly-band removed and the giant wheel laid on its side atop four marble pieces, the round table has an authoritative presence, a look of weight and timelessness.

That very first night that it stands as a table, with the fiana commanders, the king's field officers, the druids, the bishop of Britain, and Merlinus seated in attendance, Ygrane announces she is pregnant. Cheers greet the hope of their future. Merlinus bows his head and weeps silently, remembering his time in Optima's womb, that buoyant time of unalloyed bliss, and his promise to fulfill the destiny he has inherited. Like a deep chord of music, his mother's presence—*the* mother's presence—sounds in him, answering his secret prayer. All is well. For now. The people of this circle have won with small things in a dark world, where giant, terrible powers clash. They have triumphed with prayers and a hope carried by an unborn child.

Afterward, when the revelers have departed and the stars flimmer over a moonless sea, Merlinus sits alone with Ygrane and Uther. "Who is this soul you carry?" the wizard asks.

"Whomever God sends us," Ygrane answers.

"Good." Merlinus reaches out and takes Uther's hand, recalling the joyful splendor he once witnessed in the Otherworld. The wizard is still angry at the elk-king for showing Uther that hint of heaven. Few mortals exposed to such ecstatic abandon can be satisfied to stay long in this paltry world. "You have decided to reject the arrangement offered you by King Someone Knows the Truth?"

"We have decided to trust a higher authority," the king confirms. "We insist only that the soul God sends us to lead our united people shall be Christian—and so, the elk-king will have no part of our marriage."

Merlinus puts his other hand out for Ygrane, and she reaches over and takes it. "Myrddin, I must tell you that I have been studying my husband's faith, discovering the ways in my heart to mate our religions. They are not so far distant, I find."

"If anyone can find a natural union that binds these gods of desert and forest, of south and north, it will be you, my lady." The wizard sends the royal couple to their bed with more assurances than perhaps they deserve. *What choices do they have, really?* The devilish side of him knows full well that their decisions—to serve their peoples as fate has decreed, to marry as duty demands, to love as their hearts require—these things are regulated by a far greater pride than their own. Standing alone before the large round table, before the black sea and the star-whorled night, Merlinus is tempted to open his strong eye. The future lies dormant in this table, like ore in the silences of rock. Treaties will be made here, and wars. Disputes will be settled, pledges sworn. Kings and their warriors will gather at this table to shape kingdoms.

Here, on this night when the conception of the foretold savior is announced, a beginning has been made. To where will it lead? Across what battlefields? And at the end of its turning, will all those battlefields have become farms? Or is earth foredoomed the perpetual battlefield between demons and angels?

Such thoughts stymie the wizard's desire to see the future of this table. The future is an illusion; the past a dream. Only the present is real. And Merlinus is tired. Not for sleep. He is tired of the striving, of the dark magic necessary to ignite this bright destiny. He wants to feel again the joy of the unicorn, the blessing of Optima, the wholeness of heaven that, deep within each heart, breathes soft as the stars.

Falon gratefully accepts the quest to find Morgeu and deliver the witch-queen's love charm. He is restless to do something for the alliance other than pace the misty halls of Tintagel talking battle strategies. "Will the charm heal her at once, older sister?"

"The moment it touches her," the queen says, reaching up to hand him the charm while he sits his mount.

He holds it to the windy light of the moors, and its sugary glass gleams like metal. "And this demon—Ethiops—what will become of him?"

"The charm will repel him clear. The true danger comes from the Y Mamau. My talismans will ward their spells but not their arrows and blades." She holds the stare of her guardian and friend. "Be wary, Falon. I want you again at my side—with or without my daughter. Understand me, younger brother."

"I understand, my sister." He bows and covers her in his red-gold locks, touching his lips to her brow. Then he is away.

Ygrane stands apart from her escort of fiana, her robes tangling with wind as she watches Falon ride into the gray distances of gorse. The moon, like a watery ghost, floats in the day sky among spider threads of ice clouds. All that lightness does not diminish her dread that she will never see him again.

The first political meeting around the Wheel-Table takes place a fortnight later, with the arrival of the six most powerful warlords on the island. Three are Roman, three Celtic. To the cheers of the Christian populace, the Romans arrive with all the panoply of the Empire—eagle standards, glittering phalanxes of bronze-armored militia, and a boisterous parade of trumpets and drums bleating as proudly as if Rome had never fallen. The sternly disciplined men, vigilant from a lifetime of battles, look fearsome. Their beardless faces, with eyes hard as their jaws, have witnessed every atrocity of war, and many display scars from their triumphs in savage hand-to-hand combat.

The leaders wear ancient breastplates made of plaques of gold and silver and engraved with the heads of emperors of yore, some centuries old. Uther and Merlinus know these men from last winter's furious march across the countryside with Ambrosius: Bors Bona from Lindum, famous for sparing no one, not even infants, in the barbarian villages he destroys; Severus Syrax, the *magister militum* of Londinium; and, the local authority, the duke of the Saxon Coast, Marcus Dumnoni.

The brutal faces of these warlords, as boot-jawed and sullen-eyed as their troops, bear pitiless, remote expressions hardened by generations of hostility. With military rigor, they array their men in parade formation across the slate-paved courtyard of Tintagel and salute Uther. The king graciously greets them on foot, wearing the purple, wide-sleeved dalmatic of an *imperator*, chief general of the Republic, the mighty sword Lightning clenched naked in his hand. Bishop Riochatus stands behind him, blessing the alliance. It appears a magnificent show to the populace, but Merlinus reads no devotion for the king in the warlords' countenances, only a begrudging, grim loyalty.

The Celtic chiefs, for their part, arrive silently, with neither escorts nor fanfare, and are virtually ignored by the public. They are tall men, all three with large, traditional mustaches and broad, bare shoulders so admired by their culture. Lot of the North Isles, brindle-maned with a silver mustache, comes in buckskin trousers and shirtless, his thick chest crisscrossed by the straps of his shield and sword, which he carries on his back. He is an old-fashioned Celt, and many of Ygrane's fiana hail from his coastal islands.

Quite his opposite, red-haired Kyner of the Hills has brought his horse with him and wears an eclectic array of armor—Roman shoulderplates of hammered brass, Gaelic kilt, Iberian leather thong boots, and a curved Bulgar saber, the renowned Short-Life. As a Christian, he displays a large scarlet cross on his oval shield.

Last is Urien of the Coast, his white-blond hair falling to the fur belt of his wolfskin trousers. He bears no arms at all. Under his ruddy brown cloak, his bare chest and muscular back are unprotected. All that he wears above the waist is a gold torque, symbol of his thrall to the divine Mother.

Merlinus accompanies Ygrane to meet her three warlords at the cove harbor, where the barge from Maridunum delivers them, and they bluster about her like brothers reunited with a younger sister. Laughter and full-throated songs resound off the seacliffs as they reminisce and entertain each other on the coast road that leads to the bastion. Kyner lifts the queen to the saddle of his sturdy warhorse and leads the beast by the bit, recalling when, in the forested hills of his kingdom, he first met Ygrane, a spindly, lanky-haired seven-year-old sniffling sadly for having been taken by the druids to his court—a timber fortress, more like a lumber-walled corral compared to the stone parapets and spires of Tintagel, yet she quailed before the splendor of its bear hide curtains and staghead trophies. Everyone laughs, the queen as well, though with a sadder shade to her voice.

Merlinus keeps to the background, next to the grooms and attendants, yet each of the warlords, Celtic and Roman alike, makes a point of acknowledging him. Only then, on that blue, wind-broomed November day, does the demon visitor begin to understand how formidable a reputation his character has acquired. All know he is the royal wizard, famous for promoting the Aurelianus brothers to nobility and for fending off Morgeu's demons at the royal wedding.

The bishop, who still enjoys the benefit of the wizard's spell and has no recollection of demons at the royal wedding, believes Merlinus's influence wholly political and pays him only cursory heed. Merlinus is grateful for that, because they are seated together on the settle at the back wall of the counsel room, facing the Wheel-Table and the open porch above the gorge cliffs and the smashing sea. To the other side of Merlinus, the supreme druid Dun Mane sits. Together, the three attend as proud witnesses to the first war council of the alliance.

Ten high-back chairs, ornately carved with dragons and unicorns, encircle the table, their dark wood hulks reflecting in the polished surface like rocks in a pond. Four chairs display the queen's beast, four the king's, and two have both. The sword Lightning lies naked on the table, its point directed at an empty chair carved with the dragon and the unicorn standing back to back, claws and hooves rampant—the place of the enemy—the Seat Perilous. The Sacred Seat facing the hilt, where the two creatures meet in merging contours, belongs to God the Protector.

Uther sits to the right of the Seat Perilous, close to the foe, and Ygrane sits opposite, by the silver-gold hilt. Severus Syrax, looking urbane in his green silk robe and oriental topknot, opens the proceedings by protesting this arrangement. "Why does a woman—even a queen—sit here at a table of warlords? Unless she intends to follow us into battle, she should excuse herself."

"At his request, I am here," the queen replies, and motions toward the empty chair beside her. Looking across the edge of his staff, Merlinus barely discerns one of the pale people sitting in the Sacred Seat. Squinting, the wizard recognizes Prince Bright Night's dimpled profile. Merlinus nudges Dun Mane and invites him to peek along the length of his staff. The druid's horsey face shivers at the sight of the elf prince.

"Be assured," the queen says, "I have no intention to sit at council and plan war. But the Daoine Síd require me to attend—to make their contributions known."

The Romans snort and pass clenched, disbelieving looks among themselves. "Are we to believe," Severus asks, sable eyes narrowing, "that you represent the counsel of elves? That you are assigning the Sacred Seat to your heathen religion? That place belongs to God, not elves."

"The elf-folk serve God." The queen meets the mocking incredulity of the Romans with a haughty indifference. "And I serve them."

Uther puts his hands on the table and glances left and right. "This is an *alliance* with the Celts. We must make allowance for their ways."

"And our ways?" Severus inquires, a muscle twisting on the right side of his jaw that makes the thin black flames of his beard twitch. "Have we Christians become such lackeys of these hill people that we must honor their pagan gods? Did we learn nothing from Vortigern about alliances with pagans?"

"You were Vortigern's staunch ally!" Merlinus protests, and Urien and Lot rise from their chairs, fists clenched. The queen reaches out and touches each of them, whispering them back into their seats.

"I opened the gates of Londinium for your brother," Severus appeals to the king. "Tell them, Uther. I have as much right at this table as any—and I say we restrict our company to men of flesh and blood."

"An alliance requires respect," Uther says firmly, leaning forward to engage the ire in his lieutenant's swarthy face. A permanent crease between Severus's arched eyebrows makes him seem to scowl even when placid. "As Christians, we will treat them with the respect we expect in return."

Severus flexes to reply, but Kyner's dark voice booms in gruff Latin, "I am Christian. I have read the Holy Book. 'There were giants in the earth in those days.' Dragons. Unicorns. 'Have you searched the breadth of the earth and walked the depth?'"

Before scornful Severus can respond, the bishop stamps his crozier sharply on the flagstone and stands with a flap of his scarlet robes. "'Where does the light dwell? And as for darkness, where is the place thereof?' So God asks Job in the Holy Book. From the very next passage in the scripture you quote, Lord Kyner." He nods to the Chief of the Hills, then levels a cold stare at the Romans. "You at this round table are the light. Darkness encroaches with the northern hordes. Our people are being murdered and the word of Jesus destroyed by these barbarians. The Celtic bards that the Northmen slaughter are thrown into common graves with martyred Christians. We must not fight ourselves. We are the hope of Britain."

Severus sits back smugly. *The hope of Britain—elves!* All hear him scoff by the fatalistic way he crosses his arms and wags his topknot. "Then, let us begin with the counsel of elves."

Riochatus sits, and the queen speaks, "What lies ahead is what we make for ourselves with the sword. That is the same truth for the Northmen. Their first prince is murder. They believe it better to kill and steal than to build. Murder holds the hilt of their sacred sword. The name of their god is Furor." She passes a tight, knowing look to the Romans and to Kyner. "Who better to hold our sword against them than the Daoine Síd, who are the spirit of these woods we are fighting to defend?"

"Why not Jesus?" Kyner asks. "He is our savior."

"Jesus is the Prince of Peace," Ygrane says. "We cannot pit him against the prince of murder."

Riochatus, Uther, Severus, and Dun Mane begin talking at once, and Kyner's large voice encompasses them, "'I came not to send peace but a sword.'"

This time, Dun Mane bangs his druid's wand for silence, bowing his large head so far under his white hood that only a shadow seems to speak. "The Celts recognize *Yesu*—All Heal—and we accept him as savior. Let there be no further dispute. The Sacred Seat belongs to *Yesu*."

The Christians nod with murmurous appeasement, and Uther leads the discussion into strategies for a spring offensive. Merlinus holds himself apart from these debates. He already knows what perfections of war lie ahead in the darkness. His attention goes to the sword. It shines with an astral fire—with the table's reflection of seashine and sky depths. It holds the light of the original world, before the shells of darkness enclosed it in matter. The eight people and their watery reflections who surround the blade are part of a sadder prophecy.

Merlinus ignores the people and peers into the swordgleam. Wonder shoots through him. Across aeonian time, God saturates all creation. Her light shines through the shadows of reality. Ygrane is correct. What lies ahead for these shadow-people, mortals and elf-folk alike, will be made by the sword—this sword, Lightning, the enemy's own weapon, redeemed to save the people it has been created to destroy. Very like the wizard himself.

Looking deeper into its metallic depths, Merlinus realizes then that it is the sword he must serve, not the shadows around the sword. The churlish warlords, the bishop's proud robes, the druids' cowled darkness—and the queen and the king, as well—even the wispy light of Prince Bright Night in the Sacred Seat, are but ghosts. Merlinus himself is a ghost. Only the sword, only the symbol, is living.

The meeting of the warlords lasts seventeen days, during which Merlinus spends his time either sitting on the brink of the sea-cliff or picking his way along the guano-bleached footpaths, through clouds of shrieking gulls. He tries not to think about what the people on the porched terrace are planning. He feels sick with foreboding. The atmosphere is filled only with the omens of bloodlust and war.

Again and again, he calls for the unicorn. He wants to feel again the wholeness and promise of its presence. Just to know that it is still there. A way out of a bad dream. But when it does not come, he finally accepts that he must remain alone. The king and queen have each other, and their unborn child. The warlords have their war.

To assuage his dread, he sits beside the muttering sea and talks to himself about the Sacred Seat and Bright Night and the very first time the elf prince came to him—

"I took nothing with me when I left my mother's simple house. The body Optima had made for me and the dun-colored hempen cassock and reed sandals were enough. I trudged across the meadow, downslope, toward the mortal kingdoms, where lay my destiny.

"As I hobbled along, my joints and muscles aching from the great effort of the previous night, the Wild Things watched me. Fox and rabbits peered from the tall grass. Geese honked overhead on the flyway to the marshes. The day blazed gloriously—great toppling clouds, golden sunlight shining among the grassheads, coveys of birds chittering and spinning in the perfumed air—and I, saddened that my mother could never again be here to enjoy this.

"I paused to catch my breath and to pray for her. *Great Mother, Optima was Yours to take away—and now there is no freedom such as hers. Remember, she suffered to serve You. If there is a way to heaven, take her there now and keep her where we are all at one point with You.*

"When I looked up, I saw a tall, youthful man leaning against a granite outcrop with a gnarled wooden staff propped across his slender body. His bright hair stirred in the breeze like a crimson sea plant, and his long, tapered eyes shone green as the unicorn's. He was not mortal, I knew at once, though he wore the opulent garments of a mortal nobleman: a blue linen tunic embroidered with flowerets of gold, a silver-studded, red leather belt, and yellow boots.

"The stranger offered me the wooden staff. 'Perhaps this will help you on your way, grandfather,' he said in a voice as beautiful and dark as the gleaming spaces of evening. My rheumy eyes could not see him with great clarity, yet I knew then who he was.

"'You are Síd,' I surmised, though, of course, the sun was radiant and the Síd have bodies too pale to be seen by daylight.

"A cunning smile hooked the corners of his thin lips. 'You are right,' he said. 'I am Prince Bright Night of the Daoine Síd.

King Someone Knows the Truth has sent me to welcome you to the land of our demesne—and to offer you this gift.'

"'You know who I am?' I queried, still incredulous that the Síd would come to me in broad daylight.

"'Indeed.' His dimples sharpened with the cleverness of his smile. 'You are the demon Lailoken, tamed to mortal guise one year and one day by the Great Mother and Her holy servant Saint Optima. All the Síd know of you and your famous plight.'

"'Prince Bright Night.' I bowed my head deferentially, well aware of the vanity of the elf-folk. 'How is it that you are able to stand before me under the full weight of the morning sun?'

"'Well might you ask, Grandfather Lailoken, well might you ask.' He pushed off from the granite outcrop and brandished the gnarly staff. 'Do you know what I have here? It is the Stave of the Storm Tree. Its shadow is wide as a man and invisible—and in its shadow, the invisible is visible. Take it! It is a gift to you from the Daoine Síd.'

"A few years earlier, rousing the Goths to sack Rome, I had occasion to work with the Nordic elf-folk and their gods, the Æsir. I had toured their spirit realm, and they had shown me the Storm Tree, the Terrible One, the Mighty Pillar, Yggdrasil, that overspreads their world and binds the domains of their kingdom with the world of mortals and, below that, the chthonic Dragon. The power of that spirit tree concentrated so densely, it rivaled the might of the angels. I remember shivering with awe before its lunatic complexity of roots, which seemed to swarm in a bottomless night, and its delirium of branchwork darkening the shore of a starry void into which it grasped across millennia. As a demon, I delighted in that shambling might. But now, as a man—I hesitated.

"'Prince—I am honored,' I said, and took one step back. 'But how did the Síd come by a sacred rood belonging to the mighty Æsir, the gods of the north?'

"'Stolen, of course,' Prince Bright Night answered with pride. 'By the might and cunning of our chief, King Someone Knows the Truth.' His long, mischievous eyes narrowed. 'You are not spurning a gift of the Daoine Síd, are you, old man?'

"'Not at all.' I bowed again, as humbly low as my warped spine allowed. 'I only question my worthiness. I am, as you yourself say, tamed to mortal guise. Dare any mortal possess so powerful a gift?'

"'Come, come, Lailoken. You are no ordinary mortal. Saint Optima birthed you here in the demesne of the Síd, and for a year and a day we have watched over your remarkable growth as though you were one of our own. And are you not? You have grown on our soil."

"'My destiny is to work for good among mortals,' I replied with candor.

"'We would expect no less from the son of a saint. And now are we to debate what is good?' The prince's shrewd smile deepened. 'What is good in the land of the Síd is good for the Síd. We are assailed by the Æsir. They ravage our people and steal our land. But now, you are here! Surely, the birth in our kingdom of so powerful a being as you portends great good for us against our enemies.'

"'If it is God's will,' I offered humbly.

"'Bah! God's will embraces all.' Prince Bright Night's smile fell away, and the animal intensity of his green stare chilled me to the pith. 'What is your will, Lailoken? Are you with the Daoine Síd—or against us?'

"I gestured across the crazy quiltwork of forest, glade, and meadow to the thorp far below in the hazy distance. 'I am with the people.'

"A shadow of his crafty smile returned to the elf prince's slender face. 'A warrior band of the Æsir's people are moving through the forest north of that thorp right now. They have come from slaying King Cos, your grandfather. In two days, that thorp and everyone in it will be ash. The peasants who brought offerings to your mother will be charred bones, their flayed flesh the drumskins of our enemy."

"'Is this true?' I asked in a fright.

"'*Is this true?*' The elf prince cocked his head with mocking mime of my incredulity. 'You—a demon! Of all beings, you know this truth better than any. Take the Stave of the Storm Tree and go save your people.'

"I stood stunned. I had not expected to be tested so soon. I had thought there would be time to wander, to accustom myself to my life among mortals. My teeth had barely grown in, and my eyesight had not yet cleared. 'I am just an old man,' I protested. 'What can I do?'

"'With such false modesty, you will never live to be a young man.' Prince Bright Night held out the Stave of the Storm Tree. 'Take it. Do what you can.'

"I took the staff from his pale hand, and he vanished. Then I tilted the knobby pole toward where he had stood, and he reappeared, grinning lavishly. Indeed, as I held the staff high, I saw that it cast no shadow at all. It weighed nothing, and I half expected it to float when I let it go. But it fell, heavy as iron, and when I seized it and leaned upon it, it braced my weight sturdily.

"'How am *I* to save the thorp?' I asked despondently. When the elf prince did not respond, I waved the staff about. He did not appear, and, though I did not know it then, I would not see him again for many years.

"Staff in hand, I continued on my way. At the lower end of the meadow, where the sinister gloom of the thick woods began, I paused and looked back the way I had come. Morning quivered in the bare branches of the upland trees, and I peered longingly at the mountain forest's dark doors where my mother and I had come and gone. Then I turned and, leaning heavily on the Stave of the Storm Tree, I walked on into the misty dell of the lower woods, relying on courage and the arrant sun to guide me through the unraveling dark."

No one at the round table needs Merlinus, and so the wizard drifts off and mingles with the servants in the citadel and the fisherfolk of the coast towns, doing the good deeds his mother's memory requires.

After a fortnight of planning, arguing, sharing meals and battle stories, the warlords have become, if not exactly friends, at least convivial. They have agreed to take the fight to the enemy, and all of them promise a full-out effort in the spring. A war party ten times the size of what Ambrosius commanded will roll the Wheel-Table from Tintagel in the west to Londinium in the east. The united armies of Celts and Britons will then fan out across the country on either side of the table. Using bird messengers, drums, and smoke signals to communicate, they will flush out all invaders and drive them from the midlands.

Then the first winter squall chops the sea and howls like a banshee off the cliffs, stripping the forests of their last leaves. While it howls, the council debates objectives: purge the land by killing the pagan tribes, as Bors Bona wants, or terrorize them with selective acts of savage butchery, as Lot suggests? Severus, risking the wrath of the others, actually offers to negotiate with the pagans. For the Syrax family, their power in Londinium—founded on cheap labor and access to Gaul—depends upon the goodwill of the barbarian settlements. For them, profits come from turning the other cheek, and so Severus opposes driving all the pagans from the island.

No resolution is reached—no objective other than to roll the Wheel-Table to Londinium. Spurred by winter, the warlords hurry back to their own kingdoms, and a week later, a blizzard transforms the rocky landscape into a garden of the moon.

Christmas day, the bells of Tintagel chapel ring out at dawn. The sky looks like washed blood above the white lace of the forest. The king and queen summon Merlinus to the eastern terrace portico, where the round table has been moved, to spend the holy day with them.

Round table. That is what everyone has taken to calling it, though the wizard still refers to it as the Wheel-Table. Sea mist pebbles the tabletop, and servants expertly clean it with swipes of white antelope skin.

The royal couple and the wizard sit at the table beside braziers shaped like goblins that burn rare woods and waft fumes of fragrant warmth. They pray, talk about the baby growing inside Ygrane, and watch the unicorn frisk in and out of the forest in sparkling flurries and sprays of ice crystal. Then, with shouts of alarm from the rampart sentinels, a file of black-hooded wanderers in white robes suddenly emerges from out of the woods near the frolicking animal. The somber figures move in slow procession through the pristine snow to the bastion.

Nine cenobites descend from the hills in an evenly spaced ritual line. When they approach the eastern gate, they pull back their hoods and reveal that they are women with long, colorful tresses, chestnut, platinum, sable, storm gray, and several shades of sunlight. Merlinus's heart thuds loudly. These are the Nine Queens dressed as cenobites! The eldest, the silver falconess Rna, carries a candescent goblet of gold-laced chrome—the Graal.

Merlinus runs to greet them in the palace courtyard, but they ignore him, their eyes humbly lowered. He follows them into the main hall, where they genuflect before the king and the queen.

"We are the Sisters of Arimathea," Rna announces. "Eremites, reclusive worshipers of the Holy Mother. For four hundred years, our order has preserved the secret shrine of

Yoseph of Arimathea, where we pray incessantly for peace and world redemption."

"Welcome, sisters." The king greets the holy sisters with a startled expression and beckons them toward the eastern terrace, where daylight glares off marble.

"Our vows of strict solitude are in suspense only for the time we need to present you with this jorum," Rna replies, and passes the silver-gold chalice to the woman behind, who passes it on.

"Jorum?" Ygrane looks to Myrddin for a translation.

"Joram in the Bible 'brought with him vessels of silver,'" Merlinus quotes. But this is no household jorum found in the mud-brick dwellings of Judea. It is a gold-skirled mirror with the shape of an elegant goblet. In the reflecting surface, the nine women wear black veils.

The wizard rubs his eyes. The nine Sisters of Arimathea, standing humbly in the dawnlight, reveal none of the supernatural traits Merlinus sees in their reflections. Except for their black hoods and mantles and white robes embroidered with green Celtic crosses, they look like ordinary women made seraphically beautiful by serenity alone. The youngest appears seventeen, the eldest eighty. Beginning with Rna and following the Graal through the line to the auburn adolescent, they speak in turn: "The pagan tribes who scorn the Prince of Peace amass on our eastern shores and descend from the highlands."

"They worship murder. They drink from the skulls of the slain. We are sacrificed animals to their gods."

"The world goes mad for the evil that they do."

"All hope of peace rests in your sacred war, Uther Pendragon."

"History is a black beast. Be proud, rider."

"The light of the burial wagons shows the way through that darkness."

"Protect us from the raiders in the storm and the angels of death."

"Stop the invaders from overrunning this island, where Miriam, mother of Jesus, lived out her days."

"Take this jorum. We have fashioned it in honor of the vessel from which Jesus drank at his last meal—and so we call it the Holy Graal. It is consecrated by our prayers for peace and will bring blessings from God."

The youngest places it in Uther's hands, and the king's arms stagger with the surprising weight of it. "I accept for all Christendom," he affirms, and cringes within for his lusty memories of the elk-king's musical forest.

Ygrane kisses each of the cenobites, and they bless her and the child in her womb and depart in reverse order, the youngest leading them out of the citadel and back into the snowfields. Sunrise curls on the horn of the unicorn, which prances around the cenobites until they enter the crystal woods.

After their departure—as sudden and solemn as their arrival—a holy hush settles over the hall. Uther passes the Graal to Ygrane, who handles it lightly. It feels like spun glass to her.

"What does this mean, Myrddin?" she asks in wonderment, and hands him the sleek chalice.

The wizard peers into the wet shadows in the hollow of the cup and sees the turquoise light from the hall doorway pooling at the bottom. A moment's concentration reveals that the metal goblet serves as an antenna; Merlinus turns it in his hands and feels the power ebb and stream. "My lady—this is a magic vessel. The *Annwn* have fashioned it to receive power from the heavens. This will amplify your magic many fold."

He returns the Graal to her, and, marveling, she rotates it as the wizard did and feels, too, the flux of power it focuses out of the air. The invigorating current relaxes the guilty cramp in her chest. Now she has the power to revive the dragon-magus.

"It is a miracle," she finally manages to say. "With this—and the sword Lightning at our side—we cannot fail."

"We can *too* easily fail," Merlinus warns hotly. "We are

battling demons and gods who are fearless of evil. We must be careful not to become as they are."

Uther slides to his knees, ashamed of his disloyalty to this life, and Ygrane joins him, believing he kneels in prayerful thanks. With woeful joy the king lifts his face from the moment of proof and sends his personal guard to escort the nuns back to their chapel. But the nuns are gone. When the soldiers reach the tree line, the tracks end, the final steps widening to a stride impossible for any mortal to have made.

Winter is busy. Despite an unusual number of blizzards and sea storms, emissaries arrive from Armorica, the Visigothic Kingdom, Pope Simplicius in Rome, the eastern patriarchs in Antioch, and the boy emperor Romulus Augustulus in Ravenna. Celtic seers and Christian mystics visit from distant villages and hermitages to bless the unborn child Ygrane carries, and they convey awareness from the most remote corners of the kingdom that something momentous is soon to happen.

As Ygrane swells, Merlinus spends his time alert, watching out for Morgeu and her Y Mamau. Though he knows that Falon has been sent to drive Ethiops away, the wizard well knows that Morgeu's hatred of him is stronger than the demon. Reports from traders and pilgrims tell of a murderous cult in Inchtuthil devoted to the Devourer of All Things. But the dread Morgeu does not make her nefarious presence, or her alliance with the Furor, felt that whole winter. Not in Tintagel. Merlinus is unable to bring himself to use the strong eye again, to slip out of his body and visit the unholy shrine himself. His energy feels torpid and uncontrollable. Time, too, opens into a swifter dimension for the wizard. Days topple by.

Merlinus, attempting to get a grip on the slippery rush of time, attends the palace's many ceremonies—Christian benedictions, masses, candlelight processions—all accompanied by the monodic threnodies and liturgical chants of the choirs that have gathered at Tintagel from across the wintry countryside to worship the Holy Graal. Ygrane, too, and many of her fiana and druids attend these sacred services. Sitting off to the side, they join their Celtic observances with the Christian ones, rapidly locking fingers in silent rune-sharing.

The spiritual life of the diocese has never been more fervid, and Bishop Riochatus, who has been carrying a dour, emaciated countenance since his first meeting with the wizard, appears happy—actually rejuvenated, more full-fleshed, and spry. To everyone he meets—and to the bitter annoyance of the fiana and many Celts—he claims that an angel has answered his prayers and that the conversion of all Cymru has been promised by God's herald. He and Dun Mane spend hours at a time locked in vigorous debate about the scriptures, and the bishop comes away convinced by the druid that he must imitate the messiah by adhering to the dietary strictures of Leviticus and by growing his beard and temple locks in the Hebraic manner.

For Ygrane and Uther, this winter is their happiest time together. Four moons of joined magic, entwined understanding, proud purpose. Every night after the Graal celebration, they gather before a glorious hearthfire with the royal guests—the foreign emissaries, long-traveled pilgrims, warriors, poets, and opportunists drawn to Tintagel—and enjoy communion with the human dream, in all its variety and manner of foibles. And each morning after more jubilation of bells and singing worship, a carnival mood possesses the terraced courtyards and tiered ranges of the palace as musicians break into smaller ecstatic groups and accompany the denizens to their work. The citadel has never been more productive.

Many heartstrong tales play themselves out that winter, but for Merlinus the whole season distills to one vivid encounter: seeing Ygrane in her winter garden at the center of Tintagel, making her magic rinses as he watched her do seven years earlier and seventy leagues north in her summer garden at Segontium when, still garbed in animal skins, he first met her.

As before, the unicorn is there. White as the snow, it is barely visible against the frosted spires of poplar trees that wall off the circular garden. Like a sketch of itself, its virid eyes and silent hooves drift past as it circles the garden perimeter. Uther feeds the goblin braziers wood chips, saffron nodules of fragrant resins, and clear oils in separate bronze pans set on fire-trivets. Attentively, he watches the witch-queen steep small plaited bundles of herbs, mushrooms, mosses, ferns, bark, roots, kelp, and tiny shellfish, small whelks and periwinkles colorful as candy chips.

Several hours every day in the cold with Uther at her side assisting her with the rinses, the fire, and the magic, she prepares quick-heal lotions for the battles of the spring. The Graal, placed atop a frozen birdbath, draws energy into itself from the Great Tree, and the queen frequently replenishes her strength by touching her brow to its brim.

She requires a lot of energy, because she intends for every soldier, fiana and Christian, to have a phial of her healing balm. That means leaving most of the work to her servants, most of them healers and priestesses in their own right. They work diligently in the citadel preparing medicaments from the bales of curative herbs the queen has brought with her from Maridunum, and she meets with them every day to work for several more hours.

"I think you are doing too much," Uther complains even as he abets her by stirring the steeping potions and carefully controlling the heat of the aromatic flames. "Garner your strength for the spring and our child."

"Merlinus, tell Uther I've too *much* energy, now that we have the bounty of the Graal," she replies, and pauses to place her hands in the steam wreathing from the hot pans. She closes her eyes and directs a flow of magic into the elixirs. Feeling from his chest, Merlinus senses the healing power as a warm earth smell in the stinging cold. "How could I lie in bed all day? I must use this strength."

"Give it to the child," Uther recommends. "He will need all that strength when he comes into this world."

Several times that winter, the wizard wants to open the strong eye again, just to see if the child Ygrane carries is indeed male. He worries that this may not be the future king but another Morgeu. But his life-force is not focused enough for him to dare to step from his body. As it is, the very flow of time baffles him with its windrush. The strong eye is far too vigorous for him to use without the centering presence of more concentrated beings, like the unicorn or the Nine Queens.

Uther flicks a spark of glowing cinder at the wizard. "Merlinus, you've been in a daze since we left Maridunum."

"Since he rode the unicorn," Ygrane corrects. "He drifts."

"Is that why children sing stories about you now?" the king asks with a wink. Merlinus bows his head before this embarrassing truth. In his attempt to keep busy, he has gotten himself involved in several misadventures in the citadel and the nearby hamlets, creating trouble where he had tried to benefit others.

"Your mother asked you to do good," Ygrane says to him that cold, clear morning in the winter garden. "But, saint that she was, she had the heart to tell you the truth. You are not the savior."

"No." Merlinus pivots slowly around his staff, following the prancing circuit of the unicorn. The treacherous bliss he enjoys whenever he touches the creature troubles his heart with memories, and he chews his mustache. In the white glare, its squinting eyes look sly.

Uther blows warmth into his hands and approaches the unicorn. He knows well enough not to get too close. The animal shies from him and twice before has reared dangerously. One glance of those glassy hooves and no spell the wizard knows can call him back.

"Look at this magnificent being," the king says, pointing to the pink gashes of vertical nostrils jetting steam. "It is the most beautiful beast on earth." Green curved eyes close and the horn slashes like an ice dagger.

Merlinus cautiously pulls him away. "You cannot command this creature, Uther. The beast that waits on your will dwells in the underworld."

"I would not call Grandfather Vitki a beast," Uther mildly protests.

"He is far more beast than man now," the queen replies. She knows, because she feeds Wray Vitki each night with the Graal. A tower chapel has been erected for this purpose. At midnight, with the auroras furling in the starwinds, Ygrane raises the Graal to heaven and directs the flow of celestial power down through her body, through the tower rocks, into the planetary spaces below. Most of the current sluices through the honeycomb caverns to the Dragon. Its mane smokes in steam off the wintry ocean. Wray Vitki receives enough to grow stronger.

"Beast or not," the king confides, "he is in my dreams again—but now as a man. Wholly a man. He looks as my father did, from the death mask I've seen of him."

"Yes," Merlinus understands. "He wears his human face for you a last time. Even with the might of the Graal, his life will not endure the spring. We must use him wisely in battle."

The anticipation of war, as ever, hardens the king's expression, and he turns again toward the unicorn. "The time for war is not yet."

Merlinus passes a knowing, unhappy look to Ygrane, and neither of them has the heart to say what they both know and, surely, what the king must know in his heart—that war does not have a time. Inherited from the violence and fury of the stars that burn defiantly against the absolute cold of the vacuum until they explode, their death throes forging the iron of all blood, war is eternal.

Falon wanders the winter world. Through sleet winds and landscapes anonymous under their snow burdens, he travels north. Ygrane's talismans ward off were-animals and vampyres, and he makes good progress through the stormy landscape.

Three horses he wears out in the cold and blue forests. Twice, he uses the queen's gold to purchase new mounts from the stables of *coloniae* he passes through on his northward trek. The third new horse, he steals from an encampment of Picts, and flees across a frozen river that breaks apart behind him under the galloping impact of the horse's hooves.

In the wild uplands, he encounters a hermitage beset by marauders. The dozen Scoti raiders do not see him until he crashes through a thicket of icicles and is suddenly among them, his sword flashing in lethal arcs. Three are dead before the others turn on him. Valiantly, with the enormous western sun boiling at his back among storm clouds above the gray forest, he slays five more. The others flee, and Falon slumps from his steed, a wound under his arm dyeing scarlet the hoof-broken snow.

The hermits find him unconscious. After staunching his bleeding, they carry him to their stone sanctuary, which is a cluster of crude, beehive-shaped buildings on a rocky promontory. They bring him into the nearest of the cells and lower him onto a straw pallet.

While bustling to cleanse and dress the wound, they knock aside his travel pouch and spill a trove of heathen amulets and talismans—feathered rodent skulls in perplexing knots of hair, bone, and tendon, eyeholes gouged by quartz blades. A rock crusty with tiny mirrors is found in this abhorrent mess, and the whole damnable pouch is heaped up with blessed spindle wood, hard and hot-burning, and set ablaze in a lustration fire. Earnestly, they pray to dispel the deviltry befuddling this brave and wounded warrior and, lifting their voices higher, prepare to save his pagan soul from eternal damnation.

Falon comes out of his stupor at the sound of fervent chanting and howls with horror to find his warding pouch gone and the fire in the hermitage yard spooling smoke through the slanting snow. He lurches from his sick cot with another wrenching cry and heaves aside the hermits, who try to restrain him. Plunging his left hand into the flames, he retrieves Ygrane's love charm, scorched yet intact.

Falon does not wait for the mounting blizzard to abate before leaving the hermitage. He rides north into the blast of arctic night. Without his talismans, he is prey for every vile creature that the love charm attracts. Though he cannot feel the magic in the stone, wretched, soulless entities woven of shadows do.

The shapeshifting werebeasts are the worst but not the least of the night's terrors. They are plasmic beings composed of the ichor that seeps out of wounds in the Great Tree. Magi inflict these wounds to tap the ichor, from which they create astral soldiers and servants. These are the ones who have escaped their masters, the rogue shapeshifters who must eat the life-force of organic creatures to live. Most are centuries old.

Without the witch-queen's talismans to repulse astral predators, Falon must stay awake in the night, when the horribles crawl down from the World Tree. By day, he rides north, sleeps briefly at midday, and hurries into the twilight, keeping as far from other people as he can. His fiana oath forbids him knowingly to carry harm to anyone except enemies of the queen. Unshielded by talismans, the witching charm is a brilliant beacon to every ectoplasmic creature on the island.

The more clever shapeshifters plead, wheedle, and threaten from the dark, only their crimson eyes flickering in the fire-shadows. They offer him hidden treasures, secret knowledge, their lifelong fealty. But nothing they can say sways him. He knows that with their evil intelligence, they will use this power to fling open the gates between the worlds.

Falon calms himself with the knowledge that his queen has the sight. She can see the turbulent timewinds and read the flow of events that stream into the future. She can see this flux around every pebble, and surely she has seen the currents around this vital talisman. Ygrane knows that the course of events runs clear and unobstructed to her daughter. She would not throw him away on an impossible task.

Confident as a boulder, the queen's soldier sits close to the fire, naked sword in his lap, with the crystal charm tied to the back of his torque by plaited locks of his hair. Night after night, he sits thus, vigilant and untouched by the shapeshifters' ploys.

In the solstice time, with a banshee wind yelling out of the highlands and the warding fire jumping and splashing sparks, the shapeshifters depart before a less gruesome yet far greater terror. A female vampyre visits his circle of light.

She comes first as visions of Ygrane, naked, the white hourglass of her body dancing provocatively. In this way, she weakens him from inside. As with each of the fiana, Falon's life is bound to the queen's while all sexual desire is denied, directed outward to the handmaidens from whom the fiana are expected to select their wives.

Falon, who lost his first wife to Saxon raiders the winter before Ygrane summoned him, never chose another. The vampyre taunts him with images of Ygrane as his wife. The truth is that over the years pitiless desire for her has grown in him. Shame and greatness pivot on this desire. Yet, more than his fiana oath has kept him from feeling this truth until now. She is too old for him. She has been a witch-queen many lifetimes, while this is his first opportunity as a warrior.

For several nights, the vampyre taunts him with impossible images of himself in the arms of his queen. Then, on a windless night with the sky a vast commotion of stars, she arrives as herself and stands unmoving in the cinnabar shadows at the limit of his fire circle.

She is beautiful. Veins of iridescent ore glitter throughout his heart at the sight of her, and her loveliness hurts his chest. His wound has healed badly, and its poisons flare hotter as she steps wholly into the light. Her long body trembles like a white flame, and her eyes, tiny acetylene stars, pin him in place.

Sequins of chill sweat dazzle big as dewdrops across his brow from his effort to raise his sword. With her fingertip, she tilts the weapon aside and slides down next to him. Her fluent touch heals his pain—and when daylight comes it burns like acid.

Now by day, he rides through the dark glades and veers from burning shafts of sunlight. He thinks he travels north, but most of the day his mind is somewhere far away, and the bleak terrain appears as nameless as the netherworld. Only at night in the fireglow, with her lying beside him, does his mind clear. She is eating him. He knows this, even as his life-force fevers outward through his skin. He knows and cannot act to stop it because, as she eats him, she eats his pain—and all the pain of the world.

All winter, Falon shrivels in her embrace. In a soggy opal twilight, when the warrior has shrunk to a weasel of himself and his skin has the texture of mushrooms, the vampyre gauges that he is finally too weak to resist, and she pulls the torque from his throat and grasps the crystal charm.

Mouth gaping about a silent scream, Falon's whole body cramps with the exertion to draw his sword. He stands bent over, holding the hilt with both hands, the blade still wavering. The vampyre's starry eyes peer through the smoke of her hair, and her smile in the spring twilight is blue and slick. When he drives his blade through her heart, he is surprised. She is soft as moss.

Shapeshifters watching from the trees see the vampyre die, her pale body collapsing to pond scum and viscous fumes of burning black. Recognizing their chance to seize the charm from the shrunken man, they swoop out of the forest's moon-steam.

Falon seizes the torque and the attached charm and staggers back from the sudden stench. He has emptied himself into her beauty, and now he no longer possesses the strength to flee. He reels about to face his death and watches three hulks, each large as a bear, loping downhill through the moonlight toward him. Their hideously large faces swim loosely on long skulls, features warped and unreal as a smashed aftermath.

This sight inspires horror in the exhausted soldier. To his left, violet vapors smoke from a ravine, and he leaps in. Clattering among rootcoils, he descends to a shale-ledged crevice in the earth large enough for him to crawl through. At the back of the dripping, pungent interior, he curls around and waits, sword ready.

When a massive shadow rumbles toward him, he thrusts. The scream that follows burns outside on the cave ledge for an interminable time. All that night, Falon drifts between the scruffy voices that threaten him from outside and the impossible emptiness inside him where the vampyre has fed.

At dawn, he crawls into the sunlight and burns with unpronounceable pain. He does not roll into the shade but bares himself to the searing fire. He wants to suffer for his betrayal of himself and his queen, and he scorches himself until he passes out.

Out of the fever daze of noon, the unicorn appears. Ygrane has been looking for Falon all winter, since the solstice when she received the power of the Graal and could send her solar steed to help him. But the vampyre has kept him hidden in her darkness until this day.

One touch of its horn heals Falon, and he returns at once to his quest. And though there is no need to visit Inchtuthil now, for the unicorn already knows that Morgeu has left, they stop there anyway on their return south.

At the sodden site, Falon views the dilapidated shanty and lean-to structures where the Y Mamau have squatted among the Roman ruins. Scattered throughout the slum are pock holes in the ground big as kettles, where blue flames dance atop the fetid black ooze that percolates from underground.

The Dragon's presence makes the unicorn nervous, and they do not linger. On their way out through the rubble and the debris of sagging shacks and stagnant ditches vivid with fecal stench, they pass a mound of human skulls, black with baked blood, heaped about the grinning statue of dancing Morrígan.

The golden moment for the Pendragons ends with the coming of the spring storms. Never before in history have there been such torrents. Lightning tangles its hot nets among the sharp towers of Tintagel day and night for a week, and the citadel gongs and moans with thundery echoes like a temple orchestra of giants.

The dragon returns to Uther's dreams. Its webbed talons lift the earth under him, as they did when Uther went with the dragon-magus from the Otherworld to save Ygrane. The claws carry him upward, toward the huge grin of fangs and the malevolent grandeur of its cavernous, yellow eyes. Mist droplets detail the rime-crusted nostrils, and every scale looks warped and heavy as metal. Standing in the chill, mulchy breath of the ancestral dragon, before the jaws' hooked clamp, Uther sees frayed skin hanging from its chin like lepers' rags, kelpy growths and badges of cankers at the hinged corner of its mouth. And he sees that the beast is very old.

"Uther-r-r," its sea-depth voice growls like a drumming army.

Then Uther's heart beats thick, and he writhes awake in a slather of fright. Sometimes, his wife's gentle cosseting returns him to sleep, but most nights he stands at the tower window and stares. As the fog crawls the moors like the ghosts of dead millions, and fear sings out from his heart's darkest lanes of anonymity and hopelessness, he knows the time has come again for war.

The Furor sits in council with his demons, Azael and Ethiops. They squat together in the silver darkness of the Otherworld.

The nether stars breathe with the slow respiration of the Dragon.

"I will not meet you down here again," the Furor complains, his one eye glaring from within his knotted scowl. He loathes their ghastly skewed bodies, though he knows full well they are only appearances—one a bulbous skullface dangling among eelish slitherings, the other a nauseous whale hide full of nodules and laboring slug mouths fibrillose with fangs.

"Lord," the viperous Ethiops speaks in a voice pale with calm, "we are in no danger from the Dragon here among these rootcoils of your planet's magnetic tree."

"Do not think to instruct me," the Furor warns, holding his voice flat, devoid of emotion. "Two of you are already dead—"

"Not dead, lord," Ethiops blandly corrects. "Wounded."

"They are dead to this world," the Furor states more loudly. "You are no match for the Fire Lords. I should squeeze my magic out of you right now and fling you back into the House of Fog."

The demons sidle closer together. "We are your servants, lord," Ethiops assures him, while thinking how best to control him. The interference of the angels has overwhelmed him and Azael, and they disagree about how to utilize their god to ruin their enemy's strategy. Azael wants to fling the furious god and his swarms of gutsacks across the island, destroying everything. But Ethiops senses that somehow the angels expect and want that. The angels seem to have invested their power in a few humans, opportunistically creating an elite fighting force around their entranced companion Lailoken. "We have begged audience with you in this hidden place, to ask you to wait at Londinium for the arrival of your enemies."

Azael remains silent, not willing to betray his discord with Ethiops for fear of further enraging this scowling god.

"Wait?" The Furor's frown screws tighter around his mad eye. "The last time you called me to this dismal place you had me talking to a child—and you disguised as a goddess! It was disgusting. And now, you tell me to wait." He tugs at his wild beard. "I will not wait. I will crush my enemies. And you will help me."

"We *want* to help you, lord," Ethiops protests with a tinge of impatience. "The Fire Lords are scattered across their flimsy creation. They cannot long hold together this monstrosity they call civilization. We *can* defeat them. But—"

"I will not abide that word!" the Furor thunders. "We will defeat the Fire Lords! I have staked everything I am upon this."

"And we will prevail," Ethiops insists. "I tell you, the Fire Lords are spread too thin to interfere with our attacks. We can destroy empires with impunity. The Fire Lords cannot be everywhere at once."

"But!" the Furor growls. "But—what?"

"Merely this—the Fire Lords are taking advantage of our old companion Lailoken's laughable presence as a gutsack. The angels are putting far more care than usual into defending him and his circle—your human enemies."

"Why?"

"They have never had a demon to work for them before," Ethiops reasons. "I believe they are going to use him to establish their new religion in these islands—in all the northlands, if they can."

"No! He must be destroyed!"

"Yes." Ethiops leans closer, eager to press his manipulation. "You can destroy him. You are powerful enough. But the Fire Lords will protect Lailoken, and even you dare not stand against them."

"That is why you led the child to me, the daughter of the Celtic queen." The Furor begins to understand. The Dark Dwellers are experts of destruction, adept at using the most mere beings to achieve their violent results. "Morgeu is your disguise, isn't she? Your way of getting close enough to the fugitive demon to separate him from the Fire Lords so that I can kill him."

Ethiops's smile opens in his skeletal face like a bright blade. "Azael and I will distract the angels. Morgeu will kill the unicorn. That is the Fire Lords' anchor in this world. They are using its body to focus themselves on the planet's surface. With it gone, they will be scattered again, and you will have the satisfaction of destroying the one who thwarts you."

"With Lailoken ripped free of his gutsack," Azael says, glad he kept his silence long enough to fix the hook of their influence deeper in this god, "you will triumphantly sweep away your enemies and seize these islands for your own. We will kill them all."

"And Londinium is where you will stage this slaughter?" the Furor asks, the tightness of his voice relaxing.

"Londinium," Ethiops affirms, stepping back with his partner into the land of shadow, their grisly bodies wafting away, insubstantial as darkness.

With mounting terror, Merlinus feels the approach of war. He knows there will be a direct confrontation with the Furor, and he sits alone in his turret chamber at Tintagel and stares out to sea imagining that doomful event—the battle for Londinium.

How many times will this fight be waged? he wonders, hearing the surf soughing like the timewind.

The coming clash with the Furor reminds the wizard of his first—and last—human encounter with the god of war. Fear wraps him in paralysis as that memory unfolds, and he sits staring at the glinting gray sea a long time, watching the hues shift, suffering again the terror.

Night dangles its tinsels, and he begins to speak, putting to words the memories that, unspoken, immobilize him—

"I had only little fear of the Furor when I last dared to confront him as a man. I was eager to go down to my mother's people, to save them, if I could, from the fate of their king, my grandfather, who had been butchered by barbarians. I hurried through the woods to their settlement bearing the Stave of the Storm Tree.

"The people of the thorp lived in pantiled houses three centuries old, the last true citizens of Rome. Like my mother, they spoke and wrote a Latin that had been out of fashion in Rome itself for over a century. They were the Empire's provincials, the preservers of tradition who thought of themselves as civilized Romans. They worshiped the State religion, the earliest form of Christianity in which Jesus' edict to love one's neighbor required literal and daily fulfillment, so that the whole community lived and worked together as intimately as a family.

"Upon my arrival at the thorp, the villagers immediately recognized me as the old holy man who attended the eremite Optima, and they bathed me and clothed me and then offered me a hearty meal. I ate lightly, pleading, truthfully, that I was accustomed to much more humble fare. The people, gracious and accommodating, served me bread and honey. Then we all prayed together to avert the approach of the barbarians.

"With no hope of making a stand against battle-hardened storm-warriors, I urged the people of the thorp to retreat south into the forests and hide. But that tactic seemed untenable to them. The spring fields had been turned and needed tending if there was to be a summer's crop and food for the following winter.

"I offered to take the children. But the youngest of them would not be parted from their mothers, and the women were determined to stand with their men. The older children, too, would not flee. They belonged to a Roman Christian community and were determined to share their fate as they shared their faith. There was nothing I could do but pray with them and prepare for battle.

"We did not have long to wait. Early on my second morning in the community, while we breakfasted, the sentinel's cry sounded. We seized our weapons, such as they were: staves, shovels, scythes, and axes. Several of the men had the short

Spanish swords used by the legions, and two had rectangular Roman shields. The women and children armed themselves as well, for the merciless reputation of the Furor's barbarians had established itself centuries ago—though none of us, apart from myself, had ever seen a barbarian until that dreadful morning.

"They came out of the northern woods on foot and at a leisurely pace, and, at first, we thought perhaps they were a peaceable group that might be placated with winter wine and hearty food. But as they drew nearer, dread smothered that foolish hope. Each of the forty fur-clad and half-naked warriors that approached carried a throwing ax and an iron-tipped spear.

"Apart from their weapons, no two of the barbarians wore the same garb. Some had shaved the backs and sides of their heads and displayed topknots; others had sheared themselves entirely bald; still others featured long-haired styles, their wild feather-tufted braids beaded with bones. Most had tattooed their bodies blue and green, giving to their appearance an eerie, reptilian cast. A few bore the remnants of armor bedecked with the scalps and skullshards of slain legionnaires.

"A warrior wearing a rawhide helmet crested with bull horns, raised a human femur bone hollowed to a flute and piped a dirgeful wail. The savage horde bellowed with rabid glee and charged.

"Counting the women, we outnumbered them three to one, and I thought at first there was some hope of driving them back. I actually thought that. I—a demon. I who, as a spirit, had myself reveled in carnage and slaughter. I, who believed I could not misjudge evil! I had no notion how to use my demon powers. I was just an old man. And *I* rallied our defense and led those benighted peasants to meet the screeching, howling storm-warriors of the Furor.

"The axes of the enemy flew, whirling like the black blur of bats. One ax cleaved open the face of the man to my right, another split the breastbone of the farmer to my left, and in his death convulsions he snatched my arm and hauled me to the ground as if to take me into the afterworld with him. Wounded screams mutilated the blue morning.

"Spears lowered, the barbarians swarmed over us, impaling any who stood against them. I saw two women run through on one lance. Those who fell to the ground writhed as axes hacked them to pieces. Others had their brains pounded out of them with their own severed limbs. The barbarians sang jubilantly while, under their blood-mired sandals, gutted children lay weeping, tangled in their spilled entrails.

"Nothing I could do helped as I thrashed about on the ground. Whip strokes of blood spurted in bright arcs and scalded my face. I tottered to my feet, and a thick hand caught me by my long hair and slammed me face first into the burst rib cage of a felled woman whose throbbing heart beat its last hot spasms against my gagging mouth. Blood-masked, I shoved backward, and again a strong hand seized me by the hair. 'Behold the terrible might of the Furor!' a warrior screamed in my ear, and I tensed against the bite of his ax.

"But it never came.

"The barbarians hauled me around as a plaything, an enfeebled old man selected by their berserk rapture for a living death. They dragged me among the ripped-off heads and chopped torsos by my bloodied hair and forced me to watch the flaying of the corpses. I screamed for them to kill me, and the brutal, gore-filthy gang laughed. And the louder I screamed, the more crazed their laughter became.

"At the worst of it, when I lay propped up on a gory throne of beheaded carcasses with a mantle of putrid viscera draped across my shuddering shoulders and a dismembered hand splayed atop my head for a crown, the Furor himself came to me.

"Huge, globe-shouldered, his great beard slathered in the blood of the dead Christians, he loomed over me, his one good eye silver-blue as an arctic wolf's, the naked socket of his dead eye a skull-hole from which stared a piece of starless night.

"'I came myself when I heard it was you, Lailoken,' the king of the Æsir said in his profoundly sonorous but gentle voice. His kindly tone reminded me that he had lost his eye to a troll in exchange for a draught from the well of knowledge. Unlike his blood-mad warriors, he was not an uncivilized brute. 'I had to see for myself that you had taken mortal form. When my magic accidentally slammed a demon into the mud, I had no idea it was you, old friend. You helped me defeat the Fauni, and I want to help you now. I feel responsible for your predicament and I want to free you—but clearly your fall has made you crazy. I don't dare let you roam free, not now that you've taken a stance against me. And to think we were comrades once. What has become of you?'

"I tried to speak, to tell him how I had changed, but my stunned flesh could do no more than stammer hoarsely what I had been screaming all along. 'Kill—me—'

"His silver eye glittered, amused. 'Lailoken—not even I can kill a demon. As for the mortal garment you wear, I believe your punishment for betraying our old alliance shall be to wear this stinking thing until it falls away of its own decay.'

"With his massive spear, he pointed to the Stave of the Storm Tree that his warriors had propped across my chest as a mock scepter. 'You carry a splinter of the Terrible One—a splinter stolen by the sniveling Síd. Keep it. Let it remind you ever of this day when you dared stand against me.'

"I groaned in my misery, and he nodded once. 'Yes,' he said in his vibrant voice. 'Mortal life is a miserable thing. Why do you bother with it? And, worse, why do you trouble yourself with the Síd and the craven Christians? They are doomed races. Like the Romans and their Fauni that we devoured together, these puny people are marked by death. They cannot stand against my might. You know this is true.' He shook his large head sadly. 'Once, you were a magnificent being, Lailoken. How it saddens me to see you so reduced.'

"Then he touched his speartip to my brow, and his curse entered me as madness. All the death cries of the butchered children beat their charred wings against the inside of my skull. They beat wildly to find a way out, until it felt as if my head would burst. My eyes swam and strained to the bony limits of my sockets, and my throat swelled, puffed with a strangled scream in me too huge to burst its way out. Chittering insanely, I sat upon the throne of death and watched the god of murder stride across the mangled corpse of the world."

When the steely gray-and-purple storm towers retreat north and leave the sky dark blue, the Wheel-Table rolls out of Tintagel—and the king and queen carry the Graal and the Sword into the world. There is no doubt now of the two going together to war. They are the alliance, the living emblem of the kingdom, and must face together the full risk of their worth.

The march to Londinium begins with enormous fanfaronade, as if the Pendragons march in the company of Caesar himself, off to conquer the British Isles. Within a day, however, the truth of their plight sinks in.

The purple highlands of Exmoor climb before them in horizons of gorse, and out of hidden folds in the land, barbarians attack. They are a small, rogue squad of berserkers who break the volunteers' line and send the farmers' sons and village recruits scampering. With deadly efficiency, the raiders smash a dozen heads from behind before the cavalry can push through the confusion and dispatch the attackers.

Pendragon's army, bloated as it is with well-wishers, dreamers, pilgrims, and traders, makes a sorry spectacle. The ragtag volunteers continue to get in the way of the trained soldiers. So Uther creates a separate division for them—the king's auxiliaries—assigned to support the infantry of Marcus Dumnoni and Uther's cavalry. It is with them that Merlinus travels, accompanying them on their daily food forages.

At regular intervals, berserker squads howl up out of ravines across the heath. They are the religious devotees of their people, the most ardent worshipers of the Furor. At night, shallow-draft boats skim to shore from the black sea after days sailing from Frisia, Jutland, or the Isle of Gaels. The ax-wielding men they release on the moors are determined to go directly to the Hall of Heroes among the Æsir in the only way possible—by dying in battle.

The cavalry kills most of them from afar. But occasionally, as in their first skirmish, they break through the line and dance death among the panicky ranks. By the time Pendragon reaches the City of the Legion, where the Celtic army awaits him, his troops are bloodied and skittery.

Kyner, Urien, and Lot camp outside the black-walled city in a wide, colorful sprawl of tents. This is the first return of the Celts to the lowlands that they lost centuries ago to the north tribes and the Romans. They study the landscape with awe-filled attention—the river plains of their ancestors.

The allied armies of Celts and Britons roll east like weather. The barbarians fly ahead of them, as the war council has envisioned.

Outside Aquae Sulis, where Bors Bona has come down in full host from the north to greet them, a wedge of Jutes and Angles is trapped. For two days, whole clans are caught running through the woods and hiding in the underbrush. The king has a score of army priests armed only with holy water stationed at his left, and Marcus Dumnoni's lance corps for his right.

Any and all disarmed barbarians who bow before the priests are baptized on the spot and whisked off in wagons to farms for Bible study and hard labor. Those who fight are killed; defiant women and children, too. And the lance corps does its killing with a fast, precise fury. The cavalry hunts down the wild runners. Uther wants all necessary killing done swiftly, and no torture or burnings will he tolerate. The enemy slain are sprinkled with lime, packed with sod, and laid to rest under rock cairns.

Ygrane and her fiana follow a day behind the army and

work magic on the cairns. In the green mists of spring twilight, she calls the pagan souls out of the Otherworld and back to their bones. As they waft out of the gloaming, the Síd snatch them away to the Wood of the Gods. There, the blood-wet souls of hunters dance with the Piper and the elk-king and all the animal gods they hunted. Many of these souls go mad and come to the hunter's end. Only lifetimes can heal them. Others revel. The animals inside them live again and share secrets, running off together under the twisting trees and unopened buds.

After her work with the dead, Ygrane sits in her tent with the Graal. Tiny people kneel—faerïe burning bright as wicks while she swirls water in the Graal. Sky colors reflected from the open flue of the tent spin energy into the water. When she drinks, she grows stronger, the baby within her stronger as well, and her sight becomes keen enough for a while to see her brother Falon.

Worn thin as a kestrel, Falon's sun-stained face searches the southern tree line for the unicorn that leads him toward Londinium. About his neck, dangling from his torque by cords of his orange hair, Ygrane's love charm flashes bright as a spirit.

In the Cotswold Hills, smoke plumes mark Bors Bona's vehement troops and the end of the cairn magic. Among the sugary blossoms, pagan families are nailed to trees. Growing from the boughs in grotesque contortions, a pale, bruised mushroom-people has emerged. It is necessary, for an instant, to believe that these mottled, bloated gargoyles are a devil's fungus—men- and women-shapes in the tree forks, and under them the small black blossoms of children.

The king stares unblinking into the scalded faces of these corpses. His skin burns in the stink, and his horse shimmies, stung by flies and spooked by the stench of death. He sends a herald ahead to Bors with the blunt command to bury the enemy dead. That evening, the hills jump with flames. Bors laughs that he has buried the enemy with fire—in pagan style.

But the laughter stops later that night when the wind-whipped holocaust shoves the army east to the thawed bogs of the river plains. The Wheel-Table gets stuck. And far worse, the cavalry is nearly useless in this footless terrain. Out of the canebrakes, Pictish berserkers lunge, singling out the unhorsed bowmen and hacking at them with their massive axes.

Panic flares through the unseasoned village troops, and they bolt for the higher ground to the south. The veterans who have fought the Northmen before try in vain to stop the rout, but unable to ride free of the panicked mob and use their arrows, they are trapped.

Screeching and yowling in their barbarous tongue, the Picts rush down headlong from the higher bluffs. In the starlight at a distance, they are a vaporous swarming of shadow hulks. The army dissolves in a panic, scattered and separated by tussocks and black fens. Shouts and cries for order splinter against the screams of the horses.

Then, the Picts come thrashing through the canebrakes out of the south, bursting ferociously upon the army like demons sprung from another dimension. Heads shaved bald around topknots and side crests, the gruesome warriors, some with dragonskin tattooed on their broad bodies, spear, club, and ax everyone in their path. In the end, it is pitiful to watch. The horror of the Britons' death cries spurs the survivors to charge back into the ranks, causing them to collide with the regulars.

Uther proves a poor general. Separated from Marcus Dumnoni, his best military adviser, he does not know what commands to shout. From atop his horse, Merlinus sees him twisting in the saddle, bewildered, the sword Lightning held fecklessly aloft. Only a handful of people can see him in the dark.

"Dracon!" he cries, as he watches his army dissolve into the night. "Dracon Vitki!"

A riderless horse wheels by, eyes staring white with fear, and clatters into the cane.

"Grandfather Vitki!"

Merlinus hears his king shouting for the dragon-magus, and though he hoped not to have to call upon the aged magician this soon in the campaign, he speaks the barbarous words that summon the dragon-man.

Darkness shrouds Merlinus's view, but those who can see, the archers and infantry who are with him this night, witness a lightning storm suddenly rising out of the soggy ground. Swamp gas flares green flames. Ball lightning bounces over the cattails. The king's sturdy dun gelding rears up aghast with azure flames, rising almost vertically. An eerie, astral fire wafts from the sword Lightning, and by that unearthly light Uther summons his army around him.

In a conflagration of cold fire, the king leads the advance against the frightened Picts. Panic-stricken defeat reverses in an instant to violent victory. Believing the Holy Spirit has descended upon their king, the Christian soldiers themselves become berserkers. Whole squads martyr themselves in frenzied forays against the startled barbarians and overrun them by sheer numbers.

As dawn glims across the wide plains, the enraged army still slogs south under the king's banners of boreal lights. Will-o'-the-wisps and fox fire prance around them as the slaying of Picts continues, until the first shafts of sunlight shred the king's ghost fires. Then, he returns the fight to his warlords and rides wearily back to Ygrane.

Uther sits in the bright aura of his wife's magic and shadows forth all his fears. She takes them and blends them with blue in its many hues of that day and night. Glamour soothes him. Relieved of his animal woes, he accepts his destiny: seed-carrier.

Strange thing a seed—a compacted destiny made of the destiny that preceded it. Each seed is the end of destiny. It is dead—until it grows. Then it is no longer a seed but itself a seed-bearer, with its own destiny.

This makes sense now, with his green-eyed wife lying beside him in their tent. But tomorrow he must return to the field, where the sores of his heart will open again. Only for tonight do love and the child in her make sense to him. Tomorrow, he will hear again the flutes of bone and the eerie wails on the wind from the Hall of Heroes. This night, the auspicious stirrings in his wife's round belly are enough.

In a dream, asleep in Ygrane's lap, he sees down from Britain through Europe as across a deep grassy field and peers into a rocky horizon, with the vanishing point at the birth place of the savior. Jesus stands there. Not even Jesus as he imagined him in church and in prayer but actually Yeshua, the man with a Nazarene profile and the long locks and beard of his faith. He is a man. He is a swart, Semitic man with particular features, gentle, manly features as yet unmarred by the kiss of thorns.

Uther returns to his command emboldened by his dream. His stunning night victory in the marsh has secured his authority against all the blunders that follow. No one will dispute him again, though, in fact, he remains a terrible general.

The king has no imagination for killing. His wizard advises him to let his generals command the field. Merlinus is vociferous in his belief that the countryside need not be swept clean of invaders as the king's brother once attempted. It is enough to get the king and his pregnant queen to Londinium, there to give birth to a new order.

"The ordering can be done later," Merlinus concludes, "once our forces are united with Severus Syrax. You must keep him closest to your side, for he has inherited the best-paid infantry in the island—and surely he is your weakest ally."

Uther is undaunted by Merlinus's fears of lingering in the countryside, and he encourages forays to seek and destroy known bands of raiders. With the feeling of his dream kept close at heart, he finds the courage to fulfill his Jesus-drama, to be the particular man God has made him.

As time passes, each hamlet greets him and his Celtic queen with renewed ebullience. Previously isolated *coloniae* throw open their gates to Pendragon and his Celts, frantic with festivals and triumphant ceremonies in their honor. At each stop, it becomes obligatory to set up the round table and display the sword Lightning and the Holy Graal. The journey becomes a pilgrimage.

It seems to matter not at all that Uther Pendragon is a terrible general. Wray Vitki has made him great. Stories of Uther's miraculous victories against the pagans swell his ranks with zealous volunteers—more inexperienced troops that drain his supplies and slow his march. The army moves with such stately procession that word of the Dragon Lord's return flies ahead to the most remote northlands before the allies complete a third of their journey.

Pagan battle groups descend from every tribe above Hadrian's Wall, and across the North Sea the Saxon warlord Horsa mobilizes an army. Bitter from the death of his clansman, Hengist, Horsa, a chief among the storm raiders, gathers boatloads of vengeful warriors and sails up the Tamesis to Londinium. From there, they dispatch assault teams to distract and weaken the allies' procession while the Saxons harass the countryside and intimidate Severus Syrax's small, unmounted army.

The journeys between the *coloniae* become more arduous, and soon Pendragon's army progresses only a league or two a day. Sporadic enemy attacks whittle away at them. These are the very battles Merlinus has foreseen with Raglaw—brutal fights across creeks and in road ditches, with bloodspray, boneshards, and brainsludge flying.

The excellent defensive scouting of the Celts assures that no assaults surprise Uther—but there is no end to the assaults. All the pagan tribes of Europe have come to Britain to exact revenge for their humiliating losses to the Dragon Lord. Messages from Severus warn of a huge tribal gathering outside the city wall. His words hint at negotiating with Horsa.

By the time the trees are in full leaf and the maniac bands of killers in the forests and hills have become harder to see and more lethal, the allies have forgotten about driving the barbarians ahead of them. Hangers-on fall away. Volunteers evaporate. And Pendragon rolls his round table east, leaving the old stone road blackening with blood behind him.

Only Christians are buried, and those hurriedly in rock pile graves. The Celts are satisfied to be cremated, and pyres burn for them every day. The enemy dead remain where they fall, and Pendragon's Wheel rolls on. Ygrane and Uther ride with the round table, the Graal carried between them, no longer displayed but locked in a black-veiled crate on a drawcart.

Twice a day, at twilight, Ygrane drinks from the Graal. She has created a ceremony around this that includes the priests and the druids—a ritual enactment of *Yesu*'s sacrifice of healing, for the Christians a mass they use to consecrate their Eucharist, and for the Celts a rite of daily renewal.

For Ygrane, this is her chance to look for the unicorn and Falon, who stalk Morgeu. They appear small, as on a Chinese mountain. The unicorn flares ahead, foreshadowing Falon's slower path. Life-force spindles from the sun-beast—so thin these days, worn to a thread by all the queen has demanded of it through the winter.

The unicorn must lie beside Ygrane with the Graal between them and drink the sunlight, the starlight, the moonlight, and the floes of invisible light that it magnifies in its clear body. They must lie like this for a moon before it will regain the strength to carry a man.

And still, Ygrane uses her magic to take more of the unicorn's unique vitality for the child in her, more of its serenity and fearlessness. Sometimes, she feels she will go mad without the unicorn. Life tumbles inside her. Spring explodes from every hill and bird-loud valley. Yet everywhere she looks, she sees corpses. With her hands on her belly, willing the magic of life into her child, she rides in her litter, the curtains open. She does not turn away from the carcasses. These are the sacrifices to Morrígan that her life requires. God has called her to this, and she accepts it and feeds its frightful, terrible magic to the child within her: life eats life—and God alone makes this holy.

Uther has stopped looking. He watches the tumbling clouds carrying summer along the horizon, a little closer each day. The people believe he is wonderfully imperial and cheer him when they are not hiding from the roving raiders. But he is not imperial. He is appalled. Back at Tintagel in the cool autumnal days around the table, in the severe presence of the warlords, the march on Londinium had seemed so plausible. Now it is a relentless horror.

Ygrane continues to lave Uther with glamour, but protecting her child from the death shrieks and war yelps that slash toward them day and night begins to use all her strength. She wants Uther to ride with her, where they can help each other. But now that the attacks have increased, Uther will not leave the sight of his troops. The king and queen remain apart until the wide, blue Tamesis leads them to the high timber walls and smoky spires of Londinium.

By the time Horsa's horizon of tribal armies comes into view with its fields of hide tents and groves of lancemen, Uther has amassed a mighty force of his own—a host of Britons and Celts fivefold larger than the force Ambrosius arrayed on these same alluvial plains the previous year. The king lifts his face to the blue afternoon and the summer clouds sailing for eternity, and he prays with ravenous hope for peace; then orders an immediate attack.

He wants it over. He does not want to wait even the one day

it will take to combine forces with Severus Syrax. He commands an immediate full-out assault because he does not want to face again in his nightmares the dragon-magus's cruel reptile grin. All the killing there is to be done, he wants done swiftly. His impatience overrides the strategies of all his military advisers, including Merlinus. The army is exhausted. The enemy on the plains below has been waiting for them, growing stronger, frenzied by visions and visitations from the Furor.

The king will not listen to the entreaties of the battle-chiefs, and they approach the queen to intercede. But she will not. The timewinds blow every which way. All decisions are valid and none. The time for the sacrifice has come, when the king must offer himself to his fate. She stands aside.

Events, which have passed for Merlinus in a windrush of time, now whirl almost faster than he can follow. Bors Bona leads the frontal charge across the river flats directly toward the sprawling barbarian encampment. Marcus Dumnoni and two of the Celtic commanders, Urien and Lot, sweep south to attack the flank.

Messages fly by foot, boat, and carrier bird to Severus Syrax, commanding him to take the field at once. Uther leads his cavalry and Kyner's Celts along the river itself, on both banks. But Severus does not emerge at once. Confused messages return to the king, stating that negotiations have already begun with Horsa.

But by then, the battle has flared. Uther sends one more set of commands to Londinium directing Severus to come out of the city and attack the Saxon camps. Then he barricades the table, where Ygrane and a handful of her fiana remain with the wizard to guard the Graal, and he summons his sword and rides into war.

Falon follows the unicorn. Through rain and floods of sunlight, they hurry south on the indefatigable roan the fiana stole from the Picts a season ago. The decay of the vampyre slowly heals in him.

The horned beast gives no notice to the actions of Falon. It is tired. With its torpid reflexes, it must keep to higher ground or fall under the claw.

Where are the Fire Lords? it wonders as the witch-queen's magic reels it closer to Morgeu and the Dark Dwellers Azael and Ethiops. It is frightened. Death, which in the herd is a return to the one love, looms across the horizon of the Dragon's back, strewing black blossoms. Burned fields and torched villages mottle the green summer forests.

Falon, too, senses death ahead. The river plains shimmer below in haunted distances of heat haze and battlesmoke. The spoor of the Y Mamau stains the land more freshly: warm firesites, fresh hoofprints, and corpses rolling in the river, headless.

Morgeu feels vibrant and swollen with the glory of Morrígan. She rides swiftly through the woods, her fiana racing at her sides. Ethiops flushes their beasts with so much power they fly like shadows. At midday, they pass through a wind gap in the low hills and emerge from a forest that stands above them like bearded giants. The blue day widens into grasslands where the Tamesis flows in its prisms.

The brown scrim of Londinium's cooking fires drops down the sky and intertwines with the smoke from the Furor's camps. Farther off, pastures fold into themselves an imperishable green. Streaks of lightning embroider the stacked horizons of the lowlands in a summer haze that blurs south.

The Y Mamau point west. Across the wide river plains patched into farmland by thickets of dwarf evergreen oaks and low stone fences, a massive army advances. Even at this distance, where the troops look like cloud shadows drifting over the fields and roads, Morgeu recognizes the black-and-green wind socks of Uther Pendragon.

Morgeu dismounts and paces through the gillyflowers and foxgrass in the shadows of the high forest. Morrígan begins speaking in her head, suggesting a night assault when Uther's men camp to rest for tomorrow's great battle.

"Pendragon attacks!" several Y Mamau begin shouting, and Morgeu snaps free of her reverie and climbs onto her horse to see better. Unbelievably, the stable master is ignoring the basics of military tactics. He has no command camp, no formations, and no obvious sequence of attack—yet he attacks! The hordes who have gathered around him on his victorious march across the island surge toward Londinium.

Under a tree of clouds, the armies clash. Morgeu and her Y Mamau ride furiously toward the havoc. She must get close enough to inflict her wrath. Ethiops vigorously pumps her with speed and battle luck. He, too, has been surprised by Pendragon's irresponsibility. This impulsive lunge by the allies leaves him no time to meet again with Azael. He must leave his comrade to his own wicked ingenuity.

Ethiops directs Morgeu and her snout-masked dozen through the trampled fields, among ax-swinging wild men, and no arrow or lance touches any of them. The demon flings his avengers toward a central caravan, where rays of light fantail from a black-tented wagon. The Graal is there. And ahead of it on the wide road that cuts a straight line to the walled river city, a bizarre, giant wheel rolls. Ethiops is certain now, Lailoken cannot be far.

Atop a knoll swarmed about by Kyner's heavily armored fanatics, Morgeu rears her mount. The running tide of inflamed fighters drifts away before the death chill presence of Ethiops, and for a moment he exults, *Let there be chaos!*

Battle cries and mortal screams pierce the furious clanging of metal and the uproar of shouting men and horses. The small details of the battlefield—the flies and the choruses of ravens and gulls come to pick at the dead—interest Morgeu, while Ethiops feels about for Lailoken. Since the wizard stopped talking aloud to himself, he has become harder to find.

Morgeu and her warriors stare with fascination at the camphor fumes of souls that leak out of the dead and burn in the loud daylight, flames without ash. A collective shriek jumps from them at the sight of the unicorn galloping through the gritty, sulfur vapors of afternoon, corpses rocking like drowned men beneath its hooves.

Tired as the unicorn is, it has enough strength to kill Morgeu. It feels this anguished necessity from the psychic tether that binds it to the queen. Ygrane wants her daughter freed from the Dark Dweller.

Ethiops hurls the Y Mamau at the charging beast. Its tusk flashes, and four of the masked warriors burst like sausages. Hooves blur, and four more riders are flung broken into the grass. The remaining four spread out to encircle the furious thing and pierce it with their metal blades. Spryly, it capers between their swords, buckjumps, and lances each of the bitch masks.

The demon despairs before this elusive and vehement creature. He concentrates himself inside Morgeu and draws her obsidian knife—the knife of sacrifices that has long fed Morrígan's murderous appetite. If the unicorn is going to rip away the demon's servant, then the unicorn will die with her.

That instant, Falon charges out of the carbon-streaked wind, flame arrows crisscrossing in the air behind him. He bounds onto the knoll and stops the unicorn with a cry. "I have the charm!"

At the sight of the gold-flaked crust of rock in Falon's fist, Morgeu jars loose of Ethiops's possession. The blood cries of the battle soar louder and colors brighten. The young enchantress startles to find herself on horseback facing the unicorn. The sunlight breaking over the horn dazzles her with rainbow sparks and momentarily glares her view of the charm.

In that obscured instant as light inflicts darkness on Morgeu's brain, Ethiops decides to sacrifice this gutsack for the horned beast. He blows forward in her, and her horse lurches and bucks in electrocuted fury, sending her flying. Defiant of gravity, she hurls toward the starred, green eyes.

The unicorn flares backward, and Ethiops strikes with the obsidian blade. In the same fateful instant, Falon hurls the charm, catching Morgeu's shoulder a glancing blow. The impact of the witch-queen's magic throws the demon violently out of Morgeu's body, a black wind pulling banners and battlesmoke after him as he falls off the earth and plunges through the day sky toward the starved moon.

A hurricane blast lifts the arms of the dead like supplicants and whirls crows, loose helmets, and leaf litter downwind with a roaring rush as Ethiops flies past on his way into space. Limp and shivering, the unicorn lies in its black blood, its life-force a shadow widening its circle through the matted grass.

Morgeu and Falon sit numb in its shadow, which is a piece of night under a pelt of stars. Around them, saffron vapors of sunlight carry the cacophony of battle into the blue sky, but within the darkness of the unicorn's spilled life, a hush holds. The two souls stained by it, gaze mindlessly, full of the emptiness in which the animal bleeds.

The confusion of the battle engulfs Ygrane. Positioned on a broad avenue within sight of Londinium, she is supposed to ride with the Graal into the city, but Severus Syrax has not opened the way for her. The gates remain shut, and the queen's caravan and Merlinus with his Wheel-Table are stopped by burning barricades.

The infantry that Uther placed around them has been destroyed by waves of the Furor's elite warriors, Death's Angels. Plastered in white ash to resemble corpses, the deathly fighters loose volleys of flaming arrows and leap howling through the streamers of tar smoke, battle-axes flailing. Kyner's horses mill and his men struggle to pull them about before this terrifying assault.

The twenty-seven fiana posted to guard the queen loose arrows at the enemy from among toppled wagons and spilled freight boxes. But the smoke from the flaming volleys and the close in-fighting offer few targets. Battle-axes crash through muscle and bone, and horses topple screaming. Other steeds rear and scream back and churn around, seeking escape in the press of frenzied killing.

Kyner heaves about from the thick of the fray, where his broad Bulgar saber, Short-Life, flashes crimson as it hacks at the ghoulish warriors. Half his men are dead. Through the torn smoke, he sees fiery wings drag darkness across the sky as more tar-burning arrows loft toward his line. And through their veils of smoke, more corpse white howlers charge, cutting down the packed horses like top-heavy seedpods.

Signing for the drummers in the war carts to signal a retreat, Kyner gambols among fallen, thrashing horses and hacks at the gruesome ax-men rushing toward him. By deft horsemanship, he eludes them and breaks for the queen's wagon. A new line must be formed, though already he can see that defense now is hopeless. Death's Angels whirl out of every quarter. His only reasonable hope is to die before he sees his queen defiled and murdered.

The riders who can obey the drum retreat fly after him, hurrying toward the caravan where priests kneel and druids dance in prayer. Clattering onto the stones of the highway, Kyner bellows at the queen's black-draped wagon, "Show the Graal!"

Ygrane cannot hear him. From the moment the fighting began, she has been in trance, summoning the unicorn. She regrets sending it after Morgeu—and this poisonous feeling carries a bitterness from four uncompleted lifetimes as queen. Four times through history, she has presided over the defeat of her people in battle, and the blood of slain champions stains her soul. This is her punishment for betraying Morrígan by stopping the sacrifices and serving the chiefs. Her people are doomed.

In a darkness nine times the depth of night, cold rage twists in her for betraying her people. Her selfish hope of saving her child has used up her magic, and she has no power to send against the barbarians. The Graal alone offers strength, but she is too small a being to carry its glory. She needs the unicorn to conduct enough of the Graal's force to change the timewind. And she knots with rage at having sent her familiar away during this dire time.

The unicorn, feeling the queen's suffering, has hurried to return and, inflamed with her poisonous bitterness, has dared to slay her enemies. The killing inspires a deadly fury in the beast. With each thrust of its tusk, the life-forces it spills from organic bodies jolts through its antenna, and it tastes the lives of humans.

Acrid solitudes sluice through the star beast. It tastes squalid misery, fear, anguish, brutal physical pain inflicted by others of its own kind. And the ugliness of these dim, cruel lives compacts to a wrathful urgency to pull away and flee the hideous narrows of the Dragon's pelt.

Then Morgeu abruptly comes clear from the Dark Dweller's shadow. The sight of the queen's daughter jars the unicorn loose from its fury. The queen's fiana shouts as he rides closer, the charm he bears touching the air with a hot pressure like sunlight. In sudden response to this gleaming magic, darkness filled with bigness pushes from beyond Morgeu and hurls her from her mount.

The unicorn leaps back, too late. Reverberant pain cuts through the animal to the queen's core, and she cries out. Her handmaids flurry over her as she wrenches free of trance, and she pushes them aside and clutches at her swollen abdomen. The unicorn's death shadow has passed into her. And it webs as well the tiny heart in her womb.

Lailoken stands atop the rim of the Wheel-Table, despairing at the whirlwind of fighting he sees in the crowded fields. The gates of Londinium remain closed, and there are no archers on the ramparts offering covering fire. Uther and his cavalry have disappeared in the battlesmoke, and the wizard knows he must go to him. The king will need the dragon-magus. But the fighting on the highway is thick. Kyner's soldiers grapple with enraged waves of Death's Angels. If they break, the caravan's left flank will be exposed, and the trophy-mad barbarians will soon be killing each other for the right to kill the queen. The table—the Graal—all lost!

The sorcerer scans for allies and finds none near and no one aware of the queen's plight. Each of the Celt chiefs battles desperately in his own tangle of blood-mad tribesmen. The fiana and Kyner's remnants alone protect Ygrane.

For an instant, Merlinus marvels at the lethal military cunning—the evil intelligence—that has so furtively delivered the allies to this desperate moment. Someone has deftly coordinated the series of raids that has opened a path to the queen's wagon, and he squints down the length of his staff, looking for demons.

First, he spots Azael, his mammoth bulk hunched nearby. Still as a mountain, the demon concentrates on guiding the Death's Angels through the tangled mob of fighters to the queen. His unbodied, weightless shadow is the psychotic force of the frenzied tribes.

Merlinus swings his gaze along the road and sees, closer yet, Ethiops. The demon coils about a knoll on which are strewn the dead bodies of the Y Mamau. Morgeu on horseback hunches under wolf pelts in the afternoon heat, a black dagger in her rigid grip, while her head lolls and her livid hair swings like a bloody rag of clawed meat.

The wizard stands taller at the sight of the unicorn, and his heart's brails reach but cannot grasp. Shouting mutely against the uproar, Falon rides through the war mist, a charmstone in his hand shining like a piece of the sun. Abruptly, Ethiops seizes Morgeu in his coils and flings her at the unicorn. A lifetime's suffering cries from the beast as the ritual blade pierces, and an instant later, out of the black-tented wagon, the ray of Ygrane's shriek shoots from her darkness.

Before Merlinus can react, Ethiops rushes away as if from an exploding star. With black coils stretched out and vaporous as a whipped comet, he swiftly disappears over the world's brink, twinkling briefly as he burns through the atmosphere into space. Merlinus holds on to his hat, his robes lift, and branches and tufts of sod whip past in the demon's wake.

Immediately, the wizard chants protection for the queen and searches for her with his brails to be sure she is unharmed. He feels her gigantic pain—the unicorn's death killing her—and he yelps as he breaks contact. Jolted, he teeters a moment on the rim of the Wheel-Table—then freezes, his face a blur of fear.

Astride the road, the Furor towers, giant storm silver beard streaking away from his hideous face like the ferocious rays of a star.

Merlinus falls to his knees and cowers behind his staff. The Furor has won! Ethiops has put death in the unicorn—and the unicorn, the gift of the Furor, puts death in Ygrane's womb. Azael slaughters Uther's army under the walls of Londinium, where Ambrosius and Hengist died. And Lailoken cowers in dread before the rageful god.

The shouts of the wizard's demonic words whisk away in the Furor's proud laughter. Already, the music in the god's soul frames this victory to a story he will soon sing to his daughter, Beauty, and to all the shining Æsir: Their magic has given him the power to command Dark Dwellers from the House of Fog and to crush the champion of the Fire Lords!

Gray robes, vast as veils of rain, swing outward from the Furor as he aims his spear.

Lailoken stands, still shouting his futile barbarous commands. His strength against the god is as a shout against a tornado, yet he stands defiant, now that he recognizes his death is inevitable. Lightning crashes in the attic of the sky, and the Furor's one eye swivels with rage and fixes his aim with spiteful accuracy on the creature the Fire Lords fashioned.

"You and your masters want to murder the future—but the gods of this world deny you!" The Furor frowns so hard his skull seems to leer through his flesh. "Lailoken, enemy of the Wild Hunt! I cursed you once! Now you will know dying!"

The spear hurtles at Lailoken, a bolt of lightning directed by the gaze of the enraged god. "Optima!" the demon-man wails for his mother, for the Mother, for Her, who birthed him to this death.

The bolt sears past Merlinus, singeing his beard, laving him in white heat. His conical hat snaps away, and the silver hairs of his head stand straight out, bristling with a crackling static charge. In the lightning-glare of the near-miss, he sees the Furor's wrenched eye loosen with disbelief and then stupefied shock. He aimed to kill his enemy and does not want to believe what he sees.

Heat slaps Merlinus from behind, and he crouches low, staff braced crosswise in his hands to fend a blow at his back. An instant later, his alarm widens to astonishment. The war god's spear has soared across the battle plains and landed among Horsa's men—striking Azael! The river slopes where he was hunched in concentration swirl with white flakes of ashen remains, a blizzard of incinerated astral flesh that floats into the dying wind like milkweed tufts and dandelion fur.

The Furor's death-masked warriors lower their weapons, shaken by the blue bolt that has blasted the heart of their army. Sudden thunder wrings the air, and they fall back in confusion from their assault on the queen's caravan. Kyner's men hurtle after them across the fields. Swiftly, they break the barbarians' confused line and scatter them into rabid, individual fighters, enraged spin-offs to be swiftly enclosed by lancers and bowmen and pierced with death like boars.

Merlinus jumps from his high vantage on the rim of the table, eager to reach the wounded queen. The Furor's incredulous face remains only a stain in the brown air. He will stand there for days, his wrath broken, stupefied by the incense of his defeat, the sickening smell of war—spilled entrails, scorched flesh, rot, and fear.

The wizard lands on his feet, shouting for buoyancy, and the bounding recoil of his spell shoves him across the road and up against a barricade of toppled trees and upturned wagons. Exhausted from fright, he stands there senseless for a moment, only gradually becoming aware that his nose brushes a crimson slipper.

When he lifts his eyes, he meets the tired frown of Ygrane. She has crawled from the wagon and used her presence to block the god's spear. Simply placing herself in the wizard's vicinity protects him, for the Furor took an oath upon the Storm Tree not to spill the Celtic queen's blood—an oath his spear has obeyed.

When the Furor's deflected spear strikes Azael, the explosion knocks Uther out of his saddle and plops him among severed entrails. The battle stops. Fighters become gawkers in the echoes of thunderous aftershocks, looking everywhere fervidly to see who calls lightning out of the blue.

Sorcery!

The sky fills with the twilight murk of Azael's plasma, and the sun dims to a watery red moon in a purple sky. Thick mist hangs like webs in the sudden calm, motionless as the smoke of decomposed stars. Shadows flit rapidly through the gloom: Síd warriors with their rib-whittled lances stabbing the dazed, fallen soldiers of the Furor and skewering their ichorous souls to be fed to the Dragon.

The pulses of energy from the Furor's bolt, the Celtic queen's massive burst of deflecting force, and the unicorn's spilled life attract the Drinker of Lives. It rises toward the planetary crust, and its magnetic presence heaves up through the cavernous Otherworld into the landscape above.

Clouds like a jagged mane, eyes of blue Carnarvon rock and Highland shale, with its gullet in the long Tamesis, the Dragon drinks in the squandered power of gods, demons, and mortals alike. Wray Vitki rides this upsurge of dragonforce for one final glorious killing dance. Black as a beetle, with dragonish shoulderplates and a helmet of steel teeth, he manifests against the yellow lacquer of demonsmoke. He rides Uther's horse—and the surf of a roar builds as the troops spot him running through the enemy, harvesting storm-riders and Death's Angels with the sword Lightning. The allied troops surge forward with murderous zeal, thinking he is the king. And he is.

Uther slips and slides in the gore where he has fallen and struggles upright. He, too, holds the sword Lightning. Wray Vitki has copied him and the sword. Figuring that the magus has probably mimicked his horse as well, he looks for it. In the tan haze it is hard to see anything clearly, and he gropes among shadows of men lanced upright and staggering about with ghastly wounds.

He finds his horse shadowed against the broken yolk of the sun. Standing atop a fallen warhorse, he mounts his steed and rides after his forefather. The sepia battlefield glows with eerie, muffled lights and smoky flares. Renewed sounds of struggle resound dully, voices shouting as from the deep. He rides through this phantom landscape with the sword Lightning braced against his pommel, ready to swing right or gouge left. But none approach him. None see him. He is a ghost, as are his horse and his sword and his future.

In the twilight murk, Wray Vitki shines with his own black light. Uther sees him leading his clansmen in brilliant cavalry sorties, slashing in and out of the enemy ranks with a dancer's precision, inspiring his men to bold and savage attacks. He rushes to a gallop, yet still he cannot get close to the swirling horsemen.

All around the king, the feral-faced Síd reap souls with their lances. They march with the stabbed amoeba shapes of human souls to the river and feed the Dragon. In the onyx-slick water, the amorphous blobs re-form briefly into their previous shapes, and drowned figures roll into the depths and wave like clouds of krill before sinking into the black maw of the behemoth.

Above the river of souls, Londinium shines like a palace in the gloom. The gates are flung open, and Severus Syrax marches forth at the head of his elegant army. Soon, with the *magister militum's* remorseless phalanxes pressing the tribes away from the city into the killing range of the cavalry and the encircling Celtic chiefs, the rout sweeps the Furor's people—warriors, women, and children alike—into the sedges. After that, the slaughter continues in narrowing whorls.

Uther sickens and slides from his horse. With the sword Lightning for prop, he kneels and heaves hollowly over a lopped hand. When he looks up, Wray Vitki stands over him. The magus removes his steel-fanged visor and his squamous visage wrings Uther's soul. It is the adder-eyed, hasp-jawed human face of his nightmares.

"Grandfather Vitki—" the king groans.

The magus, who has lived five hundred years staring at danger, forcing the details of every difficulty to take on the intensity of magic, salutes his distant grandson. Though the young king is but a weak changeling of the lethally cunning men who preceded him, he is good. Five hundred years of battles and bloodletting to create a king gentle as a priest. Where his chest would be, the dragon-magus feels pride—a mysterious warmth that binds—a near-love. That is the emotion that he has chosen to be his last human feeling.

Overhead, spears of sunlight shred the brown effluvia, and a fresh breeze sighs from the forest and rolls the amber fog into the river. Wray Vitki's long life is over. Uther reaches a hand out for him, in gratitude for doing the killing that he could not. Grandfather Vitki turns away and does not look back. His human form scuttles to a lizard shadow in the mists.

Merlinus finds the queen in her black-veiled wagon, lying among pillows and bolsters, attended by her clever, quiet handmaids. She glows pale as a candle. The charred pain of the wounded unicorn crisps in her.

"I must feel how you hurt." The wizard stands beside her pallet and leans close, touching her with his heartflow. The drain of energy she has suffered buckles his knees, and only his staff steadies him.

Merlinus places his hand on the queen's wrist. He hears the inner wind with his fingertips, the bloodrush in the human tree, and detects a slicing whine in the wind that seems to whistle from low in her pelvis. "You bleed!" he cries in alarm.

A subtle flex of iris tells him she knows.

"Can we save the baby?" Merlinus asks her as a healer, taking her chill hand in his.

"I want you to tell me, wizard." Her eyes close. "The unicorn dies. Does that mean my baby must die?"

"I will find the unicorn—heal it," Merlinus promises.

She shakes her weary head and watches him through narrow, tired eyes. "No. Let it go. It is too dangerous. Death rides the unicorn now."

Merlinus looks to the queen, silver eyes shimmering.

"And Theo—" She grips the wizard's forearm and pulls strongly enough on his life-force to brighten her strong eye. Among charcoal scrawls of pyre smoke, Uther sits in the mud, whole yet hollow-eyed. "He suffers."

"I will go to him," Merlinus promises. Dizzy from the queen's tap of his strength, he removes his arm from her grip. "I will bring him to you."

The queen lifts her head and cocks an eyebrow at the tall wizard. "You can heal the unicorn?"

Merlinus shrugs and stares impassively.

Ygrane sinks back. After she garners her strength, she speaks again, with some effort, "I saw Theo. He suffers."

"Rest now, lady," Merlinus advises.

"Morgeu—Falon—" Her drowsy face holds a sad, apprehensive expression. "The unicorn's shadow is upon them, too."

"Ethiops—" Merlinus blames. "You were right to use your magic to drive him out, after all. He would have destroyed your daughter and the unicorn together."

The wizard turns to leave.

"Wait—" Ygrane calls quietly. "The unicorn is yours, Myrddin," she whispers, without lifting her lids. "I will call it for you. But be careful. The pain . . . It is mad with pain—Heal it if you can."

On the knoll where the unicorn was wounded, Falon and Morgeu remain. They stare up at the lovely darting of birds and at the fields of death on all sides. The whistle of the void threads both their hearts. They have felt the unicorn's dying, and they are changed.

Falon, dazed speechless, mute, dreambound, cannot seem to focus his will long enough to talk. The fiana lead him away, shaking with joy to see him alive and shivering dreadfully at the sight of him so thin and leather-tanned his eyes look jeweled.

No one will go near Morgeu, and she does not budge. The punctured bitch masks of her slain Y Mamau watch from the chewed mud. She remembers everything but feels nothing. The loss of Morrígan has deprived her of her magic but has left its hollowed imprint in her soul. What, for now, is emptiness will fill again, in time with new force, for Ygrane's love charm blasted the demon loose and yet left her whole.

Can her mother love her still? Yes, she answers to herself.

She accepts that now. How could she have been so blind? Morrígan relieved an atmosphere of hazard for the young woman, and in Morgeu's groveling gladness to possess the magic of the goddess, to acquire her own power, she ignored obvious truths. The goddess was too powerful and filled her with a wrath far more vehement than either her body or her soul could have carried much longer without damage. The realization stirs her numbness as she lies here on that field of death. Her mother is not her enemy. Indeed, she has saved her from certain madness. So, Ygrane is still the prize, the coveted source of love and authority, not to be harmed or defied but cherished and exploited.

Her mother, after all, is a witch-queen with the shadows of former lifetimes ever present. Sitting in the smashed grass with the dead for witnesses, Morgeu knows that she will never be a true witch, not in this life. She has neither the sight nor the glamour. Yet, if she works hard with the imprint of magic that Morrígan has left behind in her, she will again walk out of her body to visit distant places and she will discover for herself how to ensorcell with voice and presence. She will make herself an enchantress.

The witch-queen's charm has worked. Depths of love open their abysses, chasms, and gulfs before Morgeu. Down there, in the inmost regions of her heart, a destiny awaits. She has witnessed firsthand the advantages of political power in the duke's court where she grew up, and she sees now that she can have that influence for her own. She is the daughter of royalty, and she will, through love and the wiles of love, claim her place in the kingdom that has been won this day.

Yet, darkness pools at the bottom of her heart. The shadow of the unicorn's dying fills her with the absent love of her father, an absence which must yet be avenged by blood. She ignores the fiana's guard and the handmaid that her mother has sent to collect her. She will not hear their voices or see their gestures. Before she can leave this knoll where her magic died, she will face the one who killed her father and gave her to Morrígan.

When Merlinus arrives, looking for the unicorn, Morgeu stands. Where the etheric beast has bled, the grass has gone gray in a perfect circle four paces wide. Morgeu leaves prints as she crosses the ashen ground. Her small, tight goat eyes gaze directly at him, sharp as a curse.

The wizard slants his staff to protect himself, and the fiana edge closer, ready to sweep Morgeu away at Myrddin's nod. Bareheaded, his long, sallow skull exposed, he clearly displays aspects of the demonic in the bone-hollows of his temples and eyepits.

Morgeu pauses and opens her cloak of wolf pelts, exposing her nakedness. Blood smears her white body, streaked in brown spirals around her breasts and womb—the sigils of Morrígan.

"Love me, Lailoken," she taunts with a sultry sway. "Love me for what you've made me." With the last syllable still in her mouth, she flies at the wizard, the obsidian blade angled to pierce upward, in the manner her father taught her to kill with a knife.

Lailoken speaks love to her. But the demon Ethiops's imprint in her is too deep, and the word sounds hollow. Morgeu collides against his staff, her grimace wrathful and clear-eyed. The jet blade catches in the fabric of his robe and tears his garment as the fiana seize her violent body from behind and pull her away.

The wizard speaks sleep, and that finds ample resonance from the unicorn's shadow that stains her soul. She slumps unconscious in the fiana's arms, and they gratefully whisk her limp body away.

Merlinus watches after. She cannot always sleep, and love will not hold forever between them. Lailoken passes a quavery hand over his numbed face, the stunned flesh still tingling from this woman's hateful stare, and he cannot imagine how he can undo the fatal bond between them.

Merlinus walks the field of aftermath, through the stink of death and the last wisps from the murky smog of demon's blood. The battle has trampled thousands of corpses, crushed, and smeared them into the muddy loam. Through the amber haze of late afternoon, he is glad to see that the fighting has ended. Horsa's minions slouch south, milling at the horizon, bearing their wounded away in a weary retreat.

Across the misty fields of strewn dead, in a dark archway of the forest, the unicorn shines like a star. Merlinus stops. The maimed hurt of the creature jolts through the wizard's heartstrings, making him pull back.

The unicorn has seen him and approaches, hobbling down the green velvet hills where the wetlands bunch up against the primeval rootwall of the forest. Merlinus can see its wound, an inky gash at the base of its gazelle neck. All around it, flies hum in the fetid wind and butterflies light upon the carcasses of men and animals. Now that the fog has burned away, the clarity of the air is so crystalline he can count the flies mizzling on the blue lips of the wound.

The unicorn lies down in a muddy field littered with dead—rib cages hollowed of viscera by dogs, faces without eyes, purple clubs of thighbones—

He approaches the dying animal. It rears its head and slashes its horn sharply, then flops in the mud, exhausted by pain.

The stricken beast stares without color in its eyes—black gaps in its face. The deforming pain torques the unicorn's spine, and it twists in the mud. Merlinus brushes back the forelock while he mutters a chant.

A bubble of white light expands rapidly from the unicorn's forehead, passing swiftly through them and brightening the whole landscape. At the blinding center, the unicorn shivers with the earth's strength coursing up its nimble legs. The inky splotch of gashed flesh bleeds away in the glare, taking its poisons of pain with it.

When the wincing brightness gusts off, Merlinus holds the horn of the unicorn in his hand, and the black wound shows no change at all. Yet the beast rises stronger and rests its whiskered face on the wizard's shoulder. He rubs the animal's brow, and it slides its muzzle off his shoulder and hobbles back toward the trees. Merlinus wants to follow, but he has much else to do and so stops and watches the white beast disappear among the sunny stencils of the forest.

Merlinus finds Uther sitting slumped in the mud among the wild stones and the dead bodies of allies and enemies. Three times he has swung the gore-dark sword Lightning at his own men to drive them back from where he sits, trying to convince them he wants to be left alone. Flies haze his grimy body.

"Uther!" the wizard calls, and motions the befuddled guards to stand aside.

The king points the sword Lightning at him, waving him off, but the wizard speaks stillness to him. Merlinus has only to murmur the spell in the putrid calm, and the king begrudgingly lowers the sword and sits still. He seems neither dazed nor bewildered. An animal lucidity shines in his amber eyes, and Merlinus dares not speak sleep to him—or forgetfulness.

"The queen—"

"Sends for you. She has lost the unicorn—and she may lose your child."

Battle fatigue holds the king's brain to this hurt and something like curdled starlight in his eyes reveals tears. The child is the life of the alliance, the future of their kingdom. These truisms have lost all their meaning for him—but for his queen he imagines such a death would be a black omen, and he weeps inside for her. Before he can ask if the wizard has powers to help her, Merlinus places a calming hand on his shoulder, and he sinks back into his ruminations.

"Grandfather Vitki died here," he says, with sad ease. "Died where my brother died, in the shadow of the city where our father died."

Merlinus trembles to think of the significance of metaphor and history brought magnificently together by death—it is a demon's thought, and it feels saner for him to put it out of his mind. He drops a whistle through his beard and bends closer, hands on his knees.

The king gazes around at the corpse fields and the necrotic pall under the vivid blue sky. "War is dead," he says in the stillness of the wizard's spell.

Has the Furor's spear touched him? Dread memories of that narrow hell chill Merlinus, and he reaches out with his heart strength to share Uther's damage. But no—the king is whole, only enraptured by the huge stained altar of the earth. Savage memories of the fighting drone busily in his jarred bones and torn muscles. Horror and exhaustion have fused to an embracing alertness.

Merlinus sits alongside him in the mud and whispers ease. Uther's shoulders unlock and slump, and his head hangs. "I have failed as a king, Merlinus."

"Failed by what standard, my lord?"

"What standard?" He sighs and sweeps the flies from his face. "My standard is life, Merlinus. Look at the dead!" He sticks his sword in the ground, grips the hilt guards, and presses his forehead to the haft. "I can find no tears, Merlinus. All my weeping went out of me on the march. Now war is dead."

With another curving whistle, Merlinus shoos the flies away and turns the king's attention back to the moment. "War is not dead." He puts his arm across Uther's shoulders and gently pulls him back from the sword's hilt. "But, if you wish, I can make you forget this war—all war—"

His eyes slant angrily. "No. I don't ever want to forget." He breathes deeper. "War is dead for me, because I will never forget! Grandfather Vitki and my brother found the spirit for war. I cannot, I tell you."

Merlinus hums a quieting spell.

"Grandfather Vitki died this day, Merlinus," he explains softly. "It is a fearful thing to think I am the last of the Aurelianus men he will ever serve. For as long as I live, I will never forget the killing glory he gave me." He thrusts to his feet and points at the sword. "Wray Vitki is worthy of the sword Lightning. Not me."

He limps three paces and falls to one knee. His guard rush to him and hoist him upright. Then, straightening himself painfully, he marches from the field in locked arms, leaving his sword behind.

Merlinus removes the sword Lightning and follows Uther through the yellow afternoon to the ferny banks of the Tamesis. While he bathes in the cool water, the wizard washes the war sword, cleaning it with kelp and moss. Mounted bowmen watch from onshore, and several cavalrymen in full armor wade in to their hips. No one speaks, because the king is silent. He floats chest up, like a corpse.

Severus Syrax arrives with a parade guard of city soldiers in shiny brass and elegant plumes. Last into the fighting, he is eager to be the first to announce to the king the complete victory of the Britons and Celts over the north tribes around Londinium. Bors Bona, Lot, and the cavalry have chased down the family wagons of the retreating hordes and massacred whole tribes. Horsa himself has been taken, and his head has already been rushed to the city and paraded through the streets on a pike, to reassure the local citizenry.

The king's nostrils flare, and Merlinus speaks peace, and Uther lies back in the blond water and sinks out of sight. The wizard calls Severus aside. "Go at once to Londinium and stop all desecrations of the enemy. Prepare the way for your lord and his lady, queen of the Celts. They will have the entire governor's palace. Clear out all others and post only fiana and the king's bowmen on those grounds. We will join you there shortly."

Uther surfaces with an angry, hurt cry, and Merlinus moves to chant ease over him. But he chops his hand out of the water. "Stop it, Merlinus!" He slogs from the river and waves aside his men, who have hurried to the baggage train and back with a casque of robes and tunics. "No more spells. I want to see Ygrane—alone."

Dripping wet, he strides through the ferns to the turf-cut steps in the bank. Merlinus follows him, the sword Lightning in hand, as the king runs faster up the grassy shore to his horse. Silently, he throws a crimson riding mantle over his nakedness and gallops away, leaving Merlinus, hands occupied with staff and sword, standing among cattails in the solar drift of late afternoon.

Across a field of carcasses, under a clear sky fluttering with heat lightning, the king rides to the queen's camp. Barricades have been pulled down and stacked for bonfires, and a camp for the wounded has been erected around the Wheel-Table and the pavilion tent with its blue-and-white banner of the unicorn.

The fiana greet him somberly and escort him through a maze of wounded Celtic warriors lying on rush mats. The worst wounds lie closest to the queen's tent. The queen's priestesses, their sea-green *camisas* splattered in blood, work alongside druids and field surgeons to tie off severed limbs and stitch ruptured abdomens. Moans and agonizing cries leak from a thousand personal hells.

A handmaid lifts the tent flap at his approach, and Uther moves brusquely through the tunnel tent and the veil of pendulous draperies to the dim interior of the queen's chamber. She sits in bed, her brassy hair sprawled over linen less pale than the ghost flame of her face.

"Theo—" Her swollen lids open wider. "Is that you?"

He kneels at the side of her bed, his face immersed in her hair and the forest scent of her.

He is wet and smells of the river, and she is glad for it, because he is alive and whole. When he raises his head to look at her, she smiles strongly. "It is by your victory this day that I am feeling stronger," she says bravely.

"Are you bleeding?" He scans her face for signs. "Merlinus said the unicorn was wounded—and the child is in danger."

Her smile fails her. The child lives in her yet, but just barely. "The unicorn is gone, Theo." Her eyes brighten with tears to say this, and Uther sags prayerfully beside her.

With the unicorn wounded, he can sense her magic working against her now: She has told him before that in her trances, she sees pink, splintered bones, the glistening eggplants and white grapes of spilled entrails, death and gruesome torments. Is that morbid vision fulfilled now by his gory victory—or must she, too, bear death?

Ygrane presses a thumb to the worry crease between his golden eyes. Her pain has gradually begun to diminish now that the unicorn's tranceful energy passes from her to Merlinus. In her last trance, she glimpsed the unicorn in a halo of blue cold, wounded but not dying—suffering to live, like the rest of life. It pads through the humid light shafts of the forest, carrying its black wound heavily.

That image has faded slowly behind her swollen lids as the unicorn's magic passes. With her husband finally beside her again, it gives her a strange upwelling of peace to discover she is slowly becoming ordinary. As the sun sets, she knows she is losing all her powers—her sight and her glamour—which, over the years, have bonded with the unicorn's magic. Now, it takes them away from her, and she is glad to be returning to the way she was as a child—secret and mysterious to herself again. When she closes her eyes, she sees only darkness. Her life as a witch-queen has ended and a new future waits invisibly in the shining dark.

"Something old in the wanting has been fulfilled," the queen murmurs, her voice frayed.

Uther presses closer and prays with her, as she taught him the day they first met. "In you, God, there is no evil that is not a greater good."

He orders a bed to be made up next to hers so they can share their helplessness. Seeing themselves so weak, so small, the king and queen of the land laugh with brittle darkness. The incessant groans of the wounded in the war camp nearby remind them how far they have come from the blithe figures who met in a shrine of peace but seven moons ago.

Wrung tired, exhausted from the unicorn's pain and loss, and with no countervailing magic left to bolster her, Ygrane glides in and out of consciousness. "Theo—" she whispers down the slip face of her wakefulness. Though they laughed together, a darkness shines in her husband's drawn features, and she reaches for the words to reassure him before she glides into sleep again. "Do not doubt us . . . though war has brought us together . . . love binds us . . . "

Uther clutches her hand as she slides into sleep—or is it death? He bends to listen to her breath until he feels assured she slumbers. Then he stands and stares down at her, memorizing the wracked exhaustion in her glossy eyelids and settled features that open a deeper beauty for his inspection.

If she lives, her work will be far harder than dying now, he realizes, and so he prays for God to release her. Let her slip away into sleep, he prays. But clearly she wants to live. Her knuckles glow with their grip on the rubyflame. She and the child are indeed the story of the future. Uther Pendragon is the past—the last of the Aurelianus clan marked by the dragon-magus.

He shudders with marrow-cold remembrance of the battle. A fatigue wider than the numb ache of his tendons and joints saturates him. Seeking courage, he places his hand on his wife's stomach. From here, there will be no dragon-magus to rise up and win battles. Whoever this child is, such a soul will have to cut his own way through the war-torn world.

"You will have to be strong," he whispers to the unborn child. "Very strong indeed to make a difference in this world, without a dragon." A ripple of movement under his fingertips charges him with an even brighter alertness, as if the future listens. Against the livid groans of the wounded, he does not raise his voice but whispers even more softly, "There will be Merlinus, of course. He will protect you, as he protected me—" He tastes the saltiness before he realizes that he weeps. He wipes his eyes, rejecting sorrow, wanting a greater blessing for his child. "To help the world, to help all the other souls of your age, child, you will have to be much more than protected. You must be noble of heart—worthy of the greatness Christ proved."

Sacrifice. The thought makes him wonder what alchemy of blood and mud and these infernal cries of suffering work in him?

He kisses his wife's forehead, proud of her, and straightens, surprised enough by her cadaverous chill to feel again for her life. Assured that yet she lives, he rises, and on his face, there is a change—no tears any longer, but a look of resolution, proud as clouds folding away from the sun.

With an escort of bowmen, Merlinus carries the sword Lightning to the queen's camp. The king, in black cavalry armor over a purple tunic, has already mounted and waits for the wizard outside the camp. He calls Merlinus aside and dismisses the bowmen.

When he and the wizard ride off alone on the tamed battlefield, he sheathes the sword and points to the billows of pyre smoke blowing wider across the sky like shreds of sunset, or gusts of God's laughter. "Our enemies are dead, Merlinus. My work is done."

"Only begun, lord," Merlinus corrects. "To rule is to serve—and you have only begun your service."

"I am not the one destined to serve. You know that, wizard." He holds up a tiny, finger-length scroll of poplar bark tied with a lock of hair.

"I have fulfilled my destiny," he says with flat certitude. "There is nothing more I can give—unless I accept the elk-king's offer."

Merlinus squints with surprise. He did not see this with his strong eye. He reaches with his heartflow, feels the king's tight, unrelenting weariness, and mutters, "The kingdom needs you here, my lord."

"No." He shakes his head to keep from laughing maniacally in the wizard's face. "This land does not need a king unhappy with war. I've already told the druids, and Dun Mane has given me this. It's a spell I am to read—when we are well away from here. The druid wrote it for me on the spot with a stick of charcoal and tied it off with a lock of corpse hair. I'm not to open it until we are three leagues due west." He points his horse in that direction and spurs it to a smart canter. "Come, Merlinus. We are off to the Raven Spring."

"Lord, I do not think this is wise," Merlinus says, hurrying to keep up. "It will be dark soon."

"*Now*, Merlinus." The king directs his steed away from the killing plains toward a copse of blossoming cherry trees. Petals blow about them in flurries of spring snow.

"Drinking from the Raven Spring defies your faith," the wizard sputters.

"Another discourse with Optima's wise demon?" he asks with a sad smile. "Do you know how tired I am, Merlinus?"

"Then stop. Come back to camp," Merlinus presses. "Make this decision with a clearer head."

"My head has never been more clear," he answers, his voice hollow. They shoot out of the cherry grove into an open, empty grassland. Across the feathery field to the tall chine of the hill, they gallop, then settle to an easy gait. Below, the wide river plains of the Tamesis shine with all the laminated distances of Britain—the golden sea to the south climbing west in darkening stains of swales, rising from green effluvial basins in the east, through blue hills stacking northward, to the purple gutters of the sky.

Merlinus sees he will not be able to sway Uther from his plan easily. To fill the silence, they talk faith and philosophy, as once they discoursed among the weedlots beside the horse stables in the City of the Legion. The spell of ease that the wizard twice chanted over the king has given Uther some respite from his physical weariness. Merlinus seriously contemplates talking sleep to him.

"And finally it comes to this—" the king says. "This momentary thing called a decision. Did you not teach me that the right decision is a chisel? That it can cut the diamond of fate and shape time?"

"I might have said that," Merlinus admits reluctantly. "But that is not to say you should drink from the Raven Spring. Uther, I have seen no such end for you in the strong eye. I saw your battles—neither defeat nor victory. I beg of you, my lord. You must stay alive to decide this outcome."

He shakes his head adamantly. "No, Merlinus. Grandfather Vitki is dead. I felt him die around me—and inside me. Can you not see? War is over for me. I cannot fight for our people." He gives Merlinus a slantwise look, as if he has just realized something about them. "You think I'm sacrificing myself." He drops a hard laugh. "I am not sacrificing myself, Merlinus. What I am doing this day is *selfish*. My God, think of what Ygrane has yet to fulfill. My work is over. God made me king for this reason alone. To marry the souls of Christians and Celts. Today, the alliance is baptized in blood." He nods and holds his wizard's owling gaze, sure of himself. "And I *want* to go back to the elk-king. Remember that to the queen. I *want* to dance to that music—for a long, long time. Long enough to forget the screams."

"Yet not just now, Uther. What if Ygrane loses the child? What of the danger to come from the Furor?"

"That is why it must be now, Merlinus." He locks on to the wizard's dark gaze with an expression of incisive clarity. "I saw Ygrane. I spoke with her. Our child is alive in her. But she is dying. You know that, and you cannot stop it."

"The unicorn's shadow passed into her . . . " Merlinus tugs his hair fretfully. He cannot think of a reasonable way to dissuade the king from the Raven Spring, and he frets because he knows Optima would not want this. "Prayer may heal Ygrane. The Fire Lords may come—"

"She is dying."

Merlinus cannot extricate himself from the king's steady stare. "Yes. The fatality of Morgeu's blow passed through the unicorn to Ygrane. She may well die. The blow has already killed her magic."

He gives one nod of unceasing conviction and directs his gaze forward. "If I go to the elk-king, he will send her life. He promised me that. He *must*, to keep the child alive. He has sworn that my death will save them both."

"The one for the many," Merlinus says wearily, and they enter an oak forest pungent with damp decay and the hot pollen of flower carpets. "Who will rule the kingdom?"

"The great warrior soul that the Síd sends to be baptized my son."

"It will be a dozen or more years before he can rule—"

The king shakes his head. "I have no answer for that. I trust in providence—and you, Merlinus. You are a demon, for God's sake. You will certainly not misjudge evil. My son, my kingdom, my memory could be in no better hands."

Merlinus looks at his knobby, mottled hands and throws them up in despair. "So then—everything is in place, my lord. God has put it all together for you, hasn't She? The Britons and the Celts—Wray Vitki and the unicorn—Jesus and the elk-king—" He jabs his staff at the windows of heaven in the dark canopy. "Then why not trust in God? Why take fate into your own hands at all? Why drink of the Raven Spring?"

Uther smiles calmly, pleased with his wizard's loyalty. "God made me king because He . . . or She, as you insist, knows I can do this. I never wanted to be king, Merlinus. You of all people should know that."

"Yes, and for someone who wanted to be a priest," the wizard chides, "you are acting too much like a pagan. Sacrificing yourself!"

"My soul is in no jeopardy," Uther assures him, quite seriously. "My faith is not contradicted. I go to a pagan place now—and something pagan comes into this world Christian. What I am is not changed."

"Merely moved about in God's economy," Merlinus mocks him; then shakes his head solemnly. "Good cannot follow evil—even if done for the sake of good."

At this challenge, Uther holds himself poised in a moment of self-reflection, then asks, "You believe my bargain with the elk-king is evil?"

Merlinus pauses. "I can guarantee no truths about good or evil. But I beg you to consider that the faith of Optima that converted me from an incubus—that is what you are abandoning. Does that strike you as good?"

"I tell you, I am not abandoning my faith. That is not what the elk-king requires. I am a Christian now and hence."

"It will be difficult to dwell in pagan paradise a Christian, my lord. They dance for animal gods, you know."

"If God wills, I shall convert them." He dares a laugh, as if he well knows how frail his jest is. "What lies ahead will be easy for me. Going on will be far more difficult for Ygrane."

In good conscience, Merlinus cannot allow the king to drink from the Raven Spring. Not in his current state of mind. The man is wrung by battle fatigue and ranting about converting gods! Merlinus decides to stop him with a spell and let him rest before delivering so final a decision.

With a whistle, he calls the horse to a stop, but the king realizes instantly what his wizard is about to do. He kicks his spurs hard, and the spelled horse leaps up with a startled twist.

Aghast, Merlinus watches Uther fall. The wizard, caught in midspell, cannot shout the levity that could soften this blow. The king's head strikes the ground first, then his body. He lies on the thick, happy grass of summer, empty, already looking as if he has fallen apart.

Merlinus's heartflow clogs inside the hammering of his own heart, and he must force himself calm before he can reach into Uther to grasp his life. He finds only a husk—abandoned bones, still heart, clotting blood. For a horrified span, he listens to the crepitant noise of the body's capillaries closing, joints creaking as the ligaments begin their slow, sure tightening toward rigor mortis. Then the wizard lets go and closes the king's eyes.

Uther Pendragon is dead, the back of his skull smashed in. Merlinus's spells are of no avail, he knows, for Uther's soul has been knocked out of him and already dances to the Piper's tune.

Merlinus reels about, horrified that he has killed the king. "Not willfully!" he calls aloud, to the shard of moon. "I only tried to stop him from killing himself!"

Madness whines its shrill note in the demon visitor's nerves, like a tsetse carrying its lethal chill to his pith. He drops his staff and paces circles around the broken body, hands tugging at his hair, distraught, helpless. The angry thought tightens on him that he should kill himself.

Frantically, he grabs the king's buckler and tugs at the sword Lightning. As the silver-blue blade rings free of its scabbard, he staggers backward. Finding himself with the maker of death in his hands, a grimace of determination seizes him. He drops to the ground and begins gouging a hole in the mulchy earth beside the king's body, wanting to brace the long sword firmly, blade up.

Sobs wrack Merlinus as he works, spilling his rage at himself. When he is done, the sword stands buried to the hilt beside Uther, at a convenient slant for the wizard to heave himself upon. But, having spent so much strength erecting the blade, he does not have the necessary fury left to do the deed.

He stands swaying before the lucid steel, crazy-eyed, the taut strings of his face strumming. Behind him, blue space charges off in every direction carrying the full freight of summer—brains of clouds, bird flights, streaking dragonflies, wind-borne blossoms.

Merlinus cannot kill himself. All that he lives for denies him that fulfillment. What horrible thing he has done, contravening all his mother's prayers for him, he will have to live with, warped in his heart. He grabs the sharp blade in both hands and slides forward, slicing open his palms, feeding the pain to his hopeless remorse.

The wizard writhes, bumping his brow against the dead king's thigh, clutching his cold hand.

"You *are* changed utterly, Lailoken," a dark, gleaming voice speaks from above him. "I had never thought I'd live to see a demon sobbing for a dead gutsack."

Merlinus's bleared sight touches boottips of yellow leather, and he lifts his woeful face to the tall, angular frame of Prince Bright Night. His rubescent hair flows in an unfelt breeze across his dimpled, grinning face. The scars from his battle with the demons at the royal wedding have faded to thin pale lines in the ruddy hues of his complexion. He has picked up the wizard's staff, and he leans on it as, with his green, tapered eyes, he gazes down upon Lailoken.

"I killed the king!" Merlinus blubbers.

"Did you now?" The prince extends a hand and raises Merlinus upright. "And look at your hands!" He clucks and tears a linen strip from his blue tunic. Then, he bites the hem and rips the strip in two. "You've become near as foolish as any mereling mortal, Lailoken. I wouldn't have believed this were I not now seeing it with my own eyes."

Merlinus stands numb as water as the elf prince binds his cut hands. "Uther is dead," the wizard mumbles.

"Of course." He ties off the bandages, tightening the knots with his teeth. "He gave himself to the elk-king, did he not? They struck a deal."

"But *I* killed him," Merlinus moans.

"Not so, Lailoken." Bright Night places the sole of his boot against the sword Lightning and kicks it over. "I chose this very stone for his last pillow. And I pulled him from his steed myself."

"You—"

Bright Night passes a hand through his loose, bright hair, bends down, and plucks from the king's glove the tiny scroll given by the druid. He tugs loose the lock of corpse hair, unfurls the birch strip, and passes it to Merlinus. Written in futhorc, the spell reads:

Each pore of the flesh is the Raven Spring—
A wish is enough to join the Elfin King.

Merlinus gapes at the note, reading it repeatedly. When the sense of it finally penetrates his anguish, he falls to his knees and retches emptily into the happy grass.

Ygrane wakes refreshed and empty of pain, and she knows at once. Gone, what he was to her becomes more true. Loss and fear clash with the bounteous joy of her child's health. Life fits her sweetly. And death escapes with her mate.

She prays for Theo. She prays to his God, to her God now, and their child's God, to watch over him. And she weeps to think of him, a Christian, fulfilling the ancient love of the sacrificed king.

After her prayers, Ygrane goes directly to Morgeu, determined to end their bitterness. The fiana hold the young enchantress in a small tent encircled by torch lanterns. No one has dared raise the tent flap since they brought her here after her attack on the wizard.

Ygrane dismisses her fiana and enters the dark tent alone. Animal humidity encloses her, and the interior throws shadows from her lamp. Morgeu lies on a straw mat, curled up under her wolf pelts, asleep. Without her magic, the queen does not feel the fateful imprint of the demon in her daughter.

So, the queen sits proudly for a while beside her, listening to her breathe. Her child sleeps beside her untroubled by dreams, let alone demons. Ethiops is back in his hell and Morgeu belongs again to herself, and for that, Ygrane is glad that the last magic she worked was for love.

Prince Bright Night helps Merlinus fashion a travois from saplings and boughs, and they place the king's body on the litter behind his horse, arms crossed over his naked sword.

"King Someone Knows the Truth will keep his promise?" Merlinus asks anxiously. "He will send his greatest warrior soul to Ygrane's child?"

The elf prince tilts back on his heels with an unhappy expression. "I will favor you, Lailoken, by not telling him you asked."

The wizard frets with his beard. "It will take a great soul indeed to match the sacrifice my king offers to the Raven Spring."

"Cuchulain," the prince says, and a charmed reverence fills the air between them like a field of force. "Our very greatest warrior has come forward of his own will to protect his people. Already he swims the sea of forgetfulness in Ygrane's womb."

Merlinus nods with weary satisfaction and mounts his horse. "I will come to the Otherworld and see that Uther Pendragon is satisfied with his lot."

"Come if you wish," Bright Night says, handing him the staff. "You will find his soul blissful as all who dance in the eternal woods."

With that, he backs away and vanishes. Merlinus reaches over for the reins of the king's horse and leads it, with Uther's body trailing after, back to the battlefield outside Londinium.

They arrive out of the red haze of the setting sun. Ygrane awaits them, summoned by the cries of the sentinels. Her vibrancy, with young life somersaulting in her, persists. She waves aside her concerned handmaids and approaches.

Before she can see for herself, Merlinus falls to the ground and announces to the flame-glossed faces of the camp, "Uther Pendragon, high king of the Britons, is dead."

Ygrane does not flinch, though tears start in her eyes. She kneels quietly over his body, mindful of the life that thrives in her—his life welded to hers. She brushes the long locks of raven hair from his blue face and regards him only briefly. This grief is no surprise to her. She is a warrior's wife. What surprises her is the absence of his voice and his golden stare, gone now into emptiness, leaving behind this mere effigy of a life.

How vast seems the void into which the life of her lover has so swiftly disappeared. The whole of the past has gone ahead of him, and yet that vacuum remains as empty as before. For an instant, anger flares through her, and she wishes darkly all future to cease. But in the next instant, she feels the baby thrash in her, and her ire flees before this assertion of life.

Handmaids help her rise, and she faces Merlinus with shining eyes. "I do not think it was painful," she says, and presses her face into his chest. "For that, I am grateful."

"You know how he died?" Merlinus asks.

"My magic has passed from me," she says, her forehead against his bony rib cage, "yet I knew when he died. My weariness emptied from me, and I became well. I know how he died." She holds herself closer, and her voice comes out muffled against his robe. "The Raven Spring."

"His last word was your name," Merlinus tells her truthfully. "He thought of you—and the difficulties ahead."

She pulls away from him with frowning, drunken dismay. "What will happen to the child?"

Merlinus has not yet thought that through, and his blank look frightens the queen.

"The demons will try to kill him," she says, her voice tinged with trepidation. "The demons that made the Y Mamau. Myrddin—we must be more careful than ever. Theo cannot have died this day in vain."

"I will protect the child with my life," the wizard swears.

Ygrane closes her eyes, gathering her wits, and when she opens them, they are clear and level. "Go into Londinium, Myrddin, and find the city's bishop," she orders. "Tell him to come to my tent."

Merlinus obeys and finds the bishop not in the city but in the dusky field blessing departing souls by torchlight. Only the red manelletta on his large frame and the skullcap on his square head declare his station, for he has the muscular breadth and leathery mien of a hardened soldier. Merlinus tells him of the king's death, and he seizes a torch from one of the priests and trails the wizard through the watery glow of last light.

Outside the queen's tent, they remove their muddy boots and enter the orange, lamplit interior. Before a low table strewn with pussy willow and sugary blossoms of chestnut, the queen sits, unmoving, paying her visitors no notice. Her eyes are red, but she is not crying now. Her servants bring cushions and offer a tray of honey cakes and goblets of cider. The bishop and the wizard are hungry and eat while Ygrane sits on her faldstool, staring deeply at the flowers. "This is an altar to the *Annwn*," she tells them in a distracted voice. "I have been praying here for salvation from the invaders—and for the health of the child in me." She smiles tenderly at them. "Both my prayers have been answered."

The bishop expresses his condolences for the king's riding

accident and begins to sketch out funeral plans, suggesting a grand procession across the very plains Uther has seized from the enemy.

"Such matters I leave to you," the queen interrupts him. "I summoned you here not for my husband's soul—for that is already in God's hands." She bows her head. "I summoned you, Holy Father, for your blessing. I have decided to live out my life as a Christian."

The bishop blusters with surprise. "The druids—"

She cuts him off with a sharp glance. "Till this day, the druids have had all of me. But no more. The child I carry will be the high king of all Britain, of the Celts as well. Uther and I have already agreed. Our son will be a Christian."

"Whether son or daughter," the bishop's thick voice fills the tent, "Jesus welcomes your souls."

Ygrane kneels and receives the churchman's benediction. After a cursory catechism, he departs, leaving his crucifix among the floral offerings on the altar of the *Annwn*.

Merlinus shakes his head knowingly. "You are no more Christian than your husband was Celt—yet he died in the old way, at the Raven Spring, sacrificing himself for your child, our future."

Her face brightens. "Theo is . . . my lovea, Myrddin—my true love. And is not love the soul itself? Then, my soul is already in the Greater World, dancing, singing praises to the *Annwn*." She puts a hand over her swollen breasts. "And I am all that is left of Theo's soul in the Lesser World. I will honor his Celtic death by my Christian life."

Secluded by alder thickets, Falon and Ygrane face each other on a mossy embankment of the Tamesis. Cumulus clouds rise above the river, pink and orange with dawn, trawling fiery shadows in the placid water.

"A Christian?" Wearing traditional buckskin trousers and

boots, sword strapped to his naked back, Falon stands stunned before Ygrane. His head feels as though it carries a load of hay. In a moment, someone will set fire to it, he is sure, because he feels a flush of heat rise up in him. Is it anger or ardor? He cannot tell, because his body is a haze of aches. He most sorely misses the queen's magical medicines and her glamour. Most of all, he misses her. She seems—absent. On reflection, that seems inevitable to the fiana, for she has lost everything—her king, her magic, the unicorn—and now this difficult revelation, this loss of her faith in her own gods! He rocks back on his heels and gazes at the billowing swell of clouds. Sometimes he wonders if he is still in the Otherworld, eternally wandering, and all of this sorrow since the wedding is just a long ghost-walk.

Ygrane tells him of her conversion, of Uther's sacrifice for her dream-filled womb, of her vision of Miriam, of the living past shared by ancient Hebrews and Celts. Falon listens remotely. The unicorn's shadow still stains his soul with its otherworldly silence. What speaks to him more loudly are the daisied banks and violets that he sees over her shoulder, where a heron stands on its reflection.

Ygrane pauses. Without her magic, she cannot reach into him and make him understand. The light breeze that stirs the slender grasses has more to say to him than she does. Carefully, she studies him in the morning light, looking for damage. The vampyre has left her scar—a beet-dark vein at the side of his throat where she affixed herself each night—but that will heal. He looks harrowed by his wanderings, yet still strong. The unicorn's shadow will pass, too; she can tell from the way Falon takes in the world. He will live whole again.

Relieved, the queen steps closer and places her right hand against her warrior's cheek. "You are a brave man—and the best of my fiana." Then, she removes the gold torque from around his neck.

Falon's hand rises to intercede and stops when he meets the steadiness of her green gaze. "Older sister—what are you doing?"

Ygrane smiles softly. "You are free, Falon. Your service to the queen is accomplished."

Elbows up, hands at his throat, Falon stares with astonishment at the queen. "I don't want to leave you," he reveals. "Everything desirable is here with you."

She holds his ardent stare serenely, then tosses the torque far over the river, into the vermilion water. "The queen is gone, Falon." She addresses his startled, unreachable center as though she still possesses the power of her glamour. "The queen is gone."

"Who will rule the kingdom?"

The queen crosses her arms protectively over her unborn. "Not I. The chiefs will decide that among themselves. I am returning to Tintagel to birth the king's son." She offers him a fragile, hopeful look. "In a few years, he will need a war master. Will you come to him then?"

"Let me come with you now."

She laughs grittily. "You followed me into the Tree of Heaven and you've wandered the underworld for me, Falon. But I do not believe you want to go where I must go now." She gently takes his hand. "I tell you, the queen is gone, and she has left me a woman of peace. I return to Tintagel to found an order of worship. You are welcome."

"To worship the nailed god?" Her hand feels small and feminine, lacking entirely its vivid, silvery charge. All she has said is true—the queen is gone—and that leaves his soul feeling like a pail of water. It will be hard to carry and easy to spill. Emotions slosh in him—anger, disappointment, melancholy. He squeezes her dull, human hand until these feelings slow down enough for him to see his face reflected in the water of himself.

"He is *Yesu*," Ygrane tells him. "He has come to heal each of us. Will you let him heal you?"

Falon releases her hand and steps back. "No. My older sister has already healed me. She is queen of the Celts, witch-queen of the Daoine Síd. Her magic healed me years ago."

Ygrane nods, glad for his faith, and steps a pace back from him. But the way he looks at her makes her feel beloved, and that stirs her uneasily. These thwarted feelings set her child wrestling in the womb with its own unsuspected destiny, and she speaks abruptly, to cancel the mood: "You have served me well, younger brother. You've faced gods and werebeasts and never flinched from your devotion. I have a reward for you. The chiefs have agreed to set aside land for you in each of their provinces, so you will have homes in every corner of Cymru."

Falon starts walking backward. "No, older sister. I am *fiana*—a wandering warrior. I hold no property and am held by no one but the queen. Where she has gone, I must go."

As he turns away from her, the wind coolly touches his neck. Where he used to wear his torque, he feels a new leash— freedom.

Ygrane lives her word. After Uther Pendragon's funeral in Londinium, she returns to Tintagel, taking her vows to become a nun. Eventually, she founds the Order of the Graal. Many of her fiana convert as well; others find sanctuary with the pagan chiefs and drift west with Falon and the last of the druids.

The elk-king lives his word, as well. He directs life energies to Ygrane from the roots of the World Tree, and her pregnancy flourishes. Late in the summer, under the white star of Venus falling and the legends of blood rising with Mars, she gathers her handmaids into a circle of power and squats among them.

But the magic is gone. The next contraction is coming. That is all she knows now of memory and prophecy, all that remains of her fabled sight. She floats on her pain as on a pale, glacial lake. Clouds shimmer in the lake. They are souls. Some have died and are drifting away. Others arrive to be born. One of them is her child. He is coming. She has called him to her as she called to herself the baby's father, Uther Pendragon, and before him the demon-wizard Myrddin, and before him the unicorn, the Furor's gift . . . and before that the pale people . . . the faerïe . . . All a dream now. All illusory before the searing, exhausting pain.

Ygrane delivers a robust, fair-haired boy, with the yellow eyes of his father. When she wakes from a sleep opulent with dreams of her husband, Merlinus has to dissuade her from naming the child after Uther.

"My lady, that name would be a death sentence for this infant."

She receives him on the western terrace of the citadel above the cliffs and steaming breakers of the muttersome sea. The round table has been set up and the Graal placed at its center to honor the birth of the future king. Ygrane lies on a couch draped in floral silks, the baby at her breast. Merlinus crouches on a stool beside her, having just examined the newborn's body for the dragon's mark—and found none.

"I sore miss my magic, Myrddin," she confides. "Without it—without the trances, I cannot sense if demons are near or far. It frightens me, for I know their hate and purpose endure."

"Stronger now that you are of Uther's faith," the wizard agrees. "They and the Furor will do all in their power to slay the boy before he grows to manhood."

Ygrane gazes out at the shining sea with a smile of happy defiance and speaks in a voice that is low, pure, and clear: "Morgeu was a failure of love, Myrddin. My failure. This child must redeem that. Not just for me—or for Theo. This child must live for the sake of love itself." She strokes the pale babe in her arms. "Are you absolutely certain that the home you have chosen for him is safe?"

"If you would let me tell you, your heart would be glad for the home I've found for him."

"No. I dare not know. I fear the Furor's magic. I must not know anything about the child's whereabouts."

"Then know the name at least," Merlinus offers, wanting to give her something, for the difficult moment is upon them when she must release the child to him. "You must have that for your own."

She is silent, staring at her baby, at the life that has grown out of the inner place, the sacred place where her magic has dwelled, where she once saw the unicorn and the face of the man she would love. "There is a name," she says at last, looking at Merlinus with surprising serenity, given the consequence of the moment. "It came to me at prayer, when I was chanting the Holy Book. The passage in Matthew about loving your enemies. It was clear to me then that this child's name should be neither Celtic nor Roman, but a name that the enemy will never suspect. It must be one of their own names." She speaks to the child, "You will be called Eagle of Thunder—no." She fetches for a title. "Royal Eagle of Thunder—Aquila Regalis Thor."

The calm center of the sorcerer receives this name with kindness. The Roman eagle fused with the Celtic thunder symbol of the dragon both bespeak Uther. "Lord Thunder Eagle."

"Yes," she says with a mischievous gleam in her green eyes. "But we will call thunder by the name of its barbarian god—Thor. And that will be the name of this king of Britain, the Royal Eagle of Thor—an enemy's name—spoken in their tongue and ours, so they will understand that his greatness encompasses them as well as his own people. Aquila Regalis Thor." She lifts the baby from her breast and holds him out for Merlinus to take. Her blond face smiles so openly and with such goodness—not a shadow of doubt or withholding—that the wizard accepts the silken bundle as if gifted a robe, or a pair of shoes, and not the future king of the land.

Merlinus fumbles for something appropriate to say, but she stays him with a shake of her head that tosses hair over her face and veils the bruised sorrow beginning to surface. "Take him to his place of safety, Myrddin. Watch over him. And when he has grown strong and able, when he is worthy of his father's memory, send him back to me. I want to see him as a man—as a king. I want to give him the Graal with my own hands and tell him in my own words the story of Uther and Ygrane."

The wizard backs away, precious bundle held to his banging heart. "He will return one day," he promises. "Strong and able."

"I know." Her empty arms close around herself, and she sinks back on her couch, face shrouded by her hair, all she has left of her Uther gone from her now. "He will return. He has already begun his return. And when he comes to me, he will know me, and I will know him and call him by his name—Aquila Regalis Thor—Arthor."

—EPILOG—

Merlin: A Memory of the Future

He that made him can make his sword to approach unto him.
—JOB 40:19

Woman. Everything I am I owe to Her. *All the good and the bad in my life. All the sorcery and mystery. All the wisdom and madness. And here, in my hands is the future given from Her. From Ygrane comes a small, fragile being entrusted to my care. And from Morrígan, the shadow of his death. Between the two, I must make a difference.*

Merlinus silences his inner voice. The words come only with diminutions of his bodylight, which is his portion of magic. And he needs all the magic he can muster now.

The infant Arthor, still swaddled in his mother's brocaded silk wrappings, lies slumbering. While still inside Tintagel, Merlinus speaks sleep to him and spirits him out of the castle through a little-used passage that descends narrowly within the interior of the cliff. No one sees them emerge from a seacave that the tide hides twice each day.

Only gulls observe the sorcerer's flight among the incessant black rocks and exploding breakers. Robe flapping like a black flame, Merlinus hurries past tide pools and crescent dunes, the sea's wild vapors shredding around him as he hugs the baby to his breast. He climbs the limestone shelves that lead into the forest. At an elm knocked down by lightning, he stops and lays the sleeping infant in a hollow the owls made.

"Rest now, my king," he whispers. "When you wake, I will have found milk for you. But for now, rest a while longer. Rest on the dark brink of that deeper sleep out of which you have ascended. There will be time enough for waking to this world. Time enough—and terribly more."

Merlinus remembers the Nine Queens and the angels' plan for Arthor. He is to be a witness, awake for centuries. He is to be the first of his people's spirit-fathers.

But only if he survives! Merlinus's voice rises in him with precautionary intensity. Quickly, he silences himself, and his worry for this child's welfare throbs and glows in him like metal alive with fire. This is the raw stuff, the hot desire, from which he knows he must shape a weapon as sturdy as a shield, as precise as a sword.

With this pulsing dread, Merlinus plans to do so much for Arthor that he cannot hold it all in his mind at once. He breathes as the unicorn taught him, letting his thoughts spool away, unraveling into the energy flow of the universe, his perceptiveness calming and broadening like a river.

The shining amber grass rustles with the fetal stirrings of a storm two days away. Rains gather out of the air and out of the roaring off the sea and the furze of the bog water and all the mossy places of the forest. Rains gather like tiny thoughts. They swirl together with vast intent, gathering force to swarm into the British Isles. Dragging its chains of lightning, the storm will come and none can stop it.

This is the mind of God, he thinks, feeling the weather pouring into itself, coiling its might.

All dread passes from him. A greater intelligence will pull together all his plans for Arthor as surely as the tempest pulls together its pieces. The angels have a plan for this child. He must serve the northern race in the archaic errand of guiding the life of his people by dreams alone.

But that difficult hope remains years away, a lifetime distant. For now, the sky is clear, and a melody of birdsong crosses the woods amidst splashes of sunlight. Before the rains, there is milk to think of for the baby—and a place must be found where the child can safely hide from evil and grow strong on love.

Love! The word sounds strange. Optima's meticulous love stirs far back in his mind, behind memories of mournful Ygrane, whose love he carries with her motherless child. *Love*—and Uther dead for love.

The sorcerer must concentrate on his breathing again, to steady himself. He can hardly believe he is here among the wild cherry and rhododendron—with the king, the hope of the Britons. Optima's prophecy spills around him into the actuality of this moment. Brown, spent vines tangled like sea wrack among the old oaks hold his attention. A white butterfly, delicate as a soul, hovers a moment over the heather bells, then flutters away among sun shafts and branches and their aftermath of shadows.

He never imagined it would be like this, in a sunny wood above seacliffs, hoary and wizened as a desert prophet and growing younger. He thought he would serve the king that Optima prophesied in a palace, not a wilderness.

Slow, deep breathing restores Merlinus to the serenity that is the stage for the highest magic. Alert ease slides through him, majestic as a wide river. He closes his eyes and releases himself to the luminous darkness within.

Flowing with this energy reminds him of his darkest demon memories, touching the black spaces between the stars on his dreamless journeys to other worlds. How bitter he had been as a demon, yet even so, even in the grip of his fury, he knew this peacefulness. Under the face of eternal night, it had seemed like tedium. But since becoming mortal, since those first astonishing days when Optima snared him in her webs of blood and wove him this body, what had been tedium has become magic.

Merlinus reaches upward with his will for the portal above his eyes—the sixth gate, the threshold to prophecy. He wants to open his strong eye and peek ahead, just a little way, to find a worthy wet nurse for Arthor.

Instead, he opens his mortal eyes, and the moist sun shines in dew spangles among the grassy tufts and spider nests. Lady's-smock and celandine mix their fragrance with the spindrift whispers of the sea.

Arthor stirs, and the sorcerer hushes him with a gentle spell. The child needs milk. That is Merlin's first task as the king's guardian. Proudly he gathers the infant in the crook of one arm; then, swatting aside the underbrush with his staff, he strides through the forest's smoldering darkness.

In the ruby radiance within the earth, the Dragon feeds. A corpulent bliss possesses it, for it has absorbed the squandered energies of demons, a god, an immortal, and a unicorn, as well as thousands of tiny souls harvested by the Síd. The downdraft of energy fans the creature's hot, iron heart, and its dreamsinging flares brighter.

It sings with thoughts that, until now, have been more fugitive than deer. *All things will grow in the direction of light. Light means life.*

With vivid eyes, its empowered mind sees more sharply into its world and notices clearly for the first time the numerous shavings, peelings, ribbons of tusk that the unicorn has sent. They lie tangled in the marl of stardust that sifts through the cracks in its shell, iridescent slivers far too small to be noticed before, let alone handled and manipulated.

With its new clarity, the Dragon gathers the filaments from the dust and examines them. Seen up close, the wafers of bone reveal their secrets to the beast's stronger mind.

They are maps.

In three dimensions, they show the Dragon its other selves,

the scattered cells of its cosmic body. They show the Dragon whole.

Since confronting Morgeu in her wolf pelts on the battlefield outside Londinium, Merlinus has seen nothing more of that demon-worshiper, that spiteful and dangerous weapon of the Furor's. Nor has he seen the Furor himself. Or Ethiops. The witch-queen's charm flung him out of her daughter but did not break his power. He and the Furor will show themselves again and with cruelties that he as a demon can very well imagine—but only when they are lethally sure of success.

The child of Uther Pendragon and the Celtic queen cannot be left alive. The Furor, with his one mad eye of prophecy, can see the warrior soul of this infant and the many deaths and setbacks he can inflict on the war god's minions. And sooner or later Morgeu, with her iron conviction that Merlinus slew her father so that Ygrane could copulate with her dream lover, surely hates this issue with a terrible passion. Ethiops, too, eager to liberate Lailoken from his imprisoning gutsack, will try to slay this baby, if only to break Merlin's spirit and his mortal hold on life.

Never before has the wizard been so vigilant. From the day Uther Pendragon gave his soul to the elk-king, Merlinus has carried a profound burden. If he fails—if this child is maimed or killed—the enormous sacrifice his king and queen have offered of themselves will be canceled. The destiny his mother revealed to him, the hope that his God wove into time, will collapse to emptiness. The very emptiness in which he lost his God at the beginning of time. The very void that first inspired his demon rage.

For the hope of heaven, Merlinus dares not fail. That will have damned him to madness and, worse, to his ancient and destructive despair as a demon. So he lives with extreme caution. He avoids the strong eye, because that separates him from his body and his infant charge. Consequently, he must rely exclusively on the brails of his heart to reach into the world around him, feeling for his enemies.

On the walk through the forest to the village, he talks to the baby, to reassure him. "All shall be well, child. Fear not. I have been in far worse straits than this, I assure you, and each time there has been help—for we are not alone, you and I. Oh, not at all. There are the Fire Lords. They shall look after us. And the unicorn. Oh, yes. Though it lies wounded, it is a being of light, Arthor. It shall return to us and offer its help.

"I must tell you directly—in this our first conversation—that I should not be here now serving you except for the unicorn. It made a way for me in the world. Who would guess looking at me now, replete in my powers, that once I wandered the forests of Cos, insane, babbling in a singsong chant, yakking about murders? I had been touched by the Furor's speartip, and he drove madness into my brain.

"For years, I lurched crazed and disheveled through the dark corridors among the great trees, shuffling wraithlike into the loneliest wolf haunts, leaving shreds of clothing, hair, and flesh among thorny tangled undergrowth, and calling out in an awe-ful voice to the palpitating shadows, 'Murder, hunger, pain—the world is a fury!' And still, the dead stayed dead and the barbarians went on killing.

"When by chance I crashed out of the forest, sometimes I would see ladders of black smoke climbing to the sky from some thorp or villa put to the torch by the Furor, and I thought I could hear the mournful singing of the slain as their spirits climbed the rungs higher and higher—and not to heaven, as ignorant mortals believed. I well knew that no heaven awaited these souls above the sky's blue. I well knew that up there existed only eternal night and the cold of the void. The spirits climbed not to heaven but to the same oblivion that belonged to squashed spiders and skinned animals.

"In winter, I wrapped myself in the hide of dead beasts. I struck fire in dead logs with flint rock and stared and stared into the bleeding sores of the flames, into the ticking lives of the embers, counting their bright moments as they scabbed over with darkness and returned to the cold.

"I ate only dead things. Often, the poisons of putrescence left me buckled and writhing in agony on the forest floor. At those times, hours of retching violently left me with my lungs cracked, blood speckled on my face and arms, spent of any strength to rise or continue with my bitter harangue. Sometimes, faces like grinning dogs gazed from the sky, peering down at me through the chinks of the forest canopy. My old cronies—the demons.

"They cackled with delight at my suffering. 'Poor Lailoken—' they mocked. 'Are you happy now, brother—now that you have found God? How is the Great Lady, by the way? Has She spoken with you lately? Give Her our very highest regards when you see Her, yes? And be sure to tell Her not to forget us. We also are looking for Her. We want to be our own fathers, too—the same as you, dear friend. Yes, it looks so righteous and satisfying what you're doing, Lailoken, crawling around on the forest floor with the grubs and the worms, vomiting up your insides, eating dead things, spouting such wisdom, doing good for all humankind!'

"Cursed by the Furor, I blundered through the forests of Cos year after year, growing younger and wilder. The seasons sought their contraries, and time flowed.

"On occasion, I found myself on the high meadow where Optima had brought me into this mortal life. The hovel where she had lived had been dismantled by the seasons, and only a dodder-matted mound remained where her hearth of rude stones had stood.

"I looked in vain for the altar of smooth green riverstones, swept away in some muddy torrent of spring. But the stand of copper beeches remained. I knelt at my mother's grave in autumn fog and knee-deep snow and under the flowering wings of the beeches: Each time that my aimless rovings brought me to her grave, I knelt and my madness cleared briefly enough for me to pray, *Great Mother, Optima was Yours to take away—and now there is no freedom such as hers. Take me away, too. This is a world of death—and there is no sadder prophecy.*

"Naturally, God never answered my prayers, for I lived. Despite the hammerings of winter and the wretched abuse of my madness, I lived. Once, however, with a purple night riding tall in the saddle of the new moon, I looked up from my prayer to see the unicorn standing upon her grave. The long-maned beast raised its noble head before my wild gaze, and its nostrils flared. Yet it did not flee.

"I stood and held out a quavery bruised hand. At my touch, the unicorn's electricity hummed through me, and in my brain the blossoms of heaven opened. Their fragrance healed my madness. I jolted to my senses, and the twilight clanged around me with the vibrant clarity of a struck bell. All my raging seemed absurd. My madness had wasted energy that the world badly needed. That was the Furor's triumph—denying the world what good I might do. It felt so easy to put that craziness aside.

"I dropped to the ground and sat back on my elbows in the wet grass, gazing up at the pink-lit clouds and the silence of winter. Silence—for the first time in years! I guffawed incredulously. 'You broke the Furor's curse! In God's name—how?'

"The unicorn has been answering me ever since. In its healing presence, I not only gained freedom from madness, I calmed down enough to learn about my human body. I discovered the seven internal gates that regulate the flow of energy from the earth, through the body, to the sky. With the unicorn's quiet help, I learned for myself how to open those gates.

"Ah, but what do you, a baby, know about these gates? Well, you will learn, just as I did. And if you open even the first, you will be a great man. Of course, for me, a demon, the first gate was easy, because it is the portal of the genitals, the passage to a hell of hunger, fear, hate, and war—a hell that can dissolve into the light and the good and the truth and the love of one woman, one lovely woman, that loveliest of all women whom men call their soul.

"Healed by the unicorn, I learned about my mortal soul—my humanity. I constructed a humble but effective tree house in the upland woods near the copper beeches where my mother was buried. In the soft rains, I watched the unicorn when it visited the grave at twilight, and I worked hard on opening the other gates of my body. And all the while, I enjoyed the simple and astonishing beauty of spring in the forests of Cos.

"The more I learned about the power centers in my body, the greater my influence in the world became. With the opening of the second gate, the gate below my navel, electrical energy began to course up in me, and I acquired again the voltaic strength to affect in minor ways the stirring of the wind and the movement of clouds. My demon powers began returning to me.

"Then, with the opening of the third gate, the one under my sternum, that electrical power charged my muscles with inhuman strength. I could budge boulders and uproot trees—so long as I held that gate open. It closed once while I was hoisting a toppled oak, and the abrupt tug of gravity pulled my shoulders from their sockets. The pain knocked me senseless. Fortunately, the unicorn's magical touch repaired the torn tissue and ligaments in but a few days instead of the months it might have taken.

"A year flowed past, and I was sad the spring day when I had to leave my mushroom-studded tree house to track down the unicorn. It refused to come to me, and when I approached it, the beast retreated, leading me ever deeper into the western woods.

"Day by day, the unicorn led me farther from Cos. To keep up with it, even just to find it in the riotous undergrowth of the primeval forest, I had to open my fourth gate, the power center of the heart.

"In lines of feeling force, electrical strength rayed out of my body from that gate. I could feel deep into the world when it finally opened—and I was felt. Birds spartled through my shadow and settled on my shoulders. Butterflies haloed me. Flies, too, until I learned to focus the force bleeding from me into my surroundings.

"After I learned how to direct the heartflow energies, I could feel my way to any creature in my vicinity. Any thing, also. The unicorn was fond of hiding in obscure places, like behind waterfalls and in hedges lively with bees, until I became proficient enough to spot it before getting stung or soaked.

"I got good at tracking the elusive unicorn. I could feel its magnetic ruffling in my bosom, filling my lungs with its heaven's scent. It led me west out of the dank, trackless woods into a riverland of shimmering metals and glass.

"Mudflats and sandbars vibrant with herons, egrets, and geese streaked the dazzling horizon. Captured in a sorcerously inverted landscape, these waterfowl seemed massed like cloud strata in the sky blue of the smooth, unbroken river, while overhead, cumuli stood shoulder to shoulder, craggy as floating mountains.

"That was the first I saw of Cymru. I paused and listened to the pulmonary sighing of the forest behind me, balancing its familiar, womblike closeness with the open and wrinkled brightness ahead. The unicorn was leading me beyond myself into something grimly uncertain. But now I had come into my own, thanks to its guidance. I had opened four of my body's gates, and from them had issued potencies I had not possessed since my proud time as an incubus.

"Then and there, at the threshold of a future without parallel or antecedent in my uncanny life, I determined that if the

Furor should disapprove of my freedom and confront me again, he would face the wrath of a demon.

"But it was not my demon's wrath that thwarted the Furor when at last we did meet on the battlefield outside Londinium. It was your mother. Blessed woman.

"Woman, again, spared me, saved me for some greater good. *This* greater good, child—that I might live to know and serve you."

The wizard's smiling face presses closer and disrupts the infant's drowsy spell so that it feels again its pangs of hunger and cries.

"Oh my, hush, hush now!" Merlinus flusters, then mutters a sleep spell and hurries on his way through the smoky sunlight of the forest.

With a wet nurse from the village at his side to feed the infant, Merlinus carries Arthor north into the wild hills. This is dangerous work, because Morgeu and her Y Mamau once haunted these forests and may well again. His heartflow constantly circulates through the avenues of trees, and he senses nothing wicked on that journey at first. Then, a sudden weight of cold descends through the summer trees, and he recognizes the frigid touch of another's strong eye. Someone searches for him.

With one word, "Sleep," the wet nurse and the child plunge into dreamless slumber among plumes of fern and a spurt of dandelions. He puts his full wherewithal into the vertical river of an oak. He becomes the brilliant silence in the blazing brazier of its topmost branches. The cold gaze of the strong eye passes over them, and they are not seen.

The scent is unfamiliar, the taste of the milk strange. Arthor cries for his mother, and the nipple chokes him. After the recent comfort of his mother's warmth and before that the blissful uterine darkness out of which he grew, the forest feels alien. Wild rays of late sunlight hurt his eyes. Bird shrieks startle him. And the rooty smells of leaf rot and animal droppings cloud him with confused feelings. Where is the warmth that made him? Where is his mother?

He cries, and again the unfamiliar breast smothers him.

Far back in his nascent mind, this distress stirs shapeless memories. They flinch through him, viscerally reconstructing the first pain of losing the warmth that has nourished him always. In the crossbones of his shoulders spasming pain lives on from that fierce moment when his head was born. Squinting with unglued eyes, he struggled with purple effort in his mother's birthhold, and light burned his brain even as the cold burned his flesh.

Then, a dreamlike hallucination floated across his stuck body—a carnal vision of the kind that precedes reincarnation. And in that gruesome vision, the horror of agony was not birth but death. The pain in his shoulders became leather straps that secured him upright to a pole—a staff, no, a spear. His own spear, firmly stabbed into the earth. He hung from it, bound by tightening thongs of animal cord, so that he would die standing.

That was important. He forgets now why.

Swollen and grotesque from his wounds, he did not recognize himself as he stood apart, free of his body, watching himself die. His throttled throat wheezed blood, and his bloated head swung and drooled. Naked but for a golden ring about his throat, gold tarnished with blood. His long hair, plastered with gore, hung in hanks from his bowed head. The skin had split across his brow, and pink skull white shone through.

"Cuchulain!" someone cried in overlapping echoes.

A war whoop jumped out as if by miracle from that broken body, and the gory figure slumped dead. Stars of blood darkened in the dust at his bruised feet.

Arthor floated between two existences. The dead body of his former self bled radiance from its many wounds. The gaseous solar light hovered and swayed like *ignis fatuus* before the corpse, pulsing a brighter yellow and more sunlike. In its glare, the dead body faded to pastels.

Another figure appeared, strolling out of the sunfire—a smaller man and darker, wearing Roman armor of black leather. Uther Pendragon advanced amidst the solar haze, though Arthor-Cuchulain had no idea who he was. Another warrior—

"Yes," Uther spoke, "there will be war. And you must be a warrior again—for your people. We need you, the greatest warrior born of this land from all times past. We need you to defend your people."

A voice Arthor does not recognize—his own voice—answered: "I am sick of killing."

"There is balm for that sickness where you are going."

"No balm save death," answered the warrior's soul. "The world is a battlefield. Happy are the dead."

"No." Uther spoke kindly. "There is another balm, a greater balm, that I have denied myself so that you may have it. It belongs to the living and the dead."

"A brave death is a warrior's only balm," the unknown voice that was his own spoke. "All else is false joy."

Behind the shocking pain that still throbbed from the battle wounds and the birthgrip of the future, other memories flowed with pleasure and tumbled about each other excited and bubbling—a wonderful, enticing seductiveness of the Happy Land where the proud dead go. The lovely, unearthly side of him wanted to return there at once.

"Leave me dead—" he whispered, not strong enough to voice such weakness loudly.

"You are already born," Uther said, "as I am already dead. You will have my place in the world and I yours in the all beyond."

A great wave of sadness swept through Arthor-Cuchulain. "Then death enshadows me yet again."

"You have the strength to contend with the strongest of the living," the dark man with the amber eyes assured him. "That is why your living god has chosen you."

"The Great Dagda has chosen me?" The sun fog breathed brighter and abruptly warmer. "Then I am born of noble parents?"

"Yes," Uther acknowledged with a proud nod. "In this life you are noble. To fulfill that birthright, you must serve again your people with your very life."

"I tell you, I am sick of killing. Leave me in the Happy Land."

"And I tell you, I have the balm for that sickness—here." Uther began untying a cord from about his neck.

"Stranger, there can be no greater largeness of heart than to sacrifice one's life in battle for the love of one's own people. The letting of that blood is sacred."

"That is the truth," Uther agreed. "And here is the one who sacrificed his life for the love of all people—even his enemies."

From under his ebony breastplate, he pulled forth a small crucifix delicately carved in green stone. For all its tininess, the image was replete with wounds as gory as the badges of hell that Cuchulain's corpse had worn with distinction.

The crucifix rose before him, and shafts of dazzling radiance rayed from those many wounds and coalesced into the naked sun. The vision broke apart into the scalding colors of infant Arthor's just-opened eyes. Placental blood splashed beneath him, and as he skidded wholly forth, all memory of his former life slipped into a bottomless night lit with the untethered stars, erumpent flares, and spiritous fumes of the inner sky.

Those psychic fires glisten behind his shut eyes under the soft weight of the nurse's breast. She shifts her weight so that the warm flesh pulls away from his tiny face, and the earthy fragrances of the forest wash over him. He is frightened. He wants the familiar, trusted warmth again. He wants her back. And, as he blinks into the last brown rays of the day, his deepest self knows he will spend the rest of his fateful life returning to her.

Arthor remains in grave danger of exposure to his enemies so long as he is in Merlinus's presence. Swiftly as he can, the demon-wizard escorts the nurse and baby far into the wilderness, to the hill kingdom of Kyner. Merlin has chosen him because he is a Christian and a Celt. The future king will learn well from him both the new faith of love and peace, as well as the timeless lore of his mother's people.

His heart's brails lead Merlin directly to the camp of the warlord. Snaking coils of smoke twist above the treetops from the timber-walled enclave. The gates stand open, and a group of hunters are returning with a stag trussed on a carrying pole. This seems to the sorcerer like a propitious time to call for Kyner. From the emerald shadows of the forest, Merlinus feels with his brails through the busyness of the camp for the chief of the hill tribes.

He finds Kyner in the chief's long hall, under a wall mounted with antlers, teaching his young son, Cei, how to hold a sword. Cei is but a toddler and the wooden sword too heavy. The linen-diapered lad holds the hilt in both hands and pushes the blade along the ground like a plow. Kyner's booming laughter summons the nursemaids, who snatch the child away and leave the chief wiping merry tears from his eyes.

With a soft spell chanted over and over, Merlinus instills Kyner with the wish to stroll outside his camp. He emerges with both his hands in his red hair, his elbows high, stretching, breathing deeply of the afternoon's sylvan warmth. Adjusting his kilt, he marches into the forest, florid face uplifted to the shattered sunlight of the dense canopy.

Merlinus hushes the wet nurse to sleep out of sight under a hawthorn bush and places the infant naked on a bed of mushroom-riddled leaves between the root boles of an oak. The sorcerer waits behind the oak until Kyner spots the drowsy child and stalks toward it suspiciously. He swings his gaze all around and even searches up in the oak, looking for the child's mother. When he bends down and lifts the baby, Merlinus steps out.

"Myrddin!" Kyner gruffs, frowning off his startlement at the old man's sudden appearance.

"You do not see me, Kyner."

"I see you—" His blue eyes slim. "What deviltry are you about? I have no dealings with demons or wizards, Myrddin. I am a Christian man. Off with you!"

"I will be going, soon." Merlin chants a spell that widens the chief's eyes and opens the ears of his soul. "Now listen carefully to me, Kyner. When I depart, you will utterly forget that you saw me here. The child you hold in your arms, you will adopt as your own. He is to be named Arthor—Eagle of Thor—for he is a rape-child, inflicted by a barbarian on some anonymous village woman. She brought the infant here to lose its small life in the forest."

Kyner listens attentively to this lie, hugging the baby protectively to his strong bosom.

"You will rear Arthor a Christian," Merlinus commands, "and you will personally train him in all the manly arts. You will love him as you love your own son, Cei."

"Love him . . . " Kyner mumbles.

Merlinus slips back behind the oak and waits.

Kyner snaps alert as soon as the sorcerer passes from his sight and lets out a loud call that startles the infant to crying. Instantly flustered, the chief rocks the baby in his thick arms and hurries back toward the camp, where soldiers already rush forth to answer his call.

Merlinus gathers the wet nurse and takes her deeper into the forest. Arthor dwells in God's hands now. The sorcerer has done all he can to provide sanctuary for him, and he moves rapidly away from that place. So long as he is nowhere in the vicinity of the child, Morgeu, the Furor, and the demons have no way to identify this infant as the future king.

Eventually, Merlinus returns the wet nurse to Tintagel. But he does not go there himself. He purges the woman's mind of all she has witnessed and substitutes a fanciful memory of a treasure hunt, rewarding her with a pouch of gold coins his heartflow finds under an elm, in the skeleton grasp of a long-dead legionnaire.

Tracks covered, Merlin turns his attention to his next task, his last work for the dead king. He must retrieve the sword Lightning from the grave of Uther Pendragon.

Like ever-widening rings on water, eddies of sunset sweep aloft from a notch in the mountains where the day has died. The Furor strides over the alpine forests, wind and weather in his beard, scanning below among birch and fire-colored ash trees for Lailoken. He wants revenge. With his own hands, he wants to rip apart the fleshly body the demon has possessed and hurl the Dark Dweller back into the House of Fog.

The Furor knows he will not have that satisfaction this night. Wily Lailoken has learned much since their first meeting in the kingdom of Cos—how long ago? To the one-eyed shaman that seems only a moment ago. Lailoken had appeared such a pathetic thing then. How came he to possess the strength to deflect Blood Drinker?

"Demon!" he shouts in rage, and thunder lumbers across the horizon. He cannot accept that his Gulf spell has come to this—his magic broken, his conquest denied, and the whole world rolling faster toward Apocalypse. Irony scalds him. The one Dark Dweller that his Gulf spell inadvertently flung to earth has become the lethal sword of the Fire Lords. *Lailoken must be found and destroyed,* his hot blood cries.

The fires of his warrior's love for life, for his people, for the fertile, green-furred world burn more urgently in this defeat. He fights for more than himself and his clan. His furious passion is to defy a thing so profoundly terrible that it is greater than the gods and so to win he must be greater than himself.

Stooping through high mist to peer into dark gorges, he humbles himself in his desperate search, bending low enough to see cinnamon fern and edelweiss choking the ravines. His ivory fury even drives him to sniff for scent of his prey, and his lungs fill with the thick humus smell of autumn. But human musk is absent, and frustration bites his heart.

Since the death of Horsa, the Furor has vainly stalked these isles for Lailoken. Even the runes reveal nothing of the demon. That tempers the Furor's wrath with a little fear. If the Dark Dweller can hide from the runes, he poses a deadly threat, for that means he moves tangential to fate. He possesses magic, the true will that obeys its own divination.

The Furor chides himself for having thought that the madness from the touch of his speartip could incapacitate a creature from the abyss. He should have gutted that helpless-looking old man when he had the chance, he realizes now. The arrogance of his mockery, that is what poisoned his Gulf spell.

Sparrows bound down the wind away from the thunderstorm odor of the god as he rises and climbs into the sky with a slow, stamping rage. The red of sunset has drained away, and startling drifts and depths of luminous clouds blue as moonlight ascend the cobalt heights.

Hawks spin their rings on the wind, spiraling higher in the wake of the Furor's climb. Down the westward rim of the world stands the sickle moon following the sun behind the earth. Sunfire brightens the horizon at the altitude where the sky reaches the first auroral selvage of the Heights.

Keeper of the Dusk Apples waits there, having watched the Furor's wild pacing from above. She has drunk the least of the sleeping potion and is the first to wake. White-blond hair, wind-tangled by her long stay on this wild shore, covers her face, and the Furor turns away, not wanting to see her mocking smile.

"One Eye," she calls, her voice gentle.

Fah! Not mockery but pity! the Furor thinks, and walks away toward the brighter heights that lead to Home.

"One Eye!" Keeper calls petulantly. "Wait!"

The Furor pauses. "Keeper, I have no heart now for this. Leave me to myself."

"We have a bargain to conclude," she says, and sweeps back her knotted hair with one hand and offers a dusk apple with the other.

"What is this?" the Furor asks, frowning. "Don't mock me, Keeper."

"Lord," she says, and kneels formally, "I offer the reward I promised you for your conquest of the West Isles."

The Furor glowers. "Are you blind, woman? My enemies defeated me. The leader of my storm-warriors in the West Isles is dead. The Fire Lords have broken the Dark Dwellers I summoned from the House of Fog. I have lost."

"No, lord," Keeper says as the Furor helps her to rise. "Far below in the field you could not see, but from the Heights I have seen, and I tell you, One Eye, you have won." She puts her hand to his cheek as he shakes his head. "The armies arrayed against you have already disbanded. Their leader is dead. You know that."

"A Síd prince killed him," he mumbles. "Queer blood, those brethren. They slew their own king."

"As in Mother's time," Keeper says, shaking her head. "They sacrificed him to Elk-Head."

"Yes—Elk-Head," the Furor mutters. "I faced him down there."

"I know. You harried him bravely."

"Harried—yes, that's all I managed."

"No, lord. You did far more than that. You proved to me and to all the gods that the West Isles are ours. Our enemy's victory is hollow, and your defeat is only apparent, an illusion time will dispel. They have no one king to lead them against us, either among the mortals or the gods. Elk-Head must contend with the nailed god of the Fire Lords. They fight each other. I tell you, One Eye, they are divided and we have never been more united."

The Furor feels his heart thudding, no longer with ire but with thrill. "What you say is true," he admits, "because I want to believe it." He takes her ardent face in his hands and presses his brow to hers. She shivers to taste his hot odor with its acrid tinge of the battlefield.

Their rapport is tender, sharing, enfolding, and it shakes her, weakens her. That the king of the north gods needs her to know his own strength both frightens and ennobles her.

"I had thought you would mock me," the Furor confesses, stepping back from her, yet keeping his thick hand on her arm. "I deserve mockery for my arrogance. I was arrogant when I promised to take these isles so readily." His lone eye crinkles kindly. "But now I see, you are more gentle to me in defeat than I can be to myself."

"Not defeat, lord—not even a setback," she asserts proudly, "but a biding time. And I—and all the gods who witnessed your bravery—we will all bide with you." She offers the dusk apple with both hands. "You have won this."

The Furor demurs with a stern frown. "No—not yet. I will not taste of the dusk apple until we walk together among our people in the West Isles."

Accepting these words, Keeper of the Dusk Apples lowers her face.

The Furor lifts her chin and says, "Come, we will talk with the others, and together we will find the best way to break our enemies and spare the world Apocalypse."

Keeper, touched by some of the prescience that haunts her lord, well knows that the end will come in its time and cannot be diminished. Yet, she smiles softly and takes his heavy arm. They walk slowly but steadily, with the majesty of a certain future. Under the prosperous stars, they mount proudly toward the fluorescent summit of Home.

In Londinium, the Aurelianus brothers lie beside each other in the marmoreal vaults built atop the centuries-old columbaria of the Romans. Merlinus enters the funeral grounds at night. The torchlights of the city glimmer like tiers of attending souls on platforms stacked against the moonless sky. Above, starlight blows thinly, very thinly indeed, through the unspeakable darkness of all time.

With his spells, the sorcerer has no trouble opening the locked gates or sliding aside the marble slab that inters the young king. Necrotic vapors sigh from the crypt, filling the sepulcher with a mephitic stench that scalds his nostrils. Uther lies in the black cavalry armor and purple tunic in which he died. The sword Lightning remains in his grasp, hilt held to his heart, scabbard lying across his torso and legs.

The summer heat has done its work. White worms writhe in the soured flesh stretched tautly over his skull, and the ardent, eternal grin of his jaws already shows through the blackening shrivel of his lips. The life, love, and virtue of the man have fled this place and frolic now with the elk-king's dancers, leaving behind this exiguous flesh.

Merlinus requires spelled strength to pry the sword from the locked grip of the corpse. The sword Lightning slides from its scabbard in a transport of ethereal heft and liquid light. He lifts the sword in salute to the memory of the Aurelianus brothers and their service to the angels. In the reflectant surface of the broad blade, he shudders to see over his shoulder the blanched moonface of Morgeu.

"Is there no depravity below you, demon Lailoken?" The sorceress leers angrily. "Now I shall add desecration and grave-robbing to the evils of pandering and murder that I have witnessed of you."

Slowly, Merlinus faces about and levels the sword at the pallid creature. *Is she a wraith, or actually before me?* he wonders. The city lights glimmering through her frizzled hair lift a henna sheen from those tresses, and the scarlet silk of her robe drapes voluptuously from her nubile frame. He thrusts the blade, and it passes cleanly through her.

She flares a laugh. Quickly, he reaches behind for where he has leaned his staff against a funereal frieze, and her white face hardens. "All you have," she gnashes, "you've stolen. Your body you whored on your mother. Your knowledge you took from your past as a demon. And your weapons—the sword Lightning and the Stave of the Storm Tree—they belong to the Furor."

"Your master," Merlinus derides.

"My master is no stealthy thief, Lailoken. The Furor takes what he wants by fighting, not by craven and deceptive murder."

Merlinus snatches his staff, and the wraith backs away.

"I have searched long to find you," Morgeu claims. "Hear me, wizard."

"What do you want?"

"What I want I will have to take," the sorceress says. "I want your death. And I will have that, in time. In time."

"Not you and all the demons of the void," he swears, and stamps the staff hard on the marble floor. "I serve God."

"Ha! You serve madness."

"Begone, witch!"

"First, tell me where you have hidden my half brother."

Then Merlinus laughs, which he immediately regrets. It can only inflame her further and deepen her already-profound conviction that he is insane. Yet he finds such boundless ire in a mortal blackly comical.

"What is it you hope for, Lailoken?" Her tiny eyes tighten. "Do you really believe that the child of so obscene a lust merits a life? What is it you hope he will attain with his smutched existence?"

"He will be high king of the Britons and lord of the Celts, as were his parents before him."

"Will he?" She snorts. "I think not. The time of the Britons is over. The Furor will take their lives and their lands. This is cut in the crystal of time and cannot be undone. You should know, Lailoken. You were one of the demons who destroyed the Fauni, the only ones who could have thwarted the Furor. Now, all that was Rome's belongs to the god of the north!"

"My king will unite the Britons and the Celts," Merlinus asserts, "and the Furor will taste defeat again—" *Even if only for a generation.*

"A madman's dream," she sneers. "The Britons are doomed. As for the Celts, I am the daughter of the Celtic queen and the duke of the Saxon Coast. If there is to be a king of the Celts, he will be my son."

"And who will be the father? The Furor?"

"Mock me, as you will, demon. My kith will laugh through history at your pathetic efforts to rule this land. I am to be wed to Lot of the North Isles. This war chief reveres the old Celtic ways, and he will father true warrior-kings—by me."

"Does he know he marries a demon-worshiper? And is he aware of your alliance with the Furor? Does he want the mother of his children the pawn of an enemy god?"

Morgeu's stare flinches, hinting of fear. "He would never believe you. I have ensorcelled him with a love stronger than all your magic."

"I will not even try to break your hold on Lot—if you will leave Ygrane and Uther's son in peace."

Anger speaks in Morgeu: "Peace! Is that what you believe you cast upon the world with this child conceived of lust and murder?" She sweeps closer. "I will do all I can to destroy you and the stable master's son before you work any further malevolence in this world."

Merlinus swings his staff, and it slices through the wraith with a sound like pierced tin. Ectoplasmic fire spurts across the sepulcher, lifting the funereal sculptures brashly out of darkness—warhorses, angels, victory wreaths—only to plunge them back into deeper darkness in the next instant.

Morgeu is gone.

Quickly, with the gloom of her hatred thick about him, the wizard seals Uther's corpse in its tomb, locks the gates behind, and carries the sword Lightning away with him under the star-hooded night.

An unquenchable joy possesses the Dragon. The energy it has absorbed from the unicorn is sufficient for vivid, vibrant connections with selves that before had been faint and discordant echoes. Dreamsongs rise out of this joy and roll slowly away into outer space, toward the many worlds of the one Dragon.

In hours, the nearest worlds reply excitedly from inside their secret interiors. Pulse-thickening music returns from them. The Dragon basks in this lucid dreamsinging that it has evoked in the others by its own greater strength, and it sings more strongly yet.

Purling outward, the Dragon's ecstasy attracts an ever-wider circumference of interest. Each hour, new, more distant worlds respond with their joyful reactions. Day by day, the singing intensifies within the narrow, smoldering traverse of the galactic arc.

Searching for ways to vary the dreamsongs and deepen their beauty, the Dragon draws on the holographic models of the island galaxies that the unicorn passed along. So much comes clear with these accurate maps. The Dragon cells who possess these coordinates and who have the power can better direct their singing at the most remote worlds. Given enough time, communications can be established well beyond the galaxy, with little risk of squandering energy on the vacuoles between the galactic clusters.

The Dragon includes the sidereal holograms in its singing, enriching its neighbors. Their beatific reactions exalt the Dragon to the brink of paroxysm. Teetering happily there, it remembers how it came upon these holograms from the unicorn. They had been left in *payment* for the energy that the unicorn took for itself. At the time, without the strength to use them, the ivory peelings of horn had only potential interest for the Dragon. But now the true significance of the unicorn's gift reveals itself in the cascade of joyful song returning to the Dragon from its many selves across the deep horizons.

What has become of that fragile creature, the unicorn?

The dreamsong stops. The Dragon unfurls from its deep communion with the others and feels outward for the unicorn. Finding it is easy, for it is curled upon itself, motionless. Naturally, the beast is situated at the crest of a thick scale, out of reach, though this is unnecessary now, for its bodylight flimmers too dimly to stir the glutted Dragon's appetite.

It calls, and the unicorn stirs slowly, too weak to rise. The Dragon must listen very closely to feel the wraith chill of its contact. Its current has faded almost entirely away, and its field has little more charge than a common horse.

The unicorn sits in a grove of stunted cypress on a mossy crag where rivulets fall in threads from a rock spring. In the resined air, a falcon whistles and green finches scatter in caroming bursts through the shaggy trees.

The Dragon calls again. This time, the unicorn moves not at all. Shadows lengthen. The unicorn's silence thickens toward emptiness, and the Dragon sinks back toward its center.

"*Wait—*" the vague voice of the unicorn calls from far away, a silver mist of a voice, unraveling like smoke.

The Dragon pushes to the rim of itself, and thick fog rises from the boggy stream.

"*Dragon —* " the unicorn's voice ghosts from its still body.

"I hear you." The Dragon strains to reach out. The fog crawls up the moss shelves and into the grove of stunted cypress, and then at last the Dragon feels the unicorn's frail lightness again. "I have used the maps you gave me for my dreamsongs. I understand now your gift."

"*Help me*—" The plea floats on a wind of non-being. Its helplessness cuts across all their misconstrued history.

"How?"

"*I am dying. I want you to return my strength, so I may live.*"

The Dragon involuntarily clenches, coiling back into itself at this thought. To lose its unfading power now—to fall back from such bliss—

It stops itself from pulling entirely away. Still thrumming with the noble pride it has received from the others for sharing the star maps, the Dragon cannot deny the unicorn. The other cells of the Dragon want to repay the unicorn for its gift. They want this one cell, this dragon-of-earth, to give it the energy it seeks.

Full aware that when it gives this energy to the unicorn, it will become too weak to share the glorious dreamsongs of the others for a long time to come, the Dragon reluctantly concedes, "You will have back the strength I took from you."

"*Dragon, I need more*."

The request tears the planetary beast's heart, and thunder from below shakes dew from the cypress. "More?" The Dragon's question encloses the cypress grove in the silence of a gathering storm. "Why should I give you more power?"

"*To carry away the demon Lailoken*."

The Dragon reels backward at this, and a chill wind drives the fog off in waves across the wooded bluff. "If I give you that much of my energy, I will not have enough left to stay awake. I will lose myself in sleep."

The unicorn speaks in whispery filaments: "*Then you must sleep. The demon Lailoken has done the bidding of the Fire Lords who sent me here. I will not leave without him.*"

The Dragon wants to be free to sing, to share with the others, and so it pulls away from the unicorn and quickly withdraws into itself.

As the fog slips back through the trees like a pack of cadaverous dogs, the unicorn lies perfectly still, profoundly asleep. It is using all its tenuous strength to communicate with the Dragon.

"*Sleep—and know that you glorify the whole Dragon. Sleep, and I will use the power you give to carry the demon Lailoken away—into space—back to the fields of the sun—and beyond. That is the gift I ask for the star maps I have given you.*"

The unicorn's plaintive voice stops the Dragon. As much as it would like to, the giant beast cannot turn away from this request. The other parts of itself scattered across the universe will never abide such ingratitude. If it pulls entirely away out of selfishness, the others will spurn it when they learn what has happened, and the dreamsinging will stop forever. It must obey.

The Dragon turns back toward the surface and the unicorn. Directly into the unconscious animal, it emanates its strength. Gently, slowly, so as not to overwhelm the fragile creature's delicate waveform, the world beast pours forth its magnetic power. Dimly at first, then gradually brighter, the unicorn phosphoresces, and the fog-hung grove shines as though moonstruck.

The Dragon returns to its inmost mind, where the dreamsongs have already faded to a silence glisteny with inner lights. The songs have fled for now, and only the dreaming remains. Fatigue widens to exhaustion, and longing saturates the creature. It wants to hear again the inexhaustible beauty of its brethren beyond the galaxy. And it will, it promises itself. Now that it has given of itself to express the gratitude of the cosmic Dragon, it knows it will wake again and experience the glory and love of the dreamsongs. Eventually, it knows it will find the strength to return.

And with that resolve, the sleep of a thousand years lowers its tonnage on the Dragon.

The unicorn opens its eyes. The air glints as though hung with fish scales. Closer than ever, the Dragon's presence tightens, yet its fumes and drastic stink have thinned off, leaving the grove of stunted cypress thick with conifer resins and fiery sunlight.

The sun-stallion can see the Dragon's power aquiver in the air. It sparkles over the unicorn where it lies on its side as before, pale as a pool of fog.

The music of that power soaks the wounded creature's brain, and the motley of hurts and bruises that embroiders its long body fade. Even the black lips of the knife wound gradually smear away, like so much ink in a thin current.

By noon, the unicorn stands.

The animal touches its horn to the ground, transmitting its gratitude into the earth. The Dragon, of course, does not hear, for sleep carries it across a broad netherland, a thousand years long, where only dreams can reach.

Remembering how the sword Lightning stuck fast to the star stone until the magnetic core separated, Merlinus understands the purpose of the aerolite. It is a machine. The *Annwn* have built it for him. And with that realization, he begins to see how the stone serves Arthor's destiny.

His horse lengthens its stride on the road out of Londinium, and he feels his way across the September landscape with the brails of his heart, finding the fastest route to the star stone. Beyond the forests, moorlands range, blue horizons stacked like clouds. Many times in the coming days, when his exhausted steed cannot be coaxed even with magic, he wishes for the unicorn to gallop him across those patched distances.

When he finally climbs high into the mountain kingdom of the River Amnis, he must let the horse go or risk its life on the sheer ascent. By foot, he climbs the last steep miles into the sylvan outcrops of the cloud forest, where ferns and clubworts grow among the giant cedars that Romans planted here while the first Christians worked the busy shores of Galilee.

Looking back east from this height, into the emerald haze of the lowlands, Merlinus samples the vista Camelot will have after it is built in these tall hills. The kingdom is in his hand when he extends his arm to the horizon and paces the clear-cut promontory. Colors of silence shine from panels of sunlight in the hill forests and from silver storms over the river plains. This eagle's prospect of the countryside is a map of the rain, and the wizard is satisfied that it will serve his king well.

Construction continues. The site has been cleared on a ridge above the Amnis and the tents of the craftsmen and laborers bloom like mushrooms on the wooded bluffs. The wizard will see to it that the six warlords of the round table continue to fund construction of the fortress. With God's help, by the time Arthor reaches kinghood, he will have the finest capital in the land.

Vision shimmers in convection ripples, and a wind suddenly rises from the river gorge and blows brightly through him. Merlinus looks nervously for where the sword and his staff lie in the grass, but then an explosive wind in the nearby trees pulls his attention to the sky.

The unicorn streams through a foam of clouds.

Merlinus leaps with astonishment and falls to his knees before the creature resplendent as sun-driven snow. Its energy is so strong that, like a memory of lightning, it stains his sight when he looks away.

"Unicorn!" Merlinus shouts, squinting and crouching against the radiance. "Look at you! You are transfigured!"

The unicorn walks a circle, its white star-silence bleaching colors from nearby grass and rocks. "In truth," the telepathic beast answers in precise Latin and with a human timbre, more clearly than its voice has ever sounded before. "I am transfigured!"

"The Fire Lords!" Merlinus reels drunkenly to his feet, his heart a hummingbird. "The angels have saved you!"

The unicorn steps closer, the infinite sky above it shining like a blue halo. "Yes, Lailoken, the Dragon has been convinced to give us power—far more power than ever we have had before! At last we have the strength to ride to the black sun! Come, brother! Heaven begins here!"

The unicorn lowers its head before Merlinus so that he may mount, and the startled wizard leaps backward and falls to his haunches.

"To heaven?" Merlinus croaks, pressed to the ground by his shock. "Now?"

"Immediately!" the unicorn's voice flares. "Lailoken, I am at great jeopardy stopping here for you. Extremes become their opposites in this world very quickly—remember?"

Merlinus pushes to his elbows, his stunned head empty, his slamming heart full. "I did not expect this. I did not expect this at all. To heaven? Now? I—I *must* think."

"Demons, gods, giants, trolls, witches, and sorcerers abound, Lailoken! All wild to steal this power from us." The unicorn tosses its head impatiently. "Come! Think no more. Thought is the enemy of experience. Come! Experience heaven again!"

Merlinus stands transfixed. Yes, he must go—back to heaven! He has done the bidding of the Fire Lords and brought Arthor into the world. What else is there to look forward to? Arthor is born, and in his birth is guaranteed his death. And then, what? After Arthor, comes the millennial darkness. Why must he sit vigil on the coming of night?

The meat of his flesh hangs heavily on his skeleton, because even as he thinks these thoughts he knows why he must stay. The same knowing has haunted him whenever he has considered the possibility of escaping with the unicorn. "I cannot go with you, beautiful being," he answers, staring down at his shadow burning in the dirt. "I must stay. And you should stay, as well. We must all work together, especially those who have the power you possess. We need you here, unicorn, to stand against the evil that divides us."

"This is the abyss, Lailoken," the radiant entity states restively. "Everything is divided here—void and form, dark and light—you and me, too, unless you come now."

"We both must stay and work," the wizard insists. "Only collective moral force can unite the world."

"But why?" the unicorn inquires deeper, canting its long head at the demon-wizard. "Why must evil be answered by good? Why unite the world at all? Come away to the unity that already exists—the wholeness of heaven."

"I cannot." Merlinus shakes his head adamantly. "I have purpose in this world."

"Purpose?" The unicorn stands abruptly taller, its nostrils widening with annoyance at Merlinus's diffidence. "Ah, yes—purpose! Meaning!" It steps closer. "Lailoken—will you never learn? What is meaning? Like the distant moon, it offers no heat, only image. Come away!"

Merlinus remembers the terrible uprooting from heaven and his bones shudder with the expectation of going home. These bones want to lead the mutiny of all his senses against purpose and meaning, because they remember the wholeness; they have not forgotten the bliss. If they could speak, there would be no hesitation about joining the unicorn. But they are mute in their suffering as they are blind in their joy.

The one who speaks must answer to his soul, the woman in him that is his part of Optima, and so he says, sadly but firmly, "No, bright being. I have lived as a demon and mocked meaning—and I have lived as a man and been mocked by it. But now that I am entrusted to make meaning for a people, I feel its necessary beauty. It *needs* me or it will not exist at all. And the people of this world—they need me, too, for what hopeful meaning I *can* shape for them. They need me. Heaven does not."

The unicorn snorts, bewildered. "All meaning is promiscuous, Lailoken. There is always another layer."

"Such is life in the abyss." Merlinus shrugs. "This is where She has led me—and I will not leave without Her." The wizard steps back and raises his arm in farewell. "Go—splendid creature. I will join you, in time."

The unicorn's green eyes brighten as they search deeply into the odd figure that stands before it. And though it believes the demon-wizard is foolish to forsake this one chance to ride out of the abyss and through the black sun into heaven, it backs away. "You are no longer a demon," it acknowledges, finally understanding. "You are one of the burning ones yourself. May you carry your light strongly in the darkness, Merlinus, where your burning will shine for the benefit of all beings."

The unicorn swings about and, with a last, mute look backward, bounds into the streaming sky. Like a watery reflection, the steed wavers and breaks apart, becoming pure light, streaks of wet, brilliant colors that strobe among the clouds like a renegade sunrise.

Thunder washes over the wizard, and he sits down heavily in the feathered grass and watches heaven run off among windblown seeds.

Regret squats in him only briefly before he recognizes that the powerfully amplified presence of the unicorn has opened his strong eye. A commercial jetliner crawls down the sky, and highways follow the contours of the landscape in concrete ribbons. This is the future of Arthor's kingdom, the times yet to come that have called back to him since the spear of the Furor first drove madness into his brain.

He remembers trying to account for himself to this season

of steel. Sitting masterless and orphaned from heaven, he feels foolish now for all those times he strove to see the future and change it. That was before the sixth gate of his body opened, and the strong eye siphoned the energy from his throat into his skull, leaving behind a wake of laughter. No laughter blows through him now, because the strong eye closes as his life-force rises past it toward the seventh gate.

Merlinus sits taller in the grass, remembering the unicorn's promise to help him open all seven stations of his body. He closes his eyes and settles to the dark watchfulness of his center. With the strong eye firmly closed, he pulses softly in the dark of his skull. He directs his consciousness and strength upward.

Sudden whiteness and cold—a walloping blizzard of storm-crying wind and glaring white light. He opens his eyes and watches radiation slide from him like cool shadows. He has become as the unicorn, transfigured to light! Life-force smokes off him in viscid sheets of fiery plasma that the wind rips away. And as he burns, he shivers smaller.

All around him, a pale world watches him shrinking. Massive cedars shine translucent as amber and jade, and in their depths he can already see the raftered halls and groined vaults made from their lumber in Camelot. He can see Camelot, too: a river gorge for a defensive ditch and mountains for walls—and, upon a high ridge with a wide western prospect, a city of white stone towers whose blue tile roofs are so tall they rub their color right off the sky.

The abrupt realism of the vision frightens him, and he looks away. Juttering with the cold, he swings his gaze about and finds Ethiops far off, in the darkness at the edge of the wizard's cast light, cringing.

Rays jet from the crown of Merlinus's skull, a furnace shaft open to the harrowing cold. The intensity keeps the demon at a distance, yet the wizard can read the awe and anger in his bald face—and the sudden barbed grin, hoping that Lailoken has undone himself.

Merlinus watches himself shriveling. He gets colder as the whipping wind sweeps his life's heat out of his body and into the broadening reaches of space. The peevish thought occurs to him that maybe this, too, is a chemical delusion, the poisons of his gutsack. He suspects that maybe Ethiops has already torn him apart and his dying brain is spewing a dream.

Merlinus turns his crown-light upon himself and sees that he is whole, just smaller, shrinking and getting weaker. If he remains in this heightened state much longer, he will evaporate away. Anxiously, he searches for the gateway back down, into his physical body. He must push against the gushing energy of his own life spilling into the void.

Skittering against that strong current, he crawls around the floor of the world and finds a narrow crevice. Reduced to a boiling trickle of mercury, he slinks into that fracture and leaks back into himself. Each drop of his being gleams with global reflections of the cedar forest, Camelot's empty ridge, and his own gawky figure sitting in the grass, white-haired, bush-bearded, and with startled eyes staring from dark bonepits.

Iridescent swirlings oil the surface of each drop. And inside each one, the wizard sees a strange truth: The eruption that cast angels and demons into the void was not a singular event—not one Big Bang but many. Creation explodes into being all the time and many universes exist in the vacuum. Each universe is a rip in the cold, dark fabric of the void—rips from which the power of infinity flows.

Restored to his body, Merlinus sits alertly in the resonant afternoon, nerves sparkling from the chimes of birds. The seventh gate is the way out! He smiles at this realization: that the very body he once thought trapped him is actually a portal to the energy realms where he once lived as a demon. Now he will have the chance to learn how to live there as an angel.

If there are many Big Bangs, many universes, then creation is the spilled light not of one fall but of an endless falling, a majestic pouring forth of creation's fire.

Stunned by this revelation, he stares at his hands, not thinking, just looking at the blue bones under the taut knuckleskin. His destiny is in his grasp again. Maybe, after all, he can make his own individual dream come true, he can find Her here, as he did once inside Optima. He does not know. The same mystery that has pulled him into the womb draws him on into the future, younger each day and full of magic.

He decides then that he will, in fact and in name, make his own destiny. He will no longer be Merlinus a Briton or Myrddin a Celt but Merlin, wizard for all the kingdom's people.

His naked pride embarrasses the sorcerer, and he stretches his tired muscles and reminds himself that everything is possible but actions alone are real in this cold corner of the universe. Dreams and hope are not enough.

He is in the cedar grove, firmly in his physical body. He stands up. No demons or angels are anywhere in sight. From the skein of afternoon shadows, the cedars knit the scarves of mist that they will wear at dusk. A breeze of resin clears his head, and he gathers up the sword Lightning and his staff and resumes his journey.

Merlin descends among sharp rock tumulus overgrown with shawl moss, picking his way swiftly over the slick, lichenous boulders. He feels stronger and more nimble than ever in his mortal life. The seventh gate pours his light into the void, and his body replenishes it. He grows younger. Today he has the stamina to run along the slippery path beneath waterfalls and rainbows on the cliffs above the brown, roiling Amnis.

The steep trace twists down into the mountain shadows. Wending deeper into the verdant canyon, oak forest and rhododendron give way to willow and ivy and dragonish old trees hoarding sun shafts of fine gold mist.

In this gorge forest, Merlin locates the brook that leads to the star stone. It trickles among lotus pads, hastening away over rocky inclines of ice blue mosses, past fallen firs, and luminous islands of birch. The sorcerer moves more slowly now, memorizing the landscape in this primal scene of destiny. Here, Uther and Ygrane's barbed fate touches Arthor's future.

The brook elbows around a steep bluff, called Mons Caliburnus when the Romans had a watchtower here centuries ago. Larks soar into the blue seam of the sky between billowy boughs. At the star stone, Merlin shoves the lower rock into place, activating the magnetic strength between the two lobes. He gathers ingots of water-rubbed rock and jams them against the magnet stone so that it cannot be moved. Vines curtain the tall bank; in a summer or two the lower lobe of the star stone will be wholly hidden from sight.

Atop the bluff, the sword Lightning in hand, the wizard stands before the silver-black rock. In his strong eye, in his memory of the future, the image of the Nine Queens arrayed around the dead king on the barge to Avalon gathers spark by spark into view of his inner eye. Seen this vividly, he recognizes each of the queens—Rna, the departing falconess, and the nameless eight in every sun-struck hue of autumn, who will remain with Arthor. They have proud yet patient faces. The sky burns behind them like a ceremonial fire, a few brittle stars heralding the night to come.

Merlin cannot tell if his strategy and magic will preserve Arthor—or, as any demon would argue, sacrifice him in blood ransom to the Fire Lords and their mysteries.

The vision passes, and he is again in a flaked gold afternoon on Mons Caliburnus, with butterflies climbing ladders to heaven. Arthor himself will have to decide whom he serves. But to even earn him that choice, the wizard must act. Looking up at the tall branches chaffing sunlight, he asks of himself diligence for the work yet to be done and of all else luck, the slanderous name of God.

Bees touch the gold tassels of grass nesting the meteorite. A thrush warbles from the trees' drooping hair, and a turtle splashes in the brook. The noises mell to a kind of music, the peacefulness of what is good about being human.

Then, Merlin takes the sword and strikes the stone.

A. A. ATTANASIO is the author of *The Eagle and the Sword, The Dragon and the Unicorn, Solis, Kingdom of the Grail, Hunting the Ghost Dancer, Wyvern, Radix,* and *The Moon's Wife*. He lives in Hawaii.

Enter a New World

THE WESTERN KING • Ann Marston

BOOK TWO OF THE RUNE BLADE TRILOGY

Guarded by the tradition of the past and threatened by the danger of the present, a warrior — as beautiful as she is fierce — must struggle between two warring clans who were one people once.

Also available, _Kingmaker's Sword_

FORTRESS IN THE EYE OF TIME • C. J. Cherryh

THREE TIME HUGO-AWARD WINNING AUTHOR

Deep in an abandoned, shattered castle, an old man of the Old Magic mutters words almost forgotten. With the most wondrous of spells, he calls forth a Shaping, in the form of a young man to be sent east to right the wrongs of a long-forgotten wizard-war, and alter the destiny of a land.

THE HEDGE OF MIST • Patricia Kennealy-Morrison

THE FINAL VOLUME OF THE TALES OF ARTHUR TRILOGY

Morrison's amazing canvas of Keltia holds the great and epic themes of classic fantasy — Arthur, Gweniver, Morgan, Merlynn, the magic of Sidhe-folk, and the Sword from the Stone. Here, with Taliesin's voice and harp to tell of it, she forges a story with the timelessness of a once and future tale. *(Hardcover)*